I0772039

Chesapeake Crime Club

Chesapeake Crime Club

A MINXY BANKS MYSTERY

CECE LAMONT

This book is a work of fiction. Names, places, characters, businesses, organizations, events, and incidents are a product of the author's imagination. Any resemblance to actual persons, living or dead, is entirely coincidental. Any references to historical events, facts, objects, real people, or real places are used fictitiously.

Published by BayTown Press LLC

P.O. Box 84

North Beach, Maryland 20714

Copyright @ 2025 BayTown Press LLC

First Edition

All rights reserved. No part of this book may be used or reproduced in any manner whatsoever without written permission, except in the case of brief quotations embodied in critical articles and reviews. For information, please address BayTown Press LLC, Subsidiary Rights and Speakers Bureau, P.O. Box 84, North Beach, MD 20714.

Library of Congress Cataloging-in-Publication Data has been applied for.

Print ISBN: 979-8-9873295-2-8

eBook ISBN: 979-8-9873295-3-5

Printed in the United States of America

Dedication

This book is dedicated to Calvert County, Maryland, and particularly to the town of North Beach, which is a little like West Beach, and a whole lot more like Brigadoon. It's my happy place.

I would like to make clear that fictional Mayor Bill Hampton, the pirate, is nothing like North Beach Mayor Mike Benton. When it floods, Mayor Mike motors around in his boat to rescue people. He also lets us keep our kayaks under the boardwalk. I'm a huge fan of him and his wife Tina.

Except for being warmhearted, the mayor's assistant Sue is nothing like North Beach's Town Clerk Stacy Milor. Stacy graciously gave me a tour of Town Hall from top to bottom. She is a treasure.

Similarly, fictional Sheriff Jack Frye is not modeled on the real Calvert County Sheriff Ricky Cox. I have never met Sheriff Cox, but his biography says he's a happily married man, and not a potential suitor for Minxy.

The Calvert Cliffs Clean Energy Center (aka nuclear power plant) graciously toured me around their facility. It is the most secure operation I've seen in thirty years of national security compound visits. I've masked its security features out of respect. Minxy and Ricky could never have gotten away with the shenanigans they pulled, but reality wouldn't have made a good story.

Acknowledgments

Thanks to my wonderful friends and writer support network who have been instrumental to this book's publication. First, of course, is my wonderful husband Tom who listened patiently to every detail of Minxy Banks's imaginary life. Thanks to my amazing kids: Mark was my master plot advisor, Matthew created and manages my website, and Meagan kept me happy. Thanks to the entire Needwood Ladies Golf League for your support, especially my sounding board of Bonnie Suchman and Julie Isaac. We talked so much about Minxy on the golf course no one wanted to play behind us...or with us. Extra special thanks are reserved for another golfer girlfriend, Toby Heilweil, who volunteered to do the tech edit; I can't thank you enough for your generous soul and eagle eyes! Ione Salkoski, who knows North Beach inside and out, has been a constant inspiration and supporter at our weekly happy hours. Thanks to my co-conspirator Dr. Theresa Sabonis-Helf who keeps me fresh on science and technology. My Thrillertique writing group has been instrumental in catching mistakes and nailing down Minxy's psychiatric condition; thank you James, Elena, Steven, Brandi, and Virginia. A giant shout out to the developmental and beta readers whose comments have added so much depth and richness to the story: Jeff Ayers, Phyllis Grifman, Michael Kelley, Bonnie Suchman, Julie Isaac, and Jo Cohen Jones. Finally, thank you to *New York Times* bestselling thriller writer Robert Dugoni, whose Masterclass showed me key areas that needed work and gave me the tools to fix them.

One

WEDNESDAY, JUNE 21, WEST BEACH, MD

It wasn't the best day for a prank, but is it ever?

Running shorts and windbreaker on, I carried the large bag out my door at 5:15 a.m. I'd been preparing for this day for over a month and was bursting with anticipation. My oversized sunglasses sat on my head and controlled my hair against the stiff breeze. I wrestled with the parcel under my arm as I descended my front steps and jogged onto the boardwalk.

It was a weekday, and the West Beach boardwalk was empty this early in the morning. I'd probably see other runners before long, but no one was around now. I plodded on slower than usual managing my package that acted like a sail.

Not to put too fine a point on it, but I was sluggish today because last night's happy hour on my patio got a little too happy. Astrid Neilsen, my Danish friend, had recounted a mix up at the Danish Embassy where her husband Lars, the Ambassador, had met with a midwestern mayor seeking a sister city. The mayor had mixed up Danish with Polish and after his handshake presented Lars with a giant Kielbasa. After Lars oriented the mayor on a map, they shared the Kielbasa in the embassy café over several glasses of Danish Aquavit. They'd paired two sister cities and Lars sent Denmark's newest fan home to the Midwest with a jar of pickled herring. I'm not sure why, but we all thought that was hilarious. Probably it was because of the chilled Aquavit Astrid brought to accompany the story. It goes down easily and catches up with you fast. Celia Drexel, my friend and mentor at the Central Intelligence Agency when I worked there, had laughed so hard she'd gotten the hiccups and couldn't stop them. Not exactly our usual dignified happy hour.

Now I was a little hung over and dodging puddles on my way toward Fifth Street, which floods after every heavy rain. I'd brought the problem to the attention of West Beach's mayor, Bill Hampton, many times. He'd said he was working on it, but I wasn't impressed. The last mayor decreased the flood by putting in giant pumps. Mayor Hampton, however, had talked a lot and done little.

Turning the corner, the two feet of flood water awaited me. I pulled the 30" x 24" sign out of the plastic bag, attached the stake, and pushed it into the willing ground next to the curb. Standing back, I admired my professionally printed sign that said, "Mayor Hampton's Lap Pool: Swim in Your Own Lane." That should remind him citizens were watching. I snapped a quick photo, then shoved the plastic bag in the trash and hustled away before anyone saw me.

Giddy with the joy of a good prank, I ran down the boardwalk by the Chesapeake Bay. I was so distracted that I clipped a raised city planter bursting with June flowers. Ouch.

One of those days.

Then, as I was picking up my running pace, I came alongside Sunrise Garden across from the beach. Something unusual caught my eye. It looked like two mermaids making out. Okay, that amazed me. I'd seen a dolphin once in the bay and was surprised, but cuddled up mermaids, that was amazing. I shook my head to see if they went away, but they were still there—a shiny metal mermaid embraced by a human one with sea-foam green scales. To make things worse, the breeze whipped my hair from under my sunglasses and into my eyes.

Curiosity pulled me off the boardwalk, across Bay Street, and into the park. I controlled my hair with one hand and moved toward the tryst. The closer I got, the more I wished I'd kept running. The metal mermaid was, indeed, a lovely metal mermaid statue. The human mermaid, however, was a dead woman draped across the statue's body, her right arm clinging to the shiny flipper. The woman's seafoam-green suit was soaked through with last night's rain and a whole lot of blood. Her lifeless eyes, like the lug-nut eyes of the mermaid, stared heavenward. Maybe it was just me, but I swear they were begging God to explain their mutual torment.

No one should deal with a scene like that with a hangover.

I inched closer and felt adrenaline clearing my head, which made things worse. There was something familiar about this dead woman. I stared at her bluish-purple face and tried to see beyond the smeared makeup and wet hair. She was blond, about my height and age. I thought of all the blonds I knew in West Beach. In a strange way she resembled a messed-up version of Jenn Albrecht, my super annoying neighbor. Jenn and I had fought since I moved to West Beach.

Crouching, I put two fingers on her carotid because touching the body would convince me she was: one, real; and two, dead. It worked.

"Jenn, what happened to you?" Obviously, I had to answer the question myself and it was easy—there were multiple stab wounds in the green suit where the knife went in and lots of blood flowed out. I saw blood splatter on the ground and on the mermaid statue. Jenn was killed here. I also saw bruising around her throat. It looked like the work of five left hand fingers that had dug into her neck. The killer must have used his right hand for the knife. "Good girl. He choked you because you were telling him off."

I spent a moment taking in the demise of Jenn Albrecht and then realized the real problem. She and I had celebrated an unneighborly vendetta for years. Our petty grievances were common gossip in our tiny town of two thousand people. After all the pranks I'd pulled on her, it would be hard to explain why I was standing over her dead body. *Not good for me.*

Should I keep running and let someone else find her? My old CIA training kicked in. I looked at the lines of sight through the park and out to the streets. There were too many. If anyone had seen me here, leaving would be crazy. I'd look guilty. Only one thing to do. I pulled my cell from my pocket and dialed 911.

A female voice at dispatch said, "This is 911. What's your emergency?"

If I was thinking straight, I would have taken a minute to think this through. What would a normal woman say when she found a dead body? I thought about my friend Astrid, who was psychologically healthy, not a bell curve outlier like me. I'd channel her.

"This is 911, are you still there?"

I made my voice a little shaky. "Yes. Yes, I am. I found someone in Sunrise Garden—the park in West Beach across the street from the bay. Send the police. Please hurry."

That was a reasonable imitation of Astrid. Polite, with helpful information. I was crushing this. The police detectives would hear what they expected when they listened to the tape.

"I'm sending a sheriff's car. What's your name."

"Minxy Banks."

"Tell me what you see, Minxy."

Good idea. I should document this like in the old days. I put the phone on speaker, and said, "Uhhhh, I'm not sure. Give me a second." I pulled up the video app on my phone and started shooting. "The white, female is about my age."

"Minxy, how old is that?"

"Forty-five. She's wearing an expensive green St. John suit and, I can't believe it, but also *pantihose*." I had to take a breath because that was shocking. "This is West Beach. Why would Jenn wear pantihose to the park?"

"You called her Jenn. You know the victim?"

Oops, I let that slip. "Yes, she's my neighbor, Jenn Albrecht. She worked at the Nuclear Regulatory Commission and *always* changed into beach clothes when she got home."

"That's nice, Ma'am, but tell me about the victim's *condition*, not her clothing. I'm dispatching an ambulance."

"Her condition is *dead*. No need for lights and sirens. She has multiple stab wounds to the chest and rigor mortis has set in."

"Oh, my."

It sounds like this is the dispatcher's first murder. Murders don't happen in little West Beach, Maryland. Even if I sound emotionally detached, she'll have no comparison. I continued to video the crime scene like I'd done countless times for the CIA in Iraq, starting with the body and moving outward. A light green pump dangled from one foot. I was looking for the other shoe when I noticed the leather folio on the ground next to her. It was open, and dried blood had stained the blank paper of the note pad. The sleeve for loose papers was empty.

Now that was interesting. Why would Jenn carry a folio to a park at night? Even with the lights from the gazebo, it would be too dark to wobble on those heels and write.

The dispatcher asked, "Are you still with me?"

"Yes, just a little emotional." Astrid would say that. I, on the other hand, recognize emotion and understand it, but I don't feel it. I've been told to my face I'm a deviant for being so detached, and it might be true. That's why my New Minxy Project began.

I'm working with my shrink to sympathize more with others. So far, no results.

I could hear a siren. Judging by the distance of the sound, I had more time to analyze this crime scene. I thought my skills had atrophied but maybe spy craft gets into your bones. I looked farther from the body and saw Jenn's purse. It was a cute little Kate Spade. *When I walk around West Beach, I put my cell phone and keys in my pocket. Jenn did, too—except for last night.*

"Ma'am, talk to me. The deputy will be there in about two minutes."

I took a deep breath and said, "I'm okay. It's quite a shock, you know..."

The sirens were getting closer. Turning in a tight circle to avoid adding more of my footprints to the crime scene, I recorded the densely planted foliage of the park as I looked for papers that might have been in the folio and blown away. Seeing none, I turned off the video and pocketed my phone.

In the remaining time before law enforcement arrived, I raised the folio with two sticks and peeked under it. Nothing. The purse was zipped. My sticks couldn't help me with that, and no way was I touching it.

The sirens were very close now. I threw the sticks under a bush and prepared myself to tell the Sheriff's Deputy what he wanted to hear. I said to my former neighbor. "Okay Jenn, we had our differences, but I'm trying to do right by you. People are coming to take care of you."

I checked myself to see if I was sympathizing with Jenn. Nope. Still nothing.

The first car slid to a stop in front of the park entrance, launching the seagulls from the beach across the street. I made sure the uniformed deputy could see my hands and waited.

As he got out of the car, I realized I knew the guy. It was Charley Moore, who was part of the Sheriff's Beach Patrol. He ran into the park, looked at my hands and non-threatening posture, and focused on Jenn. As I had done, he checked for a pulse, straightening, and said, "Dead."

"Very."

Charley finally looked at my face and said, "Minxy Banks? What are you doing here?"

"Finding my dead neighbor. I didn't need this, Charley."

He shook his head and pulled out his little notepad and pen. "What's it been, three weeks since she called us about your back-yard rock concert?"

"It was Kenny G. The volume was on two. But yeah, about three weeks."

"What'd you see when you arrived?"

I gave him the details minus me checking under the folio and taking the video.

"Shouldn't you be throwing up in the bushes? That's a lot of blood."

I eyed Charley. He was the one who looked green. "It's not my first dead body. Saw them by the truck-load in Iraq."

"I know you were a spy and all. It's just that was war, and this is personal."

I shrugged. Awkward, but I couldn't tell him I'm a Dark Empath—a psychopathic narcissist with Machiavellian tendencies. That would scare even a cop. Anyway, I'm sure over the years he'd noticed there was something different about me. He just couldn't give it a name.

Charley directed me to find a seat and await further questioning. I picked a park bench with a good view of the murder scene and watched the newly arriving deputies block off Bay Avenue and descend on the park like a swarm of bees. A uniformed officer attempted to set up a privacy screen around Jenn's body. The wind remained brisk, and I bet myself that he'd lose the battle. As if on cue, a gust ripped the screen completely away. He cursed under his breath and stomped off, leaving the fluttering pile on the ground and the body visible.

Then I heard a familiar voice calling, "Minxy?"

From the other side of the newly stretched crime scene tape, I saw my friend Celia wave and then return to a heated conversation with an officer. As usual, she won. In a moment, she was ducking under the tape and hugging me before she sat beside me holding my hands in hers.

Ten years my senior, Celia knew my condition very well. She had been my mentor at the CIA when I was diagnosed. So, why all this nurturing? I said, "You *do* know I'm not upset?"

"Oh, I know, but that officer hasn't met you. I told him you were fragile."

We both lowered our heads to hide a totally inappropriate chuckle at a murder scene.

She said, "I was heading to work when I heard the sirens. Imagine my surprise when I saw you here." The officers crowding the crime scene moved apart for a moment, and Celia viewed the body. "Good Heavens, the woman was stabbed to death." Celia was tough, but even she averted her eyes.

I said, "Indeed. Oh, I forgot to mention that's Jenn Albrecht."

"You're kidding."

I shook my head, "She sure knew how to make an exit. When I came into the park, I thought she was a mermaid."

Celia looked like I'd overstepped a boundary.

"What am I supposed to say? I'm hung over and she's wearing sea foam green."

"Maybe so, but she's been murdered. We don't want the police to suspect you."

I asked, "Would I have found her if I'd killed her?"

"You were a spy. They'll expect misdirection."

"*Whatever.* Let's think about something important; the killer is still out there. This is a big deal, made bigger because the crime scene doesn't make any sense. Jenn was wearing her St. John suit, pantihose, and heels in a West Beach park at night."

Celia pinched her lower lip with her fingers and tried to catch a glimpse of the suit between the deputies. She couldn't. I pulled out my phone and froze the video on the suit.

"You videoed the crime scene? Really?"

"Old habits die hard."

Celia shook her head while focusing on the image. "Fabulous suit and so weird. No one would wear that to this park, day or night. West Beach is the most casually dressed place in Maryland. It's part of its charm."

I fast forwarded the video and then paused it. "And look next to her. Why did she bring a folio to the park?"

Celia looked at the bloody leather folio. "Must have been to manage papers. The wind was wicked last night."

"I didn't like her, but she was a professional. She wouldn't have brought work papers to the park...unless she was passing them to someone."

Celia got her intelligence-officer-at-work look and said, "That's very good. You're on to something. She was dressed for a professional meeting in a shadowy park late at night. If this wasn't West Beach, I'd think it was espionage." We sat for a few minutes watching the officers. Celia laid a hand on my forearm and said, "My first assumption is she was killed after midnight."

"Hum, maybe. After you girls left happy hour last night, I walked the dog and saw the shadows of two people behind Jenn's living room curtains. That was about 10:00 p.m. If I'm right, she was home then, so it had to be later."

Celia said, "I don't see an umbrella or raincoat. The rain started about 3:00 a.m. She left for the park well before that."

"Dog walkers would have found her last night between 10:00 p.m. and midnight. You're right. The murder was probably between 12:00 a.m. and 2:30 a.m."

"And a brutal killer got away unseen."

"Hummm. Want to bet a jar of caviar on that? I say someone saw the killer." I hoped my tiny smile didn't give me away. Serious drinkers and those up to no good walked around West Beach late at night. Someone saw the killer but didn't know about the crime. That was a safe bet.

"Sure."

We both scanned the park. I noticed a CCTV camera attached to the gazebo. Drawing a deep breath, I shook my head. *A rookie mistake.* Had it captured me checking under the folio and videoing the scene? I tracked its focus directly to the park entrance on Bay Avenue, then across to the boardwalk, the sandy beach, and Chesapeake Bay beyond. I turned back, pointed to the camera, and said, "That didn't capture the murder. It's the wrong angle to reach the mermaid." It hadn't seen me with the sticks either. Best of all it would have me entering the park when I told Charley I did and looking curious about mermaids in love.

From a distance I heard someone else call out, "Minxy?"

Celia and I both looked at the police line and saw our friend Astrid in yoga clothes, her chin-length, wheat-colored hair tucked behind her ears. She waved, then talked to the same police officer that Celia had convinced to let her under the tape. He shook his head and walked over, "Ma'am, I know you're delicate and your friends are worried. I just can't let any more people in to take care of you. It's a crime scene. Charley said he has your address. Go home and relax. We'll come to you. Just stay there until you talk to the detectives."

I nodded solemnly. "Thank you for understanding." We both ducked under the tape and Astrid hugged me.

"Minxy, why are you at this crime scene? That's Jenn Albrecht laying there." She glanced in the direction of the body, shuddered, and then looked away.

"I found her."

"*Gud i himlen.*" When excited, Astrid slipped back into her native Danish. Normally her English was better than mine.

Celia said, "It's okay. Minxy's been watching what she says and does."

Astrid let out a long breath. "That nice sheriff's deputy that lives next door told us a runner found Jenn's body about 5:30 a.m. He seems to feel responsible for Lars' security and always tells us what's happening. I'm on my way to yoga and stopped by. I had no idea *you* found her."

I said, "Hey look. One of the deputies is sliding her purse into an evidence bag."

"A suit and a purse in Sunrise Garden?" Astrid shook her head. "It was business, and who does that here?" She dropped her eyes to the ground. "Can we step a little bit away from the park. I don't want to see her like that anymore. It's making me ill."

I said, "Of course."

As we were moving away from the crime tape, rapid movement to our left caught my eye. A man let out an anguished cry so loud and heart breaking, I actually felt his pain. *Good Lord what's happening to me?* It felt like I'd been kicked in the gut. I grabbed my stomach.

Celia said, "Oh no. It's Walt, the boyfriend."

Astrid said, "Poor Walt. Can you imagine how horrid this is for him?"

To my complete surprise, I could.

Walt fell to his knees, looking at his girlfriend's body. I read his face, his posture, his eyes locked on an unimaginable nightmare. *He was devastated and I could literally feel it. No doubt about it. I felt his suffering and my own avalanche of sympathy for him. How weird.*

Celia turned to say something to me, then stopped. She looked me over and put a steadying hand on my shoulder, "Walt's suffering has gotten to you."

I nodded, then looked back at Walt and couldn't stop the pain of sympathizing with him. My therapist hadn't warned me it would hurt this much.

A male sheriff's deputy knelt beside him. The posture showed compassion. I hoped so. Walt buried his face in his hands. Like me, he was also in running gear and I saw the Marine Corps tattoo on his right bicep. The deputy helped him to his feet, took him under the police tape, and with a hand on his shoulder, led him across the park to a group of other officers.

I couldn't watch Walt's suffering. I had to turn away.

Two

Our clothes flapping in the breeze, we walked across the street to the boardwalk. All three of us leaned against the railing and faced the Chesapeake Bay.

Trying to distract me from Walt's pain, Celia said, "So Minxy, now you can stop growing dandelions. Right?"

Astrid turned to me and said, "Don't do it. I like your dandelions. They're a cheerful yellow."

Celia's clever strategy worked. I was thinking about dandelions and not Walt. I started feeling better. I said, "Dandelions are my favorite flower."

Celia gave me a side eye, and was about to speak when Astrid said, "You need to be careful. I'm guessing your alibi isn't great?"

I shook my head. "It's Mr. Magoo." My copper and white Basenji had eyesight as bad as his cartoon namesake's. Age hadn't mellowed Magoo, though. He'd bitten his previous family's neighbor—a second offense which meant the death penalty. He was hiding out with me.

Astrid shook her head and said, "Do not drag my doggy buddy

into this." She then pulled out her phone and showed it to me. "Oh, by the way," she said, "I got a photo of people taking pictures of your sign. I'll post it on social media so it goes viral. Nice work."

Celia said, "Sign?" Astrid showed her the picture. "What a day to punk the mayor."

Everyone nodded.

Astrid checked her watch and added, "Must go. Yoga on the pier in five minutes. We'll talk more at happy hour. The Chesapeake Crime Club can work Jenn's murder as a case."

Celia and I simultaneously said, "Maybe." Our hobby of solving local penny ante crimes was a lot different from a murder investigation. We solved little mysteries like who was skinny dipping in the Carter's hot tub. It was a lark, a pastime, something to scare away boredom.

As Astrid walked away, I noticed that Celia had her strict older sister look. "Back to the dandelions. You should empty those pots on your deck immediately. The police don't need more reason to suspect you."

I said, "Raising dandelions isn't a crime."

"It's not the dandelions. It's what they represented. Years of antagonism with Jenn Albrecht, well documented with police and Town Hall visits. You planted weeds upwind of her yard to torment her."

Celia was right. When I was new in town and fresh from condo living, I didn't think much about yard maintenance. I was born and raised in Manhattan, for heaven's sake. When I ignored Jenn's reprimands about unmown grass, she complained to Town Hall. An official wearing a West Beach branded polo motored over in his golf cart and threatened substantial fines. In addition, he recited the rules about trash cans. *Someone* had complained that mine went to the street too early, were taken in too late, and didn't have properly fitted lids.

That was a transformational moment for me. I became a revenge gardener.

I hired Eli, who'd been mowing lawns since the Clinton Administration. Then I raised any and every plant that would annoy Jenn Albrecht. Generations of women in my Wall Street monied family turned over in their graves thinking about me gleefully digging in the dirt with my own hands.

Trying to hide the smirk, I said, "It was just a friendly little gardening war. I wanted to kill her roses, not her."

"That's right. You planting those grape vines covered in Japanese Beetles that love roses. The ladies at the nursery will swear you insisted on infested ones."

"Japanese Beetles are so colorful. Lovely green shells..."

"Cut it. You and the beetles tried to destroy her roses."

"Those roses are terrible. They're Pepto Bismol pink, and they've survived repeated attacks." I shook my head, "But, you know what? I didn't like her, and I won't miss her..." I glanced at the park but couldn't see anything but a crowd around the police tape, "...but she didn't deserve to die like that."

Celia scanned my face for mischief and seemed surprised to find none. She said, "I believe you mean that. Let's hope someone's alibi is worse than yours."

I repositioned my sunglasses on my head to better manage my hair. My gaze wandered to Walt, the boyfriend, who was sitting on a bench with his head in his hands. I had my emotions back under control. Only an aching remembrance of sympathizing with him left me feeling off kilter. "The police may be curious about my relationship with Jenn, but it won't matter. They always blame the boyfriend. That guy is toast."

CELIA HAD to rush to work. She'd gotten a late start to CIA headquarters, and traffic was always slow after it rained. My life was blessed with no such demands. When there was nothing new to watch at the murder scene, I set off to finish my run.

I loved my adopted community of West Beach, Maryland—a fly speck of a town on the western shore of the Chesapeake Bay. A sandy beach, a long boardwalk, the fishing pier, a huge library, good restaurants and bars. What was not to love?

As in all small towns, gossip was a favorite pastime, so it was hard to keep a secret here. It could be done, but it took a rare dedication to secrecy and a well-honed skill for lying. I was confident Jenn's killer would be caught soon. Most people here were terrible at secrets and lies—me excepted. But I was a professional.

Today everyone will be talking about the horrible demise of Jenn Albrecht.

I'd only gone a block up the boardwalk before I heard footsteps behind me, overtaking me fast. Ricky Domingo came even with me and slowed his pace to match mine. He said, "Wow, did you see that mess goin' down in the park? Wasn't that Jennifer Albrecht?"

I nodded. "Sure was. Poor woman."

Ricky was a congenial Hispanic guy who worked as a computer tech at Calvert Cliffs Nuclear Power Plant, one of the major industries in the county. He was tall and muscular with wavy brown hair, brown eyes, and a Texas accent he couldn't shake.

About two years ago, I'd met Ricky at a Town Hall meeting. When he told me he worked on computers, I started my charm campaign. Who doesn't need computer help? After that first meeting, I regularly saw him around town. Funny how that happens. Turned out he was a runner whose morning route overlapped with mine.

He raised his eyebrows. "I thought ya hated that woman."

"Ricky, my friend, friction is a normal part of life," I said. "We disagreed about gardening. That's not the same as wanting her dead." It felt good to practice my defense.

He nodded, but I wasn't sure he understood. He saw me looking at him and grinned, then picked up the pace to push me faster than usual. Even though my head was clear now, I still didn't feel great. He was a few years younger than me though, so I ran faster to save my pride.

Ricky said, "Well, she certainly is dead. Awful. Her slouched there and all."

"Absolutely horrid." I said that a little like Astrid would. I'd have to remember to tell my shrink about Astrid as a role model. Why hadn't I thought of it sooner?

We lapsed into a somewhat awkward silence, so eventually I asked, "How's your garden?" Ricky was an accomplished gardener, nothing like my tactical efforts. He often told me about scoring unique plants at the local nursery.

"It's June. Everything's comin' in. I'll invite ya over to see it sometime."

"We always say we'll trade garden tours, but we never get around to it."

He gave me that toothy, Texas grin. "I know. I'm sure this time'll be different. Good talkin' to ya, but I gotta pick up the pace. I'm already late for work." He winked and took off like he'd slipped into a different gear.

My instincts pushed me to meet the challenge, but my body was having none of it. The sky was clearing, and I told myself I was happy running at a comfortable speed. It would help me think about this morning's events.

My route took me up First Street, where I saw Eli mowing a lawn. He cut the motor when he saw me and waved me over. My prediction was coming true. Everyone knew about Jenn's murder, and they all wanted to talk about it. That's what happens in a small town. Pulling off his headphones, Eli said in a low voice just for me, "I was listening to the police scanner. They found a gun in Jenn's purse."

That surprised me so much, I hoped my eyes weren't bulging. "Eli, is it just me, or is that shocking? Can you imagine her tearing out her front door with a gun?"

Eli surrendered his hands into the air, "No lie, that scared me more than a little." His hands dropped. "Anyway, police took it straight away for testing."

I thanked him for the information, and he promised to mow my lawn Friday. Eli was the first new friend I made in West Beach, and he always had my back. It was also helpful that he saw everything and reported it liberally. I ran on.

From down the block, I saw Sue step outside Town Hall for a smoke break. She was the receptionist at West Beach Town Hall. In that position she was hard wired into the town's collective brain. The week I'd moved here, I'd started cultivating her. If you needed to know something about the people in town that Eli didn't know, you asked Sue.

She said, "Funny about that swimming pool sign on Fifth Street. The mayor is totally pissed off at whoever did that. Who would do such a thing?"

From the look in her eyes, I was sure she knew I did it. "A citizen who cares. I saw it too. Pretty funny."

"Right. Hilarious. Not what he needs on top of a brutal murder."

I asked, "So you heard about Jenn..."

"Of course." She took a puff of her e-cigarette and blew the smoke over her shoulder.

"Have the police found anything on the CCTV feeds?"

She shook her head. "Don't know. They just left with the coverage from a few cameras. I copied the whole night for them on the ones they wanted."

I touched her arm and leaned in. "Come on. As soon as you heard about the murder, you checked the recording from the park camera. Right? I'm dying to know what you saw."

Sue surprised me by blushing. "Well, I did peek. The camera picked up that Albrecht woman entering the park at 12:37 a.m. She was all dressed up and walked off out of camera range. Nothing on the murderer, though. Oh, and you looked half dead going in this morning."

"You're the best, Sue. That's what I expected you'd find."

Sue said. "Minxy, the police put up with you girls meddling in those little crimes. They won't like you interfering in the Albrecht murder."

"I know you're right. Drop by for happy hour..."

"Maybe after the mayor forgets about that sign stunt." She waved goodbye.

I sprinted off, determined to finish my run. I thought I was home free, but it wasn't meant to be. Only two blocks from my house, I ran into Danny Stone. I usually saw Danny coming and switched paths to avoid him. This time I was thinking about the murder when he rounded a corner right in front of me.

Danny was early thirties, had a developmental disability, and attended some evangelical Christian church that believes in a life of proselytizing. To each his own, but it wasn't for me. I was raised high church Episcopalian. If you weren't hurting people, we tried hard to leave you alone and let Jesus sort things out. Manhattan Episcopalians wore cashmere sweater sets to mass, drank one polite cup of coffee after service, then bolted back to the world.

Danny didn't bolt. His religion was his life.

He planted himself in front of me on the sidewalk, his shoulders were slumped forward. "Morning. Miss Minxy. I haven't seen you in a while."

The clouds had blown off into the distance now, and the sun was out. I unzipped my windbreaker and moved into the shade of an old-growth sycamore tree. Danny followed. "Yeah, seems odd. Both of us walking around a tiny town and still missing each other. What's up?"

"I'm on break so I'm passing out bible verses." His hand dove into the pocket of the emergency yellow vest that he wore as a town groundskeeper and came out with a one inch by eight-and-a-half-inch bible verse he'd printed on his home computer. He'd cut the verses apart with pinking shears, leaving a tooth-like edge.

"What have you got for me today?" I asked.

Danny held the verse up close to his eyes with a large hand. He was at least six feet four inches, heavy set and powerfully chiseled from his outdoor labor. Danny intoned in a biblical, prophetic way, "'Let each of you look not only to his own interests, but also to the interests of others.' Philippians Chapter 2, Verse 4."

That simple message hit me hard. First, I'm a narcissist. No denying it. Fully diagnosed, but being open to the 'interests of others' is part of the Better Minxy Program.

Then there was the problem of not having a purpose bigger than myself. At the CIA, I'd had a mission. I'd fought terrorism, and my Dark Empath skills made me good at it. Now I was spending each day looking for something to do. My hand shook a bit when I took the little strip of paper. "Wow, Danny. That's a powerful one. I'll save this in my special place. Thanks."

He smiled, but then I watched sadness transform his generally peaceful face. "Miss Jennifer got killed."

"Yes, she did. It was a terrible murder." I didn't need to think about Astrid for that answer.

"Why did it happen, Miss Minxy? I loved Miss Jennifer. She was nice to me. I brought her bible verses all the time and she understood them. She saw them as prophecy."

Even though today's gem of a bible quote hit a chord, the whole modern day prophesy thing was bunkum. If Danny was the new Elijah, I was the queen of Sheba.

The giant's eyes were filling with tears. He ached for the woman because she was kind to him when others, me included, wouldn't spare the time. I felt just a little pinch of guilt and made a mental note to tell my shrink. "I don't know how this happened, Danny. I'm sure the police will figure it out."

"I bet it was that Marine she was dating. He should've married her. They had *carnal* knowledge. Why didn't he take care of her? I would have if she'd been my girlfriend."

His girlfriend. Hummm. Staring up at the human boulder, I felt a chill. "When you say you loved her, do you mean in the Christian 'love thy neighbor as thyself' way? Or was it something more?"

Three

Danny's cheeks colored and he took a moment, standing still under the sycamore tree. Finally, he said, "She was real pretty." He seemed lost in thought but then continued. "And she was nice to me. You know, every Sunday she'd make pie for that Marine and would save me a piece. I'd meet her at the park after work on Mondays and she'd give it to me. I didn't think it was right to go to her house, her being a single lady and all."

"Danny, are you talking about Sunrise Garden where she was killed?"

He nodded. "I'll never like that park again."

I searched his expression to gauge what he felt. He was easy to read, but I wanted to hear him say it. "Were you a little jealous of the Marine, Danny?"

"I wished she would've gotten rid of him. He wasn't a gentleman to her."

"If you'd been her boyfriend, would you have been a gentleman?" I elicited gently.

"I'd have been real good to her if she'd been mine. She would never have died in the park like that."

After a few pleasantries, I disengaged, waved goodbye, and was lost in thought about Danny's revelations for the remainder of my run. The big guy had a crush on Jenn. He was jealous of Walt and routinely met Jenn in the park where she died. He had the strength to overcome her in a fit of rage. Still, it didn't feel right. Jenn would *not* have dressed in that prissy green suit and walked to the park in the middle of the night to meet Danny.

When I finally rounded the corner to my block, I found full-on chaos in front of Jenn's house. Four county sheriff's cars were parked at odd angles in the street as though they'd chased someone, which they hadn't. The Calvert County Sheriff's Department doesn't get many high-profile cases, so this was a rare opportunity to use the lights and sirens. Jenn's front storm door was propped open, and a uniformed officer was standing near it, presumably to keep out nosy neighbors. In other words, people like *moi*.

Today was trash day and I returned the empty cans to the backyard though the gate. Then I stood in front of my house, hands on hips, and peered over the fence at Jenn's house. When I first moved into my place, I thought she was jealous because my house renovation was so fantastic, and her house was so blah. I had a double lot to her single one. A house twice the size of hers. Shake shingles to her vinyl siding. It took me a while to figure it out, but it wasn't my house she didn't like...

In keeping with Jenn's personality, her front yard plantings were regimented and symmetrical, with two pink geraniums planted in pots on either side of her door, and front beds book-ended with matching multi-colored hydrangeas. Jenn had planted pink ones, but I had secretly added aluminum sulfate to her soil, turning them blue. Perplexed, she'd tried to bend them to her pink-loving will by adding alkaline salts. The result was a hodge podge of pink, blue and purple. It was one of my finest accomplishments.

Jenn's Lexus was parked in her driveway and beside it was Walt's Subaru. His car had *not* been there this morning when I left on my run.

Jenn's car bugged me. Why had she walked half a mile to the park in the middle of the night in those green pumps? Driving would have been faster. She could have parked directly in front of the park. What would make her walk?

Another thing that nagged at me was that the car windows were down six inches on the driver's and passenger's sides. Jenn never left her windows down. Once a spy, always a spy. I watch people. When she parked, the windows went up. Every time. It made me wonder what was on her mind when she'd returned home last night.

If one thing was wrong with the car, maybe more was. I slipped between the police cars and to the side of the Lexus, casually looking through the rear windows which were up. There wasn't a single speck of dirt in the back seat. If you ran a Q-tip around the upholstery, it would come back whiter. *How annoying.*

The front seat was more valuable for judging Jenn's state of mind yesterday evening. There was a stack of rain-soaked work documents on the passenger seat by the lowered window. That wasn't like her. She didn't leave things in her car. Some people's cars are like mobile offices. Not Jenn's. She never left a paperclip, let alone work papers. Not once in all these years of watching her had she left papers in her car. But the day before she died, she'd left sensitive Nuclear Regulatory Commission reports on her seat. I was scanning the top one—something about an upcoming security exercise at the University of Maryland—when the officer at Jenn's door said, "Ma'am this is a crime scene. Please keep moving."

Crossing my arms and tilting my head, I played dumb. "Why?"

"Because we're investigating a murder here, ma'am."

"I certainly hope so. Whoever killed her is an animal."

"Ma'am, just move along."

I thought about the failed effort to screen Jenn's body at the park and considered offering the officer a tarp to cover the car. I opened my mouth and closed it again. Too snarky. Celia'd warned me to be on my best behavior. I quickly peeked at the driver's side of the front seat but saw nothing else of interest.

"Ma'am..."

"I was just leaving." I flashed a smile and returned to my yard, separated from Jenn's by a four-foot white plastic fence. The bayfront homes on the boardwalk were long, tall, and close to each other. Town code allowed a four-foot fence between front yards, but a six-foot fence from the beginning of the house to the end of your property. That was our situation.

Unlike Jenn, I had a garage on the full bottom floor of my house where I parked my Aston Martin convertible. I couldn't leave my little Bond car out in the elements. It was a very zippy ride, and green, the color of an emerald in Jackie Kennedy's engagement ring. Jackie Kennedy was my first role model. It was my good fortune to share her coloring: hair, eyes, complexion. I kept my hair cut in the sassy bob she wore in the 1960s.

I climbed up the flight of steps from the ground to my front porch. As the door swung in, Mr. Magoo yodeled his Basenji version of a greeting bark. His nearly sightless eyes struggled to see my face. He'd both smelled me and heard my voice while I was talking to the deputy and was none too pleased that I'd kept him waiting.

"Hi, buddy. How's my Magoo?" I stroked his short hair, no longer than a man's three-day stubble. His curly tail wagged, and he followed me as I moved to the living room window between my house and Jenn's. I peeked out and only got a different view of the officer at Jenn's front door.

The next room back, past the interior stairs to the garage, was a half bath. I raised the blinds to find myself looking down at a plain clothes detective looking up at me from Jenn's backyard. I'd startled him as he was writing something in his little notebook. I raised the window. "Hi, finding anything?"

He was a well-muscled guy and seemed like a no-nonsense law enforcement officer. He asked, "You're the neighbor, right?"

"How'd you guess?"

His eyes narrowed, and I regretted my flippant answer immediately.

He said, "We need to talk."

I smiled at him and responded with manipulative social grace, "Well, Sir, please come over. I'll make you a cup of coffee."

"I'll be there in five. Gotta tell my supervisor you're finally home."

Finally home? The officers must have told him I'd been released from the park. He'd been waiting for me. Celia was right about me being on my best behavior. She often complained that since I'd moved to the beach, I hadn't taken anything seriously. As usual, she was right. Most things in my day didn't matter to me. Not really. Not until Jenn Albrecht got herself murdered. That mattered.

The words from Danny's scripture felt like synchronicity.

I went straight to my spacious eat-in kitchen, painstakingly decorated to resemble a favorite Parisian bistro. It had a black and white tiled floor, cream walls, and a rack full of copper pots over the Carrara marble-topped island. The same marble covered the kitchen table and all the countertops. The room was a relaxing place to *rendezvous.*

Making a cup of coffee in my Keurig, I waited on the tufted

black leather banquette against the wall. Mr. Magoo was in my favorite part of the seat, so I snuggled up against him.

When the officer knocked at the front door, my 18th century ormolu clock said it had been exactly five minutes. He was very punctual.

Detective Reilly introduced himself. As we walked through to the kitchen, I chatted about the Washington Nationals and started making him the promised cup of coffee. He took it black. I crowded Magoo out of my seat this time. He jumped to the floor without a fight, keeping the detective under sightless surveillance. The law officer sat across from me on one of the padded rattan chairs.

I asked, "What can I do to help?"

"For the record, let's start with your full name."

"I'm Marnie Banks, but no one calls me Marnie. I've been called Minxy since I was eight years old." I thought to myself, that was the summer my mother almost got me killed. The year I earned being called Minxy.

He dutifully wrote it down without comment. Reilly's black hair was neatly cut and combed with every hair in place. His eyes were blue and as expressionless as gum balls. He asked, "You are aware that Jennifer Albrecht was found dead?"

Hands around my mug, I nodded. "I found her."

"Well, then you know we suspect this is a murder."

My resolve to be charming crumbled, "*Suspect?* She didn't stab herself that many times, so yes, I think you're right about the murder part."

Detective Reilly's posture became rigid. "You don't seem shaken up."

"I just can't imagine that this is a *suspected* murder."

He made an entry on his notepad, then looked up at me again. "When did you last see her?" As an afterthought he added, "Alive."

"Yesterday morning. I saw her leaving for work at her usual time." I nodded at his notepad, and added, "That would be at 6:00 a.m. She is—was—an early riser and so am I. Coming back from my morning run, I saw her leave."

He diligently took the details down. Reading upside down, I noted that he had near perfect penmanship. I had expected a blocky mess. Too neat penmanship signaled attention to details, and a need for order.

Reilly looked up and asked, "And do you know where she worked?"

Based on his penmanship I answered succinctly, "The Nuclear Regulatory Commission. She was a security exercise officer." *Just the facts,* I thought.

He responded positively, "So, you knew her pretty well."

"In a neighborly way. We weren't friends."

He set his pen down and studied me again. I already felt a zinger coming when he said, "I heard you two were on the outs."

I nodded, "It's no secret she annoyed me. She tattled on me to Town Hall for not mowing my lawn. Oh, and once or twice for putting my trash cans out too early. And a dozen or maybe more times for taking them in too late. She called you guys when my friends and I made the tiniest bit of noise after 10:00 p.m. Even on weekends and holidays. That's not a complete list of my felonies, but you get the idea." I thought he'd understand how irritating a neighbor like that would be.

Detective Reilly furrowed his brow. "Ma'am, those aren't felonies."

Oops. I got too far away from 'just the facts.' "I was joking. Of course, they aren't. They are minor violations. That's my point. She was hard to get along with."

"One of the other neighbors used the word 'vendetta' to describe your relationship with Ms. Albrecht. Something to do with those pots of dandelions in your yard near her fence."

In the old days I could control what emotions I let anyone see. Since I'd moved here, I'd gotten sloppy. I couldn't help smiling about the dandelions. "After she turned me in for inattention to my garden, I started growing dandelions."

"And the dandelions blew into her yard?"

"Absolutely. My property's up wind. So, yes, they blow across the fence."

"Why were you growing weeds?"

"To annoy her as much as she annoyed me. It was a prank."

He leaned on his thick forearms, took a deep breath, and said, "What grown woman pulls a stunt like that?" He looked doubtful that a rational person would do that. Trying to explain shenanigans are payback without violence would bounce off him like a ping pong ball off cement. I didn't respond.

Detective Reilly noted my silence in his notepad and continued his line of inquiry, "You seem almost happy that Albrecht's dead. Is that it? Do you feel like she got what she deserved for turning you in for those things?"

The sight of Jenn dead and still clinging to the mermaid flashed through my mind. A righteous truth welled up from a place inside me I didn't know existed. Without forethought I said, "I didn't like Jenn Albrecht, but no woman should die like that. I hope her killer is caught quickly and gets what he deserves." I shook my head. I had changed.

Reilly said, "So why were you joking?"

I gave him an answer I was sure he'd consider appropriate. "It is totally inappropriate to make jokes about the horrible death of Jenn Albrecht. All her tattling to Town Hall made me insensitive, and honestly, her death hasn't settled in yet. My neighbor *annoyed* me, but she didn't *enrage* me. The killer had to be both enraged and quite strong to hold her down and stab her like that."

Reilly leaned farther forward, "I think if someone's mad

enough, they become superman. *Or superwoman.* Tell me about last night. Did you see her?"

"No, I didn't see her get back from work, but her car was here when I walked my dog at 10:00 p.m. When I went by her house, I saw the shadows of two people through the curtains in her living room windows."

"Were you sure it was her? Who else could have been with her?"

"I can't be sure who it was. It was just shadows. Since it's her house and her car was there, I assumed one of the shadows was her. If she was home, though, it's important. She didn't go to the park straight after work. She intentionally went dressed for important business. That's significant."

Reilly wasn't writing. By the look on his face, he hadn't understood my point about the business clothes. He asked, "Could the other shadow have been a male?"

"It could have been a gorilla for all I know. Just the two shadows."

"Was the Subaru hatchback in her driveway then?"

"No other cars were there last night. The Subaru's her boyfriend's car. It wasn't there last night at 10:00 and wasn't there when I started my run at 5:15 a.m. I saw him at the park this morning and the car was there when I got back from my run."

He took particular care writing all that down.

"Besides you, do you know anyone else who would want to do her harm?"

Uh oh, I thought, *trick question.* I wasn't the only one who didn't like the way Detective Reilly said, *besides you.* Mr. Magoo picked up on the tone. He raised his head, and a low growl started. Unlike me, Mr. Magoo *did have* rage issues. I reached down and gave him a comforting pat. "For the record, I didn't want to harm Jenn Albrecht, so 'besides me,' is inaccurate. And no, I don't know anyone who would want to hurt her."

That wasn't exactly true. I was thinking about the restauranteur who'd had a little feud going with Jenn over fake "patrons only" parking signs. He'd installed them on the street next to his restaurant. It was a public street, so she parked there to make the point that he didn't own that parking. He probably didn't want to kill her, but there was no love lost between them. Someone else could tell the police about him. And then, there was always poor, jealous Danny.

Reilly asked, "What about her boyfriend?"

I leaned back in the banquette cushions and took a sip of my coffee to give me time to consider my answer. I enunciated carefully when I replied, "Walt, the Marine? He adored her. She had him wrapped around her finger."

"Love turns to hate...," Reilly snapped his fingers and added, "like that."

The snap startled Magoo and me, both. I reached down and gave the dog another pat to calm him.

Reilly asked, "Did they fight?"

"Jenn told him off once for buying pork hot dogs instead of turkey. That's the worst of it." I chuckled inside at my little joke about that being a fight.

"So that was the only time they fought."

"It wasn't a fight. More like her lecturing him on healthy eating. As I mentioned, we weren't close. I only know what I overheard when we were in our backyards."

Reilly turned his notepad to a previous page and tapped his pen on some of the words. "Mr. Hawley is a body builder. As you pointed out, the perpetrator is probably strong."

"I just don't see it. Walt Hawley is a brawny teddy bear who loved that woman." I didn't add that I could not figure out why, thus, the reason I spied on them when they were in the backyard. Those two together never made sense to me, however I believed the relationship was strong and real. Walt was a stand-up guy, and Jenn was a bossy busybody, but they loved each other.

Detective Reilly flipped his notepad shut and fetched a business card out of his breast pocket. "If you think of anything else, call me at this number." He drained his cup and pushed back from the table. I walked him out and waved goodbye before letting out a long sigh of relief.

Four

Mr. Magoo was finished protecting me from Detective Reilly and wanted out the back door to sleep in the sun. I followed him out of the kitchen onto the deck that overlooked Jenn's backyard on one side, the street on the other, and the alley in the back.

Jenn's yard and mine were the same depth but mine was twice as wide. I had an Ipe horizontal plank fence on two sides with gates on both the street side and the alley. Jenn's white six-foot-high plastic privacy fence was between us. When I rebuilt the house, I'd recommended that Jenn install a fence like mine around her property so it would all match. That plan didn't survive first contact with my adversary.

Mr. Magoo descended the circular metal staircase to the paver patio with a table, chairs, and a blue sun umbrella. After a brief sniff to make sure everything was alright, he jumped off the patio and found his sunny spot near the free-standing 'she shed' where I'd installed all the amenities.

I peered into Jenn's yard. Her prized roses lined the sunny

side by the far fence. I had to admit, they were *somewhat* attractive in a too pink, bubblegum kind of way. Jenn had bought varieties that were strongly scented, and the morning breeze swirled their perfume around me. I loved that scent but would have faced torture rather than admit it.

Jenn's faux wood deck had an outdoor table and chairs with a closed red umbrella in the middle. A straight path of pavers led from the deck to a small storage shed. The dandelion crop throughout the lawn was robust. I glanced at the giant pots of yellow-headed beauties sitting beside me on my deck and couldn't help but feel proud of my accomplishment. At the back of the yard by the gate was a single miniature peach tree laden with unripened fruit Jenn would never eat. A few feet farther were her trash and recycling cans by the back gate.

Today was trash day. The cans should have been on the street last night. She never missed trash day. *You were home, so why didn't you put them out? Was it that other shadow person who distracted you? What upended your obsessive-compulsive routine?*

Could the shadow have been Danny? He said he never went to her house, but people lie all the time. Thinking back to our earlier conversation, I wondered if he'd ever had problems with the law. He was off-the-charts intense, and that got people into trouble.

I pulled out my cellphone and ran his name in Maryland Case Search, a state app that made all criminal cases available to the public. The site grinded and then, *surprise.* There was a hit from eight years ago. I scanned the case for the charges. It read, "aggravated assault." A man speeding in West Beach had run over Danny's dog. Danny pulled the guy out of his car and pummeled him. He got off on diminished capacity.

Was Danny like the Hulk? I'd seen it before in people who care too much about something. Mild usually, but when angered, a monster. On the other hand, I could understand losing your mind when your pet was killed in front of you. Looking at Magoo, I knew what I'd do.

I dug the bible verse out of my running shorts pocket. 'Let each of you look not only to his own interests, but also to the interests of others. Philippians Chapter 2, Verse 4.'

It felt too much like an accusation. Did Danny pick these verses to make me feel guilty about being a narcissistic deadbeat? Had he told me that he loved Jenn to convince me he wasn't her murderer? What could she have done to bring out the Hulk? I understood how an irksome action could provoke rage and choices you regret.

I was enraged the day I quit the CIA.

After more than a decade chasing terrorists, they had sent me home for a headquarters tour. It was awful—too much bureaucracy and colleagues fighting for promotions and parking. There would always be another overseas tour, so I smiled and bided my time—until the disaster struck.

An agency-wide invitation to see an elected official came up in my email. After my childhood, politicians weren't my thing. However, it could be interesting to get the measure of the man. I walked to the old lobby where it was set up. Dozens of chairs were filled. I found one and sat.

The politician teed up a political rant in front of the Wall of Stars Memorial. Each star represented one of the CIA's fallen heroes. Many were anonymous. Those officers died patriots, with only family and agency colleagues to acknowledge their sacrifice. He could have made his speech anywhere else, and it wouldn't have bothered me. Just not there.

But he didn't want anywhere else. He used the Wall of Stars as a made-for-TV-ratings backdrop, and it *enraged me*. It wasn't a partisan thing. It was about respect. It was as wrong as a circus in Arlington Cemetery. I stood up and got mouthy. Secret Service manhandled me out the door.

Why wasn't everyone else with me?

I tried to call Celia, but she didn't pick up. That was it. I walked into another door of the agency, across the complex to my directorate's personnel office, and filled out my resignation papers. I turned them in that day. My boss had already gone home, and I made her come back to accept the papers, then and there. Not one more day. That night, I wrote heated letters to the CIA Director, the Director of National Intelligence, and the Chairs of the Senate and House Intelligence Committees. Talk about burning bridges...

Leaving the agency was like driving a racecar into a brick wall —a hundred miles per hour to zero in under a second. Every morning since, I've wondered what I should do with myself. Being without an important mission always brought out the worst in me.

I went into the house and put the worrisome verse about helping others into my giant abalone shell on a living room book-shelf. It held all the other verses Danny had given me. Unlike a fortune cookie, each one had hit me as true. Thus, I avoided him. It was all too eerie.

As I put the verse in the shell, I noticed that it was 9:15 a.m. *Uh oh.* I raced upstairs, washed with a cloth, and changed. I'd have just enough time to drive to Town Hall for my only *almost* serious obligation.

Sheriff Jack Frye, who knew my background from interactions I'd instigated, had persuaded me to perform a public service. I had agreed to meet weekly during the summer months with two West Beach teens arrested for misdemeanor criminal mischief. According to the statute that meant, "To willfully and maliciously destroy, injure, or deface the real or personal property of another."

The teens had dived headfirst into that charge by spray painting eco-warrior graffiti down the long side of the Town Hall building. Unfortunately for the kids, the bid for repainting that wall was $1200. Damage over $1000 could have been three years in jail. The mayor, who understood politics, had a friend paint the wall for $999, and his future voters got off with only ninety days probation.

I parked in front and ran inside the neo-classical building. Sitting at her reception desk, Sue checked her watch and held it up for me to see.

"Four minutes late, Sue. That's pretty good for beach time."

My "classroom" was on the left, just inside the main door. Looking through the glass, I was surprised to see the junior criminals playing rock, paper, scissors. I pushed open the door and said, "Hello Miscreants. What are you deciding?"

My sudden appearance startled them. Tyler's head snapped toward me. "*Minxy*." He swallowed hard, looked back at Emma, then answered my question. "We're deciding who has to tell you something." He was a fifteen-year-old male hipster with long, dirty blond hair pulled back in a boy-bun.

"Excellent." I said, sliding into a seat across from them. "Who lost?"

"I did," Emma snarled. She was Tyler's age and a female-hipster-eco-Zena-princess-warrior, with the emphasis on warrior. She was broad shouldered and muscled, with a daily habit of kick boxing. I could outrun her, but in a fight, I'd have to cheat.

"Well let's hear it."

Emma pushed her long, curly brown hair behind both ears and her hands were gripped together. "We sorta broke our promise to you. We were out after curfew."

"And?"

"We snuck out of our houses last night to meet on the beach."

Tyler's head bobbed up and down. "It was so beautiful. Windy and the storm clouds were coming in. We just wanted to sit on the beach and talk."

Young love, I thought. "Did your parents catch you?"

They both shook their heads. Tyler said, "Nah, we've been

sneaking out since we were ten. We're experts and they sleep like they're dead. It's just that we promised *you* we wouldn't violate our probation, including curfew."

Emma nodded agreement, "Minxy, you being a spy and all, we figured you had devices on us or something."

This was *so* easy. My expression remained serious, although I smiled like a girl on Christmas morning on the inside. There were no tracking devices. It was disturbing, however, that their loser parents didn't know they wandered around at any time, day or night.

I steadied myself for my performance. "Thank you for confessing before I had to confront you. I'll get you through this probation one way or the other. You can't ruin your lives. You're too smart for that."

Emma said, "We know what we're doing."

I shook my head. "No, you don't. Not yet, but when I get through with you, you will. Since your parents aren't watching you, you've got to wise up faster than most. I know a lot about that and can help."

Their incredulous stares told me they hadn't expected that response.

Emma went all puppy dog eyes, "Thanks Minxy. You actually listen to us. It's just, last night was *so* beautiful. Kinda eerie with the storm coming."

Tyler added, his words tumbling out with enthusiasm, "And we didn't smoke weed or anything. We just sat on the beach and talked."

Emma said, "But I started getting sleepy and we headed home. We passed the nuke lady. The one that got killed last night."

That got my attention. "What time?"

"About 12:30 or so," Tyler said.

I asked, "Where? Exactly. Which street and where on that street?"

Emma said, "On the boardwalk, just north of Fifth Street. She was walking in those heels and dressed up in a suit like she was meeting the mayor."

I asked, "Did you talk to her?"

Tyler nodded. "Yeah, I said something like 'no nukes are good nukes.' She said we should be in jail and that she'd call the major when Town Hall opened."

"She never got the chance."

Emma said, "While we were standing there, someone called her. She fumbled in that boojie bag she was carrying and answered her phone."

"And...what did she say?"

"She said, 'I'm on my way.' Then the person said something, and she said, 'Of course I'm walking.'"

My head was grinding on the significance of that call and what to do about it. "My dear Miscreants. That was probably the killer. She has his number on her phone."

We had to tell the Sheriff so he could check Jenn's phone. "I'm calling Sheriff Frye and you have to tell him what you told me."

Emma's eyes popped open. "But they'll yank our probation."

"It's all about choices. You took the risk. You could have run into that murderer instead of Jenn. Did you think about that?"

Both of their eyes widened. I could tell they hadn't understood the danger. I started dialing, "But most of all, this could be good. If you come forward with information about Jenn's death, Sheriff Frye might see you as civic minded. Imagine that."

Five

I was high on civic duty after The Miscreants told Sheriff Frye about last night. Walking to my car, an idea came to me, and it wouldn't be denied. Thinking about the rage of Jenn's murderer, I thought about someone who knew how to use a kitchen knife and had fought with Jenn before. That guy was always angry, but could he blow his top enough to kill her?

As I drove to the Italian restaurant, I asked myself, *Why am I doing this? I'm a civilian. Sue's right. The police don't want my help.* But the old skills and my ample curiosity were too strong to be denied. I was only going to ask Sal some questions, one citizen to another. I parked next to the sign that said, 'Reserved for Patrons of Sal's Italian. All others will be towed.' Climbing out of the car, I walked around and leaned against the passenger door, crossed my arms, and stared at the restaurant.

It took two minutes for Sal to blast out of the door carrying a broom. "Minxy Banks, either come in and eat, or move your car. You know that parking's for my customers."

"It's a little early for lunch, Sal. How's it going? Police visited you yet?" I scanned the two-story house that Sal had transformed into a Sicilian restaurant with a wrap-around porch. He lived in the upper floor. The place was quiet. The lunch rush hadn't started.

Sal leaned on his broom. "Why do you care? Why are you even here?"

I tried hard to keep the mischief out of my voice when I said, "Have the Sheriff's people came to talk with you about your conflict with Jenn Albrecht?"

Sal took that as disparaging and his anger erupted. He was that kind of guy. His face was red, and he started sweeping the walk with violence that launched dirt and pebbles in my direction. I pulled on my sunglasses to protect my eyes. Other than that, I wasn't worried. I'd always thought Sal was a blowhard. That assumption was being tested.

I said, "Okay, I'll start. They talked with me because of the itty-bitty friction I had with Jenn over my gardening."

Sal got closer with the broom. The strokes were getting longer against the concrete in my direction. He said, "Fantastic. They'll pin it on you. And what if they did talk with me? Who cares? No one thinks I'd kill her for parking in front of my business."

"You had her car towed. It was parked legally on a public street. That's theft."

"I was pissed off. She kept leaving it here just to make a point."

Sal's vigorous sweeping disturbed a crow in the large white oak in the restaurant's yard. She screeched down at him. Her noisy reprimand felt like female solidarity. That made me smile. "It's a fair point. Those parking signs are fake. I bet you paid to get her car hauled both ways."

His face was Santa suit red now. "What of it? It was worth it."

The broom was missing me by only a few inches, and I struggled not to flinch. "What did the police ask you?" He was so close

I could smell last night's garlic and this morning's coffee on his breath. I still didn't flinch.

Sal said, "They asked me about my relationship with that witch, and I told them I hated her guts but didn't kill her."

"That's pretty much what I told them. What's your alibi?"

"A girl slept over."

"*You've got a girlfriend? Really?*" Okay, I should have controlled my surprise better. It provoked him more.

Sal growled, turned his back on me, and continued to abuse the sidewalk. He didn't, however, try to hurt me.

I smiled and experienced a wonderful sense of pleasure as I locked my car and started walking home. Was this the way Jenn had felt when she'd done this?

Behind me I heard Sal yell, "I hate you as much as I hated her."

Jenn was right about one thing. Sal was a jerk.

As I PREPARED for happy hour, the evening was warm but the breeze off the bay kept things comfortable on the patio. It also carried the scent of Jenn's roses into my yard again. Was Jenn's ghost haunting me?

Celia and Astrid would have shown up for happy hour anyway, but tonight we had a crime to discuss. They would be here early because the Chesapeake Crime Club was back in action even if only to talk about the murder. Sue had warned us to stay out of police business, but what could a little talking hurt?

They walked through the side yard gate at precisely 5:00 p.m. Celia was resplendent in a bold-patterned T-shirt with a broach Madeline Albright would envy; Astrid was serene in beachy linen.

As she walked through the gate, Astrid said, "This murder has been on my mind all day. It proved what I've been told since childhood—dead mermaids become seafoam." Astrid was a computer whiz who was here accompanying her husband Lars on a four-year tour as Danish Ambassador. The Chesapeake reminded them of Danish beaches on the Kattegat Strait.

Celia's single eyebrow went up. Astrid had proclaimed her faith in mermaids and their afterlife, as if we would obviously understand. I stared at Celia, hoping she would go first to figure out what Astrid meant.

Celia said, "The mermaid didn't die. The statue's fine."

Astrid shook her head. "I saw too much of Jenn laying there in that bloody, seafoam green suit. Dead mermaids become seafoam. Celia, you always talk about coincidences."

Celia put a hand on Astrid like she'd slipped a cog, and said, "Astrid dear, why would people tell you that?"

"Obviously H.C. Andersen."

Celia's giant brain seemed to burn up a lot of energy and then she asked, "Hans Christian Andersen?"

"Of course. The Danish guy who wrote *The Little Mermaid*. She dies at the end and becomes seafoam."

What writer would kill off The Little Mermaid? "Astrid, let's keep this to ourselves. In the movie she becomes human and marries the prince. America isn't ready to kill off Ariel." I took a moment and then said, "But I understand what you mean. When I first saw Jenn this morning, I thought she was a mermaid, too." I didn't mention that I'd never thought Jenn was fully human.

That started a spirited discussion. I left the ladies on the back patio while I made something special in honor of the new crime— Vespers, the real James Bond martini. I filled a shaker and shook it while dancing to *Bad Romance* on the Lady Gaga station, then filled four frosted glasses. Three glasses went onto my grandmother's special silver tray. The fourth went back into the freezer.

I took the drinks carefully down the circular stairs and set the tray on the table under the sun umbrella where Astrid and Celia were comparing notes on what was known about Jenn's murder. I placed a Vesper in front of each of us and sat in the padded metal chair between Astrid and Celia.

Astrid said, "Thanks Minxy. I was just telling Celia that Travis, the Calvert County Sheriff's Deputy, updated us. We were right. The coroner said Jenn's time of death was between 12:30 am and 1:30 am."

I thought that Travis talking to the Nielsens so often hard-wired us into the police department's information systems—wonderful for a crime club. I said, "I love Travis. We should make up a Chesapeake Crime Club badge and give him one."

Celia said, "Or a nice trophy. I know a place that makes them."

I said, "I talked to Sue this morning. She saw Jenn enter the park at 12:37 am on the CCTV camera. She couldn't see the murder, but it was at least after that."

Celia glowed, "Our first assumption seems to be right. Time of death between 12:30 and 1:30."

I rocked in my chair and said, "There's more to confirm it. I met with The Miscreants who confessed to being out after curfew and ran into Jenn as she was walking to the park about 12:30. She got a call from the person she was supposed to meet and said, 'I'm on my way and of course I'm walking.'"

Celia steepled her French manicured fingernails, and said, "No way. That's too coincidental."

"Not really. It's a postage-stamp sized town. Wherever you go, you run into someone. We called Sheriff Jack so he could check Jenn's cell phone. The killer's number should be on there."

Celia ran her finger down the stem of her glass then said, "Why would the person she was meeting want her to walk?"

Astrid said, "That is strange. Why would he care?"

I said, "When we figure that out, we'll know a lot about the person she was meeting...who might also be the killer."

Celia leaned forward, "That's true. But we also need to keep The Miscreants on our list of suspects. Them being with her so close to the murder doesn't seem right."

Astrid said, "But they came forward."

Celia nodded, "It could be that they know they'd be on CCTV in the wrong place at the wrong time."

I liked The Miscreants. I did a personal check. Was I worried about them? Super sympathetic? No, I wasn't. That overwhelming compassion I'd felt for Walt wasn't there for them. At least not yet. Whew.

Astrid put both hands on the edge of the table. "Celia, they're just kids. They painted graffiti on a building. They aren't killers."

Celia tapped her lip with a dainty finger then wagged it at us. "We shall see."

Astrid scowled at Celia then turned to me, "Anyway, this morning, you said Jenn was home last night because you saw her shadow with someone else. Tell us about those shadows."

I rocked in my chair and said, "Jenn's porch light was on. As I walked Magoo by her house, I noticed two shadows through her living room curtains." I closed my eyes and tried to remember details. "They were both standing. Then one shadow sat down and the other walked out of the room. Jenn's perfect, shiny Lexus was parked in her driveway, but there weren't other cars parked there or in front of either of our houses."

Celia said, "Maybe the visitor walked from somewhere in town."

"Maybe."

Astrid said, "That's a late visit for a commuter. Lars gets up so early. Jenn must have, too." She folded her hands and put her chin on them. "It wouldn't be late for a boyfriend, though. I hope it wasn't Walt."

I thought hard about that. Could Walt have been one of the shapes I'd seen? I shook my head. "I don't know. His car wasn't there. He always parks next to her in the driveway. I just saw two adult-sized shapes. I imagined one was Jenn buffing her perfect nails, thinking up ways to get me in trouble."

Celia laughed. "Your inner narcissist is showing. This isn't about you. Could you hear them talking?"

I shook my head. "Curtains drawn and windows closed."

She continued, "Did anyone come or go after that?"

"I went straight to bed with a novel. I woke up this morning with the book on my face and Magoo's head on my stomach." Hearing his name, the dog cocked his head to the side, listening to see if I wanted something. He did a dutiful circle around the table getting pets from everyone, then returned to his spot and lowered his head to his outstretched legs.

Astrid said, "Deputy Travis told Lars another strange thing about the murder. Jenn was strangled before she was stabbed. She had bruises on her neck, but it wouldn't have killed her."

Celia said, "Oh my. More anger."

I said, "I saw the bruises this morning. They're on the left side of her neck, so the killer was probably in front of her using his left hand. I have the video if you'd like to see it."

They both said "No," in unison.

I shrugged, "You two are so squeamish. I think the killer choked her to shut her up. She was giving him a piece of her mind, and he lost it. He could have just choked her to death, but stabbing her too...that's rage, right?"

Celia's head slowly nodded agreement. She said, "You just made three important assumptions. You said 'he,' 'to shut her up,' and 'rage.' Those are good. *Very good.* Statistically, men commit more murders. The odds are with us on that. We know from experience Jenn would tell anyone anywhere what she thought of them. We've all wanted to choke her. Finally, the level of violence means the killer was extremely upset with something she'd done."

I said, "We're building a theory of the murder that isn't bad for this early."

Astrid said, "Don't forget about the gun. When you texted us that there was a gun in her purse, I couldn't believe it. But it makes me think she knew the killer. He didn't scare her. Otherwise, she would have pulled it out and shot him."

I took a moment, then said, "Maybe there are two different people involved. Maybe there was the professional person she dressed up for and went to the park to meet clandestinely. If she'd known him well, she wouldn't have dressed like that and they might have met in her home like the second shadow did. Then there could be someone else who came across her in the park that she knew or wasn't afraid of. She didn't dress for that guy but he could have killed her."

Astrid said, "That's an interesting theory. Jenn went to the park to meet a spy but found a different person there instead. While she was waiting to share secrets with your undercover agent, a crazy man came into the park and killed her."

Celia leaned forward. "You're both on to something. Standing there waiting, she was a vulnerable woman who could have been attacked by a random mentally ill or violent person. That's scary."

Tired of sitting, I started pacing across the patio. "I can see the scenario. Jenn's in the park late at night wearing her prissy little pantihose, when a crazy vagrant comes in to pee. She reads him the riot act about public urination. He could have choked her and stabbed her before her real contact arrived." I stopped pacing and clasped my hands in front of me. "That's right ladies. It's time to get out our whiteboard. We need to keep all these potential killers and motives straight." I thought, *What harm can it do to keep track of these theories, facts, and assumptions? It's just a pastime.*

Astrid motioned for me to sit back down. "I'll get it." She went into the 'she shed' and retrieved the three-by-four-foot white-board. I helped her hang it on screws that Eli had installed on my side of Jenn's plastic privacy fence while she was at work. The last time we'd used the whiteboard, I'd seen her glowering at it from her upstairs window.

The Garden Gnome Case was our last mystery. Someone was stealing them from yards in West Beach. Five of them had gone missing in less than a month. *The horror.*

In a week we'd unmasked the thirteen-year-old daughter of the Mini-Mart owner. She'd stashed the creepy figures under her bed. After a discussion with us, the girl had returned all the little statues to their owners. I informed the Sheriff that the town was safe again for mythic creatures. My campaign to curry his favor had progressed.

Celia dumped a reusable grocery bag full of erasable markers onto the table and we all began triaging the pile, sorting the dried-up from the viable ones. Mr. Magoo was the first to hear the knock on the front door. When I saw him stand, I heard it, too.

I jogged up the circular stairway and from the kitchen could see my guest through the front door that was original to the house —glass doorknobs and rows of windowpanes set in solid wood let in the light. It also served as an early warning system for visitors on my porch. I could smell my guest's cigarette.

As I headed through my house I called out, "You're late."

Six

My new guest was Astrid's husband, Ambassador Lars Neilsen. He was an irregular visitor to our happy hours because he often worked late. He said, "Denmark is a small, but demanding task master."

"Astrid said you were coming tonight, so I made your drink. Just don't smoke that cigarette in my house."

Lars smiled. "I wouldn't think of it." He crushed the cigarette out against the side of the empty flowerpot on the front porch, then dropped it into the sand at the bottom. In his free hand, he carried a plastic container.

"What did you bring us?"

"*Sild*...pickled herring. I know you love it."

"I do. Thanks, *mon ami*."

I curled my arm around his like Jackie Kennedy would have welcomed a Rat Pack visitor and led him into the house. Lars claimed the fourth drink from the freezer, and I carried the herring with plates and forks down the spiral stairs to join the others.

He walked to the edge of my patio and peered over Jenn's fence. "The dead woman's yard is so orderly. The roses. The deck."

"The dandelions," quipped Celia.

Lars frowned like he had a translation problem. "Quite a few. I noticed many in the front yard, so I guess it is to be expected they are here, too."

I said, "Oh yes, it *is* to be expected." I gazed up at the pots full of yellow-headed dandelions on my deck. Some had even seeded into the little puffy white globes of mischief, ready to be blown into Jenn's yard. "Weeds in a yard are like a coffee stain on a white suit. A rip in your favorite leather sofa. It's to be expected. Nothing perfect stays that way for long. I tried to explain that to Jenn, but she resisted."

Celia raised up from the marker project. "A superb point. Jenn strove for perfection."

We all nodded and forked pieces of pickled fish into our mouths. I looked up from my plate and said, "Maybe Jenn got tired of repressing herself. Let's think outside the box. She drank too much with the shadow person and dressed in her best suit for a midnight stroll to the park."

Celia said, "No, Jenn didn't suddenly become a free spirit."

I said, "I suppose not. But it was fun to imagine."

Astrid shook her head. "No. She didn't change. Celia's right. Jenn was a perfectionist and responsible. She went to Sunrise Garden after midnight because it was the right thing to do. That's the big clue we have. She was on a mission to do something good that was a secret and dangerous enough to carry a gun. It will all fit together."

Celia said, "Your *ecosystem* theory of crime." We all nodded, except Lars who looked confused. Celia added, "In an ecosystem, all the elements fit together, even though it's complex. To solve the crime, you must understand why it all makes sense."

I picked up on the tutorial for Lars by adding, "Jenn took her folio to the park, which doesn't seem to fit when you first think about it. It's too dark to write on the paper pad. But it does make sense if she was passing papers at a clandestine meeting with someone important. It fits the suit, and last night's windy conditions."

Celia said, "This morning, the folio pocket was empty."

I took one of the markers and wrote on the whiteboard 'Killer' / Motive' and under it, 'Clandestine Operative.'

Lars was sitting next to Astrid. He said, "Minxy and Celia, is it possible you see spies everywhere because of your past? This is little West Beach, not Vienna. That murder was full of anger and fear. That's not the way spies kill people. They are more... efficient."

I said, "That's what I thought—West Beach is a sleepy backwater and so many stab wounds is rage not trade craft. A spy would strike once to the heart. But the only way that meeting makes sense is if the purpose was professional and clandestine."

Astrid said, "Before you came, darling, I suggested Jenn went to meet an important secret agent, but she was attacked by a crazy person before she got the chance. That explains the suit and the unnecessary violence."

I nodded and wrote 'Random Crazy Stranger' on the board.

Lars wrinkled his brow and asked, "Are we like a citizen's council trying to help the police find the killer?"

I said, "No Lars. After I quit the CIA, Celia convinced me to move here so she could keep an eye on me. When I get bored, I cause mischief, so she dragged me into solving neighborhood crimes to keep me busy. Astrid has completed our team."

Astrid put her hand on his forearm, "We do this all the time because we're fond of mysteries. It's like that business with the garden gnomes."

Lars said, "Oh. But this is quite a lot more important than that."

Celia clasped her hands together. "Indeed, it is. But the Chesapeake Crime Club works with the crimes it gets—small like gnomes or now, big like murder. We aren't always this lucky."

Astrid said, "Oh Celia, you can't say that. Murders aren't lucky. People will think we are evil."

Astrid's reprimand to Celia made me *so* happy. For a change, someone else was in trouble for being insensitive. I added, "Tonight, we have a murder. Next week it could be another stolen mulch pile."

Astrid shook her head. "Still not appropriate but I'll let it go."

Celia looked at Lars and said, "Maybe it is a spy thing. We love putting clues together to understand a mystery...and drinking cocktails while we do it."

He nodded, "Spies are such *interesting* people."

By 'interesting' I knew our favorite Ambassador meant 'strange.' "Speaking of interesting, on my run I talked with Danny Stone. You know him. The big guy that does maintenance and gardening for the town."

Nods all around.

"He confessed that he 'loved' Jenn and was jealous of Walt."

Astrid said, "He is a gentle person, I can't imagine him hurting Jenn."

"Well, here's the kicker," I said. "They met every Monday after work in Sunrise Garden so Jenn could bring him a piece of pie."

Celia pointed her finger authoritatively and said, "Too coincidental. His name goes on the list." Astrid gave her a side eye.

I continued, "And Danny beat a felony assault charge due to diminished capacity. He proved he can be pushed into uncontrollable rage."

Now the motion was unanimous, and I added his name to the board.

"And then there's Sal..."

We all called out, "List him," in unison. Sal's anger was well known.

Celia laid a finger to the side of her pink cheek. The diamond in her ring caught the sun and nearly blinded me. "We must list The Miscreants, if only to clear them."

Celia was right. I added them to the list, convinced that I could clear them quickly.

Lars said, "When I went home to change, I saw Travis and asked about the case again. Sometimes I think he waits in his front yard so he can talk with me. He said they're interrogating the boyfriend for the second time. You know. That Marine fellow."

My sympathy for Walt's suffering welled up again inside of me, I slapped my palm into Jenn's fence. It surprised me as much as the others. I said, "They always assume it's the boyfriend. It's just not true in this case. I know it."

I needed to cool down, so I went to the kitchen to make another round of drinks.

WE WORKED for another two hours, and in the end we all approved of our hard work on the whiteboard, fueled, as it was, by the power of Vespers. It had been a rewarding pastime. The list was inclusive, meaning Astrid added Walt and me out of mischief. Names were written in the order we thought of them, not importance:

Killer? / Motive
- Clandestine Operative
- Random Crazy Stranger

- Danny
- Sal
- The Miscreants
- Minxy
- Walt
- Coworker at NRC HQ because Jenn was really mean
- Coworker at a security exercise because Jenn was really mean
- Someone we haven't figured out yet.

Like playing the boardgame Clue, we knew the murder happened in the park with a knife. Somewhere in the list of suspects might be the third element, the killer. However, in my humble opinion, Clue had ignored the most important element of a crime—the motive. *Why* did Miss Scarlet kill the victim in the conservatory with the lead pipe? Had he stolen her jewelry, cheated her out of money, mistreated her dog? The suit and folio clues look out of place in the park, but Astrid's ecosystem works because *why they were there* would explain the murder and probably the murderer. In this case, it would likely turn out to be more than Astrid's 'because Jenn was really mean.'

Or maybe not.

The hard work completed, I walked Astrid and Lars out the side gate and waved as they headed home holding hands.

Celia said, "I'll stay for a bit." She absolutely glowed. I wondered what she was up to, so I poured two glasses of an already opened chardonnay and waited for her to come out with it.

We lingered on the patio, sitting in the dark, drinking our wine. She wasn't forthcoming, so I provoked her. "You do know we'll never solve this case. The three of us will make a list of killers and think a lot about motives. We will drink many martinis. Then the prosecutor will charge some unlucky fool, and we'll never know the truth."

Celia gave me a side-eyed glance and said, "I'm almost positive the prosecutor will indict Walt. You sympathized with him in the park today. I saw it. Are you going to let that happen?"

Unfortunately for me, I couldn't quite shake that soft spot I'd developed for Walt. I could, however, deny it. "I barely know Walt. I felt something this morning, but I'm over it. I'm sure he'll get a fabulous lawyer who'll prove he's innocent."

"Come now. You *do know* he's poor…"

I nodded, "The twenty-five-year-old Subaru hatchback gave *that* away. Still, he's an entrepreneur. Those guys make stuff happen."

"Sure, *I wish I'd* owned a gym during the pandemic."

Celia was right. I said, "Well, yeah. Walt doesn't have two nickels to rub together."

Celia sat up straight, emanating her full regal countenance. I was sure in a past life she'd been royalty. At least a duchess, if not higher. She just stared at me.

I nodded, then admitted, "Okay. He may be sunk."

She took the tiniest sip of her wine and created a dramatic pause by staring at the stars. Finally, she added, "My dear, you know you could help him. His case is high stakes. Not like national security, but it feels worth spending time on. Like the old days."

Celia watched me to see if her cleverly worded punch had landed. She was the only person who could, with knowledge and forethought, get under my skin and mess with my mind. I knew she was right about this. It did sound like something I could do. Something that suited my talents.

Celia followed up with, "Everyone will believe it was Walt. Someone needs to figure out who did it. The murderer's still out there."

I thought about how good it would be to have something important to do. It would scratch the itch that my little pranks and gnome cases couldn't quite satisfy. And, unlike some Dark Empaths, I was not a complete narcissist. It bothered me that the murderer was still out there. I wanted to catch him to protect myself and the other women of West Beach. It wasn't only about me this time. I nodded agreement but remained silent.

Celia said, "So tomorrow please pick up the private investigator's license. Is that too much to ask? It's been ready for weeks."

Ahh, that was it. The PI license. On a lark, I'd told Celia I was considering a PI license. I'd never expected to do the work but it would be fun to say I was a private detective. I checked on training, and to my surprise, the state didn't mandate anything—at least not then. Changes were coming. I *did* have to sign up with a state-certified PI Agency, which could require training. That had turned out to be easier than expected, and I sent in my paperwork. All I had to do was pick up that little license and I'd be a real deal private investigator.

"Okay. You win. I'll pick up the license. They're still holding it for me." I hated it when Celia was right. This time, however, the idea of being official made my brain take its first few steps in a slow march out of the doldrums. "Walt's case will be loads more interesting than the gnome case."

"You were in your old form with that case, though. A bit aggressive for a trivial crime, but nicely done. Setting a bait statue visible from the street, and using a motion activated camera to record the theft—you got that girl dead to rights."

I shook my head, "Too easy. She was a kid. Not the same thrill as tracking Al Qaeda."

Celia said, "It's not *always* about the stakes. You like extracting intelligence and figuring out what it means."

"True, but I need the thrill of an *important* case. A real mission."

Celia glowed, "Well then, Minxy, we could save Walt from a miserable life in prison. That's momentous to him. By all accounts, he's an upstanding citizen whose only fault was loving strong-willed Jennifer Albrecht."

I wondered if helping others would feel good. *Bingo*. It would. That was it. Danny's bible verse was ringing in my ears.

Seeing my internal deliberations, Celia piled on. "Exercising that genius brain will be healthy for you. Besides, you're bored and need a challenge."

"I'm not bored. I love my life of leisure."

"Sure, you do. It's written all over you." Celia chuckled. It was a lilting laugh like I'd said the funniest thing she'd ever heard.

Celia pulled out a piece of paper from her pocket. It was folded in half and then in quarters. She handed it to me. "I found Walt's home and work addresses, and his cell number."

I looked at the sheet. I did miss the rush of the hunt. And I liked to charm or manipulate people out of their secrets. Machiavellian for sure, my shrink would hate it, but if it was for a decent cause... Figuring out who killed Jenn in the park with the knife would be more than a game of Clue. It would be a public service. That would be enough. "Let's say I might *kind of enjoy* keeping Walt out of prison."

Celia smiled. She knew she'd won. "Well then, I think we should talk with him. We can offer our services to find evidence for his case."

I said, "He was loyal to Jenn. He won't be keen on letting us help. I did bond with him once a few years ago, though."

"Do tell. When was that?"

"I thought I told you about it. He'd locked himself out of Jenn's house while she was gone. He was sitting on the porch all dejected. So, I offered to help."

"No way. You never had her key."

"True. But in two minutes I had my lock picking tools slid

inside her below-average door lock. Thirty seconds later, the door clicked open."

"Why did he let you pick her lock?"

"I had it picked before he could say no. When he got over the surprise he said, 'I thought you had a spare key.' I answered, 'Nope. We aren't that close. Tell her I recommend she get a more secure lock.' He decided to keep the incident between us."

"Maybe he'll remember that bonding moment."

I said, "So, for the sake of argument, we want to offer our services and ask him questions. In his state of mind, he won't respond to an invitation from me."

"So true."

I felt a smile break out, "If he won't come to us..."

"We'll go to him." She raised her nearly empty wine glass and touched it to mine.

I nodded. I was getting sucked into this case. My mind was racing, and the juices were flowing. It felt delightful. "Tomorrow, I'll book an introductory appointment at his gym for you and me. Two women wanting to get in shape. Let's go in alias. I'll make something up."

Celia said, "I like it. Can we do it around eleven? I can go on my lunch hour."

"I'll see what he has. You and I will surprise him in the gym, and he'll have to listen."

Celia was nodding and finished the last sips of the delightful chardonnay. "Yes, yes, yes. We'll size him up to make sure he's not the killer. Then we'll offer support, because that indictment is coming at him fast." Celia stood. "My job here is done. We working people need sleep."

"I'll walk you home."

"I'm okay. You know I've got mace on my keychain."

"Yes, but I have to get my car."

"You left your car in town and walked home?"

The smile erupted across my face. "I did. Come see where I parked it."

We strolled through the mild night air the few blocks to Sal's. When she saw my beautiful emerald Aston Martin, Celia laughed. "You left it in one of Sal's fake restaurant parking spaces? *Really?*"

I could feel myself vibrate with the pleasure of my prank. "Yes, I was pushing him to see if he could get angry enough to kill Jenn over parking."

"And..."

"He passed the test. He controlled the rage today, but who knows what could push him over the edge."

Standing by my car, I looked up at the lights in Sal's upstairs apartment. Celia followed my gaze. "Maybe Sal's girlfriend stayed over with him again."

We watched the windows for movement.

It wasn't long before we saw Sal's stocky figure moving around, visible through the open curtains. After five minutes, we were about to give up when we glimpsed a female shape moving from one room to the other.

Celia said, "So then, Sal has at least one woman who can stand him. Maybe only in small doses, but it's something."

I smiled. "But it's not a solid alibi until we know more about her." I offered to drive Celia the rest of the way, but she declined. I opened my car door but my inner devil—and too much to drink—stopped me. I closed it again and walked home.

Seven

THURSDAY, JUNE 22, WEST BEACH, MD

I put on my oversized Jackie sunglasses and walked onto the front porch at 5:15 a.m. sharp. The Vespers and my talk with Celia had left me with a tiny headache and a huge sense of purpose. I sped down the boardwalk at a pace I didn't usually find so early in the run.

More walkers and runners than usual were out early enjoying the golden glow of the sun rising over the Chesapeake. As I made the turn onto the fishing pier, I heard the slapping of running shoes coming fast from behind me. It was Ricky Domingo.

He pulled alongside me, then matched my speed like usual. "Minxy what's got into you? You never run this fast. I had to sprint to catch up."

"Loving life so much, I'm bursting at the seams."

He laughed. "That's some big-time BS, girl."

"Yeah, I know. But I did have fun last night. My friends and I had a little get together."

"That's nice. But honestly...you girls do that every night."

"What? Do you keep tabs on us?"

He smirked, "You've got a corner lot on the boardwalk. Everybody in town knows about Minxy's patio happy hour."

Predictability was a threat. A case officer who did the expected was vulnerable. I once was more cautious. "Whatever. I've got breaking news." I looked at Ricky over the top of my sunglasses. "I'm getting my PI license today."

"No kidding?"

"No kidding." We reached the end of the pier and headed back. The seagulls on the beach battled over a crust of bread.

Ricky turned to me. "Congratulations...I think. You gonna catch cheatin' husbands?"

"No. I plan to work for Jenn Albrecht's friend Walt."

Ricky ran his hand through his hair. "Uh, he's that Marine guy, right? He's gonna be arrested. It's always the boyfriend or the husband."

I shot him a glare of reproach, "Ricky, shame on you. It's *often* the boyfriend or husband. That doesn't mean it's *always* him."

Ricky smirked, "Well okay. Best of luck, Sherlock. I hope he pays well."

I gave him back my most flirtatious smile and said, "Oh no, I'm doing it for free."

He shook his head, "Minxy Banks, you are one weird chick." He blew me a kiss and took off at a speed he knew I couldn't match.

<hr>

THURSDAY, JUNE 22, WASHINGTON, DC

Walt's legal name was Walter J. Hawley. He'd served two tours in Iraq and one in Afghanistan as a Marine before getting out and opening a gym in D.C. Of course, he called it 'G.I. Fit.' His muscles bulged out his tee shirt in all the right places. He cropped his sandy hair short, and his smile was blindingly white. I'd surreptitiously monitored Walt at Jenn's for about two years. He'd always been gentle and kind. *How Jennifer snagged a man like Walt, I'll never know.*

My mind hopped to my long-term beau, Theo. I forced it to hop back.

Celia and I planned to meet in front of Walt's Capitol Hill gym at 11:15 a.m. I had made a joint appointment for us as 'Renee and Renata.' Celia objected to those names, saying they sounded like a bad German yodeling act, but the die was cast. We were supposed to discuss our fitness goals and then walk through using the equipment. We had no plans for doing either.

Arriving early to check out the location, I discreetly watched through the window while Walt supported all types of guys and gals in their midday workouts. He was like a master sculptor helping his students shape their bodies and make their fantasies come true. There was none of the hyper machismo I'd experienced in other gyms. Walt laid an encouraging hand on a shoulder here and coaxed another set of repetitions for someone else over there. My esteem for Walt Hawley rose to a remarkable height.

Celia arrived and we stood by a coffee shop two doors down to synchronize our plan. When Renee and Renata walked in, G.I. Fit was completely full of lunch-break athletes sprinting on treadmills and hoisting weights.

A door chime notified Walt of comings and goings. When our entrance caused it to sound, Walt looked up from a man he was guiding in push up technique. He disengaged and headed toward us immediately, greeting us with a smile and an outstretched hand —until he recognized me.

His smile faded and the hand dropped to his side. His voice was more accusatory than welcoming when he said, "What are you doing here?"

Celia's outstretched hand hung awkwardly until she gave up

and let it drop. She said, "We're very sorry for your loss. We'd like to talk with you."

Walt's jaw hardened and his hands balled into fists. It was a facet of Walt I'd never seen, but had expected. Even friendly Marines are trained to fight. I wasn't feeling sympathy for him now, but I could read his frustration, pain, and confusion. He said, "I've got an appointment coming in about now. I can't talk with you two." He turned to walk away.

I said, "We know. We're your appointment. Renee and Renata."

Turning back, he stared at us, as if looking for answers written on our clothing or skin. After a few seconds, he guided us with the tilt of his head in the direction of a door next to the water cooler in the back. "Let's go to my office. I want you to explain what you're up to."

Down the poorly lit but clean hallway and past the bathrooms, we arrived at Walt's office. His battleship gray metal desk was government issue circa World War II, and his faux leather chair had been repaired with duct tape. Like the rest of the gym, the room was spotless. The smell of PineSol confirmed the linoleum had been recently mopped. The three-inch pile of bills was neatly stacked. Walt sat behind the desk and pointed to the plastic chairs in front for us.

We sat. I placed my keys on the desk, then made myself as comfortable as possible in the plastic chair.

Cocking his head, he got to the point. "So why are you here?"

I said, "We're trying to figure out who killed Jenn."

That stunned him. He blurted out, "But, you hated Jenn."

My head swiveled side to side to show how strongly I disagreed. "Hate is too strong a word. As you know, we had our differences." I could see he wasn't buying it. I touched the keys I'd laid on the desk to remind him subliminally. I hoped it would buy me a small measure of goodwill.

He looked at the keys, then said, "You drove her crazy with those weeds."

I thought of several witty retorts, but the woman he loved was dead, so I bottled them up. Instead, I said, "We've heard you're the number one suspect and we don't think you did it."

Celia's head bobbed in agreement. "I checked through DHS with some law enforcement officers, your name is the *only* one on the list. And like Minxy said, we don't think you did it."

His eyes widened and he leaned back in the chair. "That makes three of us. Pretty much *only* three. They've interviewed me a couple of times. They keep letting me go but warn me to stay close. They're going to lock me up. I can feel it."

Celia said, "We can help clear you. You don't know us well, but we've got first class intelligence skills. We can uncover things the police either can't or won't find."

"I believe it. I've seen Minxy with a lock pick."

He did remember that day I helped him. I took in the humbleness of his office and added, "Oh, and we're doing this *pro bono*, so it'll save you money."

"What's *pro bono*?"

At the same time, Celia and I said, "Free."

Walt took a moment, caught my eyes, and asked, "Why would you help me?"

I thought, *an honest question deserves an honest answer.* "I'm trying to be a better person, and I've got the time and skills to do it."

He put his hands to his cheeks and rubbed the minimal scruff sprouting from the morning's tight shave. "I don't have a lawyer yet. I know I need one, but God knows how I'll pay him." He sat quietly looking at the stack of bills, then he said directly to me, "I should have been there to protect her."

That made me sympathize with his pain again. I felt his frustration twist in my gut like a viper. I said, "She was a strong-willed, independent woman. You couldn't be with her all the time. She'd never have let you."

He nodded. "She made me promise not to come to West Beach on Tuesday night. She was doing something important but wouldn't tell me what it was. She was unnerved by it though."

"*Unnerved?*" I asked. I couldn't imagine Jenn Albrecht anything but cool and in charge.

His face pinched up while he thought. "That isn't quite the right word. It was frightening, but she was on her high horse about something crucial. It was a big deal for her." He looked at Celia, "To be honest, I think it excited her. Some kind of thrill."

Celia said, "We understand such things."

I asked, "So it was work related?"

He shrugged, "I've thought about it constantly since she was killed. I don't know. She had a lot on her plate at work. She'd failed Calvert Cliffs Nuclear Power Plant on their exercise. That always took a bunch of extra effort. The facility had to redo the whole thing."

Celia asked, "Is it common to fail plants on exercises?"

For the first time since we'd arrived at the gym, Walt smiled. "It was typical for her. She said some of her colleagues just went through the motions, but she actually put those guys through their paces. They usually passed on the second try."

"Was she working on anything else at the Nuclear Regulatory Commission? Maybe something hotter than an exercise?"

He thought for a beat before answering. "She had something going on that she wouldn't talk about. She had files she would close whenever I came into her office at the house."

Celia asked, "Any guesses about what the issue was?"

He shook his head, "I don't know. Her colleagues are whiny backbiters. She called one of her work headaches a 'security problem.' She couldn't tell me much. Talk about nuclear anything and it gets classified fast. I had Top Secret clearances when I was active duty, so I get it."

Celia said, "Physical security, personnel security, or national security?"

"No idea."

I asked, "Who was she on the outs with in her private life?"

His eyes fixed on me. "You mean besides you?"

I shrugged and looked my most amiable to deflect Walt's suspicions, "Well, yeah. Other than me. I'm positive I didn't kill her."

Walt lowered his head and studied me, trying to figure out why, of all people in the world, I was sitting in his office. Celia broke the tension, saying, "We know about the tiff with Sal, at the Italian restaurant. Anybody else?"

Walt's head bobbed up and down. "In addition to Sal, she had something with the mayor. She'd called him out on some West Beach business. I admit, I didn't listen so well when she explained it. It was about contracts for town work not being done right."

"Anyone else?"

"Anti-nuke environmentalists were a problem for her. They always showed up when she spoke about nuclear power. Those folks were born angry."

I wrote down 'town contracts' and 'anti-nuke activists' on the little note pad I'd pulled from my purse. No idea what the contract problem was about, but I'd figure it out. The environmental concern was different. I'd seen Jenn's name and picture on posters advertising community discussions on future energy options. That kept The Miscreants under suspicion.

Walt leaned forward. "She was worried enough about something that she had me lend her a gun. I didn't know if it was personal or work related. But it was scaring her."

I sat up in my seat, "It was yours?"

He nodded and his lips broke into a younger man's smile. "I

brought it to her last weekend. She grew up in a small Midwestern town and was familiar with guns. I picked out a revolver because they're easy to use and took her to the range for practice. She handled it well." He was clearly proud of her. I could see his mind drifting off to the past.

Celia must have seen it too; she lured him back to the present by saying, "So Jenn was worried enough to borrow a gun? She had both professional and personal issues with people. We need to figure out what she thought required business clothes in the park late at night."

I added, "Can you help us figure out why they met there so late? They could have met at an all-night coffee shop, a gas station, an office building, even in her own living room. Why there?"

Walt answered slowly, "It's just too crazy. I've wracked my brain. I don't know. It didn't sound like Jenn. She must have thought it was the right thing to do, though."

The three of us nodded in agreement. I said, "If we can understand why she did that, we'll figure out who she met and why."

I said, "The Sheriff's Department found your gun in her purse at the murder scene. That looks bad."

We all sat silently, knowing his fingerprints were on it.

I asked, "Got a decent alibi?"

Eight

Walt scratched his chin, "Nope. My alibi sucks. I was alone in my apartment." His eyes looked toward the ceiling. "I live upstairs. I didn't see or talk to anybody after closing the gym at 10:00 p.m."

I asked, "Did you call anyone on your landline?"

"Don't have one. I texted Jenn through the night, but she didn't answer. That's why I came to West Beach."

Celia said, "We saw you yesterday about 6:00 a.m. When did you get to the beach?"

"About 5:40. I went to Jenn's place first. Her car was there, but she hadn't slept in the bed. I started running all over town to find her."

His pain stabbed through me again, and I stared at the floor. Sympathizing with his desperate situation was awful. He had no money, a dead girlfriend, and almost everyone thought he'd killed her. How do sympathetic people survive?

Shaking it off, I leaned forward. "Walt, we're experienced at digging things up. Important things people want hidden. We'll figure out what the security issue is, what the personal issues are, why she went out that night, and who she met. As we collect hard evidence, we'll pass it to you and your lawyer."

"Why are you doing this? You tormented her."

Since I shared his pain, I owed him a real answer. Celia's eyebrows were squished together, probably worried about what might come out of my mouth. I thought it over and said, "No one deserves to die like that, and you didn't do it. We all agree on those two things."

Celia asked, "So, will you let us help you?"

He looked between the two of us, then said, "I don't know. Give me some time to think."

Celia stood. "We understand. Let us know."

<hr>

CELIA and I walked to the Union Station Metro which would take her back to the office and me to my car in its parking structure. As we were saying goodbye, she said, "Walt's in bigger trouble than we thought."

"I know. No alibi. No money. The gun. Do you think he knew Jenn was meeting someone at home before the other guy in the park?"

Celia shook her head. "Probably not. And if he'd known about the park, he'd have been there. He'd have found a way. That's what Marines do."

"That's what's bothering me. He was worried enough to check on her through the night. He knew something was up."

Celia said, "To be at her house by 5:40 a.m., he had to call her earlier than 4:30 a.m. You have to be seriously worried to do that. We saw him at the park at 6:00. In twenty minutes, he'd already checked her house and found her in the park."

"The timeline's tight. He could do it though. He saw the crowd and headed toward it just like you did. Maybe someone saw him leave his garage in D.C. He might have stopped for gas, or coffee, that would help nail down his timeline. I can testify his car wasn't at her place at 10:00 p.m. or at 5:15 a.m. But he could have parked somewhere else. If he was in West Beach around midnight..."

Celia slid her bangles up one arm. "Let's hope he told us the truth." We both nodded.

She headed down the escalator to the Metro station, and over her shoulder she called to me, "Pick up your PI license."

"You know, you can be really bossy." I saw her laugh.

Walking to my car in the parking garage, I remembered a day I hadn't thought of for a long time; the day my mother died.

Early that morning, Belinda our housemaid, had brought my mother's suitcase downstairs. I found Shelly—she insisted I call her that from birth—in her bedroom. I asked her, "Where are you going?"

"To the beach house on Long Island. I need to think through some things."

To survive with Shelly, I had learned to read her moods. Something dark had infested her. It seemed like pain. Maybe fear. I watched as she gathered up her purse and jacket. I was only sixteen, but I knew she was in trouble. Whatever it was, she would be better with me as company. "I'm coming with you. You can sail and I'll read on the boat. I'll be around in case you need company."

"No. I need to be alone. But, Minxy, I appreciate your offer." She smiled but didn't hug or kiss me goodbye before she walked out the door.

Before dinner, the police knocked on the door to tell us Shelly was dead.

If I'd had a car, I would have followed Shelly to Long Island.

Walt's a battle tested Marine. Why hadn't he come to check on Jenn if he was so worried? If he's lying about being the shadow in Jenn's window or coming to the beach after work, even we can't help him.

DRIVING HOME FROM D.C., I couldn't get Walt and his troubles out of my head. I was obsessing on the Sheriff's Department repeated questioning.

When I first moved to the beach, I'd wanted to figure out who the power players were in my new neighborhood. For West Beach, that was Mayor Bill Hampton, a resort owner. Property investment, construction, and renovation were key enterprises in the town.

Calvert County, however, didn't have a single honcho. The Board of Commissioners was made up of five civic-minded souls. The divided power kept any of them from being too strong. The County Administrator kept a low profile. For the county as a whole, I found the Sheriff was the most visible leader of the 93,000 people who lived on the peninsula between the Patuxent River on the west and Chesapeake Bay on the east. That office currently was held by Sheriff Jack Frye.

Jack had seemed like a valuable contact, so every election year I'd sat in the front row of campaign rallies, asked him pithy questions, and donated significant checks. In addition, I'd sent notes to thank him for solving various convenience store robberies. On local talk radio I'd called in to praise him for catching catalytic converter thieves. On numerous occasions, I'd even manufactured bumping into him in the coffee shop near his office in Prince Frederick.

It had been a successful influence operation worthy of any intelligence officer. Whenever I called, Jack picked up.

I'd planned to get my PI credentials, but I dialed the Sheriff's office instead. I got an appointment set for as soon as I could get there. If anyone knew what they had on Walt, it was my pal, Jack.

Arriving at Church Street in Prince Frederick's town center in twenty minutes, I gave my hair a brush and added pink lipstick. This was a political meeting, so I needed to look my professional-in-a-beach-environment best. I was glad I'd worn a decent skort to Walt's gym. My beachy dress code was still a work in progress and now I'd have to rethink my image again.

The Sheriff's Department was a spacious three-story building with white siding and dormer windows on the top floor. It had a properly grand public entrance up a red brick staircase to a four columned porch and double doors. The federal, state, and county flags were on display. For a Manhattanite, the most amazing feature was parking near the front door.

I cleared security and was standing in Sheriff Jack's waiting room when he opened his office door to talk with Michelline, his secretary, about editing a letter. I usually expected a phony smile from a politician. If Sheriff Jack's wasn't real, he was an excellent faker. He met my eyes and seemed thrilled to see me.

Jack was a good-looking man—tall, dark, and muscled. His wavy brown hair was disciplined by an excellent cut. Dropping paperwork on Michelline's desk and thanking her, he took me by the arm and ushered me into his office. I saw it for what it was. The expression on his face, the way his arm curled around mine, *he was flirting with me.*

He seated me in a burgundy leather chair in front of his oak desk. Behind it was a flagpole with the Calvert County flag. That hadn't been there the last time I visited. Without prompting, he reached into a discreetly hidden mini fridge, retrieved a cold bottle of water, and set it on a coaster. "Minxy, long time no see. What was it, the fish fry in St. Leonard's four months ago?"

He's good; I nodded agreement, "Right. They had a local group playing country music. Sheriff Jack, I'm here about the..."

He cut in, "I know, I know, the murder of Jennifer Albrecht. Michelline told me. Have you got more information for me than what those kids had?"

"Yes and no. Did you get the guy's phone number off her cell?"

"Yes, but it's a burner. We pinged it multiple times and it's off with the battery pulled."

"I was hoping it was a big break."

"Unfortunate, but no. What else ya got?" He smiled at me and leaned forward.

The lean in confirmed my read. He was interested in me for real. I leaned forward to match him and raise him on the intimacy moves. "Walt Hawley didn't do it."

"Well, good to know. How'd you work that out?"

"I'll tell you mine if you tell me yours." If I didn't have a long-distance relationship with Theo, I'd be interested in Jack. I liked flirting with him. He was handsome, powerful, and *so easy*.

"I'll tell you what I can. You're almost a part of the Department with your supervision of those kids on probation. Mr. Hawley doesn't have an alibi for that evening. Also, he was a hot-tempered teenage brawler. He roughed up a classmate when he was eighteen. The judge gave him a choice: enlist in the Marines or go to jail. Now you."

I knew we only had conjecture, but I had to give him something to trade. I said, "I know Jenn Albrecht's pattern of life better than anyone. I've watched her for years. She's like a machine. That night, *for the first time ever*, she changed. She always rolled up her car windows and took everything in when she came home. On Tuesday, she left the windows down and government documents on the front seat. *Unprecedented*. She also didn't put her trash and recyclables on the curb."

"*Interesting.*" He said with no effort to hide his dismissal of the information's significance.

"What's more, she was dressed for a business meeting when she went to Sunrise Garden in the middle of the night, carrying a folio and a purse. She would never have worn a suit to meet Walt."

"Minxy, that kind of thinking led to the Iraq War and the WMD fiasco. No offense."

"None taken. I get your point and now's not the time... I know what I have is circumstantial, but we're just getting started. We believe she was meeting an undercover agent to exchange documents."

Sheriff Jack's bottom lip pooched out and his eyes went up and to the right. Finally, he said, "An undercover agent in West Beach? That's what you've got?"

"Yes. And one more thing. This I admit is squishy. Those two love birds have never had a real fight."

"My detective said you reported an altercation."

I sniffed, "I recounted to Detective Reilly how Jenn had lectured Walt about healthy eating. Nothing more. That's a mild disagreement. I'm telling you, those two were happy together."

The Sheriff said, "Well you showed me yours and now I'll show you the rest of mine. As for their relationship, a jeweler near G.I. Fit called us after the homicide hit the news. He gave us a copy of the receipt for an engagement ring. Hawley bought it two weeks ago and then returned it last week. Apparently, he asked her, and she said no."

"Oh." I could see tomorrow's headline, 'Scorned Lover Arrested in Brutal Murder.'

He continued, "She did care for him though. We read the will this morning. She left everything to him. Her house, checking accounts, government 401(k). We checked Mr. Hawley's financials. He's nearly bankrupt. That's a strong motive right there. Maybe the relationship wasn't working out.

He knocked her off before she could dump him and change the will."

I started to say something, but Sheriff Jack raised his hand to quiet me.

"But wait, there's more. At the crime scene we found a Smith and Wesson six-shot revolver with Hawley's fingerprints on it. It was in her purse. My detectives hypothesize she knew whoever she met. Like if she was supposed to meet someone for one purpose and it turned out to be Hawley. Seeing her boyfriend, she wasn't afraid, so she didn't pull the gun."

"I know. He loaned her the gun. She was afraid of something. Turns out she was right."

Jack tried to hide it, but he was surprised.

He added, "His fingerprints are on it."

"Of course, they are. It's his gun. He took her to a shooting range to practice with it. We can confirm that."

"There are only two sets of prints."

"Of course, there are. It confirms his story." I took a breath. "Jack, the clothes are all wrong for her to meet Walt. She was meeting someone for professional and clandestine reasons."

Sheriff Jack shook his head, "Sorry Minxy. I have a gun and a financial motive; you have a suit and true love. This is evidence-based policing not international intrigue."

I rose, "Just for the record I was against the Iraq War. I also know Walt Hawley didn't kill his girlfriend, and I'm going to prove it. As a courtesy I'll keep you informed."

"Minxy, one question. Why are you so gung-ho to help this guy? You've been at war with his girlfriend since you moved here."

That caught me off guard. I couldn't tell Jack that I needed a purpose and uncharacteristically sympathized with Walt. I put my hands on my hips, and said, "It's the right thing to do."

Sheriff Jack stood. The light from the windows behind him left his face in shadows that made it harder to read. He said,

"Minxy, remember you're not CIA anymore. Your talents were never intended for domestic use. And if you're collecting information for a criminal case, you'll need a Private Investigator's License."

"Lucky for me I'm on the way to pick up my creds. It's been in the works for a while. Let's put a little wager on this, Jack. If I'm right about Walt's innocence, you buy me a crab dinner at the restaurant of my choosing, and vice versa."

"That is technically a bet and generally illegal, but I'll ignore it in this case, us being friends and all. You're on. Oh, and you're not going to like the local news. You might want to keep the radio off in that cute, green roadster of yours."

Nine

THURSDAY, JUNE 22, PRINCE FREDERICK TO
WALDORF, MD

Noting that Jack had remembered my Aston Martin, I lowered the top and did exactly what he told me not to do; I tuned in to the local radio station. It usually reported on wrecks and resulting road closures. Calvert County drivers were maniacs. Then there were always reports from town hall meetings. The interesting ones were on water management and chaired by Mayor Bill Hampton in a feeble attempt to look effective. Most were about building permits for homes and businesses. The more they built, the more people moved to West Beach. I was a bit disgruntled that the world had discovered my personal Brigadoon. As an only child and a narcissist, I was not familiar with sharing.

Then I heard what Sheriff Jack had warned me about.

In breaking news from the Calvert County Court House, Walter "Walt" Hawley had been arrested for the murder of Jennifer Albrecht. The Sheriff's people and Metro PD SWAT had swept in shortly after Celia and I had left the gym. I could imagine them walking through the maze of exercise equipment and sweaty body builders. Someone would have read Walt his rights. Did they humiliate him with handcuffs?

I slapped the dashboard so hard I swerved onto the shoulder. All around, horns cursed me as I got the car back into my lane. I had almost talked myself into going straight home and picking up my PI creds tomorrow—as I'd done for months now. What difference would one more day make? My life had slowed down so much, doing three things in one day seemed like a lot. But with Walt arrested, I had momentum. I checked the clock. Plenty of time to get to the Licensing Office in Pikesville. A super nurturing woman had called several times and agreed to hold onto the credential until I was doing better after my bike accident. It was the best excuse I could think of at the time. I'd milked that for two months. Or was it three?

I bought a hearty box of chocolate truffles in a gift shop and sports injury wrapping tape at the drugstore next door, then set my navigation system for Pikesville.

THE EXCHANGE WENT WELL, and I learned something very important from the experience: limping hurts. My bike accident excuse forced me to wrap one knee in tape and hobble. Now my opposite knee ached from favoring it on the hard, green tile of the licensing office.

Once I'd bidden my new friend *adieu*, I zipped down the road to upper Marlboro. Going to my new PI office would make four activities for the day, but hey, I was back in the saddle as a newly minted private investigator. I thought, *it feels like the first day of the rest of my life.* I slapped myself for being lame, but admitted it felt good.

It had been ridiculously easy to qualify for my new career. I did a little paperwork and got special electronic fingerprints. Jojo, the digital fingerprint tech at the IdentoGO office noticed I hadn't listed a detective agency on my application. Because I'm not much of a joiner, I'd hoped to bluff my way through without listing anyone.

She'd said, "Honey, after not being a convicted felon, the most important condition for getting your license is joining an existing agency. The state uses them as gatekeepers to keep out the riffraff and train new recruits."

Jojo had hooked me up with a guy who was always looking for talent. That didn't sound good, but it did sound easy.

She faxed my documents to Jerry Mancuso and gave me his business card from a stack in her desk drawer. I'd suspected Jerry was a savvy guy if he had the fingerprint lady shilling for him. I bet she got a gift card when she sent him a decent newbie like me.

Now it was time to meet the man himself. My new employer but not my boss, Jerry Mancuso, private eye.

My PI license tucked in my wallet, I called Jerry.

He said, "Heaven help me, I thought you'd died. Did you get cold feet?"

"Nope, just busy."

"Come on by. I had to identify the last guy Jojo sent in a police lineup."

***

I FOUND Jerry's office in a strip mall above a bagel place near the Upper Marlboro County Court House. The garlic and lox smell assaulted me all the way up the stairs and through the glass door. The retro waiting room was 1970s paneling with a Formica topped counter where you'd expect a secretary to sit. The sofa was a junkyard reject. I swiped on my bright pink lipstick, finger combed my hair, then called out, "Hello, Jerry?"

"In here."

I rounded the counter and peaked through the door into the hallway. There were two offices, one on either end, with a bathroom between them. From the office on the right, I saw a heavy-set man in his fifties walking toward me, his thinning hair slicked straight back with product. He extended a beefy hand. "Hey, you must be Marnie. I didn't expect you to look like Jackie O."

I shook his hand, letting it linger a moment longer than necessary. "I get that a lot. Please call me Minxy. Everyone does." I'd batted my eyes just a bit and made sure my smile was charming.

He furrowed his brow as he inspected me. After a pause, he'd said, "Minxy suits you. Welcome."

I had the impression he'd sized up the real me and hadn't been fooled by the charm efforts. That didn't happen every day.

His office was a mess. Among the piles on Jerry's desk, I spotted copies of my documents from the IdentoGO office. He must have unearthed them when I called.

"Your application said you live in West Beach on the boardwalk. I know that town. Your address is close to that woman killed in the park. You to finally get the license to work on that."

I made sure I kept emotion out of my voice when I said, "I'm interested in that case."

"That'll get you dead real quick. The murderer's still out there."

Indeed, I thought. *My new partner is no fool.*

Jerry continued. "I made a few calls since we talked. You're ex-CIA ops. Folks like you can make a decent PI." He motioned to a chair in front of his desk.

After checking it for stains, I sat. "Jerry, let's discuss how our 'partnership' will work." I did air quotes when I said partnership. "I want to be a private investigator, but I'm the independent type."

"You don't say."

"I do my best work alone. No offense."

He rocked back in his wooden desk chair and folded his hands over his stomach. "Well, I'll tell you how the private investigation business works. I signed off on you joining Mancuso and Associates, and now you've got your certificate from the Maryland State Police. If anyone calls, I'll say you work for me. That makes you official. I'll oversee all your training to keep us both out of trouble and insured. As you can see, my other associates don't spend much time in the office." He passed me a single xeroxed sheet of paper. "Here's the list of my clients. Keep your paws off 'em. Other than these guys, it's a big state. Plenty of work out there. I'll even throw you what I can't handle."

"Perfect." I felt the 'ask' coming.

Jerry scanned my application and then looked me over with the appraising eyes of a serious businessman. "For my efforts, you owe me a thousand per month for overhead, insurance, training, and my time."

Jerry smelled money and was going for it. I looked around his office and then back to Jerry, whose suit was as unassuming as his office. I did not smell money. "That's too much. I bet your 'mentoring' service is your bread and butter. I'll pay four hundred a month, and I'll throw *you* business." I hesitated for a second, and added, "And I get to use that spare office whenever I need it."

Jerry looked at me for a long time. I waited him out. Finally, he surprised me when he smiled. "Okay. *Five hundred* and you're on the books. You're tougher than you look."

"I get that a lot. Five hundred it is." This time my smile was real. I had the sense that we would get along now that we understood each other.

"I'll send you the link to your first training course. I want to see the completion email to make sure you do it."

"I don't really have time for training right now. Besides, I've trained on everything possible about collecting information."

"You've trained on stealing it. This is domestic. New day, new rules."

"Oh." He had me there.

Jerry was quiet for a moment, then said, "The boyfriend didn't do it."

Thank God in Heaven at least one person doesn't start with the boyfriend killing Jenn.

He continued. "He'd have whacked her in the house. And it was a guy; sorry if that ruffles your feminist panties. She met him in the park because he couldn't be seen at her house. They could pass information or money or whatever and deny the meeting ever happened."

"I'll keep that in mind." I couldn't keep the smile off my face.

"If you need advice, call. I'm a sucker for lost causes."

Ten

THURSDAY, JUNE 22, WEST BEACH, MD

Finally, back in West Beach, I saw Danny mulching the crepe myrtles in the town planters by the boardwalk. A mom stopped in the middle of the street loading a minivan with kids, giving me even more time to watch him work. The planters were full of dark green leaves on the wooden branches that had been trimmed to a polite four feet. The flowers would be ruby red in the late summer. The kids were fighting with their mom about who got what seat, so I had time to kill. I pulled into street parking and walked to the boardwalk railing. A boy chased seagulls on the beach, and farther out a solo crabber pulled a pot onto the back of his boat. The wire cage looked heavy—a good haul.

Looking back at Danny, I saw that he wore his yellow vest to make sure drivers didn't miss that mountain of a man. I wondered if they had one specially made for him or if vest makers had a big and tall section.

I watched him work. He looked content. He shoveled mulch in a repeatable rhythm. I suspected if I kept watching, he'd keep going non-stop until the truck was empty.

I walked toward Danny, and when he saw me, his face lit up. "Hi, Miss Minxy. I never see you twice in a week. I'll have to tell Mom how lucky I am."

I patted him on the arm to show compassion. When in doubt, I always figured a pat or a hug was expected of me. I preferred patting. I asked, "Do you talk to your mom often?"

He looked surprised, "I live with Mom. She takes real good care of me."

I had a little hitch in my voice when I said, "You're a lucky man. What's her name?"

"Her name's Alice. Alice Stone."

"Were you with your mother the other night when Ms. Jennifer was killed."

He nodded, emphatically. "I go to bed at 10:30 every night. I never go out after that." Danny suddenly seemed to remember something and his eyes gleamed. He started digging through his pockets. "I'm glad I saw you. The verse today should be perfect for you." He caught hold of the paper's edge between his thumb and forefinger, then pulled one delicately out of his vest pocket. He handed it to me.

I held it, smiling at Danny's childlike pleasure in giving me a present. There was no guile in this man. I raised up the slip of paper and read the verse aloud, "'For nothing is concealed that won't be revealed; and nothing hidden that won't be made known and come to light.' Luke 8, verse 17.'"

I shivered. "Danny, I'm going to find out who killed Miss Jennifer. This seems directly related to that. How do you pick your verses?"

He smiled broadly and it triggered real sympathy in me. Just a little, but I felt protective of him. *Good grief. Not again.* If he killed Jenn... I wiped that thought from my brain. I couldn't imagine Danny stabbing her so violently. I made a note to self.

Schedule an appointment with the shrink. All this sympathizing was a bit much.

He said, "That's the best part. I don't pick them. I close my eyes, open the Bible to a page and stick my finger on it. That's the verse for the day."

"And you never make a special verse just for me?"

"No, ma'am. Never."

I couldn't believe that, but there was no hint of deception. I nodded. "Danny, that is literally incredible."

"I know."

I was pretty sure he didn't understand how *not credible* it was to me. How was it possible that his verses always made my hair stand on end?

He tilted his head, "Miss Minxy I don't want to be rude, but I have to get back to work. The town's paying me." He broke into a giant smile. "Nice to see you though."

He was happy as a puppy to see me, and I felt just a wee bit mean for dodging him all the time. I patted him on the shoulder again for good measure and said goodbye. Walking to my car, I pondered what Jenn could have done to make him angry enough to kill her? I couldn't imagine it, but the verse he'd given me said all the secrets would be revealed. It would all come out into the light. Maybe Danny wanted to be caught. I shook the thought out of my head and got into the car.

By the time I got home, Celia and Astrid were already on my patio with martinis. We'd all shared keys long ago, so it wasn't a surprise. The Chesapeake Crime Club was fully activated. I watched them from the open back door and knew that if they had drinks, mine would be in the freezer. I opened the freezer door and there stood my martini.

I walked catlike down the stairs and into the investigation party without being heard—except by Magoo. He was lying by the 'she shed' and raised his head in my direction. The two women were busy at the whiteboard. The suspects list had expanded, with 'The Mayor' squeezed in. Celia must have told Astrid what we'd learned from Walt. 'Because she was really mean' had been erased to pave the way for stronger motives, which they were adding to each of the names:

Killer?/Motive
- Clandestine Operative: national security?
- Random Crazy Stranger: interpersonal conflict (IC)
- Danny: jealousy
- Sal: IC
- The Miscreants: Anti-Nuke Policy
- Minxy: IC
- Walt: ?
- The Mayor: IC & $
- Coworker at NRC HQ: IC, national security
- Coworker at a security exercise: IC
- Someone we haven't figured out yet: (probably IC)

I set my glass down and walked over to pet Magoo. The ladies still hadn't heard me, so I cleared my throat, and they both jumped. I spread my arms wide and said, "Meet the newest Private Investigator in Calvert County." I fumbled my PI card out of my pocket and held it up. I'd have to order a proper case that would flip open like on the TV shows. I couldn't look bumbling with suspects.

Celia and Astrid raised their martini glasses and toasted me. Astrid called out, *"Til lykke,"* which I thought meant 'congratulations,' 'God save us,' or maybe both. We all said, *"Skol,"* then clinked glasses gently and took a sip. The freezing, almost gel-like liquid gave me a pleasant rush.

"I see you've added suspects and motives."

Astrid nodded, "By the way, Lars sends his regards and recommends we change our group's name to the Martini Murder Club. He says it sounds exciting."

I shook my head and noticed that Celia was doing the same. "This is West Beach. It could be the only murder we get for a decade."

Standing by the whiteboard, Astrid stuck her hands in her navy capris pockets. She shrugged, then turned back to the list, and tapped the possible killers one after the other with her marker. "When we thought about it, each of the suspects leads us to a different path for collecting data. We need to prioritize the most important ones."

Celia looking curvy in a little sun dress sat down next to me and relaxed. She looked back and forth between us. "That's right. We need a place to start."

"True, and I met with Sheriff Jack today. I've got news that should help us pick." I looked at Celia, "You told Astrid about meeting with Walt?"

Celia said, "Of course, and about the mayor and that Walt loaned her the revolver."

Astrid nodded, "Does everyone in America have a gun?"

Celia said, "That's right, we do."

"Stop trying to scare her, Celia."

Astrid turned to the whiteboard again. "Our hypothesis is that Jenn went to the park to meet a clandestine operative. The guy could have been fake, but it was what she believed she was doing. If the operative was real, a random stranger could have been an unlucky surprise. She was waiting for the professional and the violent stranger walked into the park and killed her. Or someone she was fighting with could have found out she was meeting the professional in the park and used it as an opportunity to kill her."

Astrid touched the names on the whiteboard with a marker. "Here are the people who had the most interpersonal conflict with her." She pointed to my name first with a naughty smile. "There's always you." She drew a line under IC for interpersonal conflict. "Interpersonal conflict is our most common motive. You, Sal, the mayor, Danny and anyone who worked with her."

"Thanks for reminding me I'm still on the list. Until we find the killer, I guess I'm stuck there."

Celia's grinned. "Maybe if you behave, you'll get off earlier."

I said, "Fat chance. I just talked to Danny again. His alibi is his mom. I'll check that one."

"That's good. I'll be happy to mark him off when you clear him." Astrid drew a line under jealousy already next to Danny's name.

I curled up in my chair. "I'm glad to see the mayor on there. Would she have worn a suit to meet him?"

Celia and Astrid both said, "No."

Celia added, "He couldn't be the clandestine professional. And she would *not* knowingly have met him in the park at any time, but especially not in the middle of the night. It's just not proper."

Astrid stood back to admire her efforts and took a sip of her drink. She turned and said, "I believe we should work on the people in West Beach first: Danny, Sal, The Miscreants, and Mayor Bill."

I said, "Good idea. Start close to home and work our way out to the nuke plant and her colleagues at the NRC."

Celia said, "Put Walt in the first batch. He's been arrested. I want to find someone who can support his alibi."

I nodded. "After what I learned from Sheriff Jack, Walt has to be a priority. He said Walt proposed to Jenn and she said 'no.'"

Astrid's hand went to her mouth, and she said, "Oh my."

Celia grimaced. "Uh oh."

I rocked back in my chair and said, "He took back the engagement ring several days ago. The jeweler ratted him out."

"Wow." Astrid wrote IC next to Walt after erasing the question mark, then said. "That had to hurt him. I still don't think he would kill her like that though."

Celia added, "He doesn't seem that calculating."

I asked, "What if she was meeting another boyfriend in the park? Someone she knew, but we don't."

Celia's tinkling little laugh filled the air. "You haven't dated in a while, Minxy. She would have worn something way sexier than that suit."

"Excellent point," I admitted. "I have worse news for Walt. The lawyer made Jenn's will public today. Walt gets all Jenn's money and the house. If she wouldn't marry him, maybe she was going to break up and change the will. That's a strong 'money' motive."

Celia said. "Good grief. This just keeps getting worse for him."

Astrid wrote the symbol for Danish kroner, caught her mistake, and changed it to a dollar sign next to Walt.

"Have I started my PI career on a hopeless case?"

Celia fidgeted with her dangly lapis earrings. She said, "It's not hopeless, but it is wicked hard."

Astrid said, "If it was a vagabond, we need to find him before he leaves town. I've got some ideas, so I'll work on violent strangers. Also, if we can get her bank statements, we can see if there was money going out or coming in suspiciously. Maybe blackmail. She might have worn a suit for that and met the bad guy in the park."

Celia and I nodded.

Astrid added at the bottom of the whiteboard: second shadow, suit, pantihose, gun, purse, folio, park, late night, trash cans, papers in car, car windows, engagement ring, and inheritance. "Here's our ecosystem. Jenn was like any animal in a habitat. She was clearly distracted because she forgot a lot of things she usually remembered, like rolling up her car windows and taking out the trash cans. She was dressed for a clandestine and professional operative. The secret agent explains the facts of the environment best."

I said, "But we have two jobs. First, to save Walt. One of these suspects will look suspicious enough to make the jury find reasonable doubt and vote not guilty. After that, we stop the killer."

They thought about that, then nodded.

I said, "So, we have our plan. Astrid, you'll find reports of a crazy stranger that might have surprised her in the park before her clandestine meeting. Celia, you'll search issues that would make a federal officer from a security agency coordinate with a Nuclear Regulatory Commission employee. I'll start working on Walt, Sal, The Miscreants, and the mayor."

Celia said, "And Danny."

"And Danny." I stood and stretched, thinking about making more martinis. Finally, I turned to Celia. "Remember Brent?"

"What agency?" Celia asked.

"NSA."

Astrid's head bent sideways like she shouldn't hear this.

I hurried to explain. "Brent was with the National Security Agency but now he's on his own. He and some high roller buddies started a company that uses advertising signals from cell phone apps to geolocate people."

Astrid was aghast. "Apps like Block Blast?"

"I can't answer that. The data aggregators are squirrely secret about which ones they track. You might not use it if you knew it was stalking you."

We all nodded in agreement. The streetlight blinked on as the night descended.

I said, "But imagine if we could know whose cell phones were at Jenn's house before the murder. What if we knew whose cell phones were at the park when she was killed? The Miscreants told us she got a call as she was walking to the park. Both phones were turned on and probably met there. Maybe we could track the killer to his home."

Astrid looked at me amazed. "Just like in the movies?"

I said, "Amazingly, yes. It's the private sector so they don't need a warrant."

All three of us took a drink of our martinis in unison. The glasses were all down to dregs. Astrid's accent was more pronounced. "That technology is a little scary."

"Not really. Brent's a good guy."

Astrid's strong moral compass was kicking in. She pinched her lips together, thought, and then said, "We have to have rules for the Chesapeake Crime Club. Rules about privacy. Oh, and for the record, Minxy, No torture..." She stood hands on hips looking at me.

I surrendered; my hands raised high. "I've never tortured anyone. I've never needed to."

"That is *very good* to know." Astrid said.

I said, "We will be mindful of privacy. Technology cuts both ways. In this case, it might help Walt with minimal harm to anyone who's innocent."

Astrid nodded her approval but still looked suspicious.

We all studied the list.

Killer? / Motive
    •Clandestine Operative: national security? (Celia)
    •Random crazy stranger: *interpersonal conflict* (IC) (Astrid)
    •Danny: <u>jealousy</u> (Minxy)

- Sal: IC (Minxy)
- The Miscreants: anti-nuke policy (All)
- Minxy: <u>IC</u>
- Walt: IC $ (All)
- The mayor: IC & $ (Minxy)
- Coworker at NRC HQ: IC, national security (Celia)
- Coworker at a security exercise: IC
- Someone we haven't figured out yet: All

Ecosystem: second shadow, suit, pantihose, gun, purse, folio, park, late night, trash cans, papers in car, car windows, fake parking signs, city contracts, gravel, national security, engagement ring, and inheritance.

I decided against making more martinis. "The plan's good, and I think that's it for tonight. Magoo and I need our beauty sleep. Tomorrow, I start my career as a Private Investigator. We'll have to wrap our evidence in a box with a big red bow around the neck of anyone other than Walt Hawley."

Eleven

After my morning run, I was planting heucheras in the dark part of the back garden. In addition to my dandelions, I planted more common varieties from time to time. To my surprise, I liked watching things grow.

My cellphone rang.

"Hey Minxy, it's Walt."

The dirt from my fingers smeared across the screen. "Walt. I was hoping you'd call. I heard about the arrest."

The Marine cleared his throat. He paused for a second, so I leaned back against the shed and waited for him to talk. Finally, he said, "I wasn't going to accept your offer, but my lawyer says I'm totally screwed if we can't find another plausible killer."

"Smart lawyer. That's correct."

"I hope he's smart; he costs a bundle. If you still want to help, would you meet us at 10:00 this morning? He's in Annapolis."

"Absolutely."

"He helped me make bail last night, and today we're talking strategy."

Wiping the dirt from my right hand onto the grass, I said, "Text me the address."

LAST NIGHT before going to sleep, I'd ordered a leather flip case for my PI creds. Sometimes my late-night shopping arrived as expected. Other times I thought my inner demon was pushing the complete purchase button. One unfortunate order was a deep discount bundle: a blanket that looked like a pepperoni pizza slice and a Doodie Head Game.

This time my order had no surprises. The Amazon truck pulled up to my house as I was washing the dirt off my hands. Inside the bag with the blue smile was a fine leather credentials holder. I fished through my wallet for the laminated plastic card, then slid it into the bottom half of the case. On the other side was a place for a gold badge, which, of course, I didn't have. I practiced a couple of times in the mirror, flipping my wrist and making the bottom section fall open.

I had plenty of time to make it to the law office, but I didn't want to be late. I went to my bedroom, and as always when I walked in, it made me feel romantic. The room reproduced a fabulous Moroccan hotel room my case officer boyfriend Theo and I had pair bonded in. Coffered ceilings, white walls, blue tiled floors, a majestic Berber rug, and a chalk washed wooden bed with breezy curtains draped from the canape. The ensuite bathroom was a tiled paradise.

I showered and changed into silk capris and a sleeveless boat-neck silk blouse, then slipped on gold sandals with ankle straps. All were designer resort wear that Celia had insisted I buy. I wasn't sure if it would be my routine PI wardrobe, but in the mirror the capris made me appear professional in a no fuss, beachy way. No doubt Jackie Kennedy would have had these capris in her closet. I scratched Mr. Magoo goodbye and pointed the Aston Martin north toward Annapolis.

As I drove through the rural countryside, I thought about Walt. I'd jumped into becoming a PI with my usual 'dive into the deep end' enthusiasm, and now I had to deliver. I liked that idea a lot. It was the purpose I'd been missing. The stakes were extreme for Walt. His future depended on the Chesapeake Crime Club finding another suspect with the means and motive to kill Jenn Albrecht. If we failed, Walt would rot in prison. I wouldn't let that happen. *Imagine that,* I thought. *I still feel sympathy for the poor guy. I'm even worried about him.*

To get Walt off, I'd point the finger at an alternative suspect. It wouldn't be all that hard to find someone who'd look guilty of killing Jenn Albrecht, a woman everyone but Walt found annoying. I would ruin the life of anyone I proposed as the killer. What if Danny was the best suspect to throw shade on? I was starting to sympathize with Danny, too. Or what about Sal? I wouldn't lose much sleep over sticking it to Sal. He probably didn't do it, but he needed a comeuppance.

It surprised me that I cared at all about those guys. It wouldn't have crossed my mind if I'd remained at the CIA. They'd driven compassion out of me like a fever.

After 9/11, I'd been seated with Celia's analysis team so she could mentor me. It was a foregone conclusion I'd be an analyst like Celia. I had stellar grades in college and was a whiz at puzzles, data, and writing.

Three days later, however, my personality test scores came back. I got a copy with an attached memo saying I'd been reassigned to the Directorate of Operations. No discussion, just a notice that management wanted me to be a case officer—to do the field work of recruiting spies and stealing secrets.

I knocked on Celia's door to ask her what was going on.

She took the report and said, "No way. I'll fight this. You're mine. You'll be a great analyst."

What did I know? I watched as she paged through it. After a few minutes her hand flew to her mouth. She nodded and said, "That's it. That's why they poached you."

"What?"

"I've never seen psych scores so high on dark personality traits. The DO is salivating over you."

"What? Say all that again."

"Marnie..."

"Call me Minxy."

She shook her head, "This is a conservative organization. You should go by Marnie. Minxy is too informal. And please, do sit down."

"Whatever." I sat.

"As I was saying, the DO looks for people who have unique skills. Successful case officers manipulate people into doing what they want. It's their core competency. Think about it. They befriend and convince foreigners to give them secrets—crucial ones—about their government. That's treason everywhere, worldwide. Few are comfortable persuading a foreigner to risk their life and the lives of their family to help the US. A lot of people who fit the bill are just Machiavellian. They're good at finding a weakness and use it to incentivize or blackmail others. They make good, but ham-handed, money-for-secrets operators."

"So, I'm not Machiavellian. That's comforting."

Celia eyed me. She looked like she was thinking hard about what to say next. I waited. Finally, she clasped her hands tightly on her desk and said, "You aren't *only* Machiavellian. You're the holy grail of DO case officer types. You scored high on narcissism, Machiavellianism, and psychopathy—all conditions closely linked to successful manipulation of others."

"Whoa." I had looked hard at her to see if she was punking me. She wasn't. "If I had all that, I'd be in a straitjacket."

She shook her head. "Most people with these characteristics, like you, are highly functional. I bet you know what every person in a room wants or needs after a few minutes of mingling."

"Doesn't everybody?"

Celia kept her eyes averted, looking at the paper. "No, they don't. As a narcissist, you can read what a target wants and use that knowledge to charm them into doing your bidding. As a Machiavellian, you know how to use your understanding of a person to manipulate vulnerabilities. Finally, scoring highly on psychopathy, the report says you are over-confident, daring and bold, boosting the power of your other skills. You can appear charming and build rapport with your targets, while being dispassionate, cold, and calculating."

"Hold on. That's just how you negotiate. I don't feel bad that I win more than I lose. A lot more...but still..."

Her eyes softened as she looked at me and said, "It isn't a moral judgment. You have a unique skill set usually developed by children out of necessity." She looked at me to see if I wanted to share anything.

I didn't.

That was ages ago. I learned to maximize my skills while at the CIA. It was good for my mental health not to care much about assets. Most were low-level operatives in a terrorist network. They had blood on their hands and needed money. No one should be emotionally invested in their future.

I smiled to myself. Since I'd walked out of the CIA, my shrink had helped me build a 'circle of compassion,' which is a stupid term, but she likes it. My empathy was less dark. Helping Walt was proof of that, even if I was going to throw other people under the bus to save him.

FRIDAY, JUNE 23, ANNAPOLIS, MD

The lawyer's office was in a much nicer neighborhood than The Mancuso PI Agency. The words 'Law Offices of Sterling, Walker, and Baroni' were carved into a wooden sign and colored with gold paint. The colonial-style building was red brick. Walking into the waiting room, the old leather furniture was reassuring. This guy at least knew how to look like a lawyer.

The receptionist was an attractive, petite blond. She asked for my name and wrote it on a steno pad, the pen gripped tightly by her polished blue nails. "Mr. Sterling will see you now. He's in his office with Mr. Hawley." She stood. "Follow me."

I trailed her into the spacious room where Walt and the attorney sat hunched over a coffee table covered in paperwork. She laid her gentle, manicured hand on Mr. Sterling's arm. The spark between them convinced me she was a receptionist with benefits. He looked the type. I could imagine his wife and three kids.

She said, "Ms. Banks is here to join you."

The two men stood, and each shook my hand. Sterling thanked his lovely minion and she returned to her post. He said, "Thank you so much for coming, Ms. Banks."

"Please call me Minxy."

His head tilted to one side, "What an unusual name."

"It's a nickname, but everyone calls me that, so I use it professionally."

"Minxy it is, then." Sterling's overly precise wording and enunciation sounded like the guy who was one scotch short of his limit at a country club bar.

"We're assessing the criminal charges." His hand directed me toward a leather chair.

I checked Walt while he was studying the papers. I doubted he'd slept since the murder. His Marine bearing tried to hide the hot mess he'd become, but I could see through it. He glanced my way and said, "Mr. Sterling used the gym deed as collateral for my bail."

I nodded. "Excellent idea. You're no flight risk."

"True. Where would I go?"

Sterling, who had forgotten to offer a first name, said, "Walt tells me you're a Private Investigator." His eyes pinched tight, and he asked, "Who do you work for?"

I felt the challenge. Channeling Jackie's charm, I crossed my hands one-over-the-other on my knees. I should have worn the pearls. "I'm a partner *with* Jerry Mancuso in Upper Marlboro."

Sterling pursed his lips, and said, "I've never heard of him."

Like there's another free PI available. I held Sterling's gaze and made my voice calm with a little dash of the Jackie breathlessness. "I'm excellent at what I do. You don't know that now, but you will. And, I come at the right price. This case is *pro bono* because I don't believe Walt Hawley killed his girlfriend."

"*Well then,*" Sterling said, again enunciating both words. He was trying to sound jovial after the challenge and response. "We *are* on the same page. I was telling Walt we need to identify other suspects with motive and opportunity to kill Ms. Albrecht. That will persuade the jury there's reasonable doubt about Walt being the killer."

I nodded. *Did he really think 'reasonable doubt' was something I wouldn't have considered?* While he was talking to Walt, I pulled out my phone and googled him. His first name was Samuel. I took a minute to assess Samuel Sterling and get his measure. His suit was above average but not hand tailored. He acted Ivy League but I got a distinct night law school vibe. Glancing around the room, I noted all the diplomas too far away to read, and the nautical décor bought at Homegoods. His odd diction was an affect to sound posh.

When his conversation paused with Walt, I asked, "Samuel, which yacht club do you belong to?"

His head cocked to the side and his face shaped into an unspoken question.

"Seriously. Is it Annapolis, Eastport, Seafarers?"

He said, "Annapolis Yacht Club. How could you possibly know that?" He seemed confounded.

"Good choice. I love that one. I just wondered." I smiled. "Moving on to finding suspects who could have killed Jenn. She had many ongoing frictions with locals in West Beach. I'm gathering more information on those. After that, I'll move to her professional life. She had to be on the outs with fellow employees and her boss at the Nuclear Regulatory Commission, and with the plant management she failed in a recent security exercise."

Sterling's brow furrowed. "Why would she have so many conflictual relationships?"

"Because she was an annoying know-it-all." I turned to Walt and feigned regret. "Forgive my bluntness, but she managed to rub *everyone but you* the wrong way."

Walt almost laughed. "Most people found her irritating. She was wonderful to me, though."

I nodded. Love. I've never understood it. Why didn't I love a nice man like Walter? Someone who adored me and stuck around? I'd fallen for Theo. A case officer who lived undercover in dangerous cesspools of intrigue on the other side of the world. It was crazier than Walt and Jenn.

I pulled myself together and asked, "If you don't mind, what evidence does the prosecution have?" Okay I knew the answer, but I wanted him to feel in control. The sucking up was unpleasant, but it was working with Sam.

Sterling nodded, "Not much. There's the gun Walt loaned

her, but it wasn't used. Jennifer refused Walt's proposal. Walt doesn't have an alibi. She left him her estate. Some neighbor said Walt and she fought about grilling..."

"Oh. That was me."

Walt's eyes pinched together. I suspected he was having second thoughts about me on his team. I turned to him. "I told them the closest thing to a fight you two lovebirds ever had was making pork hot dogs instead of turkey."

Walt appeared confused. "I don't remember that."

"Well, it was a while ago. I thought it was a funny way to tell the police you two were very compatible."

Samuel's expression was hard. "Don't joke with the police, Minxy. They don't have a sense of humor."

"So, I'm finding. You can put me on the stand. I'll clear it up."

"It would be nice if we could, but another fellow, Danny Stone, said they fought last weekend."

My mouth fell open. "*What?* Danny heard you two fighting?"

Walt hung his head. "It was when I brought her the revolver, before we went to the range. She finally explained why she needed it. She was nervous about a secret meeting, but said I couldn't go with her. The gun would be enough. That seemed crazy to me. I got loud, yelling about foolish risk taking. There was a knock on the door. Danny was standing there. He'd heard the yelling and had to see if Miss Jennifer was okay. I cooled down on the back porch, while Jenn convinced him she was fine."

This was bad. The prosecutor would say Walt came to the house with a gun and Danny caught them fighting. Three days later she was dead in the park. "You said she told you to keep away the night of the murder, and didn't tell you when or where the meeting was. That's still true, right?"

He nodded, "Absolutely. If she'd told me she was meeting a stranger late at night in that park I'd have been there anyway. Whatever it took and even if it made her mad."

I said, "We'll just have to work with it."

Sterling cleared his throat. "*I will* develop *a counter strategy.* That's it for now, though."

I smiled my most adoring smile. "Oh, yes, of course Samuel, you're the lead."

Samuel reacted well to my simpering tone. Good to know. He glanced at his Rolex watch—real or knock off, I couldn't tell. "Minxy, stay in touch. Let me know what you discover. I'll email both of you on filings and court dates." He stood, buttoned his jacket, and shot out a hand to me. "Welcome to the case."

I shook his hand. Imagine that. In two days, I'd joined a business partnership and a legal team.

Walt lingered as though he didn't know what to do, so I said, "Come on Walt, let's go talk." We walked out of the law offices together.

Once outside, I steered him to a shady spot on the sidewalk next to some well-tended holly bushes. I watched for a reaction when I asked, "Why'd she say no to the ring?"

Twelve

W alt's face turned brick red and he shoved his hands into his jeans' pockets. He took a while, then said, "She said it wasn't the right time. She was working on a super important case and couldn't take the time to celebrate properly. We planned to do it Christmas." He studied his feet as though they might do something surprising. Then he said, "She told me she loved me and wanted to be my wife. Just not now."

I put a hand on his shoulder. This is where a real sympathizer would say something pithy. Out of my mouth tumbled, "I'm sorry she said no, and sorry for your loss." On reflection, I gave myself a B for creativity and impact.

His eyes were tearing up. "I miss her. When I realize I'll never see her again, I panic. It's making me crazy."

"Grief's a tricky thing. You can't go over or under it. You have to go through it." I was getting the hang of this. That was pretty good advice. Had I read that on a poster?

He shook his head. "You're the last person I ever thought

would help me. I still can't believe it, but after seeing you work with that lawyer stiff, I think you'll get me off."

That made me laugh. "Samuel seems to be on the right track, even if he is pretentious." I molded my face into a mask of confidence. "But I have one more question. Something between just us. When did you get to West Beach? I saw you at the park around 6:00 a.m. in running gear."

He stared at his feet again. "I'm screwed right."

"Not necessarily, but if you're lying about being there during the night you might be. Did anyone see you leave your place? Did you stop for coffee or gas on the way? Walk me through your night again."

"I went to my apartment at 10:00 p.m. and tried to sleep but I couldn't so I started reading a novel. Jenn wouldn't say, but I had a feeling the meeting would happen that night because she told me to stay away. I texted her at 10:00 and 11:00, and then again at 4:00 a.m. She never answered. She had to be home so why didn't she reply? When I called at 4:30 a.m. and she didn't pick up, I pulled on running gear and jumped in the car. I had gas and wasn't thinking about coffee. I had to check on her. I told you the rest."

I thought about cellphone data. Even if he was telling the truth, it wouldn't help him. The texts would bounce off DC cell towers showing he was home when he called. However, he had the time to leave after the 11:00 p.m. text, kill her in the park, and go back home to make the call at 4:00. I'd have to check. I asked, "So, it couldn't have been you I saw through her living room curtains about 10:00 p.m."

His forehead rose and his eyes went big for a second, before he tried to hide it. "Someone else was in her house?"

"I saw two shadows in the living room at 10:00 p.m."

"A guy?"

"I don't know. I just want to make sure it wasn't you."

"No, not me. I talked to a guy at 10:00 p.m. when I closed the gym. I had to ask him to leave. He can vouch for me. I wish it had been me, though. I regret I didn't come down that night. Right after the gym closed or even earlier. I could have sat outside her house and followed her to that park. She'd be alive."

He reeked of sincerity. He hadn't known about the visitor that night and it wasn't him. While he was talking, I began feeling his giant angry convulsion of anxiety and regret. This was becoming a bit much for me.

He gave me the name of the guy he'd ushered out of the gym at 10:00 p.m. I called him and he verified the timing. Walt and I said goodbye, and I sat in the law office's parking lot prioritizing what to do next. I needed to identify a guy in the park near the time of the murder. If it was the clandestine operative, all the better, but anyone would help. It would rip the largest hole in the fabric of the prosecutor's case because I knew it wouldn't be Walt. The person in her house didn't go with her. She was alone when The Miscreants saw her. But the mystery shadow person might know who Jenn was meeting with, or at least why they picked the park after midnight. He or she could explain why Jenn was distracted that night.

Brent Smeltzer's ad data could help figure out who the late visitor was and who was at the park. He could see if Walt's phone was at the beach that night. I'd planned to call him today, but the visit to the lawyer brought me close to his house. I had dropped in unannounced before...

I drove over the causeway to the wealthy Annapolis enclave of Eastport. After retiring from the National Security Agency, Brent had started a very small, big data company that supported law enforcement as well as some private investigators. When he'd first told me about it, I'd never imagined that I'd be one of his clients.

He saw me through the window next to his door and yelled, "Minxy Banks, you promised you'd call before you showed up."

He opened the door and grabbed me in a bear hug. "I like to clean up when classy dames come around. The house is a mess."

"Brent, I didn't have the time. Breaking news, I'm a PI." I flipped open my creds case for the first official time. The bottom page fell down like it was supposed to with my picture and the seal showing. "My first client is charged with a murder he didn't commit. Did you read about the knifing in the West Beach park?"

"Of course, I did. It's all over the news. Beautiful woman dead, clinging to a metal mermaid's tail."

"She wasn't that attractive."

Brent narrowed his eyes but ushered me into his home office. He pointed to a comfy chair with a view of the docks on Back Creek. I settled into the cushions and watched Brent fire up his computer. He asked, "How much is he paying you?"

"The regular fee. He's a broke Marine."

Brent looked over his readers at me. "You've got to stop helping people for free. All those stupid things you were investigating at the beach...what was it, stolen bird baths?

"Garden gnomes."

"Yeah, right. Please charge them something. It ruins it for us working stiffs."

I didn't respond. Slipping off my sandals, I curled up and got comfortable. Brent was busy with the computer, so I watched a twenty-something guy launch his sailboat from a nearby slip. Brent's fingers tapped non-stop across the keyboard as the boat glided smoothly over the still water. It was a calming counterpoint to the staccato typing. I said, "You can imagine why this murder made me think about you."

Brent nodded his head, held up one finger, and continued to focus intently on the computer. He was about forty years too old to be a "digital native" but his work at the NSA had turned him into a grumpy old man with the skills of a teenager. He muscled his way through a lot of passwords and opening screens, then pulled up the system. After another minute he said, "I'm in. And you're right. I wish the police had come to me instead of you. They should want to know who was at the victim's house over the last week and at the park that night."

I said, "And, of course, they've got a budget. You charging me for this?"

"Fat chance you'd pay. Let's call this one a demo. *And* I expect you to talk the company up with your old friends and the cops."

"Deal." I passed him a slip of paper on which I had written Jenn's name and address, as well as the addresses of the Nuclear Regulatory Agency, Walt's gym, and at the bottom, Sunrise Garden.

"So, she worked on nukes?"

"Security compliance exercises at power plants. She loved rules."

He snorted. "I bet you two were fast friends." He slid his glasses up his nose and typed in Jenn's home address, looking back and forth at the sheet I had given him.

"Predictably, no. But the murder was brutal." When I said it, I realized for the first time that I *almost* felt sympathy for Jenn in addition to Walt. Just a hint of it, but it surprised me.

He nodded agreement. "Okay, here's what I got."

He turned his laptop toward me. I walked to the desk so I could see the details better.

"I won't have all the signals from the night of her murder until tomorrow. It takes a while for the data owners to clean it up and get it into the database. What you see is the week before she died."

There was a plot like in MapQuest, but with so many dots it blotted out most of the map. I could see the bay and some streets I recognized, but it was messy. "Yup, that's West Beach. But I can barely see my house and hers. Did I mention she was my neighbor?"

"Holy crap. No, you didn't."

"Well, she was. Those dots are everywhere. Which one's the killer."

"Patience, Minxy, patience. Like I said, we probably won't have the night of the murder until tomorrow. When we do, we can check for devices at the crime scene. We should be able to identify hers. If we're lucky, we'll find the killer's, too. But here, I'll clean up the image." He changed the date range in a bar on the side. The splotch was smaller. "There. That's more manageable."

"It still looks like a rash. What does each dot mean?"

Brent clicked on a dot and it showed a string of numbers and letters that must have been twelve or more digits long. "That's a unique identifier. Advertising agencies build a profile of that user's interests to sell them stuff. If the phone with that ID is taken to a Bono concert, the owner will start getting ads for world peace T-shirts."

"You're kidding."

"Nope. Your phone gets close to electronic displays at the shopping malls, and they show you ads for what you just searched for online. You are literally being pitched as you walk by. Personally. Just for you."

Thinking about Astrid, I said, "That's kind of creepy. You know that, right?"

He gave a look he reserved for the willfully ignorant. "We're using it for a better purpose than selling T-shirts."

I nodded, "That's true. If we find the murderer, I'll absolutely love it."

"That's the way to think about it. It's just a pointer. The cops still have to build a regular case with all the safeguards like warrants and stuff." He typed something fast. "Okay, here's the most frequent signal at her home." He pointed to a long number. "It also signals from the NRC office address, too. Bingo, a hit. I betcha this is the victim's cellphone. We can use it to track her final movements on the night of the murder when the data comes in."

"I'm impressed."

He almost smiled. "Let's identify your Marine's device." He pinched his chin and asked, "How'd he know her?"

"Boyfriend."

He nodded without comment and compared Jenn's house and then around the gym. He pushed a key and the data resolved to a single ID. "That's the Marine unless his workout buddies visited his girlfriend."

I said, "I'm betting on the Marine."

"He wasn't there after the weekend."

Walt was telling the truth so far. I asked, "So, who made all the other signals? What a mess."

He changed the date parameter again, pushed the button, and got a small cluster of dots. "The devices with fewer dots could be there or could be drive-bys. Let's focus on the multiple hits over the week. If we have to, we can dig deeper into the others."

I watched as he tapped out a command.

"There are four heavy signalers. The dead chick, the Marine, and two others. Here's number three." He brought up the long identifier and analyzed the results. "Okay, we've got a person who visited her house two evenings before she died and for a significant period of time each visit. All weeknights, no weekends."

"Can you figure out who that guy is?"

"You live next door to her. You don't remember anyone?"

"As you pointed out, we weren't besties."

His sly grin told me he could identify the person behind the device.

"I'll do a pattern of life." He pulled up the single ad ID number and tracked it to where the phone pinged during the night. "The device spends nighttime hours at this address in Solomons." He scribbled it on the slip I'd given him. "Most of the time, the bed down is the home of the phone and its owner. And here's where our person spends days." He read out the address as he wrote it on the sheet.

I punched it into MapQuest. It was the Calvert Cliffs Nuclear Power Plant address. "*Oh no*. The Marine told me Jenn failed that plant for mistakes in a security exercise. They had to do it again to pass."

Brent's bottom lip pushed out. He pulled up another signal around Jenn's house. He searched just that signal's history and got a minimum of dots.

Furrowing his brow, he widened some of the parameters and tried it again. Still the dots did not resolve into a bed down or common work location. "This one may be kept off with the battery out most of the time. It's only pinging the cell towers now and then. Always in the evening and late night near her house."

"Burner phone?" I was thinking about the phone call The Miscreants heard when Jenn was walking to the park. The phone Sheriff Jack couldn't find.

He shrugged. "Could be. Or someone with a limited cellular plan who likes to hang out near the dead gal's house at night." He rose. "That's it for today. I'll run these devices again tomorrow. The data from the night of the murder should be in by then. I'll let you know what I find." He was politely guiding me to the door.

As I stood on the porch ready to thank him for his time, he said, "So why do you care so much about this Marine? You know it's always the boyfriend."

"Thinking like that will destroy this country."

I got the stink eye, then he said, "Well, let's check all the devices on the night of the murder. Maybe you're right. The Marine's a paragon of virtue. Now, sweetheart, get the hell out of here. That's all the *pro bono* work I have time for. I'll call when the park data comes in."

I checked my watch. I had fifteen minutes until the weekly zoom call with my shrink. I was hungry and needed to find a place where I could eat and talk with her at the same time. I drove back across the causeway.

At the appointed time my phone rang and I clicked on the button to enter the Zoom meeting. "Hi Minxy." Maya's dark Jamaican face looked confused, "Where are you?"

"A sidewalk table in old town Annapolis. I'm not close to any other people." I pointed the phone around the quaint shopping area full of Federal-style charm so that Maya could see. It was all red bricks, painted shutters, and cobble-stoned streets, with few mid-week shoppers. Then I propped my phone against the umbrella pole again.

"Not usually where my patients want to have their sessions."

"It was the only option today."

"Don't do it again, okay? Too much bangarang and not enough privacy," she said in her patois. "How's your week been?"

"Maya, you wouldn't believe it." I looked at her sitting behind her desk, full-figured, gray hair, and sympathetic. The most huggable person in the world. And, oddly enough, someone I couldn't manipulate.

She shook her head. "Oh, Minxy girl, with you, I always believe it. What's happened this time?"

I explained all that had happened in one long recitation.

Unfazed, she said, "Girl, you have been busy. Just for the record, you didn't kill her..."

I shook my head. "Not me. The police are blaming her boyfriend. *When he came to the crime scene, I felt all the seething rawness of his pain. My sympathy snowballed until I could barely stand it.*"

Maya's face glowed. "Good. That's what's s'pposed to happen."

"It hurt. It keeps hurting every time I see him."

Maya nodded. "Of course it's painful. You've been unpacking the trauma of your childhood. Most of your life you buried your pain deep. You're openin' up your feelings and that hurts."

The crab cake sandwich was delivered. I pushed it to the side and leaned toward the screen. "I know. And now that I feel for Walt, I have to save him."

"Hold on girl. There's a lot you aren't acknowledgin'. It's not just about the man. Suddenly you're all about findin' who killed a woman you spent years makin' miserable. Why should you solve the woman's murder? Why not the police?"

I thought for a moment. I itched to know how the killer got the drop on Ms. Jenn Perfection Albrecht. She wouldn't have made it easy for him. She definitely gave him a piece of her mind. I imagined being in a fight with a stronger, enraged man. I liked to think I would have bested him, but that seemed like a narcissistic answer. It was all about me. Maya was watching my face. I said, "I'll have to think about that."

"Yes, please do. Just last week you were tellin' me about how much you loved your life of leisure. Now you're shifting gears into a job like your old one. That's inconsistent with bein' less manip-ulative."

"I suppose it is."

"So, all the nonsense about a life of leisure was a lie."

"Absolutely."

She smiled. "Well then, we're getting someplace. I was hopin' you'd give up that rubbish. How do you feel about the new investi-gator job? Your past will make you good at that. It's like a new version of your old job."

"Exactly. Like the old days. It makes my brain race and my heart pound."

She puffed out her lower lip, while she thought. She finally said, "Is this an excuse to get back to bein' a spy?"

"I do miss it. I feel pathetic doing nothing but garden gnome cases."

Maya cocked her head, and I knew she hoped for more.

I said, "It's always a thrill to figure out someone's secret. Even with the little things my friends and I have been doing. Jenn's murder is just a bigger thrill. It's more...fulfilling."

"And your friends are helpin' you with this one like they did with all those silly cases?"

I nodded. "Celia pushed me to finish the private investigator's license. Astrid is always there as a role model of good behavior."

Maya steepled her fingers and looked over her glasses at me. "Your reason for therapy was to become a better person. You defined that as feeling more sympathy. Do you think you can achieve that objective as a private investigator?"

"I'm feeling more sympathy..."

"One person."

"Well I did feel just a pinch of sympathy for Danny, too."

"Good."

Our chat continued until Maya checked her watch. "It's that time. This has been a big week for you. Next week we'll talk about how havin' a professional purpose that relies on your ability to deceive and manipulate will change your path."

"I'll think about that."

"I recommend journalin'..."

"I hate journaling."

Maya's face pinched, "Try it, Minxy. You need to dig deep into your childhood. Oh, and do me one favor. In the past you've not measured risk wisely. Your psychopathy makes you prone to irrationally bold and dangerous actions. You're rusty and older. Keep that in mind when you plan your investigation."

I bobbed my head dismissively and rolled my eyes, but then enthusiastically nodded my head in agreement. She was right.

We waved and the connection was cut.

I finished my sandwich while thinking about my homework. Was I regressing to my old self by being a PI? My snarky inner voice went through a list of possibilities that didn't feel right. I'd have to dig deeper.

In the meantime, I couldn't wait to find out who lived at the address in Solomons that Brent had given me. The person who was Jenn's guest several times before the night she died. It could be the person who was there the night of the murder—the second shadow in the window. `

Thirteen

I had a lot more time to ponder my motives for researching the Albrecht murder and saving Walt. Maya had dredged up my childhood. If I was going to change, I'd have to break the habits formed then. The trip would take over an hour and a half to get from Annapolis to Solomons at the far southern tip of Calvert County. *Forget about journaling. I would just think this through.*

The day was clear, and the wind was excellent for sailing. The young man who had sailed away from the dock near Brent's house kicked up old memories of catching the wind and sliding across the water. On a whim, I left Route 2 for the slightly longer Route 261 that would take me closest to the Chesapeake Bay, and through Harrington Harbor and Chesapeake Beach, both with busy marinas. As I looked at the moored sailboats, thoughts of my mother, the expert yachtswoman, surrounded me like the musky perfume she wore to activist events. Shelly had made me the woman I was, for good and for bad.

Father and Shelly both came from wealth, but Shelly's side

was far richer. They'd financed New York businesses since the Dutch trinket business with the Indians. Money allowed the women in our family to be generally unaccommodating to their husbands and everyone else. The legend was that men couldn't wait to marry and to bury these debutantes. That probably had been Father's plan. Their relationship was more merger than marriage.

Every year for my birthday, Father took me to his brokerage on the hundred and first floor of the World Trade Center North Tower. We would stand side by side looking down at the city. He explained amortization, accounts receivable, and capital gains to me as soon as I could stand on my own. Someday, I would take over for him. All this would be mine. The business, the office, the people.

After making the rounds, we'd go to lunch at Windows on the World, a few floors higher up. Father always reserved a booth close to the windows so we could look out over the city. We'd get there first and order drinks. I loved my Shirley Temple and Father seemed happy with his Beefeater Martinis with olives. He would ask for four and I'd eat two of them, scrapping them off the little plastic sword with my teeth. We made small talk as we waited for Shelly, usually a discussion of new stock offerings. I once used that knowledge to prove my deep cover as a financier.

Shelly would flounce in late, and we'd order. I always ordered French onion soup. The crusty toasted bread, the rich onion soup, and stringy cheese. I would burn the roof of my mouth, because it was too good to wait.

Then they would each give me their presents. His were golf lessons, riding lessons, piano lessons and such. Hers were political books, sailing gear, and service trips to reforest Central and South America. I was a compliant, well-disciplined daughter until the great turning point the summer I was eight. That was when I earned the name 'Minxy.'

"Marnie, wake up. We need to get going," Shelly had said.

It was the first vacation day after second grade. I'd planned to sleep in and spend the day reading the biography I'd been assigned as summer reading. Rolling back over, I'd pretended to be asleep.

She bounced herself down on the bed in a way that sent shock waves through the mattress and guaranteed I would wake up. She said, "No really. I have a surprise. We need to be in Cold Spring Harbor early." I opened one eye and saw that Shelly's long dark hair was in a ponytail. She was wearing her jean shorts with a save the whales T-shirt. If she was ready, summer better be too.

The drive to the north shore of Long Island went quickly and we unpacked the car our maid Belinda had filled with suitcases of clothes, toiletries, and books. At the beach house we didn't have live-in house help. Rhonda from Huntington came twice a week to clean and stock the refrigerator. Other than that, we were on our own.

Shelly rummaged through the fridge and made us turkey sandwiches with iced tea in tall glasses that had twined ivy around them, bottom to top. She slid back the French door and headed for the picnic table overlooking the Long Island Sound, then yelled over her shoulder, "Bring the tall spoons and sugar."

Reaching high in the cabinet, I got the sugar bowl, then picked the eight-inch spoons out of a drawer. With my book under one arm, I joined Shelly. We sat under a poplar tree and watched the boats pass by while we ate our sandwiches. She had our thirty-foot sailboat moored at our dock, its sails rolled tight. The tide was going out and the wind was brisk, so it bobbed and pulled against the tenders.

In years past, we'd taken the sailboat out almost every day all summer. We called the trips our adventures. We role played being Indians when the first settlers came. I learned that settlers really hit the Indians hard. Or we would be oystermen who would almost drown when the weather was bad. They saved themselves at the last moment. Shelly's creativity knew no limits.

I noticed her grinning. It was the look she got when she was setting up a surprise. "What's up Shelly?"

"Are you a big girl, Marnie?"

"Yes. I am." I tried to sound definitive.

"You're eight now. That's pretty old. Today you start learning about independence and responsibility."

Adrenaline shot into my head making me dizzy. *Independence and responsibility sounded important.*

"At school you always have a teacher taking care of you."

I nodded.

"At home, you always have Belinda or me watching you."

"Un huh." I tried to read her expression. What was she up to?

"It's time you know that in life you have to take care of yourself. Come with me."

Dropping the last bite of my sandwich, I tucked my book under my arm and ran to catch up with Shelly. My mother had never been good at focusing on things. Having something to read was helpful if she got distracted mid-adventure. We walked down the hill to the boat house above the dock. Maybe we were sailing to Montauk. She had friends there.

The door was unlocked and we entered the gear room where navigation charts, life preservers, and fishing tackle were stored. It always smelled briny with a hint of mold. The door to the slip was closed because her boat was already tied to the dock.

Shelly said, "Open the slip door."

I was a little afraid. Shelly was fun, but sometimes her adventures scared me. To be honest, they *always* scared me. I remembered the knob was cold on my hand and it seemed like a warning. I forced myself to twist it and pushed the door open.

Inside, tied to a cleat on the dock, was a brand-new Sunfish. The tiny sailboat was less than half the length of Shelly's boat and only around four feet wide. The hoisted sail was almost a perfect triangle made of bright blue and green striped sail cloth.

I climbed aboard, dropped my book in the hull, and touched every inch of the boat, the ropes, the sail, the tiller and dagger board. *Mine, all mine.*

"Sailing means taking care of yourself and the boat. It means responsibility, which leads to independence." Shelly flipped the switch and opened the slip door to our cove and farther out, the wide expanse of the Long Island Sound.

"Are we going sailing right now?"

Shelly put her hands on her hips. "*You* are going sailing. Hold on and I'll push you off. Don't come back for at least three hours."

"But Shelly..."

"I believe in you." She pushed the boat out of the boathouse and into the sound. The sail began filling with the breeze.

"But Shelly, I need a life vest."

Shelly grabbed one, and running to the end of the dock, threw it toward the little boat. She missed but I fished it out of the water.

That was the first time I knew what pure terror was. That day was also the first time I'd learned that Jackie Kennedy would not have stood for such nonsense.

FRIDAY, JUNE 23, SOLOMONS, MD

The car behind me honked, when I didn't start rolling immediately after the light turned green. I snapped out of my ponderings as I neared Solomons, an upscale community on the Patuxent River that fed into the Chesapeake Bay. At least a half-dozen top-shelf marinas contributed to the nautical frenzy. A very fine six-sided lighthouse and Maritime Museum drew visitors year-round. Solomons Island, the downtown area, had streets lined with art shops, restaurants, and coffee places. The water separating the island from the mainland was so narrow you could almost jump across it.

My roadster slid to the curb several houses down from the address Brent had given me. The address was on the outskirts of Solomons and had its own boat dock and a lovely little Catalina sailboat. The sailboat appeared to belong with the two-story, shake-shingled house with those real shutters that you could close when hurricanes threatened. They were painted a cerulean blue. The door was painted a glossy navy with a brass anchor for a door-knocker. The house sat on the top of a rise to protect it against storm surge. I was impressed. It was built to last and it had.

I knew property values pretty well throughout the county. The owner of this historic beauty had a better than average income. I had a strong signal on my phone, so I pulled up the tax records for Calvert County, entered the address and bingo, there were the names: Andrew Cunningham, and probably a wife named Barbara.

A quick 'people finder' search told me Andrew was fifty-nine years old. LinkedIn gave me what I needed. Andy not only worked at Calvert Cliffs Nuclear Power Plant as Brent had suspected; he ran it. He was the Site Vice President. He'd trans-ferred a few years ago from another nuke plant in California.

Jenn and Andrew were at least professional acquaintances. She was the regulator, and he was the manager. That could be a contentious relationship. Especially after she failed his plant's security exercise. That was a blight on his record. Why would Cunningham visit Jenn's house several evenings the week before she died? Why didn't they do their business during the day like normal professionals?

A woman in her fifties with red hair came out the Cunningham front door wearing a sun hat. She put in ear buds and fiddled with her phone until she was hearing a beat that caused her head to bob. She put on gardening gloves and knelt slowly protecting her knees. She hadn't noticed me but was facing my way behind a circular garden in the center of the front yard. She clawed at the dirt with a trowel, making headway with her weeding. Handful after handful went into a pile, and she kept moving in time with the music.

I was considering what ploy to use so I could introduce myself to her. New neighbor a few streets over? Looking for a landmark and no cell coverage? Looking for my dog? I liked the dog story. I pulled Magoo's leash out of the glove box, then climbed out of the car, and walked up the sidewalk calling for Magoo. I would ask if she had seen him, introduce myself and start our relationship. I was just ready to wave to get her attention when a Mustang driving too fast for the neighborhood screeched to a stop in front of the Cunningham house. The driver jammed it into park but didn't bother turning it off or closing the door. The younger red-haired woman was crying. She ran to the older woman and pulled one earbud out of her ear and spoke to her while pulling her to a standing position. Words I couldn't hear were exchanged and suddenly the two women were racing toward the house. The older woman threw off her gloves, leaving them where they landed. I strolled past, reached the end of the block, and doubled back.

By the time I was in front of the Cunningham house again, the older woman had changed her shirt and walked onto the front porch clutching her handbag. She stared into the distance with tears tracking down her cheeks. The younger women locked the front door and guided the dazed woman to the Mustang.

With such a display of sorrow, you didn't have to be a genius to know something bad had happened to the Cunningham family. I wasn't going home until I figured out what it was. Luckily, I knew who could help me.

Fourteen

I needed a source who could tell me what was going on with Andrew Cunningham's family and how hard he had taken the failed security exercise. I had a bad feeling about the display of grief I'd witnessed. I needed an insider at the nuke plant. I thought of Ricky, who worked at the plant as a computer tech.

He picked up on the second ring. "Domingo." I heard people in the background shouting orders.

"Hi Ricky, it's Minxy."

"Hey, Minxy."

He sounded happy to hear my voice. "I need to ask you a few questions. I'm working on my PI case."

"I'm kinda crashin' on somethin'. It's been a crazy day here. My shift's over in a few minutes. I could meet you somewhere at the beach."

"So, you're at the nuke plant, right?"

"We prefer to call it the Calvert Cliffs Clean Energy Facility, but yeah."

"I'm in Solomons. Why don't we meet at Vera's. I'll buy you a drink."

"My AA sponsor wouldn't like that."

Humm, Ricky had a drinking problem. Who knew? "Then I'll order you a coffee. I'll meet you on the deck by the creek."

"Okay, then. See you there in thirty minutes."

Vera's was a cross between Elvis's Graceland and a roadside attraction, which was almost redundant, but not quite. I rarely drove by without stopping. Vera had been a Hollywood starlet. When she married an optometrist, he resettled her three thousand miles away in her own kingdom and indulged all her fantasies. She decorated everything with marble and leopard print.

The restaurant was on St. Leonard's Creek, attached to a marina. I snagged a table on the back deck and immediately got rid of two of the four chairs. I left the remaining two close together for our little *tete a tete*. Once settled, I watched boats of all kinds and sizes slide back and forth in slow progression to avoid kicking up a wake so close to the dock. The life-size, fake palm trees fluttered in the breeze like real ones. Below me on the white sand beach were tiki bars serving frozen umbrella drinks.

Sally promised to put on a fresh pot of coffee for Ricky and brought me an iced tea with an umbrella in it. They make great fidget toys. I kept watch for Ricky's arrival through the windows of the restaurant. When he walked in, the hostess greeted him like a regular and pointed him in my direction.

Ricky was waylaid as he walked through the bar by a gaggle of women enjoying an early happy hour. Some had forgotten to remove their badges, so I was sure they were from the nuke plant. His light olive skin and fine bone structure, probably inherited from Spanish conquistadors, certainly were a crowd pleaser. After saying quick goodbyes, he headed my way.

Ricky's suit and tie looked great on him but weren't at all what I'd expected. Of course at the beach I'd only seen him in running gear, or shorts and a T-shirt. That wasn't the problem. He'd told me he was an IT guy. They climb under your desk to figure out why your computer doesn't work—like because you've kicked loose a cable connection. They wear khakis and a polo shirt for obvious reasons.

I started right in on him as he came through the patio door. "You're no IT person. Suits don't lie. You're management." I patted the table at the seat next to me.

That made him laugh. Ricky wasn't stingy with laughs, and I'd developed a habit of getting him going. He laughed at everything, and I knew why. He did it to fit in. Who doesn't love a guy who chuckles at feeble jokes?

He held up his hands and said, "Guilty. I told ya I worked with computers, but I left out I'm the senior plant computer systems engineer."

"Wow. Good for you. I thought you plugged in wires and said to restart the machines. So, sit. Sally'll bring your coffee."

Ricky took off his tie and jacket, hanging both over the back of his chair, then he rolled up his dress shirt sleeves and rubbed both hands together. "Better?"

"Much beachier." I watched him rubbing his hands and noticed his ring: a cabochon-cut carnelian stone set in an ornate silver setting. "Is that new? I don't remember it."

He shook his head. "You just haven't focused on it when we're runnin.' I never take it off. It was Dad's. Carnelian is a thing in Mexican families like mine."

I leaned in to look closely at the raised silver dots and swirls circling the domed orange gem. "What a beautiful ring. You're lucky to have it."

He touched the stone reverently with his other hand. There was no doubt that Ricky's heritage and its manifestation in that ring meant a lot to him.

Sally came through the doors and set the coffee mug and little plastic single-serve cream containers in front of Ricky, then winked at me. The way I'd positioned us, I couldn't blame her for thinking it was a date. It didn't help that written over the door was, '*What happens at Vera's stays at Vera's.*'

When Sally was safely back at the bar, I gently touched Ricky on the arm. "Thanks for coming. I've got a question about Andrew Cunningham, the head of the nuke plant."

My question rattled him. "How did you know about that?"

My brain pinballed through a full catalog of response options. In the end, it came down to two choices. I either admitted I knew zip about Andrew Cunningham, or I lied. That wasn't a viable choice for me. "You're my best but not my only source at the plant."

"It was *such* a shock. He was a healthy guy. Fit, you know? Then he had that heart attack at his desk. Massive. *Bam.* Here one minute, gone the next."

I nodded, to give myself time to connect some obvious dots. Andrew Cunningham was dead. That's why his wife and probably daughter were distraught. "Did you know him well?"

"He was my boss. I met him at seven every mornin' to go over taskin's. I gotta tell you, he was fine when I left. Couple hours later...gone. Creepy."

"That early, do they serve coffee and donuts?"

"We always had tea. That's what he drank. I brought it for him, you know, to kinda brown nose him."

"*No way.* You wouldn't brown nose a boss."

He gave me that boyish smile. "My budget has doubled in two years. Ya do what ya gotta do."

"What was he like?"

"Not everyone liked him, but I did. Pushin' sixty. Knew how to pick his battles and build a team. He was kind of dogged, you know? He'd go to the end of the earth to figure somethin' out. Most of all, he treated me real good."

I didn't feel bad about the death of a man I didn't know, but I needed to say something. I finally said, "Heart disease is a ticking time bomb. Sorry for your loss. Did he know Jenn Albrecht very well?"

Ricky looked confused. Like he was trying to understand why I was talking about both his dead boss and my dead neighbor at the same time. "You mean the gal killed in West Beach?"

Elbows on the table in front of me, I rested my chin on my hands. I've practiced it in the mirror. I look amazingly attentive when I do that. "Yes."

Finally, he said, "She was with the Nuclear Regulatory Commission. He'd have met with her. We have NRC folks resident at the facility. But when a non-resident NRC person comes, our PR people have Andrew schmooze 'em. He would have met with her before and after."

"What about you? Did you meet with her? You're head of IT. That's gotta be a big deal in a nuke plant."

"I had to brief her. Pretty standard stuff. I'd seen her around town but never even talked to her before that exercise. She didn't recognize me, so I didn't say anything about us both living in West Beach."

That made sense to me. Why would anyone talk to Jenn more than they had to? Trick questions are a great interrogation tool. Walt had told me the answer to this one. "Did you pass Jenn's test?"

He sighed like he didn't want to talk about it, but said, "Eventually, but not on the first go. She was tough."

"In what way?" I asked.

"Usually, the NRC tester suggests improvements and passes us, but not her. It wasn't anything bad. Just a little problem with access control. We didn't limit where our people go in the plant because they badge into each room. We can always see where they've been and reprimand them if they're in places they shouldn't be. It shows trust. Unfortunately, that's a violation of commission rules. We've already fixed it." His jaw set, "You're not one of those anti-nuke people, are you?"

"Heck no. Nuclear plants are great. At least if they're secure."

"We run a safe plant, Minxy. Those two reactors have been hummin' along accident-free since the mid-seventies."

I did the math in my head. "Isn't that kind of old? I mean, technology changes."

He gave me his big flirtatious Texas smile. "It's all part of a plan, you know? We stress test everything. Equipment's changed out all the time. There aren't many original components left."

I took the umbrella out of my drink and fiddled with it—open, closed, open, closed—while I thought about how they'd rehabbed an old plant. "So, you gave it face lifts and knee replacements. Good to know. But Jenn was a colossal pain. She must have driven Cunningham crazy."

"Don't get me wrong, Andrew hated that we didn't pass, but it wasn't his first rodeo. He's got..." he caught himself, "...he *had* thick skin. Her visit was just part of the job. We fixed the problems and moved on." He looked down into his coffee.

Everyone lies. Sometimes they do it for understandable reasons, and sometimes because they like messing with people. I did the latter quite often. I'd been watching Ricky carefully, looking for lies. When he said Cunningham simply *moved on* from a blemish to his reputation, he was lying.

Cunningham and Jenn had some kind of major interaction to get him to her house twice after the test. Maybe he'd pled his case and didn't want it seen by the staff. Maybe they'd tangled before. A self-righteous woman from D.C. had lectured and embarrassed a hard-working plant manager. I bet Cunningham wanted to throw her into the reactor and watch her burn.

I needed to match Ricky's lie with one of my own. He needed to think I'd bought his story. In memory of Vera's brief acting career, I leaned forward as though sharing a confidence and said, "Well, that is *such* a comfort. Cunningham didn't kill Jenn. One more person I can rule out."

"Yup, what's-her-name's murder wasn't about the plant. I heard the police arrested your client, PI Banks."

I groaned and pushed my hair behind my ears. "They always investigate the boyfriend. They have no imagination."

Ricky was about to sip his coffee, but stopped and said, "So, you're goin' full bore on this Private Investigator thing?"

"That's correct. I'll get Walt Hawley off."

The good old boy's eyes twinkled when he said, "Show me your badge."

I explained about not having a badge while I pulled my creds holder from the side pocket of my purse and flipped it open. "It looks official, doesn't it?"

"Oh yeah. I can see you bein' awesome at PI work. Sorta back to your spy days."

"Yes, it is. Between you and me, it feels wonderful."

We finished our drinks and after a brotherly hug initiated by Ricky, we separately headed up Route 4 toward West Beach. I was left with the feeling Ricky had cared about Cunningham and was protecting his boss. Jenn must have started a real ruckus at the plant. I wasn't any closer to figuring out why Cunningham had visited her at home, though. I needed to know that before I talked with his widow.

Fifteen

The drive back to the beach helped me focus on what to do next. Celia's commute depended on traffic and work demands, making her arrival unpredictable. Astrid would be there right at 5:00 p.m. though. Punctuality was a Danish thing. I needed to talk with her about this Andrew Cunningham business. Were Jenn and he working together or was one of them threatening the other? Those late-night meetings were as unusual as Jenn's suit at the park. It wasn't proper business behavior.

Before going home, however, I had one important stop to make. I wanted to talk with Alice Stone about where Danny was the night of the murder. His eerily predictive Bible quotes unnerved me, but I liked the guy and hoped his alibi held water.

The People Finder had given up the Alice and Danny Stone address easily, and I was soon sitting in front of the bungalow they called home.

Halfway up the front walk, a voice called to me from inside the screened door. "May I help you?" It wasn't a friendly welcome.

"Are you Alice Stone?"

"I am."

"Then, I think you can help me a lot. I'm Minxy Banks." I reached into the side pocket of my purse and marveled at my own dexterity as I flipped open the creds. It excited me more than a little to show them. "I'm a private investigator for Walter Hawley."

"The dude who killed Danny's friend in the park?"

"That's the police allegation. We'll prove he didn't do it."

Alice pushed open the screen door and walked toward me. "So why are you here? I don't want my son mixed up in this mess."

I did a one second assessment. Alice was still living in the 1970s. She had on a vintage Led Zeppelin T-shirt and Birkenstocks. Her hair was an all-natural, some-brown, mostly-gray tangled pile on her head. She'd clearly had Danny later in life. Her stance and attitude seemed protective of her son. I liked her for that.

I said, "No ma'am. I'm hoping to keep him out of this."

"Minxy Banks. I've heard about you messing in people's business. Coupla times I've seen you make an about face when you see my boy on the street in front of you."

In a pinch, case officers fall back on tradecraft. The first rule we learned was that 'plausible deniability' works. Never admit to doing anything wrong regardless of how lame it makes you look.

"You know Alice, I'm scatterbrained. Sometimes I find myself walking several blocks out of my way because I'm lost in thought. If you saw me turning around quickly, that was probably it."

"Humph."

She didn't buy it, but she let it drop. I said, "I'm only here to confirm Danny's alibi. If I'm right, he'll be off the list of possible suspects we're building. Can you prove he was here with you that night? The night of the murder."

"I'm not talking to you about the murder. You'll twist what I say and make Danny look bad."

"Alice, I want to help him. I know about the assault charge and the reduction for diminished capacity. That makes him a target for Walt's lawyer if his alibi's squishy."

She crossed her arms over her chest.

"Just confirm some things Danny has already told me. He says he goes to bed at 10:30 every night. Was that true the night of the murder?"

She thought for a minute and finally said, "Yes."

"He never goes out after 10:30 pm."

"Also, yes."

Time for a curveball. "He could slip out of the house without you knowing, right?"

She harrumphed at me again like I was crazy. "He's a sleep-walker. I've alarmed his bedroom door and window. It's more like a siren. I close them every night when he goes to bed. When either opens in the middle of the night it wakes me up."

"What if he needs to go to the bathroom?"

"We share a Jack-and-Jill. Those doors aren't alarmed, but I'm a light sleeper. I'd hear him come through my room to get out, if that's what you're wondering."

"So, you're sure you'd have known if he left his room?"

She nodded. "Positive. He hasn't gotten out since I put in the alarms months ago. It's so loud it wakes up the neighbors. They hate me."

"And he couldn't have turned it off somehow?"

"Lady, he can hardly work a microwave, let alone a fancy alarm."

I didn't need to know for the case, but I was curious, so I asked, "What caused his disability?"

The way she looked at me, I could tell she knew this was me being nosy. She answered. "None of your business."

I could read her pain for her son, but didn't feel it. Thank goodness for small blessings. I crossed my arms and said, "Alice, let me test that alarm system and take a picture of it. If it works, I promise I'll keep Danny out of this."

"You're not coming into my house. Believe me or not." She walked inside and slammed the screen door.

Oddly enough, I believed her. Just to verify, however, I went to her neighbor's house to ask if they'd ever heard the alarm. The neighbor said, "Oh my goodness, it sounds like a fog horn. It's gone off every night this week."

I asked, "Even Tuesday night? The night Jenn Albrecht was killed in the park."

She told me to come in. We walked to the kitchen where a calendar hung from a nail next to the refrigerator. She stubbed a finger at Tuesday. "See. It went off Tuesday night well after midnight. When it hits seven days, I'm calling the cops."

On Tuesday, written in red ink, was "1:27 a.m." That was too late to murder Jenn.

WHEN I GOT HOME, Astrid was standing at the white board on the patio. It was slightly modified:

Killer? / Motive
- Clandestine Operative: national security? (Celia)
- Random stranger: crazy, interpersonal conflict (IC) (Astrid)
- Danny: jealousy (Minxy)
- Sal: IC (Minxy)
- The Miscreants: Anti-nuke policy (All)
- ~~Minxy: IC~~
- ~~Walt: IC $ (All)~~
- The mayor: IC & $ (Minxy)

•Coworker at NRC HQ: IC, national security (Celia)
•Coworker at a security exercise: IC
•Someone we haven't figured out yet: ?

Ecosystem: second shadow, suit, pantihose, gun, purse, folio, park, late night, trash cans, papers in car, car windows, fake parking signs, city contracts, gravel, national security, engagement ring, and inheritance.

Astrid had used a marker to cross out my name and Walt's. She heard me walk onto the deck and looked up. "Celia will be late. Something came up at the office."

Mr. Magoo was leaning against one of Astrid's legs as she stood by the suspect list.

"What did Walt and I do to make it off the list?"

She looked up at me over her shoulder. "It made the list too unruly. However, I'm still watching you two."

Walking down the spiral stairs, I saw that Astrid had opened a chardonnay instead of making martinis. I looked at the label. "French. Lars has been to the embassy's duty-free commissary."

"They just got a new shipment with some nice ones. I thought it would be a fun change. There are more bottles in the mini fridge."

Next to the wine, Astrid had laid out brie with crackers to go with the wine. I poured a glass. *Magnifique.*

After I caught her up on today's events with Walt, the Cunninghams, and Danny, Astrid marked out Danny's name on the whiteboard. The fierceness of his mother's love and the weariness of his sleep-deprived neighbor convinced us he was home on the night of the murder.

With her marker poised to write, she said, "We should add something about Cunningham. His visits make no sense. She failed his plant. That's conflict, but he comes to visit like a social call."

"The data from the night of the murder will explain a lot. Maybe he was the second shadow. That would make three late night visits. If not, we might have another suspect."

Astrid thought for a second, then said, "Those meetings had to be more than long lectures from Jenn. He was a powerful man and wouldn't have put up with it. Regardless, she'd passed the plant by then, so it was something else. They both know nuclear things. I think he was helping her or threatening her about her clandestine mission. The reason for the meeting with the operative in the park."

"You might be right. I just assumed she was nagging him, but that's me being me. It makes sense that her big security case had something to do with nuclear."

Astrid smiled, "Let's put his name on the suspect list to figure out those meetings. I suppose he could be the killer if he was at her house, left, and surprised her at the park. Celia can figure it out. She loves a challenge."

She had her naughty look when she wrote Cunningham, then Celia's name next to a lot of question marks. "The price you pay for being late to happy hour."

Astrid, her straight, blond hair swinging loose from its usual perch behind her ears, scooped up a piece of brie on a cracker. She took a bite. With a hand in front of her mouth she said, "I researched crazy strangers on community social media boards for Calvert and Anne Arundel Counties. It was very interesting."

"How so?"

"People report anything as suspicious that they wouldn't do. Like sitting at the nature overlook for more than thirty minutes. Or feeding vultures cooked liver in their backyard."

"Okay, that *is* strange."

"Vultures need love, too."

"That's debatable."

"Anyway, the point is that no one has reported a threatening stranger near here."

Mr. Magoo shifted to a grassy spot where he faced us both. He sniffed audibly using smell to make up for what he couldn't see. Convinced we were safe, he rested his snout between his front legs.

I said, "A crazy stranger who did that to Jenn would have threatened someone else."

"Maybe there are people who know something but aren't on social media. We should interview people who might have seen something. Especially here in West Beach. Could The Miscreants do that for us?"

"Great idea." I stood up. I pulled my phone from my hip pocket and called Emma. She picked up on the first ring.

I asked, "Can Tyler and you come to my house ASAP?"

"Crap! We can't be in trouble. The Sheriff said it was all good."

"You're not in trouble. Imagine that. I've got a civics project for you. Will your parents let you come?"

"They won't care because they won't know. Still at work."

"Get over here then." The softness of my tone belied my gruff words.

I looked up from my phone and watched Astrid cover the whiteboard with a beach towel. She said, "They don't need to know they're on the list."

The Miscreants walked through the side gate in ten minutes and dropped into seats at the table. Emma eyed the wine. "Do we get a glass?"

"No, my dear Miscreant. But I'll get you both a Coke." I pointed to Astrid. "This is Ms. Astrid. She's Danish. We're working on the Albrecht murder case, and we need your help."

I winked at Astrid. "Keep them out of the wine and fill them in on the project."

As I went to the mini fridge in the 'she shed', I heard Astrid say to the kids, "In Denmark you could drink wine at your age, but you would have to do it responsibly. If you made mistakes, we would hold you responsible."

Coming out of the 'she shed' with the cold Cokes I watched Magoo walking around the table sniffing the new arrivals. He didn't growl but he didn't go up to The Miscreants either. Instead, he went back to his spot in the grass and resumed his sightless watch.

I brought cookies with the drinks. Astrid was wrapping up. "So, we are trying to find out if people in West Beach have seen a violent or just suspicious person in the last few days. Ask as many people as you know, as well as your parents' friends, and shop-keepers. Ask them, 'Have you seen anyone acting crazy or being violent in or near West Beach in the last five days,'" She sighed, "That would be fantastic. If there isn't such a person, we can mark 'random killer' off our suspect list. If you find out about a violent person..."

I broke in, "If you hear about a violent person, call me. Don't get anywhere near him. Or her."

Emma bristled. "I can take care of myself."

I smiled broadly, "I know, but you'll get Tyler killed."

It was a joke and I shouldn't have said it, but it was true, and I couldn't help myself. Emma could take down a bull moose, but Tyler was a poet at heart and would get squashed trying to protect his lady.

"Tyler bristled, "I can handle myself, too."

Astrid and Emma glared at me, so I spread my hands in surrender, adding, "It was a joke. What I meant to say is: we won't confront violent or suspicious people. We'll call the police. They have guns and handcuffs and other metal stuff to control them. You'd still be citizens of the month for identifying him. Or her."

The two teens exchanged glances. Tyler asked, "Okay, this is a cool mission, but why are we doing it?"

"Oh, I forgot to tell you, I'm a Private Investigator now." I pulled my flip creds and let them drop, getting the usual rush. "My friends and I are working for Ms. Albrecht's boyfriend. He was arrested for her murder."

"Really?" they said in unison.

"That's right. And now you're on the case, too."

Tyler said, "The dude didn't do it."

I cocked my head, "And why is that?"

Emma answered for him, "He's the only person who liked her."

My internal happy meter registered off the charts. Literally everyone besides the Marine had a better reason to kill her.

Tyler pointed a finger at me, "And anyway, they always blame the boyfriend. That's just stupid."

"Exactly right. You get a cookie." I pushed the plate toward him. "So, take your Cokes and cookies, Miscreants, and go save this community." Belatedly I added, "And an innocent Marine." I asked them to write up their report for the record.

They readied themselves to go with an enthusiasm I had never seen in them. They were so whipped up, they bumped into Celia on their way out the gate. I yelled after them, "Be home by your 10:00 p.m. curfew."

"Our parents don't care. Even the Sheriff didn't seem to." Emma yelled over her shoulder.

"I care and I'm the enforcer."

After her encounter with The Miscreants, Celia readjusted her golden four-inch, articulated crocodile pin that probably had belonged to Wallis Simpson back in the day. It was an excellent accompaniment to her Bahama Mama T-shirt. We stood together watching The Miscreants race away. "What's gotten into them?" She turned toward the table.

Astrid leaned in on her elbows and said to Celia, "We put them to work interviewing West Beach citizens about seeing crazy or violent strangers."

"Smart move. Someone out there knows something that could help." She eyed the French chardonnay. Before she could reach for it, Mr. Magoo came over for a head scratch. She knelt and petted him with a lot of babytalk greetings. When she stood, she said, "I checked the FBI 'See something, say something' database for Calvert and several adjacent counties. There's odd stuff happening all around here, but nothing that fits our violent suspicious perp. I also talked to my FBI buddy. They're hush hush about active cases, but he convinced me there were none related to a nuclear power plant threat."

I handed Celia a glass of the French wine and she took a seat at the table. She twirled the wine in the glass, waved her hand above the rim to smell the aroma, and finally tasted it. It passed her test, and she took a second sip. "I also asked the DHS infrastructure protection people about threats to domestic nuclear power plants. There are general warnings about cyberattacks to infrastructure by all kinds of bad guys. However, the nuclear plants hedged against cyberattacks by keeping most of their command centers analog. They still look like the 1970s. Some data can come in from the reactors, but the Command Center can't control their functions."

I said, "You mean the Command Centers look like a scene from the movie China Syndrome?"

"Yes, believe it or not."

Astrid filled Celia in on the app data, who Cunningham was, and ended with, "Oh by the way, he's dead."

Celia stopped drinking mid-sip. "Dead? How?"

I said, "Massive heart attack. We should focus on Cunningham. He was at Jenn's house two evenings. Maybe he was the second shadow I saw the night she died. We'll know for sure when we get the rest of Brent's phone data."

Astrid said, "He could have been helping Jenn or working with the killer."

Celia nodded. "Okay, he's a person of interest."

Astrid looked up from a doodle she was making with a marker on a takeaway food menu. "What if he pretended to help Jenn, told her he was leaving the night of the murder, but didn't. Instead, he followed her to the park and killed her before she met with the clandestine operative. He wasn't a natural killer, so the guilt weighed him down. It caused the heart attack."

Celia said, "It would have been easier to kill her in the house. Cunningham was more likely involved in supporting her secret mission. The reason for the clandestine meeting in the park. That means he knew what she knew."

We all three nodded. Astrid went to the board with her marker and underlined Cunningham's name.

Killer? / Motive

    •Clandestine Operative: national security? (Celia)

    •Random crazy stranger: interpersonal conflict (IC) (Astrid and The Miscreants)

    •~~Danny: jealousy. (Minxy)~~

    •Sal: IC (Minxy)

    •The Miscreants: Anti-Nuke Policy (All)

    •~~Minxy: IC~~

    •~~Walt: ? $ (All)~~

    •The mayor: IC & $ (Minxy)

    •Coworker at NRC HQ: IC, national security (Celia)

    •Coworker at a security exercise: IC <u>Cunningham</u> ????? (Celia)

    •Someone we haven't figured out yet: ?

Ecosystem: second shadow, suit, pantihose, gun, purse, folio, park, late night, trash cans, papers in car, car windows, fake parking signs, city contracts, gravel, national security, engagement ring, and inheritance.

The buttery chardonnay distracted me for a moment. Wine really does make me more creative. I was sure of it. After swallowing, I said, "I wanted to pin this on Cunningham, but now I'm thinking he's one of the good guys and the case is about the nuke plant. Maybe he talked to his wife about why he met with Jenn. We can ask her."

Astrid had resumed her doodling and looked up from the growing mix of circles and lines, "Give the widow a few days to grieve before you call."

"Oh, right. Of course." Oops, another sensitivity demerit for me.

Celia said, "Good idea. Then we ask why her husband's phone signaled from Jenn's house. She knew he wasn't home. Maybe she knew more."

Astrid brightened, "Until then, I can tell my neighbor to match the fingerprints from Jenn's house with senior leaders at the nuclear power plant. Just a little tip..." She rose slowly, stretched and headed to the 'she shed' to get another bottle of the French wine from the mini fridge.

Celia laughed, "You know, Minxy, Astrid really is a little devil."

"No, she's not. That may be what we need to do. But we have to wait. No police until we understand what those two were up to."

THE HAPPY HOUR wrapped up early. After the ladies left, I lingered in my backyard. I was still thinking about my first solo sailing misadventure. Magoo sensed my need and joined me on a lounger with his head on my stomach.

I remembered every detail of that late Spring day decades ago. Pulling away from the dock in my new Sunfish, I had shaken so hard I couldn't properly hold the tiller or manage the sail. The wind was too brisk for me, and I struggled to tack after leaving our cove. As I got farther from it, I looked back wanting nothing but the safety of that sheltered inlet, but if I went back early, Shelly would be mad.

For what seemed like a long time to my eight-year-old self, I sailed close to the shore, getting caught in the breakers. They tossed the little boat around like a cat with a toy. I'd get really scared and go farther out, only to return, seeking proximity to dry land. Then I saw a deep cove and headed down it.

With relief from the strongest gusts, I practiced maneuvering. I wove back and forth in the long but narrow harbor. I was getting better but was far from in control. My coming about was sloppy. Shelly would not be proud of me for that. Worse, I'd been in the midday sun for too long. My legs and arms were an angry red and my face hurt. I'd had all I could take. I lowered the sail, pulled up the rudder and daggerboard, and beached the boat the way I'd learned to do at summer camp with canoes. I grabbed my book from the hull, then stripped off the life vest and threw it on the ground. There was a shady maple tree up the hill. Leaning against the trunk, I lost myself in my biography of Jackie Kennedy.

The book had lots of stories about Jackie as a girl, as a newspaper photographer, and as the First Lady of the United States. The author said that she made her own path, and whatever problem came her way, she would overcome it. I loved that she took super good care of her daughter and son. I cried when her husband got shot. Then she remarried and had a lot of adventures.

She even did good things for New York City, like saving Grand Central Station.

I read it so fast that my head was dizzy with all the ideas. The two biggest: I looked a little like Jackie. The wide set brown eyes, the dark hair and light complexion. That's why my teacher assigned it. *More important for me at the moment, Jackie knew how to get what she wanted.* She was charming. She could talk people into doing what she needed them to do for her. I wanted to be like Jackie. She wouldn't be stuck in this cove, sunburned, and sitting under a tree. She would have insisted on sunscreen and water and help from Shelly to learn how to sail the boat and...

Enough. Tired and thirsty, I threw my book into the boat as I pushed it away from the shore. I had belly flopped into it and was working on the sail when I saw the life vest laying on the ground. I thought, *just leave it.* The boat was off the sand, and I was almost underway toward home. I looked toward deep water and back at the vest. I couldn't do it. I hopped out into the water, pulling the boat with me. I ran to the vest, pulled it on, then raced back to the boat that was slipping away. Flopping back in, I raised the sail and headed out of the cove on a path home. I'd be early, but I didn't care. The sail filled with the brisk wind. I pulled away from dry land and the breakers. I was headed into the Long Island Sound and felt great about it.

That's when the wind shifted, and a huge gust capsized my Sunfish.

It was early June and the water in Long Island Sound was frigid. I tried a dozen times to right the boat, but the sail was heavy with water, and I was too light. I clung to the hull, trying to climb on top, but it was too slick. Instead, I bobbed in the water like a buoy while the boat and I drifted farther out into the sound. I was terrified. When I was passing our cove, I yelled for Shelly, but she didn't hear me. What would Jackie do? Jackie was a good swimmer and so was I. Maybe I could swim to shore before I got any farther out. I could see dry land and wanted to get back to it. I let go of the boat.

The life vest made it hard to swim, but I made headway with a kind of breaststroke. The current kept carrying me farther down the island away from our house, but I was getting closer to land. I stroked and stroked, closing my eyes and thinking about Jackie Kennedy. She'd make it to the shore.

I opened my eyes when I heard yelling. An old man was out on his dock waving his arms at me.

I waved back. "*Help. Help me.*"

He hopped off the dock into a motorboat and headed my way.

Killing the motor and coming along side me he said, "Hey, kiddo, what are you doing in the water alone?" He reached down and picked me up under the arms and set me in the boat. Then he handed me a beach towel.

I wrapped myself up and hugged myself to warm up. "Thank you *so* much. I was really scared."

"Why were you in the water? Where's your family?"

"My boat tipped over." I pointed to the Sunfish, which had drifted farther and was barely visible now.

He looked me over, "I've got a grandchild about your size. She's nine."

Still hugging myself, I said, "I'm eight. I'm kind of tall for a girl."

"Come on kid, we'll go get that boat then get you home. Where do you live?"

I pointed. "We're in a cove that way." I sat in the swivel seat next to him. In a bucket, I saw bottles of water. "Could I please have a bottle of water? I'm really thirsty."

He handed me one. "Didn't you have water on your boat?"

"No Sir."

He headed in the direction of my boat. "I bet your mom's going to be righteous angry at you."

"What time is it?" He showed me his watch. "No, she won't be. I managed to stay out the full three hours."

"Oh. So, your mom sent you into the bay for three hours by yourself?" He rubbed his scruffy chin. "She and I need to talk." We came alongside the Sunfish and the man righted it quickly. He lashed the two boats together then handed me a coffee can and told me to bail while he lowered the sail. In no time we had her tied with a long rope to a cleat on the back of his boat.

As we rounded into our inlet, Shelly and her friend Camie were sitting in Adirondack chairs. They were sharing a cigarette, passing it back and forth when they noticed my new friend—his name was Mr. Dave—and I coming toward the dock. They met us there.

"What's up?" Shelly said more to me than Mr. Dave.

"I was so scared Shelly. It's too dangerous out there. The wind capsized my boat, and I had to swim to shore. And I lost my library book. My teacher's going to be mad."

Mr. Dave said, "I found her swimming alone. If she hadn't had that life vest..."

Shelly said, "I'm sure she'd have been just fine. You're fearless, aren't you, Marnie?"

"No, I'm not fearless. I was really scared." I thought about what Jackie Kennedy would do. "I'm not going out there again by myself. I don't want independence or responsibility."

Shelly put her hands on her hips and said, "Well then."

I stood in the same position, hands on my hips, chest out and demanded, "Oh, and I want more Jackie Kennedy books from the library. I need them today."

She looked at her newly demanding child. "You never talk to me like this. Your sailing adventure has turned you into a proper little minx."

Mr. Dave patted me on the back. "Minxy suits you. You're a tough little girl." To Shelly, he said, "If I see her out alone again,

I'm calling child protective services. That was stupidly irresponsible of you."

Shelly waved goodbye to Mr. Dave with her middle finger as he pulled away from the dock.

Every time I demanded something from Shelly after that, she called me Minxy. My demands were frequent, so the nickname stuck. The funny thing was, she *had* taught me independence and responsibility. I began running my own life because I no longer trusted Shelly's bad judgment.

I locked up and went to my bedroom. Magoo jumped on the bed, and I thought how nice it had been sitting in the lounger, so I opened a bedroom window to let in some fresh air. Below, on the boardwalk, a guy leaned against the boardwalk railing, playing games on his phone. He wore sweat pants and a hoodie. I couldn't see his face, but I had a bad feeling. Magoo sniffed and let out a long, low growl. The guy walked away with his back to me. It was odd enough to convince me fresh air was a bad idea. I lowered and locked the window.

<h1 style="text-align:center">Sixteen</h1>

SATURDAY, JUNE 24, WEST BEACH, MD

I guzzled my pre-run water and started at a fast pace. It made for a very quick circuit around town, even with all the people setting up for the Farmer's Market. In the shower I decided today I'd check the CCTV tapes in Town Hall, but they weren't the most interesting lead in that building. It was the weekend, but on the last Saturday of every month, Mayor Bill Hampton held office hours for voters who couldn't come during the week. He'd be there today, and poor Sue would be with him. Mayors are like Santa. They can't work without a helper.

As I slipped on a flouncy skirt and simple sleeveless blouse, I was thinking hard about Jenn's conflict with Hampton. Our previous mayor had walked the streets of West Beach saying hi to all the people he would undoubtedly help in one way or the other. Bill Hampton, on the other hand, was in it for himself. He remained the full-time operator of a luxury resort and marina farther south in Calvert County. The mayor's job was a step toward building a second resort in West Beach. To disguise his ownership, a corporation had already bought the land and petitioned the zoning commission. Hampton influenced them from the inside. Jenn's complaint had to be small ball compared to that level of self-dealing. Maybe Walt was wrong. It couldn't only be messy contracting practices. There should be juicier crimes to find. Mayor Bill was a pirate, and I'd made my opinion known in town hall meetings.

I called to see if Bill was in yet. Sue said he was and planned to be around for a couple of hours, even for me if he didn't know I was coming. I put on my sandals and flip flopped over to the West Beach Town Hall.

Walking in I asked Sue, "Did you tell him?"

Sue shook her head, and her mouth curled in the smallest of smiles. She walked around and opened the staff door. We had a discrete little fist bump, and I walked the few steps to the mayor's anteroom, and through it to his office.

Knocking on the door jam, I called out, "Hi Bill, you got a minute?"

He wore khakis and a polo shirt and sat behind a laminate desk in his small office. Harsh overhead lights made up for one tiny window near the ceiling. Bill's thinning hair was neatly combed, and he had a dark suntan from working at his resort. I didn't have a problem with that. Being mayor didn't pay a salary you could live on. He looked up, and the politician's smile lasted until he recognized me, and he let it slip. "Minxy Banks. If I'd known you were coming, I'd have run out the back door. You're my number one suspect for that stupid flooded lap lane sign on Fifth Street."

"Sign? What sign?"

The mayor scowled, then said, "You want something. What is it?"

"Well, you're right, Bill. First, look at my newest acquisition."

I pulled out my flip creds from my pocket and opened them as I'd practiced. "Minxy Banks, Private Investigator."

"Okay you're scaring me. Minxy PI will be a disaster. Does it come with a license to kill?"

"Unfortunately, not yet. But the good news is I have my first case. Walt Hawley hired me."

"Nothing like starting a job with a loser. I suppose you'll want to sit down."

I moved to one of the uninviting wooden seats and sat gently. "Bill, I need to review the town CCTV feeds for the night of the murder. All the cameras."

"How about just the ones we copied for the cops? They wanted the ones in Sunrise Garden and on Chesapeake Avenue in front of this building."

"That's not enough. I want them all. Particularly the cameras on Seventh Street and the Fishing Pier."

"Knock yourself out. Sue can set you up. Better bring No Doz."

"Thank you. And now for the tricky part. You know Jenn Albrecht didn't exactly have a lot of friends in town."

"I don't want to speak ill of the dead, but that women didn't have any. We all hated her. I heard the police talked to you about your gardening war."

I nodded. "Yes, they did, and my alibi is an old, blind dog. But I didn't kill her."

"And the Sheriff wrote you off the list with that alibi?"

"Not yet, but they're fixated on my client. I'm looking for others who had the means and motive." I stopped there and sat silently.

"So how can I help you?" He started shuffling papers.

"Jenn was concerned about improper contracting practices by the town. Specifically...by you. I'm expecting you to confess to her murder."

Hampton's face reddened and he slowly exhaled through his nose.

I held up my hands in surrender, "It's not just me. Sal, who is also on my list, pointed the finger at you."

"Sal's a jerk."

"He said you and Jenn had some issue about favoritism in assigning a public works contract."

He took off his reading glasses. "I will not miss that woman."

"Same here. What was she talking about?"

"Minxy, I didn't kill her. I was in DC with my wife for a getaway. We saw a show at the Kennedy Center and stayed at a fancy hotel."

"Lucky you. A decent alibi. Not bullet proof if you're a criminal mastermind, but it could fly. Where'd you stay? Did you take time and date stamped photos at the bar about midnight?"

"It was the Sheraton, and we probably did. That's Kathy's department. She takes family pictures. Definitely have some at the play during intermission. We had champagne on the balcony."

Shifting in the hard chair, I asked, "What about the contract?"

He shook his head like he couldn't imagine having to explain himself to me. "I issued a sole-source contract without competitive bidding. That's it. Just paid some contractors who've worked for me before to fix some city property. I understand the capabilities of every contractor in this town. I know who's drugging, who's lazy, and even who'll get the job done to specs and on time. Oddly enough, I chose the latter. But for Albrecht, there needed to be a process where I had all those other guys apply, then picked the one I wanted anyway. What a waste of time."

I nodded. "The last major repair was the boardwalk after the big storm. Was that the one?"

Bill leaned back in his chair put his hands on his head, fingers laced together. "That's the one. It was a bigger project than maintenance could handle quickly. I gave a contract to Woolsey and his boys to put it back the way it was. Nothing fancy. He did it in a coupla days. Albrecht had no problem with the outcome or the price, just the process."

A little light bulb went off in my head and reminded me that Bill was a pirate. "Well, I heard you got a kickback. You know, for being so helpful." I was making it all up, but knowing Bill, it was probably true.

Bill fell forward to his desk and he cradled his head in his hands. "That woman drove me nuts. Woolsey had some leftover gravel and kicked it outta the truck and into my driveway. They had to put it somewhere. No big deal."

"Welcome to the list of suspects. You'll find us a rowdy lot."

With that he stood, "Always glad to meet with a citizen. Now get the hell out of my office, Minxy. I've got to stop the flooding you keep complaining about."

"Well, thanks for the chat, Bill. I'll be looking at the videos if you need a PI."

"Yeah. Right."

SUE, the everything woman, set up a computer for me in my Miscreant classroom. First, I went through the files the police had copied. I started with the camera in the park on the centrally located gazebo, positioned to capture the entrance and the koi ponds. That had the secondary effect of also catching traffic and the front plates on some diagonally parked cars on Bay Avenue.

I fast forwarded through vehicles moving south to north on the one-way street. I recognized some of the driver's faces. They were waterfront residents coming home late.

When Jenn entered the park, I paused the video. She looked so resolute in that prissy green suit. I started the video on slow motion and watched as she stood for a moment, her head high, looking around, then she walked beyond the camera's range toward the mermaid statue and her fate. It gave me a chill. She didn't appear to see anyone. She didn't look frightened. I repeated the part with her several times, then played through the rest of the tape. It was hard not to acknowledge that off screen the murder was happening. No one came in and no one left through the entrance until I jogged in at sunrise. The confusion on my face made me relive that two-mermaid moment.

After I examined what the police had taken, I skipped through the images from the camera on the fishing pier. Melancholy people leaned against the peer railing and peered into the darkness. A few couples were making out in the dark.

Next, I checked the footage from the Town Hall camera mounted on the front of the building above the entrance. Chesapeake Avenue was a major thoroughfare going both north and south. There was more vehicular traffic than on one-way Bay Avenue. Maybe one of the drivers would be a lead. A few walkers stumbled home after drinking with friends. So far, there was nothing I could use.

Then I saw The Miscreants doing exactly what they had told me they'd done. They walked side by side, engaged in conversation. No camera had captured their interaction with Jenn, but at the time Jenn entered the park, they were on video blocks from the park headed away from it toward Emma's house. They were officially off my list. *Great kids,* I thought. *If we can get them graduated and off to college, they'll be fine. Humm, I'll have to tell Maya that those two are in my circle of friendship. I have a real warm spot for those two. What a week.*

There was only one more camera in West Beach, proving once again, it wasn't London. That camera monitored the commercial district...all three blocks of it. It was set up at the corner of Seventh and Bay and caught anything happening close to either street. The owner of the wine bar brought in boxes of wine from her SUV. It looked like a long night of stocking and accounting for her. The Mexican place closed at 11:00 p.m. but patrons lingered on the patio.

Then I saw it. A medium-height stocky man walking toward the park within fifteen minutes of Jenn's time of death. His stubborn walk was unmistakable.

Seventeen

The late-night angry man was Sal. So much for his girlfriend alibi. He was walking down Seventh Street toward the bay looking as angry as he had been when I parked in front of his restaurant. Arms swinging, muttering to himself, his walk was more a stomp than anything else. He rounded the corner onto Chesapeake Avenue and quickly was out of the camera's range, headed in the direction of the park. I saved that video clip to the thumb drive as a file called 'Sal_the_liar'. I copied all the rest of the videos and closed down the computer.

I'd made progress. The mayor had admitted to less than kosher contracting and a gravel kickback—both about as bad as jaywalking. Not exactly a reason for him to kill Jenn. Similarly, she would not have risked her life to meet a cop in the park after midnight dressed professionally to turn over evidence of bad procurement practices. If this was the important security business she told Walt about, she would have taken the evidence to the Sheriff during business hours. A quick call confirmed Bill and his wife had stayed at the hotel in DC that night. The mayor was a dead end.

Sal was a different story. He was walking in the right place at the right time to have committed the murder. I had to tone down my enthusiasm for sticking it to him. I needed a solid motive for this to work as reasonable doubt. I said aloud, "Where were you going that night?" It didn't seem plausible that he'd kill her over fake parking signs. And it still didn't explain why she would be in that park.

On my way home from copying the videos, I walked by Sal's restaurant to imagine what he'd been up to the night of the murder. Standing in front of it, I followed his path on the video. I passed other restaurants, the brewery, the building that once housed a gypsy fortuneteller and stopped where I'd lost him on the footage. He had turned right, which would have taken him in the direction of Jenn's murder.

I was close to Astrid's house so I walked over and knocked on her door before entering as usual. "It's Minxy. You home?"

Before Astrid had a chance to answer, I was standing in her sunny, Euro-style living room. She was dressed in tights and following yoga poses with an instructor speaking what I assumed was Danish. When I wondered where that channel was on the TV, I realized that she was casting a YouTube video from her phone. She struck a warrior's pose and said, "*Hej hej.* What are you doing today?"

"Working on our case. I brought you the CCTV feeds to see if you can find clues in them. I also need to run something by you."

"May I keep going with the poses. I promised myself I'd get in a full session. Lars will be home any minute to go for a hike."

"Of course, I insist." I sat cross legged on the floor beside the TV so she could see both me and the incredibly limber yoga instructor at the same time. "I've got news."

Astrid looked at me and nodded, then shifted into another pose.

"First the good news. The Miscreants were caught on the Town Hall camera at the time of the murder. They were walking away from the park just like they told us."

Her smile brightened the room. "I'm so glad they are off our list. I like those kids."

I continued, "And second, the police have zip, nada, nothing on the videos they copied."

She nodded acknowledgment then stretched upward into a tree asana, balancing on one foot. Her muscles tightened and she was steady as a steel girder.

"But I searched farther from the park and guess who I found on a video just about the time of the murder?"

She broke her pose to look at me and said, "Walt?"

"No because he's not guilty, remember."

"I think he's innocent, but you made me wonder. Who did you find?"

Astrid knelt on her yoga mat following the instructor in a move I thought would dislocate her shoulder. "Sal."

"Oh my." She stopped the pose and paused the YouTube video with her cell phone. Sitting cross legged she asked, "When?"

"About the time Jenn was killed."

Astrid's face lit up. "Well, that was lucky. You may have solved the case. That will ruin our happy hour fun but for a good reason."

"No worries about that yet. Before I confront him, I need to know about the girlfriend. She was his alibi until I destroyed it."

"What's her name?"

"Don't know."

Astrid stood up again and restarted the video. "Find me a picture. I have very fine facial recognition software."

"Deal. I'll send it when I've got it."

I laid the thumb drive on the coffee table and waved goodbye as Astrid restarted the video and arched her back into a perfect cobra pose.

I NEEDED a photo of Sal's woman and I had just the tool for getting it at my house. When I walked into my sun-filled living room, Mr. Magoo was napping and only thumped his tail in greeting. He'd been wide awake when I got up. I wondered if that guy playing games had been back outside again.

In my office closet I rummaged through my electronics cubby and held up one of the little battery-operated cameras I used just for fun. They weren't CIA issue; I'd turned in all that equipment. This one was the next best thing, bought directly from Amazon. It had the capability that five years ago would have been unbeliev-able in the spy world. Now the public could buy them. *Americans should give up on privacy*, I thought. It was impossible if the adversary was aggressive.

The camera was round and about the thickness of three quar-ters in a stack. It had a U-shaped clip attached to the back and was mounted on a swivel so I could direct the lens a few degrees. When I thought about where I would plant it, I chuckled. *Serves him right.*

Saturday lunch at the Italian place would be busy with a steady stream of customers. I hoped that Sal and all his wait staff would be too occupied to notice what I was doing in plain sight. I swapped my flip flops for loafers, then walked back to the restaurant.

Sal's girlfriend had to come and go through a door, and I thought he would bring her in the front. Even he wasn't boorish enough to sneak her in through the loading dock. After thinking about that for a moment, I downgraded that assumption to about a fifty-fifty chance.

Laughter and loud conversations filled Sal's outdoor deck seating on a busy Saturday. Stopping near one of the fake parking signs, I leaned my hip against the post and removed my shoe, pretending to shake out a non-existent pebble. It was a classic magician's misdirection. My other hand slipped into my pocket, pulled out the camera, and attached the U-shaped clip to the top of the parking sign. The move had come to me while watching Astrid doing that one-footed pose. The camera was on the sign closest to the restaurant door. It could record the front door as well as the windows of Sal's apartment upstairs. When convinced it was properly adjusted, I let go and slipped my foot back into my shoe.

I glanced around to see who might have observed me. A gray-haired woman appeared sympathetic. She had fully bought into the pebble ruse. I nodded back and smiled, confident from the woman's expression that she hadn't noticed the camera.

I started walking home as Sal came to the open door wearing an apron and standing with his arms crossed over his chest. He yelled at me, "You again."

I threw up my hands in a particularly New Yorker way. "What? Now you own the sidewalk, too?" The observant gray-haired lady gave Sal the stink eye.

Back at my house I pulled up the feed on my laptop to check the signal. Not bad. It captured the door and all the windows as planned. It would continue transmitting for seventy-two hours and was saving to the cloud. His woman had to come out sometime.

By late afternoon, Emma called to say they'd finished their report. I could tell from her voice she was proud of their work and eager to show it off. They'd be at my house in fifteen minutes. I phoned Astrid to come for the presentation, too. She was back from their hike and would be right over. I didn't call Celia, because it was Saturday—her errand running day. That's sacred for a working woman. She'd be over when she was finished.

I uncovered the whiteboard and erased The Miscreants before I placed my laptop on the patio table. When Astrid arrived, she noticed the change to the whiteboard and smiled.

The teens had barely sat down before they slipped a thumb drive into the computer and pulled up their presentation. Standing behind them, Astrid and I leaned in close to the screen. I had told them to "write it up," but didn't expect much. What do I know about teenagers? To my surprise, the kids had prepared a full PowerPoint slide deck with a format that included a title box with a light gray background and blood red letters. Some had red drops of blood falling from them.

The opening slide was titled, "Miscreants' Random Crazy (Maybe Serial) Killer Research."

I asked, "Serial Killer? We only have one body." Thinking about Cunningham, I wondered if that was true.

Tyler's head popped up. "Oh yeah, we figured whoever killed her that brutally wasn't a 'one and done' murderer. We watched a Netflix special. Serial killers often have a type, but they don't target a particular individual. Since we don't know if our victim was his type or just unlucky, we think everyone is still in danger. We asked everyone about seeing a suspicious person who seemed capable of that kind of violence."

Emma added, "We talked with nineteen people. I was surprised... When we told them what we were doing, they treated us respectfully."

I felt a warm glow inside. "There's a lesson in that reaction."

She nodded then moved on, "We didn't put all the people we heard about into our report. For example, we didn't count the angry, old guy who ran off from the nursing home and got lost in his motorized wheelchair that night. That would be a silver alert not a psycho killer warning."

Deadpan, Astrid leaned on her elbows, "Excellent judgment. How many suspects do you have?"

Tyler said, "Wait and see. We have a slide for each one we thought you'd like and a list of the ones we cut so you can check our decisions."

Promising talent, I thought. "Okay then, let's go."

Emma pressed the forward key and moved to a slide that had a large, red '#1' in the header. Next to the number was, 'Cigarette Man.' Emma said, "Mrs. Wilson lives in that Bay Avenue house covered with what Mom calls 'gingerbread trim.' Her house is four houses down from the park. She said she saw a suspicious guy in his thirties, parked in front of her house a little after midnight when J Al was killed. He was leaning against his truck's front bumper smoking and looking up the street all ghosted like."

"Wait," I asked, "Did you say J Al?"

Emma said, "Yeah, Jennifer Albrecht. It's like J Lo without the talent."

I couldn't help smirking, "I get that." I noticed even Astrid chuckled.

Tyler continued, "Mrs. Wilson saw his cigarette's red tip when she was going to the bathroom. Being an old lady with nothin' better to do, she watched him."

Astrid said, "That is a very exciting discovery. If she can describe the truck, I can find the license plate from other CCTV feeds. I bet he was one of the drive-bys."

He said, "Mrs. Wilson said his truck was candy apple red and real shiny even with only the streetlight. The guy had dark hair and was wearing jeans. He yelled at someone farther north on Bay

Avenue and walked on the boardwalk in the direction of the park. He was gone for a while. When he came back, he stomped out his cig and drove off all mad like."

I made a note to myself to recheck the park camera footage. "Well then, Cigarette Man is now a murder suspect. Fabulous work. What's next?"

Emma pushed the button and '#2 Rage Rover' appeared on the screen. "I talked with Sarah at the Wine Shop. She was working late doing inventory when Mr. Salvatore went by the store about the time of the attack. Since he's an angry jackass, we put him down as a possible killer."

I couldn't quite control my urge to laugh. "Language, Miscreant, language. But yeah, you're right. Why do you think he's a 'Rage Rover'?"

Emma said, "I mean seriously, that guy always looks like he wants to kill someone."

Astrid said, "Isn't it odd he runs a restaurant where people expect him to be nice to them?"

Emma said, "In the restaurant he yells at the staff to keep from yelling at the customers."

Tyler said, "Anyway, Sarah didn't know where he was going exactly, but it was toward the vicinity of the park."

"Vicinity is a great SAT word. Don't forget it. You already sound like a real detective. We'll keep Sal on the list."

Emma advanced to '#3 Crazy Drunk Contractors."

Tyler said, "Our friend Preston watched two women construction workers stumbling around a white panel van closer to the pier than the park. He said he was sure it was within minutes of J Al's death. It was in the parking lot by the ice cream place."

Astrid said, "What was he doing out at that time if he's your age?"

Emma said, "Let's just leave it at...he was in his yard for some fresh air."

I said, "Got it. He was smoking a joint."

Tyler nodded, "He's a musician. He makes techno music late at night. Regardless, he said he hoped they lived close because they were hammered."

Astrid and I shared a look. "If they were that drunk, they probably aren't murder suspects."

Tyler shook his head, "Don't wash them out too easily. Preston said they were both super muscular and one was really tall."

Emma added, "We need to tell you something we remembered. We thought a lot about what happened when J Al answered her phone while she was bashing us for breaking curfew. We realized it was a dude that was calling. We heard a man's voice."

"Any accent?" I asked.

"He only said, 'I'm here. Are you walking?' Not enough to get an accent."

Astrid said, "Think back, please. Did she say anything to him that gave some information away? Call him something? Was she formal like he was a stranger, or did it sound like she knew him?"

The Miscreants looked at each other. Emma said, "More formal."

Tyler sat up, "Oh, and we wanted to mention that she was carrying her notebook thing full of papers. It was weird, because when she answered her cellphone, she sort of fumbled it. I could see there was at least an inch of loose sheets and a pad of note paper. It was packed."

Astrid and I made eye contact. *We were right. Jenn was going to pass documents to someone. The killer took them.*

Without waiting, Emma pushed the button again to a slide named 'Others'. "And here are the wash outs. I put you on there, Minxy, since a couple of people talked about you because of the weeds and all, but we know you didn't kill her. You'd have done way worse than just stab her."

The Miscreants thought I was a ninja. *How wonderful.* I scanned the short 'also ran' list. "Me, and I didn't do it. Bob the local drunk. He's always passed out on a boardwalk bench about that time. A guy cursing while changing a flat tire on an SUV. The silver alert for the guy in the motorized wheelchair. That's it?"

They nodded.

I stood up straight to stretch my back after leaning over during the presentation. My arms folded over my chest. "I don't want this to go to your heads, but nice work. You're officially junior private eyes. And..." I fished out two fifty-dollar bills from my skirt pocket and gave each Miscreant one, "...this is a paid gig. We can use all these as leads on the case." I looked away and then back. "Oh, and don't buy drugs."

The two smiled and pocketed the cash. "Can we go now? We've got a ride to the movies."

"Sure, go. I'll be in touch. This work goes on the plus column of your permanent record."

They saved the file to my Desktop, bounced up, pulled the flash drive out of my computer and with a quick wave, left through the gate.

I closed it behind them. "Amazing. I never expected they'd be that successful. These are actual leads."

Astrid nodded. "You may have to stop calling them miscreants."

"Nah, I like the nickname too much."

Eighteen

SATURDAY, JUNE 24, WEST BEACH, MD

Astrid and I added Cigarette Man and the Drunken Contractors to the suspect list in the space where The Miscreants had been. We added CCTV to the ecosystem line and made a note about Sal on the video. Our list was longer and more specific.

Killer? / Motive

    •Clandestine Operative: national security? (Celia)

    •Random crazy stranger: interpersonal conflict (IC) (Astrid and The Miscreants)

    •~~Danny: jealousy. (Minxy)~~

    •Sal: IC, on CCTV video (Minxy)

    •Cigarette Man

    •Drunken Contractors

    •~~Minxy: IC~~

    •~~Walt: ? $ (All)~~

    •~~The Mayor: IC & $ (Minxy)~~

•Coworker at NRC HQ: IC, national security (Celia)

•Coworker at a security exercise: IC_Cunningham,_?????_ (Minxy)

•Someone we haven't figured out yet: ?

Ecosystem: second shadow, suit, pantyhose, gun, purse, folio, park, late night, trash cans, papers in car, car windows, fake parking signs, city contracts, gravel, national security, engagement ring, and inheritance, CCTV videos

We were strategizing on how to use The Miscreants' information when my phone rang. I said, "It's Brent."

Astrid looked confused.

"The guy with the telephone tracker software." I pushed the button to connect.

"Minxy, I got the rest of the data."

I blurted out, "Please tell me Walt the boyfriend's phone wasn't in West Beach that night."

Brent said, "I didn't find his device there until the morning you found the body."

I signed with relief, then asked, "Did you find the killer's phone? Oh, and I have my cell on speaker." I pushed the button. "My associate can also hear."

Brent chuckled. "Associate? You're already growing your business?"

"Yes. Crazy, isn't it?"

"Anyway, that phone that bedded down in Solomons, the one I gave you last time? The device that had been in the house twice the week before the murder. It also signaled there the evening she died. It left at 11:00 p.m. heading back to Solomons presumably with its owner. The interesting thing is that every time that device was visible, so was the other one—the one that doesn't signal much and might be a burner. I hate coincidences."

Astrid asked, "So, when Cunningham was at Jenn's house, the other person's phone signaled in there, too?"

Brent said, "No. It's the one that only signaled from *around* her house. The one with no bed down. It hovered outside the house and up the street. I think it was surveillance."

I made a face for Astrid then said to Brent, "A watcher *outside her* house is *outside mine, too.* We're neighbors."

"Well toots, that would make me uncomfortable."

Astrid said, "Why would a surveillance person carry a phone when he's quietly watching outside a house? He wouldn't be talking on it."

Brent laughed. "I think he used it to play games with the sound off. No one has the patience to just sit and watch a house anymore."

I thought back to the guy in the hoodie I'd seen on the board-walk playing games. "Any other signals from that one? I mean anywhere, any time?"

He said, "Ding, ding, ding, you win the prize. It pinged around the dead woman's house the night of the murder. I checked it against the murder scene. It was there, too. In fact, that night, I tracked it and the dead woman's phone from her house to the park at the time of the attack, like he was following her. It was turned off a little after 12:45 a.m."

I asked, "Could you track a home address this time?"

Brent said, "Nope. It only signaled from the victim's house to the park, then went dark."

I drew a deep breath, but didn't say anything.

He said, "You're going to hate this last part. The data aggre-gator sent early signals for yesterday. The signal is back."

"Really. At the park? At night?"

"No, Minxy. The pattern is around your house now. The owner of the device is surveilling you."

Astrid was sympathetic. It comes as naturally for her as unnaturally for me. I adored her for that. We talked it out and I convinced her, and to some degree myself, that surveillance was benign. I wouldn't worry too much until the person took more direct action. It was an opportunity. The guy was showing himself. I could turn that to my advantage.

After an hour of examining the situation from every angle like a Rubik's cube, Astrid was comfortable that I wouldn't be dead by morning. She and Lars had dinner plans, so I sent her home contented that I had this under control. That left me time to strategize before Celia arrived.

It wasn't my first experience being the bug under the microscope, but I cautioned myself not to minimize the threat. In a dangerous situation like this, I liked being at the middle point of a continuum between blasé and terrified. That's where my senses were heightened, but I wasn't on edge. It allowed the kind of bold action Maya had warned me against. I remembered her warning and pledged to myself that I'd be careful.

I pulled out more miniature video cameras from my stash. Sitting in a back deck lounger, I decided where to put them. The back of the house was easy. It would go on the deck with a view of both gates, and some of the alley beyond. The gates would be locked, but locks could be picked. I installed the back one.

Walking to my master bedroom, I pondered what to do next. I stood by the French doors to the deck and gazed out at the street and boardwalk below. I looked at the spot where the guy with the hoodie had stood. No way was that guy a pro. This is little West Beach. At best he was a skilled amateur. He'd stay on the boardwalk close enough to hear the louder sounds in the house. If he was spooked, he might add more distance, but then he'd have to use audio-visual equipment. I considered the bay beyond. Boating would be a problem. Few people in West Beach went out in boats at night. It wasn't a thing. The harbor was too shallow for sailboats with sleeping berths. A kayaker would stand out and be noticed.

My focus floated back ashore from the blue bay. *No,* I thought, *this man will keep doing what he did at Jenn's. He'll walk down the boardwalk and up the alley. There's always someone walking around West Beach. It would look perfectly normal.*

I got back to work, attaching a camera to my bedroom deck railing and a motion detector on the French doors. The last motion detector went on the front door. If any exterior door opened, it would make my phone vibrate.

As I was finishing my installation, Celia arrived for happy hour. Her glowing skin made it obvious she was coming straight from a spa treatment. "I got the works. A massage, a facial, a mani-pedi. It was fabulous."

Her nails were a perfect shade of mauve that matched her shorts. Tonight, she had black pearls.

I filled her in on the video feeds from the town's CCTV and the resourcefulness of The Miscreants. She laughed when I told her I was using the signpost at Sal's restaurant to spy on him. Served him right. I left Brent's report on the phone signals for later. I wasn't ready to hear her nag me about the threat. First I'd get pictures of the guy, then I'd take more action.

I was refilling her wine glass when my cell rang.

This time it was Astrid calling on What's App. She was requesting a video chat and I accepted.

"*Hej hej.*" she said. "Is Celia back?"

"But of course," she said, leaning over my shoulder and photobombing the shot.

"We miss you," I said.

"I know, but I'm making dinner for Lars' tonight. It's a rare event and I'm very pleased with my meal. I had my searches running while I was cooking." She pointed to her computer, "I have lots of information for you on The Miscreants' leads."

"Really? That was fast. I'm propping the phone against a book on the patio table so we both can see you." Celia and I sat side by side in front of the phone's camera. I said, "So tell us everything."

Astrid was sitting in her office filled with birch furniture and a cool green and blue decor that reminded me of sea glass. The late evening light filtered through lace curtains. She said, "I identified both Cigarette Man and The Drunken Contractors. I used the information the teenagers gave us and then went through the CCTV videos you brought me this morning. I saw a dark-haired man drive by in a red truck and caught him on another camera where I got the tag number. Same with the women in the van. I have names and addresses."

Celia said, "Wow, fantastic work. Tell us about Cigarette Man. That one sounds like the best lead."

Astrid put on her arctic blue reading glasses and peered at her screen. "His name is Al Behnam, and he lives in Upper Marlboro." She pulled off the frames, holding them in her hand. "Isn't that funny that he is Cigarette Man and he lives in a place named Marlboro?"

Celia had a lop-sided grin. "The irony did not escape me."

Astrid slipped on her readers again. "LinkedIn says he works as a Nuclear Equipment Operator at Calvert Cliffs Plant."

Celia said, "Coincidence or suspicious? It sounds like an important job. Significant responsibility. A reason to get crossways with Jenn in the exercise."

Astrid leaned on her elbows and stared straight into the camera. "Most important of all was the information I found in Maryland Case Search. He was convicted of hitting his girlfriend a few years ago. He spent six months on probation."

I said, "Bravo, Astrid. A woman beater so close to the garden at the time Jenn was murdered. That's great for Walt."

Celia said, "It could be the alternative suspect the lawyer wants."

"I was thinking so, yes." She nodded. "And I have more. I found the two drunken contractor women. They didn't leave the beach until the morning."

"So, they aren't from West Beach?" Celia asked.

"No, but close. That cute little neighborhood north of here—Shady Side. They have a house there."

"Together?" I asked.

"Social media explains that they are married to each other."

Celia and I nodded. I asked, "Anything about their work?"

"They are quite fine carpenters. They call their company Builder Chicks and they do excellent renovations. I found pictures of beautiful bathrooms and kitchens. Even some outside construction like patios and decks."

I asked, "Any criminal cases for those two?"

Astrid's smile was sly. "It is no surprise that both have driving under the influence charges."

"That explains why they didn't drive home that night," Celia said.

"Yes, it does, but I have no idea where they stayed. I've got to go now. My kitchen timer is going off. The *coq au vin* is done. It's Lars' favorite and it goes nicely with the French Bordeaux he brought home. I'm emailing you the addresses and phone numbers. All the details you'll need to make contact."

We all waved goodbye, and the screen went blank.

Celia and I filled our glasses with the French chardonnay Astrid had left for us.

I started. "Al Behnam is a game changer. A woman beater near the park. How lucky can we get?"

Celia looked at her nails for a moment, then said, "It looks good superficially, but we need to know a lot more about him."

Celia was in serious analyst mode—new information means

virtually nothing until it's vetted and put in context. "I know. You're right. But he *appears* to be perfect."

"Indeed. A bit too perfect. I can imagine a dozen explanations that get him off the hook."

"I'll dig deeper. But come on, it's *a tiny bit exciting.*"

Her smile was brilliant. "Okay. He could be Walt's salvation."

I loved knocking her out of analyst mode like that. This was a good time to spring my surveillance problem on her. I said, "With an alternative suspect in our pocket, we can work on the guys at Jenn's house the night of the murder"

"Brent got the signals."

"Yes, from the night of the murder and beyond. Cunningham was the second shadow I saw in the window and left at 11:00. A person was surveilling Jenn's house every time Cunningham was there, including when he was there the night of the murder. Brent tracked the watcher through West Beach following Jenn to the park."

She sat upright. "You've got to be kidding me. He either killed her or saw the murder."

I nodded.

"So, the murderer could be Cigarette Man or the watcher."

"Either or both together. We know Behnam walked toward the park, was gone for a while, then came back. Maybe he's working with the watcher. The two of them could have converged on Jenn in the park and killed her together. We need to ask the woman who saw him exactly when Behnam left and how long he was gone."

"Then he might lead us to the surveillance guy."

"That's right. Oh, and Brent says the watcher is still out there."

"What?"

I took a sip of my drink to give her time to process that, then said, "Look at the bright side. We know where he is. I just installed motion-activated cameras and sensors on all the doors. If Brent's right, I'll see him on the feed tonight."

Celia crossed her arms. "Psychopathic energy makes you too bold. Aren't you working on that in therapy?"

"We had to prioritize. I'm working on sympathizing first." *Plus, what's so bad about being a little bold?* "But it's getting dark. Celia. Time for you to go home. I need to draw this guy out—or both guys." I took her empty glass.

When she saw I was serious, she stood. I let her out the gate. "Text me when you get home." She hugged me hard, and I could see she was afraid for me. "I'll be fine. I'm still a professional."

I locked the gate and kitchen door, then went to my bedroom balcony. I kept the lights off and checked for the watcher. He wasn't there. Magoo was calm and curled up on my bed; another sign there was no threat out there. I gave him a good petting. "Magoo is my best guard dog."

Celia texted that she was home.

After checking all the locks again and making sure the garage door was secured, I went into my office and got comfortable in my desk chair. First, I checked the motion-activated counter-surveillance cameras in the backyard. I saw myself saying goodbye to Celia. The front one had registered a lot of folks strolling on the boardwalk. I made a mental note of the faces.

I brought up the feed from Sal's. It had only been eight hours since I'd put out the camera, but it took a while to search through the feed. The restaurant was busy, and the location had a lot of foot traffic. I fast forwarded through the people who were caught in the camera's eye.

After about forty-five minutes I hit the jackpot. Close to the end of the video, Sal walked behind a woman and held the door for her as she entered the restaurant. She always had her back to the camera, except for a brief profile that didn't give us enough for facial recognition. It did leave a strong impression of her, however.

She was young, olive skinned, had long, dark hair, and a killer figure.

The woman's profile was frozen on the screen. "You're a beauty. Why on Earth would you date grumpy, old Sal?"

Tomorrow, I thought. *I'll capture a clear face shot when you leave. When you come out the camera will be waiting.*

Nineteen

SUNDAY, JUNE 25, WEST BEACH, MD

The next morning, I went out the door early again for my run. I jogged down my steps inspired by the cool morning breeze. My pace had some zip in it and I felt engulfed by the beauty of the sun rising over the bay. I was thinking hard about The Miscreants' most significant finding: Cigarette Man aka Al Behnam being near the park at the time of the murder.

Al Behnam was a convenient suspect. We didn't have to prove it was him. His proximity to the attack and history of violence toward women were enough. Most significant, he worked at an important job at the plant Jenn had just failed. Jenn's inspection criticism might amplify Behnam's anger against women. She might have disparaged his performance. She was good at scathing criticism.

To play devil's advocate, could we pitch Behnam as helping with the security case she was working on? He might have met Jenn in the park to discuss a nuclear security problem. Would he have been suit worthy?

I answered my question out loud with gusto, "*No, he's not the* operative, so maybe he's the killer." A nearby runner heard me and sped away creating a safe space between him and me talking to myself.

From the fishing pier, I could see the house with all the ornate gingerbread trim. I needed to talk with Mrs. Wilson, who'd seen Cigarette Man that night. Maybe she would remember what time he walked off and how long he was gone. Maybe she saw him with papers. It would add a lot to our case if he had Jenn's papers with him when he came back. I'd pass Mrs. Wilson's house on my running route and check if she was up.

It flashed through my mind that I was inappropriately dressed, and it was Sunday morning when people might not appreciate company. Nah. I'd give it a try anyway.

At the end of the pier, I jogged in place and watched as the sun lit up Tilghman Island across the bay. The water was calm, and some guys were already kayaking. A fine June day. Turning, I ran back toward the boardwalk and saw Ricky in the distance. He was ahead of me on the circuit. Maybe I'd catch up with him tomorrow and ask about Behnam.

Running by Sunrise Garden, I noted that the crime scene tape was down, and the metal mermaid statue was alone in its alcove, except for a couple of bunches of flowers for Jenn at the base. I'd wondered if they would remove the installation. Glad they didn't. It wasn't the mermaid's fault.

Mrs. Wilson lived four houses down from the park. The colorfully painted Victorian home stood out. As I caught my breath on the sidewalk in front of it, I looked for signs that she was awake this early. Her curtains were drawn but I could smell coffee. Still on the sidewalk, I peeked at the backyard. There were too many flowers to see anything helpful.

Then I saw one of her curtains move. She was watching me watching for her. I was probably standing feet away from where

Behnam had stood that night. The front door opened, and a short, blond-haired woman in her eighties came out to meet me.

I asked, "Are you the Mrs. Wilson who talked to my mentees Emma and Tyler about the park murder?"

"I am." She was bright-eyed and jovial.

"I'm Private Investigator Minxy Banks and I apologize up front for not being professionally dressed. I wanted to ask you about the man you saw the night of the murder."

"Well come in then. Call me Joanie. I've got coffee."

For a woman in her eighties, she moved well and had a young woman's smile. She looked excited to have company. Following her through the home filled with collectible statues—I recognized Hummel and Lladro—we made small talk. I noticed her bookcases were jammed full. She seemed to read a lot of history from my quick skim.

"What is your favorite historical period?" I asked trying to make a connection.

"Unfortunately, all of them. I read about war. The period doesn't matter. The decision to go to war is fascinating. If the Presidents had read *The Peloponnesian War*, we wouldn't have been in Vietnam."

I did not see that coming. I reassessed my view of Joanie as a sweet little old lady into something spicier.

"Please have a seat. I'll get you that coffee." She pointed to a mid-century modern table and chairs that weren't reproductions. The white kitchen cabinets were topped with dark granite countertops. The kitchen was fresh and cozy.

I sat. "Ma'am, could I have a glass of water instead."

Looking at my running gear, she said, "Of course. Ice?"

"Yes, please."

She placed the glass in front of me.

"I'm the Private Investigator for Walt Hawley. I apologize again for my appearance, and I don't carry creds when I run."

She sat beside me with her coffee, leaning on her elbows. "Not a problem," she said. "What can I tell you? I'm happy to help."

Was she lonely, living here by herself? Would this be me in forty years? I pushed those thoughts aside and got down to business. "Emma and Tyler said you saw a man smoking by his truck the night Jennifer Albrecht was murdered. Could you see how he was dressed?"

She folded her hands in front of her on the table for a second or two, then said, "Well, it was after midnight, so it was dark, but the streetlight isn't far. What I remember was blue jeans...and a light-colored T-shirt. It had words on it, but I couldn't read what it said."

"What did the man look like?"

"Very young. Probably in his thirties." She took a sip of her coffee and had that far off look people get when they are digging around in their memory banks. "Average height, slender, dark hair. I couldn't see his face all that well. He was smoking."

"Mrs. Wilson, I'd like to ask some timing questions. My mentees said the man saw something in the direction of Sunrise Garden. He walked that way and eventually returned. When did that happen, and how long was he gone?"

She was looking at my face intently. "When? Maybe 12:30 give or take. He yelled at someone, crossed the street and walked away on the boardwalk. He was gone for about ten minutes. Less than fifteen. After that he got in his truck and drove off."

"Ten to fifteen minutes." I thought, even if she's off by a bit, that's enough time to kill Jenn. "Was he carrying papers when he came back? A thick pile of loose sheets?"

"No. Definitely not. He walked back like he was angry and didn't have anything in his hands but a cigarette."

I finished my water. "Mrs. Wilson, you've been a great help. Thank you so much."

"Please, call me Joanie."

"Thank you, Joanie."

She walked me to the door, and I shook her hand. She looked like a hugger, but I was way too sweaty. I kept my distance.

She said, "Nice to meet you, Jackie." She put her hand to her mouth and reddened. "Oh my goodness. Forgive me. I was thinking you resemble a young Jackie Kennedy. It just slipped out."

It was official now; I liked this woman. "Thanks. It's a huge compliment."

"Private investigation must be interesting work. I was a Navy nurse in the Korean and Vietnam Wars. Put in a full twenty years. I remember how hard it could be as a woman in a man's world."

A montage of this small woman crashing around in war zones zipped through my mind. I bet she had great stories. "You don't by chance enjoy a happy hour cocktail now and then?"

"I drink like a fish, dearie." Her smile was radiant.

I hadn't anticipated her exuberance for alcohol. "Well Joanie, I'll be in touch about happy hour. Thanks again."

I was building my running speed to a good clip while thinking about what I'd learned. Behnam didn't take the papers, and Jenn wouldn't wear that suit to meet him. He could be the killer, but if he was, did the watcher take the papers in Jenn's folio? If he and the watcher killed Jenn together, why would the watcher take the papers. Behnam had the truck, and the watcher was on foot.

And I would definitely invite Joanie for happy hour.

I'd hit the wall on thinking about Behnam and the watcher as killers. My thoughts turned to Sal as a suspect. I didn't like him, but was he a killer? Probably not, but he was a convenient villain. It was worth figuring out what he was up to that night. Since his alibi was the mystery woman, I had to identify her, and figure out why he left her to take an angry walk? I thought of someone else who might have seen Sal with the girl in public. Cassie at The Circle, a local bar and music venue, interacted with lots of people.

She was like every bartender, a talented listener, and an even better gossip. She might know about Sal's girlfriend. I ran down the street that would take me by the bar.

As I came close, I saw her bringing in supplies for the day.

Slowing in front of the building, I took the steps two at a time and walked down the walkway to the door. Cassie heard my knock and turned, ready to shoo off whoever thought the place was open. When she saw it was me, she dried her hands on a dish towel and came to the door.

"Minxy Banks. Long time, no see. Why have you abandoned me?"

Bending over to catch my breath, I took a few deep breaths and stood straight again, pushing my hair out of my eyes with one hand. "Never. Your dirty martini is the best in the beach. We're simply in love with this weather. Until it gets hot, we're in my backyard. I told you to sneak over. Your staff can cover for you."

"One of these days. What's up? Want to come in?"

"Nah, quick question. I saw a young woman going into Sal's place with him to stay over. Upstairs. He says it's his girlfriend. Do you know who it is?"

Her face pinched, "Why do you care? I know you can't be jealous."

I filled her in on being a PI for Walt, then said, "and Sal's alibi is this girl. It sounds sketchy. No one could put up with him."

She laughed. "People have told me about a dark-haired, late twenties or early thirties woman who visits. Like they date awhile and then she disappears, only to come back six months later."

"Got a name? I'd like to know more about his girl before I confront him."

Cassie threw the dishtowel over her shoulder. "No idea. She's not from here. She never goes anywhere but Sal's place."

I said, "Sounds like a hook up. Why the mystery? Dating would improve Sal's image. *A lot.*"

"I hear ya, but I've got nothin'. I'll keep my ear to the ground and call if I find out anything."

"Thanks."

She nodded "That Marine is a saint to have put up with Jenn Albrecht. Get the guy off and I'll buy you girls a round of drinks."

<hr>

As I jogged back to my place along the stretch of bayfront homes, I thought, *do people wonder about my love life?* I fell for Theo the first time he walked into a CIA Station meeting in Rabat. Tall, fit, and all that thick, dark, wavy hair. He was one of those bad, but good boys. Naughty, but very nice. We were each other's type. As we worked surveillance and dead drops together, things went from interested to flaming hot in hours. After ten years our relationship remains. He was the only man I'd ever wanted, but he couldn't give up being a case officer. At least he couldn't yet. I thought about the last time he'd showed up on my doorstep. The days we'd spent together had been glorious. Physics books say that two particles can be entangled and know what the other one is doing no matter how far the distance between them. That was us. We knew when the other one was in trouble.

Arriving home, I did a little dance to Taylor Swift's song "Shake It Off" that I heard in my head when I thought too much about Theo. Magoo pawed at me for a pet, then followed me around the house like he knew I needed a friend. I drank another tall glass of water, then made a cup of coffee to take to the office where I began examining the restaurant video. No joy. The mystery woman hadn't left yet.

The counter-surveillance feeds from my place were more interesting. Late last night, the camera's motion sensors tripped in sequence. I caught the watcher in the front and then minutes later in the back. The camera pulled in enough streetlight to see a shape walking by, dressed in black with a hoodie. Over his face, the man wore a gaiter. Average height, medium build. In all, I'd captured eight images of him from four circuits around the house. I compared them all side-by-side, picked the clearest one, and printed it.

It was time to be serious about security. I opened the closet door in my office and knelt in front of my safe that was bolted to the floor. I worked the lock open, and retrieved my Glock and two clips. I put it on my bedside table.

I showered and dressed in a yellow, sleeveless golf dress. I padded around the house barefoot, thinking what I should do next. Magoo followed me wherever I went. Finally, I turned to him and stopped. "Magoo, you understood this way before me. What do you think about us calling in the cavalry? With that guy watching, it's time. We need to learn a lot more about Al Behnam and why he was parked by the beach late on the night of the murder. He might lead us to the watcher."

Magoo listened attentively, his head cocked to one side.

"Jerry Mancuso didn't look busy. He could do a surveillance gig for us. While I chase down the contractors, my partner could surveil Cigarette Man."

Magoo pawed at me again. It made me feel uneasy. I looked out the windows but saw nothing.

I slipped on little black flats. Scratching Magoo behind the ears, I said, "Buddy, keep the place safe. I'll be back soon."

SUNDAY, JUNE 24, UPPER MARLBORO, MD

I wanted to talk to Jerry about the gig in person. He agreed to meet me in *our* offices in half an hour. As I left home, I'd grabbed a plant from the kitchen windowsill. It would be the first step in laying claim to the empty office. It was like a stake in the dirt—literally. Since I didn't want to be there much, I'd chosen a cactus that wouldn't be too needy. I walked into our reception area. "Anybody home?"

"I'm in here Minxy. I knew you'd be asking for work."

He stood to welcome me, which I do enjoy. That act of courtesy has never blunted my feminist principles. I said, "Actually, that's not why I'm here." I held up the cactus. "I brought this plant to put on my desk."

"Hey, I never said you could have that office. You can *maybe* use it now and then. You know, to look legit. That's it."

"Yup, that was what I was thinking. This place will build my credibility. Bricks and mortar."

He tilted his head, "You're jackin' with me."

I winked. "Yes, I am, but only a little." I set the cactus on a small clear space on Jerry's desk and sat. After Jerry lowered himself slowly into his chair, I said, "I do need your help, just not more work."

A smile snuck up the corners of his mouth. "Having trouble with your training assignment? I'm still waiting for that confirmation email."

"Right. I'll get to that *very* soon. Truth is, right now I need manpower. Would you do a stake out on a suspect in the Albrecht murder? I'm wondering why a guy who beat up a woman and worked at the nuke plant Jenn failed was by the park when she died. I'm particularly interested in whether he keeps coming back to West Beach at night and who he visits."

"Obviously, it's not the Marine."

"Absolutely not." I gave Jerry the highlights about Cigarette Man, ending with, "And he lives here in Upper Marlboro. If he comes to the beach again tonight to do heaven knows what, follow him. I want to know where he goes and who he sees." I didn't tell Jerry about the watcher surveilling me. If they joined up, Jerry would let me know. I passed a sheet of paper with Behnam's name, address, and tag number over the detritus on Jerry's desk.

"That's a great lead. If this pans out, it's enough for an alternative to the Marine. How much?"

"I checked. Going rate's sixty dollars an hour. Should be about a twenty-four-hour project."

"Where you gettin' the money for this gig?"

No way would I tell him it was out of my own pocket. "Walt's got a go fund me page."

He nodded. "Remind me to send Jojo flowers. You're alright."

I picked up my cactus. "And I'm putting *my* plant in *my* office, partner."

Jerry chuckled. "You're not my only mentee, you know. The others use that office, too. I'll get some grub and start the stakeout."

I reached across the desk to shake his hand. I liked Jerry Mancuso. He knew how I played the game, and he was onboard with it. We were both on the same wavelength.

SUNDAY, JUNE 24, SHADY SIDE, MD

After leaving the office, I headed east to Shady Side to check out the address Astrid had given me for the female contractors. The trip from Upper Marlboro was quick, a little over twenty minutes to reach the contractors' house.

I rolled up to a ranch style house with bright yellow siding and a cheerful orange front door. It looked like a two-bedroom, one-and-a-half bath house built in the seventies. Their yard was strewn with contractor leftovers: lumber, pipe, cinder blocks, bricks, two by fours. The white panel truck's roof rack was full of crown molding in twelve-foot pieces. It was parked in the driveway with the rear door open. The license plate matched the one Astrid had given me.

Putting on my sunglasses as I got out of the car, I called out a greeting to ensure I didn't get shot. With everyone on edge these days, you can't be too careful.

Walking into the carport, I picked my way around five-gallon paint buckets, tools, more lumber and plumbing parts. They had clear walking paths around the piles, and I decided it was organized chaos. There appeared to be three distinct projects. Wonderful for them. They had plenty of business.

A big, blond woman in cutoff overalls and a T-shirt came out the side door into the carport with a shop towel over her shoulder. "Who are you?"

I was ready with the flip creds. A dopey smile broke out across my lips, and I realized how much I liked the new me. "Minxy Banks, Private Investigator. I'm working on the murder case in West Beach. You're Ashley Bridges, right?"

"Yeah, but what's the murder got to do with me?"

Leaning against one of the supports, I said. "We have an eyewitness who says you and another woman were getting stuff out of this van about the time of the attack." I tipped my head toward her vehicle.

"So what?" She pulled the shop towel off her shoulder and started rubbing at grease on one of her hands.

"Did you see anything unusual?"

She folded her arms over her overalls. "Didn't see a murderer, if that's what you're asking."

"Is your partner here? Maybe she saw something?"

"She's my wife, and she ran to the store for groceries."

I nodded in acknowledgment. "Congratulations on your marital happiness. Did you or your spouse see any unusual activity? It might be more important than you think."

Ashley thought for a moment. She closed her eyes, opened them, then said, "We were both drunk. Big celebration for a payday at the end of a project. We couldn't make it home, so we couch surfed with some friends at the beach."

Nodding agreeably, I pushed off the carport support and walked closer toward her. "Got it, but you were at your van about the time the victim was heading to the park. Did you see anyone?"

She was getting annoyed. "Yeah, I saw some blond woman, busty, dressed in a business suit, walking down the street. She was fancied up like she was going to an office or something. She had her little purse over her arm and frankly looked just adorable, in a Junior League kind of way. It being West Beach and me totally loaded, I thought I was hallucinating. I mean a beautiful woman in a designer outfit? She was even wearing hose."

Ashley was exceptionally observant. Then I wondered, *was Jenn busty?* I added, "Pantihose in West Beach surprised me, too. Where was the blond woman going? Anyone with her?"

"Alone. Headed toward the boardwalk going south."

"The park?"

"Yeah, I guess."

"Did you follow her?"

Ashley's eyebrows pinched together and she looked at me like I wasn't paying attention. "Like I said, we were fried, and the lady was walking fast for those heels. We barely stumbled to our friend's house after locking up the van."

"Well then, you're one of the last people to see the victim alive."

Ashley's blue eyes opened wide. "You're kidding me. That was her?"

I nodded.

"Wow, I can't wait to tell Sarah. We thought we were trippin' you know? It gave us the giggles." She realized the incongruity and added, "No disrespect for the dead."

"Understood. Anything else? It's important. Please think hard."

"Just some beach guy in black sweats and a hat."

Trying to keep the excitement from my voice, I asked, "How would you describe him?"

"Medium size, medium height. He was just walking at a steady pace down the street going the same direction as the lady."

"My friend, that may have been one of the murderers. We

think he followed her from her house where he'd been surveilling her."

Ashley's arms flew to the top of her head. "*Holy crap... That's weird.*" Her head bobbed for a minute, then she added. "I need a beer. Want one?"

Ashley and Sarah had seen the watcher and Mrs. Wilson had seen Behnam. I was pretty sure one or both of them killed Jenn. I smiled. Either way, Celia owed me caviar and Walt's future was looking brighter. Thinking for a second about the beer, I said, "Sure, if it's not lite. I hate lite beer."

She glowered. "*No.* We're picky. We only drink the good stuff."

"Well okay then, I'm in." The wind was blowing, and I held my hair back from my face with my hand. "We can hang out until Sarah gets back. She might remember something else."

Ashley pulled out her phone. "I'll text her to hurry."

SARAH RETURNED about ten minutes after we had cracked open two fine craft beers made by a Baltimore brewery and had taken seats on wicker furniture in a screened porch. Sarah put the groceries in the kitchen then curled up next to Ashley on the sofa. She wore calf length tights and a long, sleeveless tunic. The definition of her arm muscles was truly amazing. Lifting lumber had its benefits.

She asked, "Did we really see the killer?"

I said, "It's very likely you did."

"So, we saw that Hawley guy? The Marine?"

"No, that's my client."

Sarah said, "So, if it wasn't him, who'd we see?"

"That's the question. Think back. Can you remember something about the guy that stood out?"

"He was about Ashley's height."

"Which is…"

Ashley said, "I'm five ten."

Making a mental note, I said, "That's average for a guy."

They nodded.

"Think about his clothes. Anything that you can recall. Branding. Fit. Even something small that seems insignificant."

Sarah started. "He surprised me. He was close before I saw him because he was dressed in black sweatpants and a black hoodie."

Ashley said, "Yeah, but the hoodie wasn't up. He had a hat on."

"That's right. A ball cap. Dark but not black."

I said, "Maybe blue?"

Sarah said, "I think it was a Nats cap with the curly W."

No surprise. The local baseball team would be the most likely and least noteworthy to wear. "Anything else? Did he carry something?"

"Only a phone. He had one in his hand. But, you know, the distinctive thing about the dude was his runners."

I said, "And…tell me more."

Ashley looked at her wife with surprise. "You remember his shoes?"

"Well, yeah. He had those On Cloudflows that I like. They're a medium blue that fades to almost white on the toes and have a red band across the heal."

"Sarah's a runner. She's training for a marathon."

Sarah nodded. "I might buy a pair like the ones he wore. They're for running on hard surfaces like pavement. The women's sizes only have a white band. The red looks cooler."

Pulling up the brand's website on my phone, I checked out the Cloudflow model. "Stylish. You're right. The red band is great."

She beamed.

I finished my beer and said goodbye. The guy following Jenn was involved in the killing, I was convinced of it. Sarah's observation of his height and the distinctive shoes might be a break. Seeing him walking after Jenn matched what Brent had given us. The guy was surveilling Jenn's house and then followed her to the park.

Then it hit me.

Pleased that I had new information about the man in black, I hadn't recognized the significance. Parking my car on the side of the road next to a field, I pulled up my home video feed on my phone. The man they described was, of course, the same man surveilling me. In the low light conditions there wasn't much color, but in one of the shots I could tell his shoes were the same On Cloudflow brand and model. That was our guy.

Why was that predator watching me? It had to be my research into the case. Did he know I was watching him? I didn't think so. My surveillance cameras are tiny. I stared out the windshield into the pasture beside a farm. The wind was blowing the ornamental grasses and I could see a horse grazing in the distance. It felt as safe as my house used to feel.

There was an opportunity here, but I had to figure out how to take advantage of it. Was he working with Behnam or alone? What if I went on the offense and set a trap for both of them? It made sense to wait until after Jerry's surveillance of Behnam. I'd know if it was one or two of them.

There was nothing significant in my texts. Then I checked alerts from the camera at the restaurant, scrolling through them until I saw what I wanted. Bingo. There was a picture of a young, dark-haired woman hugging Sal in the doorway with a clear image of her face. I forwarded the picture to Astrid so she could run it against her facial recognition database. That would make or break the investigation into Sal.

Starting the car, I pulled onto the winding two lane road from Shady Side south to West Beach. Things were breaking our way.

If Al the Cigarette Man joined my watcher tonight, Jerry would get more information about him. All this is about the nuke plant. He and Cunningham both worked there. Jenn failed the plant. Walt said she brought her NRC work home…She'd had the evidence she was passing to the clandestine operator in her house that night. Maybe she'd brought a lot more home.

Astrid picked up on the second ring, "I know Minxy. I'm trying to find out who that woman is, but there isn't a hit yet."

"Okay, but I was calling about something else. Would you meet me at my house in about twenty minutes?"

"What's up?"

"For the next line of investigation, I need a spotter."

"What is a spotter?" she asked.

"You'll keep watch for me while I try something that will either jumpstart this case or get me thrown in jail."

Twenty-One

When I opened my front door, Astrid was cross legged on the floral chintz sofa giving Magoo doggie treats for sitting. He was in front of her on the antique Persian rug I'd bought from a bed and breakfast owner to match the blue irises on the yellow background of the sofa fabric. It was the centerpiece of the room, reminding me fondly of an English country manor I'd once used as a safe house.

I said, "You'll spoil him. He sits without bribes." I stowed my handbag in its spot on the floor-to-ceiling bookshelves that covered two walls.

Setting the treat container back on the coffee table, Astrid said, "He looked unhappy, so I was cheering him up."

"He's been acting funny for days."

"Poor boy. What is wrong in your doggy world?" She petted him and he came closer, leaning against her leg to be more available for affection. She kept petting while she asked, "What did the Shady Side women say?"

Flouncing onto the overstuffed chair upholstered to match the sofa, I draped my legs over the arm and said, "They convinced me they were too drunk to be the killers. They also saw Jenn walking to the park, and best of all, the watcher following her."

"Did they know him?"

"No. They couldn't see his face, but he was dressed in dark cloths like the watcher does. He was about five feet ten and wore a pair of distinctive On Cloudflow runners."

"On Cloudflow? Never heard of that brand."

"Me either. The ladies were very observant. They noticed Jenn's purse and were admirers of her suit right down to the pantihose."

She scoffed. "Drunken women saw hose in the middle of the night?"

Nodding I said, "They thought they were hallucinating since no one dresses like that here. There's a streetlight by the parking lot, so it's possible. Anyway, our new Shady Side friends were probably the last people to see Jenn alive, and the only ones who saw that guy. The Miscreants and you are getting a promotion."

Astrid put her chin in her hand. "Now we only have to find out who the man is."

"I talked to Mrs. Wilson this morning. Cigarette Man was gone for less than fifteen minutes. The two of them could have killed Jenn together, but Cigarette Man definitely didn't take Jenn's papers back to the truck. The watcher must have kept them."

"So, we have two possible killers. Cigarette Man will be the best for Walt's case."

"We still have Sal, too. He's shorter, and was in jeans and a T-shirt, like Behnam. So, we have three suspicious men near the park when Jenn was killed.

Astrid asked, "What if all three are linked?"

"My partner Jerry can help make that linkage." While telling

Astrid about Jerry's surveillance gig, I texted him asking where Behnam was and if he had company.

He wrote back, "home alone."

I replied, "All day? Please get pictures of anyone who visits." He sent back a thumb's up emoji.

"Jerry says Cigarette Man's hanging out at home." Because Astrid had stopped giving Mr. Magoo treats, he walked to my chair and nosed my arm to get a pet, which I provided.

"You and Jerry are getting along?"

I nodded. "That guy's alright. If Behnam is linked to the watcher or Sal, he'll find out." I took a moment to take a screenshot of men's On Cloudflow shoes and texted it to Jerry. If he saw anyone with those shoes, I wanted a picture.

Astrid said, "I'll be happy to know who's sneaking around out there."

You and me both. "Let's talk about my new project. As Lar's wife, you have diplomatic immunity, correct?

"Yes, I do." Astrid's lips pressed together.

"You're sure? The old Minxy would have just talked you into this, not worrying about the consequences for you. The new Minxy cares."

"They won't throw me in jail."

"Well then. If I do something sort of illegal, and you help me, the worst they can do is send you home."

She gave me one of those cryptic Nordic looks. "What are you planning?"

"I'm going into Jenn's house to investigate. You'll watch for someone coming to either door."

She shrugged her shoulders. "That's hardly against the law. It belongs to Walt now and you work for him."

"The police might not see it that way. Walt might not see it that way either."

"Will we wait for night? That's what they do in the movies."

I scratched Mr. Magoo. "Flashlights cutting through the darkness is dramatic, but today I can search without any lights to give me away."

"It's more boring."

"And more effective. Are you in?"

"Sure. Lars will regret suggesting more hobbies for me."

I changed out of my yellow dress and into a pair of shorts and a T-shirt. I unearthed a backpack from my closet for evidence collection. I didn't need my lock picking tools for this effort, because Walt had hidden a spare key in Jenn's rose garden after he'd locked himself out.

Astrid moved my rear surveillance camera so it covered Jenn's backyard including her door. She sent the feed to her cellphone. She and Magoo sat on my bedroom deck with a view of Jenn's front entrance. When we were both ready, I walked out my back gate, down the alley, and into Jenn's gate by the peach tree and the trash bins. I pulled on latex gloves, then smelled the roses while picking up a false stone with the key inside. Walking at a steady pace up the stairs to the back door, I was in her house in under two minutes.

I had never been inside and found it to be what I'd expected. The nautical décor, the proper thing to decorate a beach place, was everywhere. What surprised me were all the affectionate photos of Jenn and Walt. "You actually loved him," I said, holding up a picture of them dressed for a party, arms around each other. The realization of her being capable of positive emotion was unsettling. There was a lot more to her than I had known.

I walked through the living room with its matching love seats at right angles to each other. A circular coffee table decorated like a giant compass sat in the middle between them with two empty wine glasses on it. I thought back to the night of Jenn's death. Cunningham and Jenn must have been enjoying a social drink. Their meeting may have been less confrontational than I'd thought. If that was true, why wasn't his car in the driveway? Why all the sneaking around?

I eyed the staircase. The motherload of information would be in her office. I expected it to be in an upstairs spare bedroom at the back of the house, like mine. I often saw a light there late at night when Walt's car wasn't in the driveway. That would be the one.

Passing the master suite, I took a quick and nosey peek. The bed was made but looked like Jenn had napped on top of the pink duvet. There was no nautical theme here. The room was a pale blush color with high quality but fake roses in vases, and framed garden prints on the wall. I nodded my head, "She's recreated her rose garden." The room even smelled like roses. There was one of those air freshener devices plugged into an electric plug. I checked the trash can. All that came out when I dumped it was a wad of paper. I stuck it in my backpack for later.

I opened the door to the middle guest room and closed it again. No surprises there. Then I stopped in the open doorway of Jenn's office.

The room was decorated like Sterling the lawyer's place. There were painted oars on the wall, a sandy colored rug and light blue walls. There were pictures of the couple everywhere, but in this room, they generally had a water theme. Them sailing. The two of them smiling in snorkeling masks. Photos from the local beach in swimsuits. I had to give credit to Ashley and Sarah's discerning eye for women—Jenn was a good looking, well-built woman. I had never noticed.

The sofa and curtains were a richer, darker navy. By the rear windows, I stood in front of Jenn's white wooden desk. There was a particularly attractive photo of the couple on the West Beach boardwalk with runner's numbers pinned to athletic clothes. Out of an abundance of caution, I checked Walt's shoes—*not On Cloudflows.*

A computer had been on the desktop, but the police must

have taken it. The power cord lay there, waiting for its unlikely return. There were papers in a several inch high stack, and I got excited for a moment. One was a huge compendium of nuclear plant security exercises. I scanned the table of contents and saw Calvert Cliffs on the list. Flipping to the pages, I was disappointed to find that the section had been cut out. The slice was clean, like it was done with a razor blade. If it was me, and I was walking to a park in heels, I'd have done the same to avoid carrying the five-pound document. The butchered report went in my backpack along with the rest of the pile. In another neat stack, there were bills. I flipped through, found several recent bank statements for Astrid to review, and slipped the pile into my bag.

A manila folder was open and stapled sets of pages spilled out across the coffee table. I studied the top one. It was the security report on an Iranian American employee of Calvert Cliffs Nuclear Power Plant. *Iranians?* Had Cunningham brought those to her? I slipped all the reports into my backpack.

I dumped the trash can on the rug and could almost physically feel Jenn's disapproval. I rooted through it, finding a few things of superficial interest. Another wad of paper, like the one in the bedroom, a receipt from the local hardware store. I scooped it all up and crammed it in the pack to examine in more detail later.

I checked the closet, which Jenn had organized as supply storage in an obsessive-compulsive way. It resembled a shelving section from Office Depot. Rooting around behind and under the supplies proved fruitless.

It occurred to me that the police may have taken the good stuff.

On one wall was a set of floating shelves. Several books were displayed, held upright by anchor shaped bookends. I had a set of those shelves. They had weight restrictions. I had chosen carefully what I put on mine. Maybe she did, too. I started going through each book left to right.

First book, nothing.

The second book hid a birthday card from Walt. I read the note he wrote. It was nice to know the guy had been an ardent lover.

Third book, bingo. Inside *The Coral Reefs of Australia* were papers folded in half. One was a picture of the Ali Hosseini Khamenei, supreme leader of Iran since 1989, speaking behind a lectern with his hands clasped over the edges. Behind it was a photo of General Qassem Soleimani, the former commander of the Qods Force, Iran's special forces. He was killed in a U.S. drone strike in 2020. In the photo he had a wise-guy smile and was scratching his beard. *What's with all this Iranian stuff?* I had the buzz I experienced when a puzzle piece was almost ready to fit into place. Flipping through the rest of the pages, I found boarding passes for a flight to Houston, Friday before last. The Friday before she died. Why would she hide boarding passes for a trip with a bunch of Iranian stuff?

The Iranian printouts and the boarding passes went into the backpack. I pulled my phone out of my pocket and googled 'nuclear plants near Houston.' Southern Texas Power Project Electric Generating Station was in Bay City. I reached for the last book.

Just as the hardback copy of Hemingway's *The Old Man and the Sea* came off the shelf, my cell buzzed. It was Astrid. "What?" I held it between my chin and shoulder while flipping through the book. The book contained photos of a younger Jenn with a different man than Walt. He was older than she was. They were on an ocean beach and were clearly a couple.

Astrid said, "Go out the back door *now*. A police car is parking at Jenn's house."

I crammed the book and pictures into my backpack and raced down the stairs, hearing the thud of boots coming up the steps to the porch. I froze at the bottom of the stairs. If I went into the living room, the officer could see me through the door's windows.

The sound of boots stopped. I heard Astrid talking to the officer, asking his name and what was going on. I heard him walk to the edge of the porch to be closer to her on my balcony. She was buying me time.

I zipped across the first floor to the back door. Like my house, Jenn had an open floorplan, and the back door was visible from the glass windows in the front one. I slipped out the door and closed it, then leaned against the siding so the officer couldn't see me as he reached the front door. There was knocking and then he buzzed. I heard him try the doorknob. Then I heard boots receding down the stairs.

I sprinted for Jenn's gate and slipped through it as I heard the officer fighting with the catch on Jenn's front gate. I sprinted down the grassy strip in the middle of the alley to avoid the sound of crunching gravel. Wedging through my half-opened gate, I threw off the backpack and my latex gloves, then dropped to my knees by my back garden. The gloves laying on the ground looked suspicious, so I crumpled them into a ball and lodged them under my knee. My hands grabbed at weeds in the garden as I kept my head down and took deep breaths to tamp down the adrenaline.

The police officer had gotten through the gate. I heard footsteps in Jenn's backyard, then on her porch. The officer was ensuring the door was locked. Oh no. I forgot to turn the latch. It wasn't locked! I reflexively touched the key I still had in my pocket.

My weed pile was growing.

The officer went inside. I had a few minutes now. The best thing I could think of was to hide the backpack in the 'she shed' and double down on gardening. I picked up the latex gloves and pack and as calmly as I could, opened the door and threw them in. As I was backing out, I saw my earbuds on the side table by the door. I put them in my ears loosely and without music so I could hear, then I went back to the garden and detached a whole lot more weeds.

It seemed like years before the officer finally closed the back door and locked it. I heard him wiggle the doorknob to make sure. Standing on the deck, he could see me over the fence. He came closer to my yard. "Excuse me ma'am. Have you seen anyone at the Albrecht house?"

Turning my head, I saw a uniformed sheriff's deputy I'd never met. "Hi. What did you say?" I pulled out the ear buds.

"Suspicious activity. We got an anonymous call about someone inside the Albrecht house."

"Really? What did they steal? First, a killer on the loose and now a break in next door. What's happening in little West Beach?" The manufactured deep sigh felt a little too real.

"Nothing seems to be missing," he said. "So, you didn't see anyone?"

"No, but I appreciate the warning. I'll keep an eye out."

He held out a card. "Call me if you see anything."

I came over to the fence and accepted it. "I sure will." I imagined standing on the stage in Town Hall accepting citizen of the year for my superb show of support.

He thanked me for my cooperation, stepped off the porch, and walked through the gate to the front yard.

I took a deep breath and kept weeding until the officer's car pulled away from the curb. As soon as it was gone, Astrid and Magoo appeared on the back deck. I sat on the grass and stretched out my legs. "Thanks."

"Glad I could help. Where's your backpack?"

Before I could answer, Magoo smelled the wind and started barking—which for a Basenji sounds like a cross between a child's scream and a yodel. I heard footsteps crunching gravel in the alley as a person sprinted behind my house. It took a second to link the runner with Magoo's warning, but when I did, I jumped up and raced to the gate. A blur rounding the corner. Taking off after the runner, I got to the street but there was no one. I ran to the next corner but the runner had vanished. I checked in every direction, but it looked pointless to continue searching.

Walking back to my yard, I felt the prickle of fear. In the yard, Astrid had shut the gate and was comforting a worried Magoo. I locked the gate behind me. "Let's go inside." I grabbed the backpack from the shed, then climbed the spiral stairs to the kitchen. After I put the pack in the kitchen, I backtracked, unhooked the whiteboard from the fence and brought it upstairs as well. I locked the kitchen door and knelt to pat Magoo. "Good job boy."

Looking up at Astrid, I said, "The only way anyone saw me go into Jenn's house was if he was watching from the alley. I thought the watcher was only active at night."

Astrid's breath caught in her throat, "You don't think it's..."

Twenty-Two

SUNDAY, JUNE 24, WEST BEACH, MD

I took a deep breath. "Absolutely it's the surveillance guy, and he could be the killer. He's getting aggressive. Running by us was a taunt."

We looked at each other and said nothing as the new reality sank in.

After texting Jerry to see if he was still on Behnam, I cleared a countertop and set the whiteboard there leaning it against the upper cabinets. I laid the markers beside it. The room looked like a college class being taught in a French bistro.

Jerry returned a thumbs up, and a text that said, "still home alone." The runner wasn't Behnam. I was also positive it wasn't Sal. He couldn't run that fast. Because Astrid had moved the rear camera to view Jenn's back yard, we didn't have any images of him on video either.

Sitting at the kitchen table, we spread out all the materials from Jenn's house except for Jenn's copy of *The Old Man and the Sea.* I laid it on the baker's rack for later perusal. An old relationship didn't fit this investigation. On the table, all our new items were individually visible. I sat on the banquette with Magoo curled up beside me. Astrid was in a chair on the other side. Handing her the stack of bills, I said, "There's bank statements in here." She dug into the pile.

I flipped through the large nuclear plant report with missing pages, looking at the information for other plants to understand the format. It looked like a write-up of exercises and outcomes. I made sure that only the Calvert Cliffs chapter was missing, then I dropped it on the floor. The link to the plant grew stronger. She'd taken the cut out pages in the folio.

Astrid laid down the bank statements. "No unusual money going in or out. She wasn't being blackmailed."

She touched the open folder with the Iranian American employees' security reports, briefly looking at the top one and laying it back into the folder. "I know America has problems with Iran; Denmark does, too. After the *Jyllands-Posten* newspaper cartoons about Muhammad, Iranians hate us."

"I think every country but Russia has trouble with Iran."

I pulled out the photos of the Ayatollah and the General and laid them in front of her. "Jenn was collecting Iranian materials. These photos combined with the security review files of nuclear power plant employees worry me. Remember Celia told us about foreign threats to infrastructure? Maybe Iran is planning an attack that would affect the electrical grid."

Astrid studied the two photos while I reached for the folder. There were three security reports, each a few pages long and individually stapled. After paging through the first two quickly, I said, "These guys seem like upstanding Americans..." I picked up the third file, and it stopped me in my tracks. "Astrid look."

Even reading upside down she immediately recognized Cigarette Man's name and said, "He is really *Ali* Behnam, not Al. Check the surname on Google. Is Behnam Iranian?"

The name was, indeed, of Iranian origin. Now we had

Behnam's picture and a full background report which I read aloud so we could both know. His parents came over after the Shah fell. He was born a U.S. citizen. The report described a talented employee with stellar performance. It also confirmed his single conviction and probation for hitting a girlfriend.

Astrid said, "We still have to prove he's a threat. Being Iranian American isn't a crime."

"True. But he sure looks suspicious. Walt said Jenn had a security problem. Cunningham and she were investigating a three Iranian Americans, and one was by the park where Jenn died when she died. Behnam could be the killer, and *we may have uncovered an Iranian threat to the nuke plant.*"

Astrid said, "Well Jenn and Cunningham uncovered it. We just found the trail they left."

"*Whatever.* We've beat the police to it, that's something. It explains why Jenn and Cunningham met secretly at her house instead of at the plant. Why Cunningham parked somewhere else when he visited. He wouldn't want the Iranian employees to find out they were collaborating against them."

Astrid stared at me, eyes wide. "When one or all the Iranians figured out Cunningham and Jenn knew about the threat, they killed them both. Now they know we're on to them."

I nodded. "That explains the gun."

Leaning on her elbows amid the papers, Astrid said. "Why didn't Cunningham go with Jenn to the park? He was in on this. He was here but he left."

I hoped for a light bulb moment, but nothing came. "Maybe she didn't tell Cunningham everything. Maybe she wanted to meet the fake FBI alone. That's the only agency with jurisdiction over domestic Iranian threats. We need Celia to look at this."

Astrid looked at her phone. "She texted. She'll be here soon."

"Jenn was smart. If they set up a fake FBI ploy to get her to the park, it had to be convincing."

Astrid had that gotcha smile again. "You're starting to sympathize with her."

"She will be remembered without fondness as a colossal pain. But I respect her a little for putting this together."

I could see that Astrid wasn't believing any of it. She stepped to the whiteboard and in the environment line at the bottom added 'fake FBI agent.'

The crumpled papers from the trash cans sat in the middle of the table. I picked up a piece of paper that was stuck together and pulled at it. It was a wad of gum wrapped and discarded. The other wadded paper was the same. "Do you see Jenn as a gum chewer? Or Walt?"

Astrid shook her head. "Not her for sure. We can ask Walt."

The boarding passes from Jenn's trip to Houston were in front of me. "Why did Jenn go to Texas? Why did she hide boarding passes?"

Astrid asked, "Are any of those three men from Texas?"

I flipped through the files again. "Two of them. One was Behnam. I googled it and there's a nuke plant there but what was she looking for?" I rocked my head back and forth while I thought. "Jenn was killed because she was getting too close. Then it was up to Cunningham to tell the cops. Why didn't he call as soon as Jenn was killed?"

Astrid said, "Save it for Celia. I know she will have an answer."

THE NEXT OBVIOUS move was to find out what Walt knew about Iranian threats, the Houston trip, and the gum. Astrid stayed below to explain to Celia why we weren't on the deck, and I sent him a Zoom link from my computer upstairs. Walt responded immediately and could be on the call in five minutes. The box with his name showed and then his image appeared in his office sitting behind his big gray metal desk. "Hey, Minxy. What's up?"

"I've got news and need to ask you some questions." I leaned in to see the screen. "That's your gym office, right? You're working."

"Was that a question?"

"No, I just wasn't sure you'd get back at it so fast."

"Better to work than go crazy."

Work didn't appear to be helping. His shoulders were hunched and strain was obvious behind the pretense of normality. "I get that. We have two leads. First, we have video footage of Sal walking toward the park about the time of the murder."

"So..."

"It might be enough for reasonable doubt. A guy she fought with was near her attack. You weren't. In the video he was stomping like a man in a lather, and we have an eyewitness that can confirm that. I'm trying to nail down what Sal was really doing. He's a pig, but I don't actually think he killed her."

"Okay. Sounds good." Walt seemed confused about what I wanted from him.

"The better lead is another man closer to the park at the same time as the murder. He works at the nuke plant Jenn failed. A couple of years ago, the guy was convicted of beating up a woman. A witness saw him walking toward the park and there's CCTV video of his truck leaving the beach shortly after Jenn was killed. He's Iranian American, which might fit with Jenn's security concerns. It makes it a *national* security issue."

"Wow. Great work." He looked impressed.

"Did Jenn ever talk about Iranian threats to nuclear power plants?"

Walt thought for a minute but shook his head. "No."

"Why did Jenn go to Houston the Friday before she was murdered?"

"How'd you know about that?"

"A little bird told me."

Walt frowned. "That was a pop-up trip. Planned one day and she flew out the next. She was checking on the security background of some guy who worked at a nuke plant there a while back. It was a discrepancy in his original investigation file that she wanted to research in person. In the original interview someone told the investigator that the guy didn't add up."

"What? She reinterviewed a contact from an old security clearance investigation?"

"Yup. That was it."

"Was he Iranian American?"

"No idea. Two families lived next door to each other for twenty years. The neighbor woman told the investigator that the employee's family ate the wrong food to be whatever they said they were. The neighbor thought they were lying about their identity, but the investigator only made a note for the record. Jenn told me that part because it was so quirky. She was excited about it."

"You're sure she didn't mention anything about Iranians in general?"

"No, never."

I nodded, "I'll think about that. Anyway, our second question is easier. Did Jenn chew gum?"

His head went side to side with vigor, he said, "Absolutely not."

"How about you?"

"Not since Mom cut it out of my hair. I think it was grade school."

"That's it for now. Keep up your morale. We'll figure out why she took that trip. It could be about the killer."

Walt's voice caught when he said, "Please do, Minxy. I care more about finding who killed her, than I do about getting off."

I WALKED DOWNSTAIRS to find Astrid sitting on the banquette staring at the whiteboard, while Celia examined the photos of the Iranian Ayatollah and General. When she saw me, she laid the photos upside down, saying, "I can't look at those two troublemakers. There's so much blood on both of their hands even if their rings are nice." I slid into one of the chairs. Celia handed me a glass of a fine Chilean chardonnay. She said, "I've been shopping. You'll be surprised at the variety of wines and gin I've found."

"I love surprises. At least this kind."

Celia said, "We'll need these supplies to get through your first PI case."

Astrid said, "I asked Celia our question about Cunningham. As expected, she had an answer. Tell her, Celia."

Celia shrugged. "It's easy. Cunningham didn't know about the watcher. He would expect no one knew he was working with Jenn. He'd been discreet about meeting at her house and even hiding his car when they met. He thought she was meeting with the FBI, but she turned up dead. He wasn't used to the secret world and didn't know what to do next. Cunningham thought he had time to figure out who he could trust, but he didn't move fast enough."

I asked, "So why did the killer wait so long to kill Cunningham? He obviously knew they were working together."

Celia shrugged. "I'm still working on that."

"So, we're sure Cunningham was murdered?" Astrid asked.

Celia and I nodded.

Celia said, "Yes, it's too coincidental. We just don't know how. It could have been a nerve agent or a poison that affected his heart. That's the way the Russians do it, so it would confuse Iranian involvement. We should get the coroner's report."

I tapped Celia on the arm. "Oh, and you owe me a tin of

caviar. Mrs. Wilson saw Behnam, the contractors saw the watcher. One of them is the murderer."

Celia pursed her lips. "We shall see. We'll need a little more proof. If you're right, you can come with me to a place in Alexandria and pick out what you want."

Astrid said, "I told Celia about Jerry's surveillance, the Shady Side ladies, your collection adventure, and the watcher being here during the day."

The jolly expression faded from Celia's face. "I'm worried. If the watcher reported you and ran by, then he's becoming aggressive. We already know he was involved in Jenn's murder, if not the murderer himself."

I nodded. "Duly noted."

Celia said, "He'll wonder what Jenn had in the house that could implicate him."

"He sure will."

She held up the Behnam file, "Linking Al to Ali Behnam is a big revelation. Maybe the watcher is one of these other two guys."

Astrid looked up. "And there was never a clandestine operator. It was all a lie to get Jenn to that park."

I said, "I think that's right. It looks like Behnam, or the other Iranian American guys from the nuke plant were playing her."

I looked at the three reports spread out so we could see each face. "If we're lucky, Jerry's surveillance will link them together." Mr. Magoo hopped up on the other chair. He turned several times and settled in. He was calm; the watcher was gone for now.

Celia nodded, "While you were talking to Walt, I ran the other two through Maryland Case Search. Super clean. Not even a speeding ticket. The Iranians would want them to be clean so they didn't raise suspicions."

Celia said, "Do you think the watcher was reading our whiteboard."

Astrid nodded. "We can only hope. With so many dead ends,

he'll be confused for weeks. Let's update it." We agreed and Astrid stood by the board marking out a lot of people and motives we'd ruled out. She wrote new clues in the ecosystem line and sometimes in other appropriate places. Celia played hostess, dutifully refilling our glasses and placing crackers and cheese on a cutting board. When it was done, the list was unwieldy but starting to focus on a motive far worse than interpersonal conflict.

Killer? / Motive

- ~~Clandestine Operative: national security, (Celia)~~
- ~~Random crazy stranger: interpersonal conflict (IC) (Astrid and The Miscreants)~~
- ~~Danny: jealousy. (Minxy)~~
- Sal: IC, CCTV video, near park, weak alibi with mystery woman (Minxy/Astrid)
- Cigarette Man on video, near park, violent, Iranian American, works at plant with two other Iranian Americans. (Jenn and Cunningham were looking at files)
- ~~Drunken Contractors:~~
- ~~Minxy: IC~~
- ~~Walt: ? $ (All)~~
- ~~The mayor: IC & $ (Minxy)~~
- Coworker at NRC HQ: IC, national security (Celia)
- Coworker at a security exercise: IC, <u>Andrew Cunningham ?????, Behnam, other Iranian Americans</u>
- Someone we haven't figured out yet: ?

Ecosystem: second shadow, suit, pantihose, gun, purse, folio, park, late night, trash cans, papers in car, car windows, fake parking signs, city contracts, gravel, national security, engagement ring, and inheritance, CCTV videos, fake FBI agent, On Cloudflow brand shoes, Iranian threat, Cunningham murdered, Houston trip, wrong food, gum

Astrid said, "That board is still impossibly messy. What if I take a picture of it so we can erase all the things we've crossed out?"

The idea seemed unwarranted at first, but after a moment we all saw the wisdom of it. "Share the picture so we all have it."

She squatted to the perfect height to get the best image. Her phone camera snapped three times. She checked the photos and then shared the best one. "It's done."

Astrid erased all the crossed-out parts, sometimes moving the clues to a new section. In the end the new and improved whiteboard said:

Killer? / Motive

•Cigarette Man aka Ali Behnam: truck on CCTV video, near park at time of death, violent, Iranian American, works at plant with two other Iranian Americans. One may be the watcher. Houston trip, national security/Iranian threat?

•Sal: IC, on CCTV video, near park, weak alibi with mystery woman

•Coworker at Nuclear Regulatory Commission HQ:

•Coworker at a security exercise: Jenn and Cunningham working together

Ecosystem: second shadow, suit, pantihose, gun, purse, folio, park, late night, trash cans, papers in car, car windows, fake parking signs, city contracts, gravel, national security, engagement ring, and inheritance, CCTV videos, fake FBI agent, On Cloudflow brand shoes, Iranian pictures and security reports, Cunningham murdered, Houston trip, wrong food, gum.

I said, "So, what do we work on next?" I looked at Celia, because I could tell she was thinking of something.

Celia said, "This is much better. The board is starting to tell a story. The Houston trip is the thread to pull."

Astrid said, "Sal doesn't fit so well in the list now, but there's still no facial match for the girlfriend. Not having a photo in the database means she hasn't had problems with the law or worked in any high-security jobs."

We all nodded.

My lovely golden clock said it was after 8:00 p.m. "I think we've done all we can for now."

Celia slipped out of the banquette and adjusted her clothes. "Yes, we need enough sleep to be strong tomorrow."

"Oh my," I said. "I'd forgotten."

Twenty-Three

I was up earlier than usual. Today was Jenn's funeral and it promised to be a rough day for my client, and thus, also for me. I've always been aware of what would hurt someone, but caring that they hurt is new, and frankly, exhausting.

The first thing I did was check the feeds. After the ladies left, I'd repositioned the backyard camera from Jenn's yard to mine, and made sure the gates were locked. I pulled up the feed. Last night there had only been two passes, but it was the same guy. I compared the photo I'd printed yesterday to the new image. The physicality was identical. And he still wore the On Cloudflow shoes.

I prepared for my run quickly and was out the door. My pace was faster than ever. Apparently, my body, without my knowledge, was burning off the tension of the case through physical exertion.

I heard a familiar slapping on the boardwalk about halfway through. "Hey Minxy, are you trainin' for the Olympics?"

I saw Ricky's big grin as he matched my pace. I said, "No, just feeling zippy this morning. I'm glad to see you. I've got a question."

"Okay, shoot."

I mentioned all three Iranian American employees and asked if he knew them.

Ricky gave me a distinct side-eye. "Why are you asking about those guys?"

"They came up in my investigation."

"I don't know where you're getting all your info about my plant, but it's making me worry you know something I don't."

"So, do you know the guys?"

"Not really. None of 'em are in IT. Seen 'em around, that's all."

"But two are from Texas."

"It's a huge state, Minxy."

I said, "I suppose it is. I'll let you know if I find anything interesting about them."

"Thanks. That would be great. I'll help you where I can. You goin' to the funeral?"

I nodded.

"Me too. Since she worked with our plant, it seemed like the right thing to do. In fact, I've got to get movin.' I'm teleworkin' and have to get some things done before I go. See you there."

Ricky slipped into a sprint and ran on. I noticed he wore old Nikes.

The serenity of the morning offered some time for hard thinking about what we had uncovered.

The pieces that wouldn't let my mind rest were centered around the Calvert Cliffs Nuclear Power Plant. Jenn and Cunningham were collaborating on a security issue, and now they were both dead. Iran was involved somehow. She had the picture of the Ayatollah Khamenei and General Soleimani in addition to the three Iranian American security reports. There was the proximity to the park of Ali Behnam so he could be the killer. She went to Texas to check his or one of the other Iranians' clearances. But it didn't make any sense that his family in Texas would pretend to be Iranian if they were really another nationality. The only nationality more suspicious than Iranian is North Korean.

An image of Samuel Sterling the lawyer, came unbidden. I hadn't heard from him, and he would be talking to people also. Maybe he'd found something useful. I'd Zoom him.

WHEN I GOT HOME, Mr. Magoo leaned against my leg while I called Sterling's secretary and set up the appointment. Sterling was available in twenty minutes. That wasn't a positive sign. If he was successful, he'd be harder to schedule. I sent the link to his email address. With my buddy staying close to my heels, I made a cup of coffee, brushed my hair, and put on a white shirt over my running gear.

Magoo and I settled in front of the computer screen.

Checking the time, I said, "Magoo, I bet you a dog treat he can't open his own Zoom call."

Recognizing the word 'treat,' he cocked his head to the side. I pulled one out of the drawer, setting it on the desktop. He blindly faced it, smelling the reward.

A box filled with the law firm logo and in a few seconds, the face of the secretary appeared above her tight V-neck top. "Mr. Sterling is ready for you."

"Terrific, because I'm ready for him."

She left the screen and Sterling sat down. "Minxy. I'm glad you called."

"Morning, Sam."

His jaw clenched and his cheeks reddened. I guessed he didn't like being called Sam. He said, "Good morning, Minxy."

I said, "Now down to business. We've had a couple of breaks in the investigation. The restauranteur who feuded with Ms. Albrecht was on CCTV walking toward the park about the time of the murder. I'm about to crush his alibi."

He stuck his lower lip out and nodded, then said, "Good work."

I said, "But wait, there's more. We have a man at the park very near the time of death. He was convicted of assaulting a woman. He works at the nuclear power plant that Jenn failed in a security exercise."

His eyes bugged out just a little. "Excellent. That could be very good."

"We washed out some other possibilities. One quick question. Have you found anything related to an Iranian threat to the Calvert Cliffs Nuclear Power Plant?"

He looked surprised. "Well yes and no. I called Ms. Albrecht's supervisor at the Nuclear Regulatory Commission—Ms. Romanescu. She said Ms. Albrecht was obsessed with a national security threat involving Iranians. She didn't mention Calvert Cliffs plant though."

"Good to know."

He said, "Nice work."

He was playing nice, so I dosed him with a lot of charm. "Samuel, I appreciate catching you up. I think we're becoming a great team." I smiled like I adored him. "So, anything else?"

"Just information about the arraignment. Dates, time, court room, that kind of thing. I'll have my girl email it to you."

"Yes, have *your girl* do that. I'll keep you updated. Goodbye, Samuel." I decided to save 'Sammy' for when I was mad at him. I doubled down on cute and gave him a little finger wave—probably the way his loveable secretary waved when he left the office.

I clicked the end meeting button.

Mr. Magoo continued to face the treat. "I know I won the bet, but I'll give it to you anyway." He jumped up resting both paws on my leg, and I fed him the prize on my flat palm.

I was still petting him when the phone rang.

"Hey Minxy, it's Jerry."

"What's up, partner?"

"Stop calling me your partner. I'm the mentor and you're working for me."

"I am never a minion. Anything interesting with Cigarette Man?"

Jerry laughed into the phone, then said, "I think so, but you tell me. He never left the house yesterday. Later in the evening a girl showed up. He came to the door and his reception was smokin' hot. Seemed like she had come back from a long absence."

"Love conquers all. What'd she look like?"

"I've got pictures. Late twenties. Dark hair. Curvy but not fat. Dressed all sexy. I pegged her for one of my tribe."

"You mean, like Italian?"

"Yeah, specifically Southern Italian."

I knew where I'd seen a similar young woman. "Jerry, I'm sending you a photo from my surveillance feed. See if this is the woman." I tapped the picture on my phone and shared it.

"Same woman?"

"Yup. That's her. Isn't that Sal from the restaurant place hugging her?"

I said, "I'm about to break into that song, about a lover's triangle but I won't out of professional courtesy."

"For the record, she's still with Behnam. No one's left the house yet."

"No one else came to visit?"

"Nope."

"Jerry, that wasn't what I expected to happen, but it's something I can work with. Thanks. I'll get back to you." I clicked off the phone.

Today was going to be busy. It wasn't an ideal time to confront Sal, but I was too curious about the relationship of Behnam, the girl, and him. In under five minutes I was standing with my back to the restaurant door and hands on my hips like the fearless girl statue on Wall Street. I listened for the door to open and Sal to storm out. Instead, footsteps came at me fast from the side of the restaurant. I turned in time to see him take his last few steps toward me. He was so close I could see his nose hairs.

"*You.* I heard you're asking around about my girl. It's none of your business. You're as much of a witch as that Albrecht woman."

"Oh, I'm way worse than she was."

"Why can't you just leave me alone? It's enough that I can't get good help, and imports from Italy take more than a month. It's all I can handle. But you. You're ruining my life."

I continued to stand my ground and straightened my posture to be as imposing as possible. "I've only started destroying your life. What were you doing the night Jenn Albrecht died? I mean *really* doing."

"I was with a girl."

"Not all night. I've got you on CCTV stomping down the street toward the park near the time of the murder."

I watched as that puckered Sal's entire face. He flinched and was at a loss for words, probably searching for a flimsy lie that would keep him out of hot water. Finally, he went into rage, the go to for men without a decent explanation. He yelled, "So, what? I needed fresh air."

"Did you find it in Sunrise Garden? Were you angry that night, too? Did you see Jenn alone and take out your anger on her with a kitchen knife when no one was watching?"

Sal marched twenty feet away and screamed to Jesus to

preserve him from women like me. From a distance, as if he was afraid of what he'd do if he got closer, he screamed, "I didn't kill her." Spittle hung from his lips.

"Well, the police say Walt the Marine did it, but I'm building a fine alternative to that theory. You fought with Jenn. You have rage issues as we see right here and now. I have CCTV footage of you heading to the park a little before the attack. If I was the jury, I'd suspect you killed her. So, Sal, what were you doing that night?"

"It's none of your business."

"Ah, but it is. Mine and the entire jury pool of Calvert County. You see I have an image of another guy, younger than you," I put my finger to my lower lip as though considering, "and way better looking, who was also near the scene. Oddly enough, both of you share the same girlfriend. We know she was with him last night. A fine little love triangle. I'm guessing Jenn got in your way at the wrong time. You were mad about being jilted. It took a lot of anger to stab her that many times."

Sal ran at me, furious. He stopped inches from my face. If he punched me, it would be recorded on my little camera on the sign. I could take a punch. Cooking Sal's goose would be worth the pain.

To my surprise, he was shaking with anger, but he controlled himself. It must have taken every last scrap of willpower, but he did it. He yelled, "You're spying on me."

I shrugged. "It's what I do."

He didn't like that answer. His face got redder. I took the opportunity to change my tone and mess with him a little more. "Sal, I don't think you killed Jenn. It's just that I'm working for Walt and you're the best defense we have. Tell me about that other guy and why you were out that night. If it ruins my case, I'd rather hear it now than on the witness stand."

He turned away again and pushed his hands into his pockets.

He started pacing around the yard. Abruptly he stopped and glared at me. "So, you're sure she was with him last night?"

"Positive."

"That girl..."

"Tell me about her. What's going on?"

He was no longer angry. He was broken. I changed my tone to match his and asked in a quiet voice, "Sal, what is it? Who is she?"

He stood still, his head drooping. He let out a long sigh, then said, "She's my daughter."

I couldn't hide my surprise. "*Really?*"

Sal stood up straight. His posture was both cocky and proud. The emotion was as strong as his anger had been. "Yeah, she's my sunshine. I had a thing with her mom way back. She had Trish but we never married, you know? Over the years Trish and I've gotten close. She comes to me when she needs advice."

"Wow. I didn't see that coming. But I have to tell you, warn her about that guy. He's a woman beater."

"*That's why she was here.* He hit her. She had to get away from him. He knew she was with me. He parked by the beach and called her the night of the murder. I went to meet him instead of Trish and told him to get lost."

"So, you two talked. How long were you with him."

"I yelled at him for at least five minutes maybe more like ten, and then he went back to his truck. I saw him shoot me the bird when he drove by me."

I believed him. I could feel sincerity oozing out of him. "If he was with you, he couldn't have killed Jenn either. See anyone else while you were near the park?"

"Nah, I was pretty focused on telling that guy to leave my girl alone."

That was all I needed. I was done here. Unfortunately, Behnam was not the killer or even linked to the killer as far as I could see. Damn. I'd have to try harder to identify the watcher. I said, "You've got a real problem with your daughter and Behnam. If you need help, I'll do it."

His eyes pinched together in surprise. "You hate me."

"Not as much as I hate woman beaters." I shrugged. "Besides, a lot of people I couldn't stand are turning out to be okay. I'm reevaluating."

"You're talking about your neighbor."

"Maybe. Turns out she wasn't as bad as I thought she was. See you at the funeral." I started walking backward away from Sal. "And call me if he hits your daughter again. We'll take him down."

Twenty-Four

I let myself in and enjoyed Mr. Magoo's delight that I was back. After showering, I slipped into my "go to" little black dress which was appropriate for funerals even in West Beach. I put on the pearls. The three stranded ones like Jackie's.

I sat on my bed and then flopped on my back, staring at the coffered ceiling. Almost instantly Magoo was beside me, laying his head on my stomach. His presence comforted me. I hated funerals. They reminded me of Shelly's funeral as well as Father's. They were both bad in different ways.

When the Coast Guard found my mother's body after she wrecked the sailboat, she had been underwater too long for an open casket. Father did well by the wife he hadn't loved. Instead of putting her in the Chanel dress she only wore because she had to, he'd sent her favorite T-shirt, a hippie skirt, and hoop earrings to the mortuary. That was what she would have wanted.

The service was set for St. James Church at 2:00 p.m. The staff were invited, as were Father's employees from the brokerage. We'd cast a wide net to invite all of Shelly's friends and acquaintances. Our maid Belinda picked out a nice dark Gucci suit for me. It fit my teenage frame and looked sophisticated. I only needed a nicer purse and I'd be ready. None of my purses were grown up enough.

Father was on the telephone finalizing the reception at a restaurant a block from the church. He requested that the full catalog of Steely Dan songs be played on repeat, once again, doing this event the way she would have wanted. I went barefooted into Shelly's room. The lack of conjugal bliss in their marriage had been owned up to early on, and both parents had their own bedrooms.

The decor was a cacophony of colors, bright neon yellow walls, a daring blue carpet. Peter Max and Andy Warhol originals hung next to original Che Guevara posters. Liberal political books and manifestos lined the bookshelves. I had never played in my mother's room. There was no draw for me. No makeup lessons, because she wore none. No girl talk about guys to help me transition into a woman. That would have been too trivial for Shelly.

I thought of Jackie's many worst days. For her, there was competition for worst of the worst. She'd had two miscarriages and buried a baby who only lived a short while. That had to hurt. She'd buried her older husband Ari Onassis. She'd even buried her confidante and brother-in-law Bobbie Kennedy. But the drama and violence of JFK's murder with her by his side, his blood all over her, was always the worst.

If she could be composed through all that, so could I.

I pushed open the door to Shelly's walk-in closet and went to the shelves in the back where she stored her purses, including the one Shelly had been using when she died. The staff must have brought it back from Long Island. Shelly's tastes were too adventurous to be proper for a funeral, but there was a clutch-sized silver one with a chain strap that would do. I slipped the chain over my shoulder and checked out the suit and purse combination in the mirror.

As I turned, my eye was drawn to her current handbag. It was a dyed leather hobo and was unzipped. I looked inside. What was important enough to be in her last purse? Among other things, there was a chapstick, a joint, and a letter. I pulled out the letter. It was from our family doctor. Slipping the two sheets out of the envelope, I started reading with no sense of guilt. Privacy stops when you hit the shoals in the Long Island Sound.

It read:

Dearest Shelly:

I have tried to reach you several times, and knowing you as I do, it is clear you are avoiding me. I understand why. No one likes to hear the diagnosis of pancreatic cancer, but it is what it is. You can extend your life for a significant amount of time with the pharmaceutical and radiation treatments I have proposed on the attached page. It will give you time to finish up your many projects and to see your lovely Marnie graduate high school—maybe even enter Harvard as planned. I know two years sounds like so little when you were hoping for forty but it's not to be so readily dismissed.

Please call, Shelly. We've been friends for a long time, and as your doctor I need to make sure you have all the information.

Respectfully,
Dr. Robert T. Briscoe

My eyes stopped focusing on the letter and I imagined the

minutes before she willfully plowed into the rocky shoals. My mother knew that stretch of the Sound like she knew every inch of this bedroom. We had navigated those shoals for many years. The day she died was breezy but nothing she couldn't handle. She was a daring and accomplished sailor.

Tears came unbidden when I admitted the crash was no accident. My mother had run aground on the rocks because she couldn't face the indignity of cancer treatment. Worst of all, she hadn't said goodbye. No words of wisdom. No proclamation of her love for me. She just went away. That was the cruelest pain of all.

Magoo sensed my sadness and shifted his head so he could lick my arm. I shook off the memory and sat on the edge of the bed. He repositioned himself against my leg and leaned in. I know why people love sympathizers.

It was time to put on my shoes and go. I checked my makeup and hair. Before I left, I moved my wallet and keys to the little silver bag with the chain I'd used at Shelly's service.

I stopped first at Astrid's, and then we walked together to collect Celia. It wasn't far to St. Anthony's Catholic Church. A lady at the door handed us a program that explained how Jenn had been a regular there. I had no idea. Even though I'd had a front row seat to my neighbor's life, I still barely knew her.

The funeral was a proper West Beach event. This was the first murder in anyone's memory. A lot of people came just for the spectacle. Those folks had never met Jenn and cried the loudest.

The rest of the church was full of locals in their finest dark colored clothes. Funerals are one good reason to dress in West Beach. The Miscreants came all emo in black jeans and hoodies as a sign of respect. Some showed up in flip flops, black shorts, and tees, also considered respectful. On the other end of the spectrum, Astrid had a Eurofit black sheath perfect for her lithe body and accessorized with fabulous Danish modern jewelry. Celia had a short-sleeved coat dress, a black hat, and a sapphire broach the size of a clam shell.

We sat at the rear of the church so we could see all the attendees. Conventional wisdom has it the killer shows up at the funeral. I wasn't so sure, but if there was something to see, I didn't want to miss it. I also wanted to ensure Walt didn't make a spectacle of himself. His demeanor would be under a social microscope.

Celia tapped my arm. "There's Danny."

She pointed and indeed, he was with his mother and dressed in black pants and an open-collar dress shirt. He was a mess. His eyes were red, and he carried a wad of tissues in his hand. His mom guided him into a pew.

I was still watching Danny settle in his pew, when I saw Walt in my peripheral vision. He stood ramrod straight, wearing a dark gray pin-striped suit, light gray shirt, with a black and gold tie. He was eying the throng with trepidation.

I had taken the seat nearest the aisle and moved to his side, laying my hand on his shoulder. "We're over here." The look of relief on his face made me sympathetic again. I nodded toward the ladies and said, "Come on."

Celia and Astrid scooted down, and I slipped in next, letting him sit on the aisle. He said, "I'm so glad you ladies are here. I could use some backup in this crowd."

I whispered in his ear, "Not to worry, I brought num-chuks and a stun gun if things get nasty."

Walt let out one of those little surprised 'ha' laughs. After that, he turned into a statue. He stared straight ahead at the golden coffin of his beloved Jennifer Albrecht and didn't move.

We all sat in silence watching the people file in. To my surprise, Sal came, dipped a knee as he stopped at a pew five rows ahead of us, and crossed himself before taking a seat. I kept studying the crowd and saw Ricky sitting at the front of the church, close to the wall. He was talking with a young woman to his left when the organ began the processional.

Celia and I followed the program and helped Astrid and Walt with the readings, singing, standing, and kneeling. Father Sullivan led the service. During the eulogy, he spoke of parishioner Albrecht and her service on the Liturgy Committee. She helped ensure that church doctrine was represented accurately in all the Sunday School Classes. She taught special classes on the liturgy. That did sound like Jenn and her love of rules. I nudged Walt. "Did you know she did that? I mean where did she find the time?"

He nodded. "I attended with her. I was planning to convert when we got engaged."

I wasn't fond of rules, but Jenn was and she'd made them her purpose. It must have meant a lot to her. At the same time, I'd been finding stolen gnomes, and solving mulch mysteries. I was glad to have what felt like a purpose now.

One of the communion hymns started and the priest invited all Catholics to share in the sacrament. I stood, and Celia pulled on my arm. "Minxy...communion is for *Catholics* only."

"Explain that to Baby Jesus." As an Episcopalian, I could easily pass as Catholic, and did so sometimes. I wasn't going to today, however. I wanted to walk around and get a better look at the congregants.

My hands clasped in front of me, I looked at every face in the sanctuary. Winding forward in the long line, I finally reached the priest. I crossed my arms over my chest, the sign I wanted only a blessing. Those are free to people of all faiths.

The line returning to our seats snaked along the first pew and up the aisle by the wall. We passed where Ricky had been seated, but he was gone. The Miscreants and Sal were also missing. I remembered when I was young the cool kids left after communion. They walked as though returning to their pews but kept going out the door. It was appealing even now, but I needed to stick with Walt. I returned to my seat and waited for the end of the service.

When the recessional began, we were first out the doors after the priest, the acolytes, and the coffin which was then solemnly loaded into the hearse by the funeral home staff. It would have been too awkward having Walt as a pallbearer, so I'd advised him against it.

All of us donned sunglasses against the morning sun and for Walt, to shield his tears. We milled around waiting to go to the cemetery. Walt had asked me to go with him to the graveside so he wouldn't be alone. He had plenty of room for us all. His Subaru was in the parking lot across the street, and I marveled at how clean an old car could be. I rode shotgun, with Astrid and Celia in the backseat. We followed the hearse for fifteen minutes in silence. The Sheriff's Department stopped traffic along the route, allowing us to pass in one long line.

The cemetery was peaceful. Stone angels prayed by the pond. Benches under trees offered shaded rest for loved ones. Lots of plastic flowers were fading in the bright June sun. A small group, which I noted included Danny and his mother, crowded around the casket sitting atop a metal platform. The priest committed the body to the earth with a prayer that was perfect in its two-minute length. We were finally done. Amen to that.

Walt stood at the casket, his whole body shaking with his sobs. I could feel the pain as if it was my own again. With a head nod, I gave the girls the signal to give the man some space. We found a tree and chatted in its shade until a pulled-together Marine joined us with his sunglasses on.

As we were walking back to the car, Danny came up from behind, grabbed Walt's shoulder, and spun him around. Danny was hopping mad, his red and blotchy face was streaked with tears. With his mother trying to control him, he held Walt by the biceps and screamed, "Why weren't you with her? You should have been there to protect her."

Walt was emotionally gut punched but held himself together. He put his palms gently on Danny's chest to add some space between them and said, with a voice so full of emotion it made my heart ache, "She wouldn't let me, man. You don't think I wanted to be there? When you heard us fighting, that's what the fight was about. I needed to protect her."

Danny's mom pulled his arm and Astrid pulled on Walt's. I stepped between them. "Guys, that's enough."

The two separated a few feet and stood facing each other. Walt seemed to be aching with regret and said, "It was some nuclear security thing. Classified. I'll always regret not being there."

Danny looked at Walt and to my surprise closed the space between them and cried on his shoulder. He said, "I miss her." Walt hugged the big man tight.

Twenty-Five

Walt dropped off Celia at her house to telework on open-source research for the rest of the day. Astrid got out, too, saying she'd walk the few blocks home to stretch her legs. She had a project to send to Denmark and it was getting late in Copenhagen.

Walt and I were hungry, so we went to the fish restaurant for lunch. He wasn't in a hurry to get back to the gym and seemed eager for the company. We chose an outside table toward the back to avoid gawkers. Every citizen of West Beach was well informed about the funeral and Walt's demeanor by now. When I'd noticed one person walk by three times, I tipped the umbrella toward the street to avoid his prying eyes.

We both got fish and chips. The waitress came quickly, told us she was sorry for our loss, and showed up quickly with our orders. Once we began eating, I saw my opportunity to find out more about Jenn's Texas trip. "So, Walt, let's talk about Houston. Maybe you'll remember another detail to help explain it."

"I've told you everything I can remember."

I said, "Let's just try again. Jenn decided to go on Thursday and flew there and back the next day. The more I thought about it, that's faster than most bureaucracy works."

He nodded. "It's faster than Jenn's office worked, too. She said she took leave and paid for the trip herself."

"That's important. It wasn't only work. It was important to her personally. She must have learned something she couldn't ignore." I was thinking about Andrew Cunningham's visits to Jenn's house. His information could have driven her actions. I added, "Personnel security and counterintelligence are a lot different than running plant security exercises."

Walt's lips curled into the tiniest of smiles. "That's what her boss told her. She didn't listen."

"Were there two people to check in Texas? Maybe some Iranians Americans that worked at the Calvert Cliffs Plant?"

His eyes looked up as he thought. "No, I'm sure she said it was just one guy. She never said anything about Iranians. What's up with Iran?"

I lied. "Nothing really. When in doubt, I always blame the Iranians...or the North Koreans."

Walt shook his head. "No, I'm sure she was talking about one guy. About ten years ago, that guy's neighbor said the whole family was fake because of the food they ate. It was kinda nutty and we had a good laugh about it. It had her all lit up."

"Did Jenn think I was Japanese? I eat a lot of sushi."

He laughed at that. "Nah. But she did think you should Febreze your fishy trash cans."

Just when I was starting to respect Jenn, Walt had reminded me how annoying she was. "Think hard Walt. Why was an old security clearance review so important?"

Walt's face went blank as he thought hard about the conversation. After a moment, his focus returned to me. "Jenn said that it was the key to everything she was working on. She said she'd be in trouble with her boss, but only until the story broke. That's when her boss would feel like a jerk for not trusting her."

I nodded. "The 'key to everything.' That's something. Any idea why her boss didn't trust her?"

"I don't know."

"Anything about the employee she investigated?"

"Nope. Nothing but the old lady and the food."

The waitress stopped at our table and refilled our water glasses. It gave me a moment to think. I still couldn't figure out how Iranians not eating Iranian food would be important to anyone. "So, after ten years the people are still neighbors?"

"The employee's parents were dead and the old lady with the food issue was in a nursing home. She was frail but her mind was good. You could ask Jenn's supervisor. She'd probably know more about it than Jenn told me."

Walt was right. My new friend Sammy Sterling had talked with the supervisor. If anyone was going to understand the Iranian connection it would be Jenn's boss. I cocked my head, "What's her name again?"

"Valery. Valery Romanescu. She and Jenn didn't get along, but the supervisor should know all the details Jenn couldn't tell me."

I made a mental note to talk with her as soon as possible. "How was Jenn over the weekend after her trip?"

"Nervy. She borrowed the gun and seemed distracted all weekend."

I thought about that. She learned something important in Houston. That knowledge triggered the clandestine park meeting and transfer of evidence. She must have found the missing piece that put a bow on her research.

We finished up, and I patted his shoulder as we left the restaurant. "Hang in there, buddy. I'm close to a breakthrough. We'll find reasonable doubt for your trial. Then I'll catch the killer."

He smiled weakly, "Don't tell me his name. I really could kill him."

I nodded. "I won't say a word until he's in lockup."

ON THE WALK HOME, I let the pieces of the puzzle float around my mind to see if they would connect. They didn't. Ali Behnam didn't kill Jenn. He'I couldn't remember the name of the other Iranian American from Texas. I'd have to look it up. Maybe he was the guy she checked on in Houston. Imagine if he was the watcher and the killer. He was coincidentally only yards from his Iranian American colleague from work when he killed her. Celia would hate that coincidence. I walked up the stairs to my door, fumbled with the key, and opened it. "Hi, Magoo."

Silence.

Placing my keys and purse in their usual spot, I waited for Mr. Magoo to greet me. No bark, no happy tail-wagging dog.

He hadn't been sleeping well because of the watcher. Maybe he was in a deep sleep. I walked into the kitchen to his favorite napping place, but still no dog. Then I saw that all the papers from Jenn's house were missing from the table and the backdoor was ajar.

"Hey Magoo, I'm home." I stood completely still listening. I heard a barely audible whine and a muted tail thump coming from upstairs. I slid a knife out of the block, slipped off my shoes, and headed up toward my dog.

My bedroom door was open. I checked behind the door, on the deck, in the ensuite bathroom, and in the closet. Nothing.

The guest bedrooms were the next rooms down the dark hallway—one on either side. I cleared them without seeing anything amiss.

Only the hall bathroom and my office remained. Outside the

closed bathroom door, I saw blood on the blond wood flooring. Not a lot, but it was clearly drying blood. I opened the door and Mr. Magoo's eyes searched blindly for mine. He whined and tried to stand but couldn't. I whispered "Good boy. Sssssh."

Holding the knife low at my side, I approached the last room, my office. The door was open and as I moved closer, I could see chaos. The intruder had rummaged through all the drawers and pulled the supplies out of the closet. The desktop was completely empty. The burglar was gone and had taken my computer from here and the evidence from the kitchen.

I took a deep breath and backtracked to the bathroom. Magoo tried to stand again, but I helped him back down. Kneeling beside him, my hands worked inch by inch over his copper coat, looking for wounds. He wasn't bleeding, but his ribs were so tender he growled when I touched them. The blood in the hallway wasn't Magoo's. I smiled at the little dog. "Good boy. You bit him." I dialed the vet.

Per my vet's instructions, I slid a large cutting board under Magoo and the bathmat he laid on, then carried the bundle downstairs to the living room sofa. I pulled out my phone, "Astrid, I need your help. Can you come over right now?"

She must have heard the intensity in my voice. "On my way."

True to her word she was through my door in five minutes still holding the half-eaten yoghurt that must have been in her hand when I'd called. I could tell from her breathing that she had run. She saw Magoo's distress. "What's wrong with my buddy?"

"The guy who broke into my house kicked him."

"What?"

"All our research and my computer were stolen."

"They must have known we'd be at the funeral."

"Yes, they did. But they left a calling card. There's blood in the hallway upstairs. Magoo must have bitten the guy. Would you call 911 and have the Sheriff's Department check the crime scene. Especially that blood."

She appeared confused, "Where are you going?"

"If the killer broke into my house, he knows we're getting close. He's seen what we have. We need to get this thing solved. The way to do that is to talk with Jenn's boss."

"About the Iranians?"

"Exactly. She can tell us why Jenn went to Texas and about the Iranian threat. Plus, Jenn may have the originals of the documents in her desk, and a memo about what she found in Houston. It could solve this case"

"What about Magoo. He needs a vet."

"On the way. Mine does house calls."

Astrid nodded. "I'll tell the deputies I came over to walk Magoo and found all this."

I nodded back, "And you don't know where I am and can't reach me on the phone. I don't want the killer beating me to the NRC."

Twenty-Six

MONDAY, JUNE 26, ROCKVILLE, MD

Traveling to the Nuclear Regulatory Commission from West Beach required driving halfway around the always frenzied Washington, D.C. Beltway, and then a few more miles up traffic-clogged Rockville Pike. The high-rise headquarters was protected from bombers by boulders the size of Volkswagen Beetles. Calling from the road, I scheduled my meeting with Ms. Romanescu. I found street parking a few blocks away and made my appointment time with a few minutes to spare.

Internal security mirrored the external protective mind set. No way I was getting into the building without an official escort and a trip through the metal detector. The Administrative Assistant said he would fetch me, so I sat in the foyer eyeing the guards who eyed me right back. To my surprise when the elevator opened, a bear of a woman wearing a severe suit and a matching temperament marched toward me, hand extended.

With a brief dip of her head, she said, "Valery Romanescu. Pleased to meet you. Follow me."

We went up several floors on the elevator, then walked

silently through a warren of halls and rooms. *So, this was Jenn's boss.* My sympathy for Jenn continued to grow. This woman looked like she could personally upend a rugby scrum. And it wasn't just her wrestler's physique topped by a helmet of graying hair. Considering how to describe her countenance, only 'battleax' came to mind.

In contrast to her bearing, Romanescu's office was light and bright with large windows looking down on the miles of small shops along Rockville Pike. Seated facing each other across her desk, the awkward silence continued. I broke it saying, "Thank you for meeting with me, Ms. Romanescu. I have a few questions in my investigation of Jenn Albrecht's murder."

Her voice was husky, like a serious smoker, "It's Mrs. Romanescu, and please explain who you are and who you work for."

Her question was fair. It was one I would have asked if I was in her size twelve pumps. "I'm a private investigator working for Ms. Albrecht's gentleman friend, Walter Hawley."

"Please show me your badge."

Reaching into the side pocket of my purse, I said, "Sorry, but that's the thing with PI's...we don't get badges." I palmed the leather case and let the lower half fall open to reveal my card. "Here are my credentials."

Romanescu sat upright with elbows on the desk and her forearms stretched out in front of them. Her hands balled into fists as she looked at the creds without touching them. "Good enough."

Seizing the initiative, I asked, "Was Ms. Albrecht working on anything sensitive? Something so consequential that someone murdered her?"

The woman's fists released, and she clasped her hands together in front of her, fingers clinching and releasing, as she considered her answer. "Jennifer performed nuclear power plant security exercises. She oversaw an exercise at Calvert Cliffs facility because she lived closer than the rest of us. There were problems with it."

"Could you be more specific? What problems?"

"That's classified. It is a nuclear power plant, you know."

"I worked at the CIA before I became a private investigator. The Intelligence Futures Alliance still holds my clearances."

Romanescu cocked her head in challenge. It was clear she didn't believe me. "Ah, but there's the problem. Unless you pass them to me, I can't know that."

"Their security officer can send them to yours in five minutes. What's the contact information?"

She wrote from memory a number using blocky square numbers carefully drafted. She slid the paper to me. "Make the call."

I did, then asked, "While we're waiting, how would you characterize Ms. Albrecht as an employee?" Complaining about Jenn would keep Romanescu busy while we waited.

"Well, as I told the police, she was difficult."

"*Really?*"

Mrs. Romanescu's hooded eyes pinched together. She didn't seem to like me any more than she'd liked Jenn.

I said, "I mean, from my other interviews, Ms. Albrecht comes across like the most diligent employee you could find."

Romanescu pursed her lips at that nonsense and leaned back in her chair. Her hands gripped the edge of the desk so hard her knuckles turned white. "Oh, she was hard working and thorough, but she didn't take directions. Not at all. She always thought she knew best, which caused problems in a small office with not enough resources to cover all we're expected to do."

"For example?"

"The Calvert Cliffs exercise identified a significant security problem. They passed after the retry. Done and done. We had Albrecht scheduled to do another one with the University of

Maryland campus reactor, but she took unplanned leave the Friday before she died. That left us scrambling. No real explanation. She said she had something important to do and just didn't show up."

"And you didn't like that?"

The woman sat silently for a moment, then she said, "I had the impression Jennifer was conducting official business on personal time. If she was doing that, it was something she knew I wouldn't allow. We follow the rules here."

Just then, the young Administrative Assistant arrived at the door. He waited for an invitation to enter, and Romanescu waved him in. He dropped a single sheet of paper on her desk. When he received no recognition or further directions, he awkwardly backed out of the office.

She perused the clearance verification, memorizing every word. Not very trusting. She finally laid down the document and clasped her hands over it. "Well, Ms. Banks, you do indeed have clearances. I thought you were faking it."

I gave her what I thought was a pleasant smile. "Now, what went wrong with the security exercise?"

"It was an access problem. Employees are supposed to have badged access only to the places where they perform their duties. That plant was like a social club. Everyone went anywhere in the whole plant. They tried to hide it during the exercise, but Jennifer checked the logs. They faked restriction, but she figured it out."

I remembered hearing the same thing from Ricky at Vera's. "Sounds impressive to me. But you were upset with her."

She nodded her head. "Please understand, it wasn't for her work on the Calvert Cliffs exercise."

"So, what was it?"

She said, "Are you familiar with the story of *Moby Dick*."

I waved away the stupid question. "Of course."

"Ms. Albrecht was like Captain Ahab. The Intelligence

Community has told us Iranians might have sleeper agents attempting to infiltrate energy facilities somewhere in the U.S., through any means possible. Our commercial nuclear power plants are an ideal target. Ms. Albrecht saw Iranians everywhere. She hunted for that white whale and wouldn't let it go. She thought she'd found a bad one at Calvert Cliffs. Mind you, there are three Iranian Americans employed there. They all passed their security reviews. They were hard working children of immigrants, like me. After the exercise failed, she dug deeper.

"Did she find evidence of anything?"

"Nothing valuable. I told her to stop wasting our time. Then, I learned she didn't quit. She took leave, then flew to Texas using her own time and money to continue the investigation. I'm sure it had something to do with her search for that damned White Whale of Iranian infiltration."

"Was she back at work Monday and Tuesday before she died?"

"Yes, but when I asked her about it, she wasn't forthcoming."

"How did you find out she went to Texas if she did it on her own?"

"She met with the security officer at the facility in Houston that originally hired the man in question. He faxed her the minutes of their meeting for her records. She never saw it. My AA found it on the fax machine after she died."

Who dislikes a worker for showing initiative and caring if America's enemies blow up a nuclear power plant? I took a breath and said, "So, you knew there wasn't Iranian infiltration because they've never done that before. Why would they be able to get in now?"

Her eyes brightened and she leaned back in her chair. "Exactly my point."

Romanescu's stunning lack of imagination was familiar. It was the reason for 9/11. "So, if she had anything she thought was evidence of Iranian infiltration, she wouldn't have shown it to you."

Romanescu looked at me and remained silent.

"Where's the response from the security officer?"

"The administrative assistant put it in Albrecht's cubicle after I read it and before we knew she was dead."

"Have you cleared out her desk?

"No. Not yet."

As politely as I could muster, I asked "Would you mind if I looked at her desk?"

Joy flickered in Romanescu's eyes. I'd given her a way to get rid of me. She stood. "You've got a need to know and higher clearances than anything that would be at her desk. Come with me."

She led me to a standard-issue, government cubicle, with a five-foot by three-foot desk, a swivel chair, and a shelf for books and papers. There were two short filing cabinets. A picture of Jenn and Walt holding hands while sitting in deck chairs was pinned to the insulated partition. Perched on top of the bookshelf, Jenn's ivy had wilted from lack of care. I sat in the seat and Mrs. Romanescu said, "Nice meeting you. When you're done, have my AA show you out." She whirled quickly and I heard her office door close from across the sea of cubicles.

The giant room was quiet. I guessed there were only two or three employees still at work. Apparently, this was an early to arrive, early to leave kind of workplace.

In the single drawer, Jenn had stored supplies: lipstick, hairbrush, toothbrush and toothpaste, pens, and paper clips. Nothing unusual.

The stack of papers on Jenn's desktop looked promising but proved to be routine correspondence. Most were exercise-related forms that nuclear power plants were required to file in preparation for exercises and in response to infractions.

One filing cabinet was locked. It took me three minutes to find the key hidden in a hollowed-out face powder compact. I found a special section where Jenn kept her classified materials. They were filed by classification and had the proper cover sheets stapled on. I checked them and found nothing useful. Behind the classified stuff, there were files on many past exercises. I flipped through them looking for personal notes. One after another, they were recounts of exercises where the red team tried either physical or cyber-attacks, and the courageous plant security officers and staff heroically fought them off. All the demerits were minor security flaws, a lack of paperwork on software updates, a malfunctioning door lock, and the latest at Calvert Cliffs, unchecked access to sensitive parts of the facility.

I found the heated response from Ricky Domingo justifying the relaxed access program important for the speedy movement of his computer systems team. He argued that the threat was mitigated by constant security reviews. His people knew where they were supposed to be and didn't go into areas where they were not authorized. *Yeah sure.* But I agreed. If anyone should have the run of the place, it was the cyber crew.

Regardless, Jenn won the battle, and Cunningham had required an access plan where workers could only badge into areas related to their jobs. Even if they had access, the new system recorded who went where and when. It still sounded too benign. Who would kill Jenn for that?

The last file was labeled "Cyrus."

I knew that name. Shelly had sent me to the United Nations International School from kindergarten through twelfth grade to make me a citizen of the world. The son of the Iranian Representative to the UN was named Cyrus. After I had teased him about his name, he'd set me straight. It was the name of the founder of the First Persian Dynasty. The boy's family was related to the original Cyrus in a long, cumbersome way.

Paging through the folder I found it was all unclassified. I checked every page to be sure. This was her Iranian file. I found duplicate photos of the Ayatollah Khamenei and General Soleimani on the top of the file; the same ones I'd found in the book in her house. Next were copies of the Director of National Intelligence's unclassified threat assessment, with the Iran section highlighted in yellow marker. It warned that Iran had deep cover agents in the United States who were a threat to infrastructure. The Department of Homeland Security had put out a National Terrorism Advisory System Bulletin warning of domestic retaliation following the U.S. drone strike killing of General Soleimani.

I leafed through the stack and had a revelation. She was passing documents in the park. *Of course, she would only pass unclassified papers. She followed rules.*

Next, I found her list of all Iranian American people working at nuclear power plants in the United States. She'd been on the hunt for quite a while, and a lot of names were marked through with red ink. Most were at plants farther north, but she listed—and marked out—the three working at Calvert Cliffs. Jenn had duplicate copies of their security reports that I'd found in her home. If they were still on her desk at home, did that mean she'd left them out of the documents in the folio, and if so, why?

Reading through them again I was slow and methodical. They all had stellar records. Romanescu was right. They were the talented children of highly motivated immigrants. They were second generation Iranian Americans whose parents had left when the first Ayatollah took power. Cigarette Man's file was last, and I decided to have a little one-on-one talk with Ali about dating etiquette. He was too smart to be such a jerk.

I wasn't finished with the Cyrus file, but my eyes fell upon the Houston security officer's report on one corner of Jenn's desktop. It wasn't classified. It was an average bureaucratic memo capturing a discussion for the record.

The document described Jenn's questions and the security

officers' answers. He had shown her a copy of the original security report for—I swallowed hard—*Ricardo "Ricky" Domingo.*

Ricky?

The file included the original investigator's unpublished notes recounting and dismissing Ricky's neighbor's comments about the family eating Cuban not Mexican food. Despite the woman's concerns, the final report had recommended clearances for the young and talented electrical engineer. The memo ended by documenting that he had shared the identity of the neighbor with Jenn.

Of course, Jenn had tracked the old woman down in the nursing home. She would have documented the interview. Those notes weren't at her house, so they had to be here somewhere. Maybe she had twin white whales: one Iranian, the other Cuban.

So, Ricky was Cuban? So what? Cuban emigrants were cool, leaving communism to breathe free in America. Who would try to hide that?

Turning back to the last documents in the Cyrus folder, I found they didn't make any sense. Jenn had Ricky's updated security report from Calvert Cliffs nuke plant. The investigator's review was stellar. Ricky was a model employee, liked and respected for his work and management skills. I thought back to his welcome by coworkers at Vera's. That wasn't a surprise.

The next papers in the file were Jenn's handwritten notes from the Texas interviews. She must have written them on the plane home. Her handwriting was loopy and girlish, making it very readable. She had documented her talk with the old neighbor who suspected Ricky's family of being Cuban. Why had she misfiled this and Ricky's security report in her Iranian file?

Taking my time, I read her nursing home notes. The old woman had said more than just the food wasn't right. The Domingo family was outwardly friendly, but they didn't show any concern about Mexico or its culture. They never had family visitors. They went to church for the major holidays but weren't active. The old woman couldn't prove it, but she didn't believe they were Mexican and beyond that she thought something bigger wasn't right about them. Jenn had written in the margins, "No one ever believes women!"

I thought, *You go girl. You got that right.*

Then I saw Jenn's conclusion about Ricky.

Ah Jenn, I didn't give you enough credit.

Twenty-Seven

MONDAY, JUNE 26, WEST BEACH, MD

In her final paragraph, Jenn had concluded that Ricky Domingo was a deep cover Iranian sleeper agent. Just reading it made my skin prickle. Had her search for the White Whale of Iranian sleeper agents made her jump to an unsupportable conclusion? My brain was screaming "yes" and "no" at the same time.

Behind the Houston notes from the interview, there were several think tank articles about Iranian and Cuban cooperation from 1980 to the present. Iranian families stayed in Cuba for extended periods. They integrated into society. They learned to speak fluent Spanish and to eat Cuban food. Jenn wrote in the margins, "Dark hair, brown eyes, and light brown skin helped them blend in as Cubans or Mexicans."

Hummm. Cubans or Mexicans?

In the margins of the report, Jenn had written "'heat' not big in Cuban food." Cuban dishes reflect a more African and Caribbean heritage. Cubans eat spicy but not very hot food; Mexicans go for the hotter peppers. Unfortunately for Ricky, the lack of hot peppers gave his family away to the neighbor.

Reading that think tank report made my case officer cylinders start to fire. It was a dry, academic piece, but Jenn's analysis in the margins spiced it up. If you wanted to sneak deep-cover agents into the United States, Iranian expats weren't the ticket. Iran has been our enemy for a long time. When asked about their heritage, loyal Iranian Americans say they're Persian because Americans are terrible at geography and history.

If Iran smuggled in dark-haired and brown-eyed Iranian families fluent in Spanish as *Cubans*, they would still be scrutinized. Castro had sent in plenty of Cuban secret agents of his own over the years. Also, Cubans have special immigration treatment. When they arrive, they are formally reviewed and documented.

However, an Iranian family who had spent long years in Cuba could pass as Mexican after getting fake Mexican identity documents and an on-the-ground cultural orientation in Mexico. It may have taken months or even years, but Qods Force plays the long game. When ready, they would smuggle the family into Houston to blend in with other undocumented and unreviewed Mexican immigrants, set them up, and let their seeds grow to fruition. Ricky was that seed.

It was a genius move, but they rushed it. *The Domingo family hadn't stayed in Mexico long enough to break their adopted taste for Cuban food.* I could imagine a Houston dinner party where the Domingos pushed food around their plates without eating any because it was too hot. No one figured it out except a sharp-eyed, Mexican American woman who was ignored.

Well, Jenn also had figured it out. Or maybe Jenn and Cunningham. He had to be the one who brought her Ricky's current security review. Ricky Domingo was Iranian. The thought made my head spin.

Then it hit me. Jenn had the same photos of the Ayatollah and Soleimani in her Cyrus file as she'd hidden in her books. Why hide pictures printed from the internet? I slid the photos out of the file and looked at them carefully. Turban, robes, gray hair and beard on the Ayatollah. The man's hands gripped a podium... *That was it.* On his finger was the same carnelian ring that Ricky wore. I looked at the Soleimani photo. *He was wearing the same ring also.* Jenn had noticed Ricky wearing his and had connected the dots. The ring had been from the old country like he told me, just not from Mexico.

I slipped Jenn's Cyrus file into my purse. For good measure I unpinned the photo of her and Walt and slipped that into my purse, too. Finally, I looked on her bookshelf and found the big compendium of exercises, this one with all of the pages. I grabbed it, as well as the report faxed from Houston. All were unclassified.

Jenn's ivy needed adopting. It was coming home with me.

My thoughts were full of questions about Ricky Domingo. How had he pulled it off so successfully? If he was a spy, he was probably the watcher, and the killer. Smiling, happy-go-lucky Ricky Domingo.

On my drive home I played devil's advocate. What if Jenn was wrong. Valery Romanescu had accused her of an unhealthy obsession with finding an Iranian sleeper agent in a U.S. nuclear power plant. She had built a circumstantial case against Ricky based on assumptions about the Qods Force, the Domingo family's appreciation of Cuban food, and a ring.

Driving back in stop-and-go rush hour traffic, I considered the linkage between Iran and Cuba. They were both enemies of the United States. That had kept them close after the Iranian revolution and throughout the end of the cold war. Since then, who knew?

I needed a timeline. When could Iran have resettled the Domingo family?

Traffic came to a dead stop, and I googled 'Iranian revolution.' Just as the results came, I saw what I wanted—verification that the fall of the Shah was in 1979. The Ayatollah Khomeini, the first Ayatollah, quickly had created the Islamic Revolutionary Guard Corps as a loyalty-tested military unit to protect the Islamic State from both domestic and foreign enemies. I knew from CIA work that the group was made independent and turbo charged in 1988 when it took on the new name of Qods Force. Its new duties included unconventional warfare and military intelligence. When Khomeini died in 1989, he was replaced by Ali Khamenei.

Traffic stopped at a light, and I googled Cuba and Iran. When in doubt, try Wikipedia. There it was. The two had good economic relations. Iran even worked at an electronic jamming station outside Havana to block Radio Marti, the U.S. effort to get unbiased news into the country. Typing fast, I got a honk for not rolling as soon as the light changed. The results for Radio Marti would be waiting at the next slow down.

I couldn't remember ever wanting traffic to slow to a stop before today. When it finally did, I checked the results. Radio Marti started broadcasting in 1983. From his security report, I knew little Ricky Domingo was born in Houston in 1986. The timeline worked. Two years in Cuba, one in Mexico, then to the U.S. in time for his birth. If they'd worked in another Cuban position before Radio Marti, their accents would have been even better.

I made a face in the rearview mirror at the honker behind me, set my phone aside, and focused on both driving and thinking. Rubbing the three stranded Jackie pearls gave me inspiration.

There was another date I remembered quite well. The Berlin Wall fell in November 1989. Losing Soviet support was hard for Cuba. The newly minted Russian state was focused more on itself and less on its old allies. Cuba would have been looking for new partners. Iran was a smart choice. If Jenn was right about the Qods Force using the Iran-Cuba-Mexico-U.S. pathway to imbed sleeper agents, it could still be happening. Slow and easy, like the Qods Force likes to play it.

I had convinced myself Jenn was right. Ricky wasn't a Cuban masquerading as a Mexican. He was an Iranian masquerading as an American.

THIS WAS one of those situations when I considered what would Jackie do, or WWJD? Jackie would act boldly. What was I going to do about Ricky Domingo? I believed he was an Iranian agent. I also believed he'd killed two people. He'd stolen my computer and evidence. *Worst of all, he'd kicked my dog.*

I silently apologized to Jenn and Cunningham for any disrespect, but I really loved that dog.

I already knew what I was going to do. Fingering the three strands of pearls again, I parked in front of Ricky's house. He didn't respond to the knock on his front door, but his truck was in the driveway, so he was somewhere close. The gate to the backyard was to the right. It was part of a six-foot privacy fence like Jenn's.

As I walked toward it, I called out, "Hi Ricky. You back there?" Just as I reached the gate, he opened it, wiping his hands on a towel. He flashed his Texas charmer smile. "Hey, you're still wearing your church clothes. How are ya Minxy?"

"I've been better. Saw you at the funeral. It was nice—as good as one for a brutally murdered woman can be."

"Yeah, the priest did a bang-up job."

"You attend there?"

"Only the holidays."

Smiling, I tried hard to give off our usual flirtatious vibe. "I'm stuck on the Walt Hawley case. Can I ask you some more questions? You're my best source at the nuke plant."

"Sure, I'll answer what I can, but I still don't know why you're linkin' our facility to the murder." His hand directed me to the low platform deck about two feet off the ground, with a single long step all the way around. There were four chairs and a table with a green sun umbrella. Slipping into a chair with my back to the house and a full view into the backyard, I considered each plant in Ricky's garden, one at a time. "Your garden's amazing. The hydrangea is beautiful. Mine's stuck between pink and blue." I thought of how I'd spilled some of the treatment I used on Jenn's in my own yard.

"Ya gotta pick a color and add chemicals. I can help if ya want."

"You make it sound easy. Mind if I take a picture of yours to remember what I'm aiming at?"

"There's usually a fee, but in your case, go ahead."

Raising my cell camera, I snapped several pictures that captured the full backyard. Then I tilted my head and smiled adoringly at Ricky. "That should cover it."

He said, "I don't have as many trees as you do. Your yard's too shady. Mine's a lot sunnier."

The comment hit me as I made the connection. He knew so much about my trees because he was surveilling my house. He was the man in black. The man who had kicked my dog and robbed me. Checking my rising anger, I kept the conversation going. "Yup, shade plants aren't very colorful."

"You've got all those heucheras. They're boring."

That level of familiarity cut right through my resolve. It was hard to hold back. I said, "But back to the reason I'm here. For Walt's defense we need another suspect who might be the killer. There's always Sal. He and Jenn had a real hate-hate relationship.

But somehow, I don't think it was him. The jury won't believe it either."

Ricky nodded. "He's a super cranky guy, but he can butter up customers. That's the Sal you'd have on the witness stand."

"Maybe. He can be pleasant in spurts, but he always goes back to angry." Turning to him, I said, "So, I know your facility failed the exercise because of access issues. Had Jenn found out something else was wrong with the plant?"

He sat for a moment looking at me, his face expressionless, and then he shrugged. He'd stolen our evidence and had found nothing about him except the pictures of the Ayatollah and Soleimani with their rings. He was trying to figure out where I was going with this line of questioning. I said, "I asked you about those three Iranian American guys who work at Calvert Cliffs." Watching for the smallest possible change in expression I dragged out the reports of the three men I'd gotten from the Cyrus file in Jenn's desk. Copies of the documents stolen from my house hours earlier. Stolen, I was sure, by Ricky.

I kept my eyes on his face, waiting for a tell. If I was right about Ricky, he was trained by the Qods Force. His reaction would be small. Indeed, there may have been a slight double blink, but his face was blank.

"Like I told ya, I hardly know these guys. What about them?"

"Do you think any of them are spies for Iran?"

Mock surprise covered Ricky's face like a mask. "Are you kidding?"

Watching his face told me nothing. Then I got a bigger, more rock-solid tell than I'd hoped for. The fingers of his right hand were beating out a nervous rhythm on the chair's arm for a few seconds, then he forced it to stop. Better yet, there were new rings of sweat at the armpits of his long-sleeved T-shirt. They hadn't been there when I arrived.

"That's what Jenn was working on." Fishing in my bag, I

pulled out the unclassified Director of National Intelligence threat assessment and laid it on the table. "She had this document. The DNI assesses that Iran's sleeper agents could be in this country."

Ricky struggled hard not to react. His fingers started the tapping again, but as quickly as before he forced them to stop. I couldn't help looking at the carnelian ring.

He had to wonder how I had replaced our evidence and now had more. Probably the same documents that he had taken from Jenn when he killed her. I read aloud, "'Iran also remains committed to developing networks inside the United States—an objective it has pursued for more than a decade.'"

Watching his efforts to hide rising discomfort, I continued, "It even says that Iran targets key infrastructure, like water facilities in Israel. Why not nuclear power plants in the U.S? They think the Israelis and the Americans were behind the Stuxnet attack. It would be pay back." Stuxnet was the computer virus that brought down uranium centrifuges in Iran by making them spin out of control, while masking the activity on the system monitors in the operations center.

Ricky's eyes were shifting right and left. He picked up the three security reports I had laid on the table and leafed through them probably to buy time. Shaking his head, he turned one of them my way. "Like I said, I don't really know these guys, but I think they're hardworking and dedicated. If I had to start with any of them, I'd work on Ali. He goes by Al to fit in."

"Why Ali?"

"He has access to the reactor. Nothin' beyond that. I can't imagine any of them bein' a spy, but if you say so, I guess one of 'em is."

Packing the reports back in my bag, I said, "Thank you *so* much. I'll start with that guy. Got to get home. Mr. Magoo is under the weather." I stood and turned, seeing Ricky's running shoes lined up by the wall behind where I was sitting. Next to the old Nikes, there was a new pair of On Cloudflow dark blue tapering to almost white runners with the red band across the heel. "Nice shoes. Are they new?"

"I'm breakin' 'em in by walking around town."

Grabbing my arm, he said, "I don't think you've ever seen my indoors plants. Let's go look at 'em."

I pulled against his grip. "Got to get home. Maybe next time."

When he wouldn't let go, I grabbed his left arm above the wrist where I could see a bandage-sized bulge under his shirt sleeve. He winced and I pinched harder. It had to be where Magoo had bitten him. He would have used his left arm to defend himself when the dog attacked. Our eyes met. No more pretending.

"No time like the present." He pulled me so hard I lurched toward him.

"*Ricky let me go.*"

Twenty-Eight

MONDAY, JUNE 26, WEST BEACH, MD

The reprimand in my voice made Ricky's neighbor stand up on his deck to see what was going on. It was a guy I knew from the Saturday farmer's market. "Hi Bill," I said.

Ricky dropped my arm.

Bill looked surprised, "Oh hi, Minxy. Hi Ricky. I thought I heard trouble."

Ricky shook his head and said, "You know women. Always squealin'." He stepped back toward the house, clearing space between us. "Just let yourself out. I'll be seein' ya again real soon."

As I opened the gate, I said, "I count on it. Bye Bill."

When I walked into my house, Astrid and Magoo were cuddled on the sofa. "How is he?"

"The vet says you're right. Mr. Magoo was kicked hard. He has cracked ribs and a lot of bruising, but he'll be alright in a few weeks. No long walks and he has mild painkillers to take twice a day."

I sat gently next to the dog and scratched his head. "My poor boy," I cooed. I felt guilty for not sensing the danger I'd put him in. "When's his next pill?"

"Bedtime."

"And the Sheriff's Office? Did they take the report?"

Astrid's eyes glowed with amusement. "They were a little confused about me filing a break in for you, but it's West Beach. They just went along with it. They sampled the blood and are running it against their databases. They dusted for fingerprints upstairs and on the back door, but I think the intruder wore gloves, right?"

I nodded agreement. "Probably. The blood will be the key." Heading to see the mess in my office, I gave Magoo another scratch. "Celia's on her way. I called her from the car. She'll be here any minute. I'll tell you both what I've got when she gets here."

"Where are you going?" Astrid asked.

"To see what kind of mess the Sheriff's guys made in my office."

Astrid stood up and stretched her yoga-taut body. "Sorry, but I have to go. Lars and I are opening a Danish art exhibit tonight. I'll be by in the morning to catch up." She looked at me very seriously. "Be careful tonight. Whoever got in this afternoon can do it again."

"You're right, and I'll be ready for him." The reveal about Ricky could wait. She would think too much about it and not her role at the event.

Walking Astrid to the door, I thought about hugging her. I know that's what she would do if the situation was reversed, but I made do with an honest statement of my appreciation. "Thanks a lot for helping with Magoo."

I think she appreciated my reserved but sincere response as me being me. She, however, gave me a giant hug.

Leaning against the door jam, I watched Astrid leave. At the corner she stopped to talk with Celia, resplendent in raspberry shorts and a T-shirt. While they chatted, I ran upstairs and checked my office. It was the same mess I'd seen earlier but now coated with fingerprint powder. This was the only room in the house I hadn't put my decorating stamp of approval on. This mess would kick start that project. Maybe 1940s film noir, like Sam Spade's office in The Maltese Falcon. That would be good for a private detective.

When I was coming back downstairs, Celia walked through the door. The ruby pendant she wore was so big it made me forget what I was going to say.

She said, "So, you got robbed. And instead of sticking around, you met with Jenn's supervisor. Something's up."

"Everything's up. I know who murdered Jenn and Cunningham. I know why he killed them. And I know who broke in. I need one more piece of evidence to prove it all."

Celia stopped abruptly, "Well then, I'm impressed. You had a very productive afternoon." She headed to pet Magoo.

"Be careful with him. The burglar kicked him."

She spun around, "*What*. Astrid told me about the laptop and papers but not about Magoo."

"It's been a long day since the funeral. I'll make Vespers. Just one. I need my wits about me tonight and tomorrow. Stay with him, I'll bring them in here."

The evening was cool, with a gentle breeze off the water. It was a shame to waste it, but after the runner yesterday and the break in today, caution was important. She shrugged and settled in next to Magoo, telling him in detailed babytalk that she would find the rat who'd hurt him.

I poured the gin, vodka, and Lillet Blanc over the ice. The

shaking was a comfortable ritual. The drink splashed into two martini glasses, plop went the lemon rind, and they were ready. Before saying anything, I took a gentle pull of mine and the gin provided its promised kick.

Putting the drinks in front of us I curled my legs under me on the other side of Magoo, and said the four letters, "B.L.U.F." In the CIA they trained analysts, case officers, and probably the janitorial staff to give the 'bottom-line up front,' or B.L.U.F. Their customers were wicked busy, and the writer or briefer had to get the key message to them right out of the gates. Celia's curiosity was aroused.

I said, "Ricky Domingo murdered Jenn and Andrew Cunningham. He stole our reports today and kicked Magoo."

Celia went wide eyed. "Minxy, that's delusional."

"He isn't the man he pretends to be. He killed Jenn because she'd discovered he wasn't Mexican. At first, she suspected his family was actually Cuban, but she found out the truth. He's Iranian"

"You lost me." Celia said.

"There was a note in Ricky's security file that his Mexican American neighbor in Houston thought the Domingo family was Cuban, not Mexican. Jenn dug into it deeper and had just uncovered that even the Cuban identity was wrong. Ricky Domingo, which is not his real name, is Iranian."

"What on earth are you talking about? He's Hispanic."

"No, it's a big lie. Iranian engineers have been stationed in Cuba to help with all kinds of things."

"That's irrelevant."

"No, it's genius." I filled her in on Jenn's Cyrus file. "Somewhere along the line, the Qods Force realized most Americans couldn't tell fluent Spanish speaking, light-brown-skinned Iranians from Hispanics."

Celia took a sip of her drink, set it on the coffee table and began pacing from one end of the room to the other thinking all that over. Her heels on the hardwood made click, click sounds with each step. Her giant brain was weighing evidence. "That's insane." She paused for a moment, thinking and then went click, clicking some more. "Or the most fabulous deep cover story I've ever heard."

Celia said, "Imagine how thrilled Jenn and Cunningham were about their off-the-books espionage investigation. They met clandestinely. They wondered if their suspicions could be real."

I said, "Someone at the plant mentioned to Ricky that Jenn was going through Iranian American security files. Ricky starts surveilling her, and to his surprise sees Andrew at her house, with his car parked elsewhere—all clandestine. He knew the two of them were collaborating on finding the Iranian mole."

"Even with the Cuban Mexican America story, what convinced Jenn that Ricky was really an Iranian? She wouldn't have gone to the authorities with the wrong food story."

"Ricky's ring convinced her."

Mentioning jewelry was enough to make Celia's sit down and pay attention.

I found the photos of the Ayatollah and Soleimani in my bag, then handed them to her over Magoo's head. "See their rings?"

"I noticed those before when I looked at the photos. Lovely carnelians. Nice silver work."

"Ricky wears one *exactly* like it. She might have seen it during the plant exercise."

"That works. She'd looked hard at the leaders' images and made the connection when she saw Ricky's. The ring gave him away."

I said, "Exactly. The ring cinched it for Jenn and Cunningham. Their continuing to meet cinched it for Ricky. He called her pretending to be FBI and learned about her trip to Houston and suspicions. He had to move fast. He probably said her efforts might compromise his ongoing investigation into Ricky."

Celia said, "If she helped him, however, she would get part of the recognition for catching an Iranian spy. I bet he asked for all her evidence in one package delivered to that clandestine meeting in the park. The suit represented her professional pride in the discovery."

"Once Ricky knew what Jenn knew, he had to kill Cunningham, too."

"And now he knows that I know. He's my watcher. When I was at Ricky's house this afternoon, he had On Cloudflow shoes on his deck just like Sarah the contractor said."

"Did you say you went to Ricky's house by yourself? Minxy Banks, what were you thinking?" She jumped out of her seat and started pacing again.

In accordance with Celia's disapproval, I made a show of letting my head drop so she knew I'd heard her dismay. I stared at the floor just long enough to look contrite before confirming it. "I stopped by to verify my suspicions. The whole Iranian connection is conjecture except for the ring. Now I've got the shoes and more."

Celia's voice got louder. "It's still conjecture, and you could have gotten yourself killed."

I shrugged. "He's been surveilling me and stole all our evidence. It would be hard to make myself a bigger target now that he knows what I know. But after my visit, we also know that Ricky has an injury consistent with a dog bite. He was wearing a long-sleeved T-shirt with a bulge on his left arm where my guard dog bit him." I petted Magoo with considerable pride.

Celia looked at Magoo. "The blood in the hallway floor will match Ricky Domingo?"

"Absolutely. That's not conjecture, but it only proves he broke in and stole my stuff."

Celia stood behind a chair, leaning against it. "How'd he kill Cunningham?"

"Before he was sure I knew the whole story, I got a picture of his backyard. He loves unusual plants and made tea for his boss every morning. I bet some of his plants caused heart attacks like that old Russian case."

She nodded. "I know that case. The dissident who moved to Austria or Switzerland and died of a heart attack. Their intel blamed it on poison added to an herbal cup of tea. I can't recall which poison, but I'll check it in the files tomorrow."

"Thanks. I bet it comes from a plant in Ricky's yard. Tomorrow I'm going to see Mrs. Cunningham. I want that tea mug. If she hasn't picked it up already, I'll talk her into getting it from her husband's office. It should still have residue of the poison. Cunningham's secretary would know if Ricky brought it that morning."

"That puts a bow on it," Celia agreed.

"So, I just need to get it done before he comes after me or attacks the facility."

Celia said, "Ricky oversees IT control systems for the plant. If he's really Iranian, it would be an elegant payback to disable the facility with the Stuxnet code."

"Why wouldn't he go all the way?"

Celia's brow wrinkled. "You mean not disable but melt down the reactors?"

"A meltdown and explosion would blow radioactive material into the wind."

Celia added, "They're probably fifty miles from Washington DC. If the wind was right, it would cover the city."

I took a deep breath to calm myself down. "Very satisfying for a man who dedicated his life to attacking America."

Celia stood tall and shook her head slowly, back and forth. "Minxy my dear, I thought a little sadistic murder would be a good warm up for your professional return. You know, sort of get you back in the game. Now we're close to a radiological disaster."

Twenty-Nine

MONDAY, JUNE 26, WEST BEACH, MD

Celia had a new thought. I could see the change in her eyes. It was a worrisome thought. "I think he'll come after you."

"Why wouldn't he? He's seen my evidence. I know what Jenn and Cunningham knew."

"Minxy I know you too well. Your condition makes you too daring. You've got to sleep at my place tonight."

I shook my head. "If I stay with you, you'll be in danger, too."

"We can take turns keeping watch. I have a gun, too, you know."

The thought of Ricky trying to kill Celia scared me to the core. I had that radiating fear that started in your belly and spread outward to consume you. The adrenaline tunneled my vision to just Celia. The woman who treated me like a sister. The only one, except for Astrid, that I could count on to be there for me when I needed someone. *Celia, we can't do that. I can't lose you. You're all I've got.* The intensity of my outburst froze us both.

Finally, Celia gave me the big sister look. She came over to the sofa and gave me a tight hug. "I'll always be here for you. You're not alone. But we both have to fight your brazen instincts to keep you alive. Don't you have an office now? What if you stayed there. It's one night. Tomorrow you get that mug."

Had I ever realized how much I depended on Celia? I couldn't remember it if I had. The recognition made me shaky all over. I made a mental note to discuss it with Maya. Shifting gears back to neutral, I thought about my office at Jerry Mancuso's. It was clean, but ratty. It had a bathroom. I could blow up a mattress and take Magoo. No. Only one way in and out. Then I realized the real problem. I looked up at Celia, "No. If Ricky can't find me here, he's going to your house. And Astrid's. You'd still be in danger."

Click click click click. Her pacing was faster. "You can't just sit here."

I looked at Magoo while I considered my options. Celia went back to her seat to take a sip of her drink. She leaned forward, waiting for me to say something. Finally, I said, "What if we play offense and lure him here? He sees me in the house alone with all the lights on moving around like usual, visible through the blinds, and decides I'm an easy target."

"Another Minxy-as-bait ploy. You *would* be an easy target. If he's an Iranian agent he's trained and dangerous."

I was starting to like the plan. "We set a rattrap and Ricky's the rat. Entice him to try again. Killing me is his only hope of getting back to normal."

Celia sat back. "If that's the case, he'll have to kill Astrid and me also."

"More reason to take him out of action fast. Your idea about my office made me think. I'll hire Jerry to back me up. We'll jump Ricky when he comes in. His blood will match the sample they took upstairs. The contractors saw a man his size with those running shoes heading toward the park. My camera picks him up as he surveils me. I could pick up the tea mug. We could unravel everything."

Celia shook her head back and forth. "It reminds me of Tashkent."

"Tashkent worked. Remember?"

Exasperated, she said, "Barely. Sometimes luck runs out, Minxy. How about a real plan this time?"

I had a good feeling about this plan. This would work. "I'm calling Jerry."

"Listen Banks, I like the pay. I really do." Jerry was sitting at my kitchen table looking around as though he'd been dropped into a foreign country. "The money helps with the bills. That's great. However, this plan is bat shit crazy."

Celia was looking at me as if to say, 'I told you so.' I leaned back into the banquette's padding. Mr. Magoo was on the floor next to me. "It'll work. We lure him in, then take him. The responding police will have all the probable cause they need to break this open."

"You mean the case about the nuclear plant guy being an Iranian spy by way of Cuba, masquerading as a Mexican? Did I get that right?"

I smiled. "Yes, you did. And you can see why we can't go to the Sheriff yet. Who would believe us, even if Ricky's blood matches the sample from upstairs? The most they'd get him on is breaking and entering and theft of my computer and the documents I took from Jenn's house."

Jerry nodded, "Stole."

I shrugged my shoulders.

Celia was sitting in the chair next to Jerry. She said, "Have you ever worked in national security?"

He shook his head.

She continued. "I agree Minxy's plan is insane because it could get you both killed. The funny thing is the whole Iranian/Cuban/Mexican/Texan scenario is believable."

He looked between us and huffed. "You know, I like you two. I wish I didn't feel like you're a danger to yourself and others."

I said, "Come on Jerry. You know operations like this happen. You just can't believe there's one in little Calvert County."

Jerry fiddled with his half empty coffee mug. "That's right. I've never met an Iranian sleeper agent who wants to attack the nuclear power plant."

Celia said, "That doesn't mean she's wrong."

I asked, "How would you feel if you could've stopped it, but didn't try? If he doesn't break in, you lose a night's sleep and walk out tomorrow with a wad of cash in your pocket."

Jerry nodded.

"And if something goes down. If he comes for me like I think he will…"

He met my eye. "We'll wrap him up." He slapped his hands and rubbed them together, startling all of us, including Magoo. Jerry leaned back. "Okay. I'm in. I'll only feel a little guilty taking your money." He held out his hand.

I shook it. "Excellent. Celia, my dear, it's time to drive you home with your little doggy houseguest. Mr. Magoo would blow our cover when he smells Ricky, and he'd get hurt worse trying to protect me."

I wondered, *what would Ricky expect to see?* He was familiar with a certain pattern of my life, modified now by what I'd learned about him. That meant I would be security conscious and take precautions.

Once Jerry got over how unusual the case was, he was a good partner. He drove Celia and Magoo to her house and left his car there. After walking back, he sneaked into the 'she shed', where I joined him, and we scripted the evening's activities like we were writing a play. We would spoon feed Ricky's expectations back to him. When we were done, I went into my house and he remained in the shed, sitting comfortably on the sofa in the dark.

I turned on more than the usual number of house lights so Ricky could see me moving around. The camera feeds went to both Jerry's and my phone, which were set to silent, with the screen lights so low they were darker than fireflies.

We both agreed that Ricky would come in through the back fence and the back door. He would pick the lock on the gate, and our comms to confirm we saw it was 'a.' When he picked the lock on the back door, we would share a 'b.' Just in case Ricky didn't follow our plan, we had letters for all other entry points.

And so, our production of 'Minxy the Bait Minnow' began. First, I was in my office moving things around, repairing the damage from the break-in. That was easy enough because it needed to be done. Then there was the dinner preparation part of the script, followed by me eating at the kitchen table. There was the reading in the living room scene that eventually moved to the bedroom like usual. Finally, I made a show of patrolling the inside, checking doors and windows. I turned out the lights, then changed into black leggings and a long-sleeved black T-shirt. My shoes were rubber soled, which allowed me to move downstairs soundlessly.

The plan was to let Ricky enter the house and then trap him in the living room. I would hide on the stairs to the garage until Ricky passed me. He'd be heading toward my bedroom, where he'd assume I was. Then I would confront him. Jerry would leave the shed and wait at the base of the back staircase until he heard my voice, then he'd join me. We both had guns.

By 1:45 a.m. I was starting to think I'd made a mistake. I had expected the attack to happen by 1:00. Ricky would want to get in and finish this. I could almost hear Celia's voice in my ear telling me that assumption was me being impatient. In the back of my mind, I was thinking about the snarky way I'd face down Jerry tomorrow when he was taking the cash and saying he told me so.

Then the camera picked up movement in the alley. A dark figure walking briskly stopped at the gate. Jerry and I both shared 'a' texts. Moments later, Ricky was in the yard and heading, as expected, up the spiral staircase to the deck and back door. The 'b' texts were exchanged. Then I heard it. The scratching of the lock picking tools, the click of the lock disengaging, and the slight squeak of the door hinge opening. Then there was a padding of footsteps on my kitchen tile. He was in.

Show time.

Thirty

In the darkness midway down the stairs to the garage, I waited until Ricky passed my position before confronting him. He walked slowly forward through the kitchen. I breathed in time with his steps—left foot breathe in, right foot breathe out. I suspected he held a gun in his hand and was ready to use it. Jerry would be at the bottom of the spiral staircase by now, to block Ricky's retreat if he got spooked.

Step by step, Ricky made steady progress. His shoes made little noise on the kitchen tile.

He was now crossing into the living room, his training evident in his deliberate and methodical movement. I willed my breathing to be as quiet as humanly possible. He stopped beside the wall that hid the garage stairs and me, less than five inches of lumber and sheetrock away from him through that wall. The hair on my arms stood up. He stood silently on the other side, while I held my breath.

I'd been told you can smell fear. I'd never been able to, and I didn't want to find out if Ricky could. Him standing there still and silent, was worse than if he'd come toward my hiding place. I could feel his presence through that wall. Finally, he took another step forward into the living room. I drew in a slow and deep breath. Three more steps and he'd be where I wanted him. One. I raised my gun. Two. I put my leg silently on the stair above. Three. I raced up the remaining steps yelling, *"Hands up."*

The streetlight through the windows lit him in silhouette. He straightened, standing tall with his back to me. His hands rose, including the gun pointed at the ceiling. Jerry had heard my voice and was running to join me.

I said, "Ricky, this is it. It's over."

Jerry yelled, "Put the gun on the floor, pal. Real gentle like."

Ricky didn't move and didn't speak.

I said, *"Ricky,* put down the gun and kick it to me." He turned slowly, facing us, his gun still in the air. He wore a gaiter like in the video feed, and the black clothes, hat, and On Cloudflow shoes. I said, "Come on, be smart. It's over."

Silently, he crouched, putting the gun on the floor. He pushed it my way. As he was rising up again, I saw his play, and yelled to Jerry, "Other hand. Watch out..." I fired twice at Ricky as I closed my eyes.

The flashbang erupted in light and sound. It was all immersive. My sense of direction was confused, and I refused to open my eyes.

DEPUTIES RESPONDED QUICKLY to reports of shots fired and an explosion. Several cars were parked outside, and uniformed officers were checking my house to ensure the intruder was gone. He'd left his gun, but the serial numbers were filed off it and I'd seen his gloves. We all agreed he had used the flashbang as a diversion to flee through the front door. It had been a backup plan.

The detectives weren't eager to take my statement. It seemed odd, but it was okay by me. I could barely hear and even though I'd closed my eyes, my sight was not back to normal yet.

Just as I was pouring Jerry and me a stiff bourbon, another Sheriff's car pulled up with lights but no sirens. Walking out on the porch, I wanted to be a good hostess and greet whichever new deputy was arriving.

To my surprise, it was Jack Frye, the Sheriff himself. I sat down on the top step watching him as he got out of the cruiser and came my way. As he reached the bottom of the stairs, he took off his hat and asked, "Having a busy night, Minxy?"

That made me laugh, even though I'd read his lips and wasn't sure he'd said what I thought he'd said. "I can't hear you too well. Someone let off a flashbang in my house. What are you doing here? Your whole night shift is checking my house."

He cocked his head, "A second break in, shots fired, and an explosion were enough to get me out of bed. When they gave me the address, I admit I was a little worried about you."

I'd read his lips, and said, "Well then, welcome. Come on in and I'll get you a bourbon. That's what we're having."

He ambled up the stairs and followed me into the house, past the burned hole in my beautiful blue living room rug, through the smell of the explosive charge, and into the kitchen. Jerry was sitting at the table rereading the intel assessment about Iranian sleeper agents in America. The two met eyes and Jerry said, "Hiya Jack. Long time, no see."

Sheriff Jack looked back and forth between us, "Well if it isn't the investigation firm of Beauty and the Beast. Imagine that— Minxy working for a salty dog like you."

Jerry said, "I have no idea what you said. I can't hear."

Having read Jack's lips, I cleared my throat and said, "Respectfully, I work *with* Jerry, not *for* him. It took him a while to accept it, but it's settled now."

Jack passed on the bourbon but accepted a cup of black coffee. We sat awkwardly quiet around the table. Finally, he said, "Care to tell me about the gun shots and why this looks like a stakeout?"

We shared a look, and I answered, "The guy who robbed me and hurt my dog, came back. We thought he might. We were ready for him."

Jack shook his head, "And why didn't you call us?"

"I think you said, 'why didn't we call you.' If there'd been a police presence, he would have waited until you couldn't waste the manpower anymore."

"Did you hit him?"

"No blood anywhere so I missed. Well, none tonight, anyway. Your guys have the sample from when my dog bit him earlier today. Once that's processed, we'll all know who this guy is."

"So, you couldn't see his face?"

"Wore a hat and a gaiter."

"Any chance of fingerprints?"

"No. Just like when he broke in earlier, he wore gloves."

Jack looked at me and I could tell he was not buying my story. Finally, he said, "You know a whole lot more about this than you're telling me."

Smiling, I said, "I can't hear you."

He nodded but I could tell he knew I was not giving up who I thought the guy was. Glancing at the documents scattered across the table, he focused on the three security reports for the Iranian American plant workers. "What's going on with the nuke facility? Aren't you working the murder case?"

Curling up on the banquette, my legs tucked under me, I said, "We are. It's taken a few twists and turns, but I think we're close to naming the killer of Jennifer Albrecht. That's why the guy broke in to steal my evidence and then came back to kill me."

He whistled. "That's some high stakes stuff. You agree with her Jerry?" Jack pointed at the documents my partner was reviewing. "This somehow links up with Iranian Americans at a nuclear power plant?"

Jerry lowered his head and looked up at Jack over his reading glasses. "You talking about the threat to the nuke facility? If so, this is the craziest shit I've ever seen. We're onto something big."

Jack nodded and sipped his coffee. He was clearly gathering the right words to say something significant, so I waited. Finally, he said, "With all that went on tonight, and after burying Albrecht yesterday, I need to know what's going on."

"Jack, I'll tell you soon. I promise. There's one last piece of evidence. It'll be the proof linking the killer to both murders."

He cocked his head my way and asked, "Did you say *both murders*. As in plural?"

Sipping from my bourbon tumbler bought me time to decide how much to share. "Yes, I did. This is way bigger than Jenn's murder. Do you have a relationship with the local FBI field office?"

Jack said, "Yes ma'am, I do. The FBI shows up real fast whenever I catch their bad guys." He said it so loud and distinctly, even Jerry heard him.

"Well get ready to call them. By happy hour tonight this thing will be over."

Thirty-One

TUESDAY, JUNE 27, WEST BEACH, MD

About 4:00 a.m. the break-in after party was winding down. The deputies who had responded to the incident were leaving. The officers had taken photos of the backdoor and gate locks, Ricky's discarded gun, my shots at Ricky that had ruined a first edition of *Uncle Tom's Cabin*, the flashbang casing, and my burned rug. They confirmed the assailant left no finger or footprints.

Jerry had left earlier after Jack called for a marked county car to be posted outside my house. The officer was told to stay until 8:00 p.m.

Jack asked, "That will be about when happy hour wraps up, right?"

I smiled. "That's right. I stand by my promise. This is done by happy hour."

"So, you suspect the guy who broke in twice here was the same guy who also killed your neighbor and someone else. That's either great detective work or pretty crazy."

I took a deep breath and gave Jack a mysterious smile.

He continued, "And you knew he'd come back and didn't call me."

My hearing was almost back to normal. "You want me to tell you who it is, but I can't. Not yet. The blood sample from this afternoon will prove who broke in. When it comes back from the lab, you'll have the name. Everything else is circumstantial. It wouldn't get you a warrant to search for evidence of the other murder. I don't need one."

I looked at Jack sitting in the chair across from me, drinking coffee. He appeared comfortable hanging out in my kitchen in the early morning hours, and didn't seem ready to leave. I knew I was right when he put his hand over mine, and said, "Don't break the law Minxy. I can't help you if you do."

The extent of his intimacy wasn't lost on me. It was obvious in a lot of macro and micro ways. If Theo wasn't in my life, Jack Frye would make an excellent suitor. Resting my free hand on his, I said "My plan is legal. It'll get the evidence one hundred percent above board. And then, I can give it to you to clear my client."

Checking his watch, he stood reluctantly, "I love seeing an innocent man go free. Just..." he gazed into my eyes, "be careful."

"Always. Let me walk you out." Taking his arm in mine, I walked him to the front door. "Thanks for coming."

Jack started to say something more but thought better of it. He pulled a business card and pen out of his pocket, wrote his personal cell on the back, then handed it to me. "My spider sense tells me you'll need me later today. Just call."

"Expect that call."

IT WAS TOO late to sleep, and no way was I going running with a target on my back. Ricky knew I would be coming for him, and he also knew I hadn't told the police his name. They'd have been at his door if I had. I needed to finish this case as fast as possible. That meant getting Cunningham's tea mug and stopping Ricky from sabotaging the power plant. With me still alive, he might consider blowing the reactor as his last option.

The phone rang, startling me. I rummaged through the piles of documents on my kitchen table and found my cell.

It was Celia. "Minxy, I found it. I came in early and dug out the old poisoning case we were talking about."

"Excellent, but before you tell me, how's Magoo?"
She chuckled, "He was none too pleased staying with Auntie Celia, but he eventually fell asleep at the foot of my bed. I walked him, gave him his pain pill, and left out food and water."

"Thanks for taking care of him. Things got wild here last night. He'd have gotten hurt."

"What happened?"

"Don't worry. No one's bleeding. Ricky broke in but got away. At happy hour I'll tell you the whole story. What about the poison?"

"That's going to be some cocktail story. It was in Belgium, not Austria. Anyway, a Russian KGB agent, Natalia Rostikova, killed an expat journalist in Brussels using a cocktail of oleander and foxglove in tea. The file says the poison makes the tea a little bitter, but milk cuts the sharp taste. Add sugar too, and it's virtually undetectable. Causes a major heart attack within a couple of hours. The journalist drank the tea in the morning and was dead by noon."

My pulse sped up. I put Celia on speaker and rummaged through the photos on my phone until I found the ones of Ricky's garden. "What does foxglove look like?" I asked.

She said, "Tall spikes of bell-shaped flowers. Usually pinks and white."

"Got it. I know oleander—long leaves and more pink and white flowers, five petals."

Celia said, "That's right."

"Well, I'm looking at a photo of the two plants thriving in Ricky's backyard."

"Circumstantial."

"That's why I need that mug. I want to get him for both murders. Ricky gave Cunningham spiked tea at their morning meeting. The boss was heading to the morgue by 1:30 p.m. when I was surveilling his wife."

"His Qods Force handler would know about that poison. They may have told him to do it." She cleared her throat. "It's time to call the FBI or at least the Sheriff."

"Sheriff Jack came by last night. I told him I'd let him know by happy hour. I need the teacup. With it, we've got proof. Even Ricky's blood from the dog bite might not be enough for a Cunningham murder search warrant."

Celia's voice went up an octave. "Tell me you aren't going to break into the nuclear power plant and steal the teacup."

"Celia, please, I'm not stealing anything..."

<hr>

TUESDAY, JUNE 27, SOLOMONS, MD

About 7:00 a.m. I called Andrew Cunningham's widow to see if she was home. I wanted to surprise her in person, not on the phone, but didn't want to waste the drive if she wasn't there. She picked up on the third ring, saying, "Hello. This is Barbara."

I started speaking fluent French asking for Jean-Claude. Mrs. Cunningham was apologetic and said, "I think you have the wrong number." It was helpful to know she was polite to total strangers. That would come in handy for what I had planned.

I sped south on Route 4 toward Solomons on a cloud-covered morning that threatened rain. I had spent my entire life influencing people. From my self-absorbed parents to the disinterested household staff who raised me, I had to work hard to get what I needed. Thanks to my study of Jackie Kennedy, I got very good at it. One of my earliest lessons was, people hate to say no to your face. 'No,' can easily turn to 'yes' with the proper encouragement. That understanding of human nature was at the core of today's plan. Barbara Cunningham had no reason to trust me, a total stranger, but I was pretty sure I'd get her to give me that tea mug.

Soon I was parking in front of the Cunningham home. I had dressed in 'no nonsense' clothes—black long pants and a tucked white shirt under a blue blazer like an FBI agent in the movies. I'd added aviator sunglasses as the final touch. If Barbara thought I was a G-Woman, so much the better for me. I knocked at the door, and she answered quickly.

Holding my credentials in my palm, I said, "Hello, you're Mrs. Barbara Cunningham, correct?" I stood as erect as possible and projected authority that I certainly didn't have.

Barbara leaned against the door jam, behind the storm door, using it as a protective barrier. "I am. Do I know you?"

I looked at her through my aviators and decided to use my given name, because as Celia had warned me long ago, people expect security people to be conservative. "No, ma'am. I'm Marnie Banks." Flipping my creds faster than ever, I slapped them back together and in my pocket in about a second. "I have information about your husband's death that you'll want to know."

Barbara's head snapped to the side. "Information? Andy had a heart attack. What could you add to that?"

"May I come in ma'am?" I reached for the storm door handle and let my hand rest on it, waiting for an invitation from Barbara.

The woman hesitated. For a moment I worried she wouldn't open the door. Then her head bobbed just a bit, and she unlocked it. "Of course, please come in."

She motioned me into the living room. It was cozy with overstuffed chairs, dark mahogany tables, and lots of family pictures on the wall. Apparently in addition to the daughter that I had seen the day of Cunningham's death, there were two boys, one older and one younger than the girl. I saw Andrew and Barbara standing side by side at a dress-up event of some kind. I took a moment to linger over the photos, while Barbara turned on an antique brass table lamp. She motioned me toward a chair. I sat on the edge of the seat, my elbows on my knees. "Mrs. Cunningham..."

"Please, call me Barbara. May I get you anything? Water? Coffee?"

"No thank you, Barbara. I want to share something with you. If I was you, I'd want to know."

Her hands were neatly stacked in her lap, her back stiffly pressed against the sofa. "What are you investigating Ms..."

"Marnie. The death of Jennifer Albrecht. I've found something that links her death to your husband's."

The shock was instantaneous. "Really? How could that be? Didn't that Marine stab her in the West Beach park?"

"The police *allege* he killed her. He didn't do it, and I'm close to proving it was someone else." I took a moment before I spoke, which focused Barbara's attention completely on me. "Barbara, I believe the man who murdered Ms. Albrecht also murdered your husband."

She went so pale that I worried she might faint. "*What?* He had a heart attack. He wasn't *murdered.*"

"Ma'am, you don't look okay. Can I get you some water?"

Her eyes were tracking something on the carpet that didn't exist, lost in her imagination, thinking about what I had just said. She didn't notice that I went to the kitchen and returned with a glass of water until I pressed it into her hand. She looked up, confused, and said, "Oh. Thank you."

"No problem." I sat beside her on the sofa and rubbed her

back to comfort her just like Astrid would do. When I thought she was past the initial shock, I said, "It's hard to believe people we know could hurt us, but I can prove it to you. If you help me, we can catch your husband's killer."

She turned toward me, looking pensive and said, "It was strange, Andy having a heart attack. I mean, he was the only man we knew in his fifties that wasn't taking heart medicine. The doctor had been amazed at his low blood pressure."

Minxy nodded. "I believe he was poisoned. A coworker drugged his tea at the office. Have you collected his belongings from the plant yet?"

"No, I was too busy with the funeral."

"Would you go with me to retrieve that tea mug? If I'm right, the residue will prove he was murdered, and the killer's finger-prints will be on it."

She shook her head in disbelief. "What if you're wrong?"

"No harm done. I'll have helped you do something that you shouldn't do alone."

Barbara smiled, "Why are you doing this?"

"It helps free an innocent man, but most of all it catches the killer. That man's killed two people. It's personal for both of us. Jenn Albrecht was my neighbor." The next words caught in my throat for a moment, but I got them out. "She was a decent woman."

Barbara's backbone straightened with her resolve. "Let's go, Marnie. I took Andy's badge when I identified his body at the morgue. It should help us get around after the guards let us in."

Smiling, I said, "Why don't you call me Minxy. It's a nick-name, but that's what everyone calls me."

Thirty-Two

Barbara changed clothes while I paced around the living room looking at her photos. Pulling out my phone I took a snapshot of a particularly good picture of Andrew and Barbara. There would be time later to think about my epiphany.

When she reappeared, she was dressed in a skort and collared shirt that she wore with her deck shoes. Her smile made her seem game to do this, but closer observation showed her hands trembling so badly she was holding them together to hide it. Helping her lock up, I insisted we take my Aston Martin.

The drive from the Cunningham house to the Calvert Cliffs Nuclear Power Plant was about fifteen minutes. Barbara and I chatted about her past as I built rapport.

I asked, "This may seem random, but did your husband chew gum?"

"Absolutely. It was a habit he picked up when he quit smoking."

I nodded.

At one point she grew quiet, and I asked if she was alright.

She said, "Have you ever been told you look like Jackie Kennedy? In her younger days when her hair was shorter."

"Yes, ma'am. I always take it as a compliment. She's my hero."

"Mine, too. When I was burying Andrew, I thought how brave she was at Jack's funeral. The whole world was watching. If she could do it, so could I."

"Same for me. At both my mother's and father's funerals, all I thought about was what would Jackie do." I didn't mention how hard Father's funeral was. His brokerage firm was on the hundred and second floor of the World Trade Center North Tower. On that fateful day in September, Flight 11 crashed into the building between the ninety-third and ninety-ninth floors. He called me after the impact, but I was in class that morning and had the ringer off. He left a message that still breaks my heart when I listen to it. In the end, I arranged his bodiless funeral. I was twenty-one years old and swore I'd join the CIA and catch the men who did that to us.

Rolling to a stop next to two security officers, we showed our drivers' licenses. "Oh, good morning Mrs. Cunningham," the older guard said. "I am so sorry for your loss. Your husband was a good man." He radioed the front desk and wrote up a parking slip with his thick felt tip marker to place on my dashboard. It allowed us to park in the Site Vice President's reserved spot.

We walked down the sidewalk with pairs of two-story red poles with lights on the top. The Administration Building was obviously a new upgrade to the older facility. It was two stories tall and Scandinavian modern in its clean lines and glossy materials. We walked in the door to find an open airy lobby with security at the back, behind the symbol of an atom with a seashell in the middle. The Scandinavian theme carried into the interior. The walls were covered in four-by-four-inch white tiles floor to ceiling. The carpet was corporate plaid in a gray beige color that I'm told is now called greige. All the furnishings and the exposed heating and cooling pipes were primary colors. The vibe was friendly and open.

In industry, senior leaders get top-shelf treatment, so the widow of the Site Vice President was welcomed with dignity. Barbara was accustomed to this treatment. She told them politely that she was there to pick up her husband's effects. We watched everyone scramble to take care of her.

Barbara had wanted to call ahead, but I had stopped her. I didn't want Ricky getting wind of our visit. He knew I'd try something, but I was pretty sure he wouldn't expect this. He'd keep thinking the nuke plant was a Minxy-free zone.

The Asian female at the security desk apologized to Barbara. "New policy, Mrs. Cunningham, we'll have to escort you and your friend. Sorry but it's our new access protocol." Turning her attention to me, she looked suspicious. "Ma'am, what was your name again."

"Marnie Banks, here to support Barbara. You can imagine how difficult all of this has been on the family." I handed over my driver's license again.

The guard nodded reflexively while she prepared our visitors' badges with a great big V on them. "Yes, ma'am, of course I know this has been hard. Just one moment."

Barbara glanced at me like a co-conspirator as she slipped Andrew's badge back into her purse, then watched the woman make a quick phone call and hang up. "Mr. Cunningham's Executive Assistant, Clara, is on her way. She can escort you anywhere you need to go. She has complete access to the plant because of her role with your husband."

While we waited, I politely chatted with the armed security guard standing by the desk. The guy had the biggest gun I'd seen in a while and plenty of clips stored on his bulletproof vest. He looked like a counterterrorism SWAT member. I was glad he was on our side and wanted to keep him that way.

A pert young woman arrived, tearing me away from my appreciation of the security at this facility. She was in her late twenties wearing a full skirt fitted at the waist and a tucked in T-shirt. She went straight to Barbara and hugged her. "I'm so sorry for your loss Mrs. Cunningham. Your husband was the best boss ever. I can only imagine what your family is going through."

Barbara nodded graciously, "Sorry about not giving you notice. Minxy offered to come with me to get his things. It was a spontaneous idea."

My hand out, I said, "Minxy Banks. Friend of Barbara's."

We followed the athletic young woman, who was probably an avid soccer player from the calf muscles and bounce in her step. We rode the elevator to the second floor. Clara held out her hand for us to go left and down the full length of the hallway. The executive level was slightly fancier than the lower floors, but no Manhattan executive corridor like my father's had been.

"Andrew Cunningham" was engraved on the plaque next to the metal door painted a rather delightful blue at the end of the hall. We entered the waiting room, appointed with two sleek leather sofas in one corner, with a stylish metal and glass table and lamp between them. News magazines were neatly stacked. The wrapper of Clara's power bar breakfast was evident on her desk.

Clara took Barbara's hand and said, "I'm afraid it's a mess in there. I locked his door and haven't let anyone in since the EMTs came for him. I figured we'd get his personal things to you when you were ready."

"Thank you, dear."

I asked, "Has anyone tried to get in there? An employee..."

"A few, but I'm the only one with the key. It doesn't open with the access card."

That made me smile. Cunningham hadn't trusted the access system either.

Clara dug in her purse until she found the key with the tag saying 'Boss's Office'. She unlocked and pushed open the door.

The room was spacious and appropriately executive. Another metro sofa and table sat under the plate glass window, with a very fine view of a pine forest. Andrew's desk faced that window from across the room. There were plaques on the wall, and a case of memorabilia. I turned on the light to brighten the room; only time could fix the stale air.

Barbara remained at the door, unable to make herself come any closer to the site of her husband's death.

Analyzing what I saw, I suspected Andrew had been at his desk when the heart attack hit. From all the papers and the laptop on the floor by the left side of the desk, he must have fallen that way sweeping them along with him. Had he stood to go for help or tumbled from his seat, too weak for anything more? The EMTs or Clara had pushed his desk chair into the corner to get closer to the body. A large ceramic mug sat prominently on the right side of the desk next to a landline phone.

Clara leaned sheepishly against the wall, with her hands clasped in front of her. She looked ready to assist but unsure of what to do. She said, "Mrs. Cunningham, I heard him fall and call out. I went straight to him. He was rubbing his chest and left shoulder, and all the way down his arm. I called 911 and tried to make him comfortable until they came." She stared at her feet, then whispered, "It was too late."

Tears slipped down Barbara's cheek, but her voice was strong. "Thank you for your kindness, Clara."

I gauged that we'd endured more than enough sentimentality. It was time to get on with the real business of the visit. I placed my hand on Clara's shoulder and said, "You've been wonderful. May I ask you some questions?"

"Of course."

"Who brought him the tea the day he died? And is that the same mug on his desk?"

She seemed relieved she'd gotten questions she could answer. "Oh, that was Ricky Domingo. He and Mr. Cunningham had tea together every morning during their coordination meeting. Always at 7:30. That's his mug. I haven't touched anything in the office." She blushed. "It was too hard to come in where he'd died and all."

"Thank you. Why don't you find a box for Barbara. She can look around for what she needs to take home." I pulled out a folded reusable shopping bag from my purse. "We'll start gathering the smaller mementos." I steered Clara out the door.

Barbara had turned very white. I positioned myself to catch her if she dropped on me. I asked, "Are you okay?"

"No, but that's just the way it is now." She stared at the mug on the desk understanding now that it might be a murder weapon. It read 'Hangin' ten in Haleiwa' and there was a picture of a stylized surfer on it. She said softly, "One of the boys bought him that when we vacationed in Hawaii."

I took a photo of the scene, and then a couple of close ups of the mug. Photographing the insides, I saw dregs in the bottom that had dried out over the days since its last use. Just as I was pondering chain of custody, the use of latex gloves I'd gotten from Jerry, and where to store the evidence, I heard a male voice in the waiting room say, "Mrs. Cunningham, I heard you were here and wanted to..."

Ricky appeared in the doorway. He came full stop when he saw me standing by the mug. We both knew that his fingerprints and traces of poison would be on it. He also knew I'd figured out the poison came from plants in his backyard. It was an awkward situation when a killer and the person chasing him have a meeting of the minds in a public place. In private, he'd have tried to kill me. Here, he was stuck wishing he could kill me.

So much for the myth of a Minxy-free zone.

He shook his head to clear it, then said, "I wanted to extend my condolences to you, Mrs. Cunningham. Your husband was a fine man."

"You're Ricky, right? I met you at the funeral. Andrew talked about you frequently." Her expression darkened. Then she said, "That young woman, Clara said you brought the tea to Andy the morning he died. Is that true?"

"Yes, ma'am. It is. There's no denying it. Not now." He turned to me. "Howdy, Minxy."

"Back at you, Ricky."

His eyes locked onto mine, and I would not blink first. Eventually he looked away. "Well, just wanted to say hello and see if I could get that mug as a remembrance of Andy. I reckon that's not happenin'. I'll be goin' now. I've got a lot to do." He spun on his heel and left so fast it could only mean one thing. He knew the jig was up and had a Plan B.

Thirty-Three

I nodded at the tea mug. "Stay with this but don't touch it. Don't let anyone except the Sheriff or his officers take it from you. Don't leave it for a second."

She was shaken, knowing that she'd been talking with her husband's killer, but nodded that she understood.

Then I added, "And give me Andrew's access badge."

She rummaged in her handbag for it while I pulled Sheriff Jack's business card out of my pocket. She handed the access card to me, and I gave her Jack's business card. "This is the Sheriff's personal cell number. Call him now. Tell him we came for the mug that Ricky Domingo used to kill your husband with poisoned tea. *Tell him that Minxy Banks needs him and the cavalry ASAP.* Have you got all that?"

Barbara repeated, "Ricky poisoned Andrew. We have the mug. You need him and the cavalry ASAP. I'll tell him. And you think he'll believe me?"

"Mention my name and he'll believe anything." Placing the card in her palm, I turned and ran through the door.

When he was leaving, Ricky had bumped into Clara who was returning with the empty box. She appeared confused by the ruckus.

I asked, "Where's Domingo's office?"

She gave me a room number on the first floor, and I told her to lock Barbara and herself in the inner office. "Promise you'll stay there with her until the Sheriff's people come." Over my shoulder I yelled to her, "Above all, don't let in Ricky Domingo."

Clara put her hand to her mouth but did what I'd said to do.

I raced to the elevator. The doors closed before I could get there. I was pounding the button so hard I cracked the plastic cover. When the car finally returned, I pushed the button and tried to calm my breathing on the trip down.

When I arrived at the first floor, there was no one on the long, industrial greige carpet. Each door on this floor was made of metal and painted a primary color. I couldn't detect a pattern, but the numbers and names beside the doors took care of that. I checked them for the number Clara had given me as I jogged by.

Near the end of the hallway, I reached Ricky's office confirmed by Domingo on the name placard. The door was locked but I used Cunningham's access badge on the card reader and the door clicked open. There was no one in the anteroom where I would expect a secretary to be. I went down a hall by three small offices before I found Ricky's larger one. He wasn't at his desk, but there was another door. It was locked, and I opened it.

On the other side of the door were racks of servers and cubbies and a band of techies hard at work. I walked swiftly by them without anyone challenging me and slid along the wall to a corner and peeked around it. A burly man with arm-sleeve tattoos was sitting with his back to me at a cubical desk, his access badge was in the holder on the keyboard. He was typing steadily with his ear buds in, so I surprised him when he saw me.

"Who are you?" he blurted.

"Where's Ricky Domingo?"

The man was winding up to give me the third degree, but the seriousness of my expression gave him second thoughts. My national security wardrobe probably helped, too. He said, "I wish I knew. Ricky missed our morning meeting."

Pulling out my creds and flipping them so fast no living human could have read them, I said, "Look, where would he be if he wanted to damage this plant with a computer virus."

"Whoa. You're the FB freakin' I." He kind of froze for a second and then was on board. "He might go to the IT office in the reactors building. Maybe."

Not correcting him about the FBI, I said, "Come with me buddy. Show me that room."

I URGED the IT man to run, which was not a common thing for him. We headed out of the administration building and into the building around the base of the reactors. "Buddy run faster."

"I'm Bryce. My name is Bryce," he barked out between ragged breathes, "and I'm doing the best I can."

Bryce badged through the outer security door, and when I saw guards in the distance, I ripped off my visitor badge and slipped on Cunningham's lanyard around my neck—picture facing toward me. We breezed by the heavily armed security detail who asked, "What's the emergency?"

I yelled, "No time. If you see Ricky Domingo, detain him."

The hallway had the same greige carpet as the administration building, but the walls were all painted off-white. We entered an enormous room above the turbines. It was hot and rumbled with the power of the giant machines spinning. Bryce led me through several turns in the warren of hallways, until he stopped before a door that said, 'IT Reactor Services.' He badged in, then took the step up into a small room with a couple of standing workstations and a long worktable covered with engineering schematics. Two dozen lockers were mounted on one wall with names on them. The ceiling housed industrial strength lights that made the white paint on the walls almost glow.

One of the workstations was operated by a bearded man in his forties, swarthy like his family came from somewhere around the Mediterranean. Exasperated by our invasion, he yelled, "What's going on here?"

Bryce was recovering from the run, so I said, "We're looking for Ricky Domingo. Where is he?"

The man shook his head, "He just came through here running like you two. Didn't say anything, just went to his cubby, unlocked it, and took a laptop with him when he ran out."

"Where'd he go?"

"I don't know, but he was in as big a hurry as you guys."

I asked, "How many rooms in this building?"

"More than I've ever counted."

Taking a deep breath, I said, "Can you see who's logged onto the system?"

"Sure."

Bryce was able to talk again and said, "There's several hundred employees here."

I checked the men's badges. Both were administrators. "How many have administrative rights like you do?"

"Maybe a dozen."

"One of you bring up the administrators and find Ricky."

The bearded man nodded in appreciation of the strategy. He was already logged into the system, so he did the search. The list of thirteen popped up, identifying the locations of all who were logged into the system.

Checking the names, I found Ricky. "This says he's logged in on the first floor of the admin building. He wasn't there."

Bryce said, "He might have doubled back."

Shaking my head, I said, "No. He wouldn't have needed a laptop if he was going back to his office.

Bryce asked, "You can't log into two computers at once. How's he going to log into the new computer if he's still logged into the admin building one?"

"He has a fake badge and has given that one administrative rights as well," I said, because it was obvious that access issues had been part of his plan. "Look at the other names. Any you don't recognize?"

In a low baritone the bearded man said, "There's a name I've never seen. Darius Nassari. That badge registers from the big machine shop in this building."

I thought for only a second. The answer was obvious. "That's him. He's leaving his calling card for the investigators who come after the attack. Take me there."

Bryce said, "Attack?

I didn't answer.

The bearded man said, "Can't. Ricky changed the control system so that only senior executives have access to that space. Ricky has it but not us. New policy."

Pulling off the Cunningham lanyard, I checked the man's name on his badge and then handed Andy's to him. "Carlo, check if Andrew Cunningham's badge still works."

Carlo preened when I called him by his name and did as I requested with a shy smile. He tried his dead senior boss's badge in his card holder. Touching it seemed to have jolted him. He was getting caught up in what possibly was the only excitement he'd seen in months. Adjusting his glasses, he leaned into the computer screen, and said, "It's been turned off. A few minutes ago."

I smiled at him, "Turn it back on."

Thirty-Four

I took the reactivated badge and tried it on the door. It worked. "We need to get to Ricky."

Bryce wanted no more running, so he logged into one of the computers and told Carlo to help me. "Carlo knows the building better than I do. He'll take you to the room where Nassari's logged on." He handed Carlo and me walkie-talkies for communications. The thick cement in the building limited cell coverage.

I clipped the device onto my belt. "First, dial up your Command Center. I need to talk with them."

Bryce cast me a long, side-eyed look that explained no one just called the Command Center. He saw I was serious and did what I'd told him.

"Calvert Cliffs Command Center, Shift Manager Westman speaking. How may I help you?"

I tried to sound my most authoritative when I said, "Officer Westman. You have a problem. You can't trust any digital system. Darius Nassari is initiating a cyber-attack on your reactors. You can prove I'm telling the truth by verifying he is logged in as an administrator. You won't find anyone by that name on your employment roster."

"Who are you?"

I didn't answer, asking him another question instead. "If you're uncertain about your reactors' safety, is your protocol to shut them down?"

"Why are you asking that? Who are you?" His voice was getting more strident. Sensing their leader's distress, the background noise of the watch went silent.

I said slowly, emphasizing each word, "Answer the question."

"Yes. If we aren't certain about safety, we shut them down."

"You've got me, who you don't know, calling from a telephone in the reactors building. I'm warning you about an attack on the reactors. Darius Nassari is logged into your system as an administrator. That's a lot of uncertainty about security. *Please do your job*." I hung up.

I could see Carlo was impressed, "That took nerve. Let's go, lady. I'll take you to the machine shop."

We checked the radio frequency with Bryce, as we headed toward Ricky. Bryce agreed he'd call Shift Manager Westman to help him position plant security and get the Sheriff's people brought through to us.

Carlo led the way down the maze of hallways with endless metal doors painted blue on either side. I stopped trying to remember the route after the fourth turn. Focusing on what I would do when I found Ricky, I wished I had a gun. My mind went through the range of possible improvised weapons I might find here. I was hoping for a screwdriver. Preferably a Philip's head. That would have to be good enough. All I needed to do was slow him down until the Shift Manager shut down the plant and Jack arrived.

The reactor building reminded me of being below deck in a cargo ship. It was clean and well-scrubbed but had the same smell of grease and the feel of claustrophobia. As we ran down the hall-ways, I was steeling myself for my confrontation with Ricky. I was thinking about what Jackie would do. She'd distract him from what he was doing to buy time.

Finally, Carlo stopped in front of a door like so many others, but with a plaque saying 'Engineering and Monitoring.' He whispered, "This is it. Let's go."

Shaking my head, I told him. "Sheriff Frye and plant security will be here any minute. You need to get plant security and him through this door. Keep it open. Stay in touch with Bryce on the ETA of the Sheriff and his people and get them inside."

"ETA?"

"Estimated Time of Arrival."

Begrudgingly he watched me disappear inside.

THE ENGINEERING ROOM was a large open floor workspace with machines but no people because of Ricky's lockout. It had two supervisory offices along one wall. The other wall had an amazing view of the Chesapeake Bay. The room seemed to be the place where workers modified and tried out pieces of equipment before installing them in the plant. A few machines hummed with life; the rest were off. I stopped to listen for Ricky over the machinery's hum. Nothing for a moment, and then I heard the tapping of computer keys in one of the offices. Hugging the wall, I moved silently toward the sound.

A quick glance around the door jam, and I saw Ricky at a desk, working on a laptop. His lanyard with the fake access card was in the computer slot. He kept muttering to himself and cursing.

I sat down across the desk from him.

"Well look who's here. Minxy Banks, the weed gardener. The

woman who tends all the weeds in West Beach. Have I made your list of misfits?"

"I don't know what you're talking about."

"Come on. You do. That woman with all the jewelry. The crunchy Danish yoga gal. Those annoyin' teenagers." He stopped for a beat and then appeared perplexed, "How'd you get in here?"

"We reactivated Cunningham's access badge."

"Remind me to fire the traitor who did that."

I playfully said, "I hate to deliver bad news, but you won't be working here much longer."

He mirrored my mood, eyes twinkling, almost flirtatious. "I suppose not."

"So, your real name...your Persian name, is Darius Nassari."

That took him aback. His eyes softened and he paused typing for a moment. "It's been a long time since I've heard it spoken out loud."

"Darius, it's nice to meet the real you. Tell me about killing Jenn Albrecht."

"Surely, you've figured it out by now. It's simple if you know I'm Iranian, which you clearly do."

"Humor me. I'm still trying to puzzle out why she met you in the park. She couldn't have known she was meeting you. She'd figured you out."

"Nope, of course not. She was all thrilled with huntin' me and fell for a scam. Catchin' me was her higher purpose. She'd even talked to our nosy old neighbor in Houston and linked my ring to Iran. I had to stop her."

"So, you distorted your voice and told her you were FBI."

He looked at me, "Speaking of FBI, you look like you came here from Quantico. Did the guards believe you?"

"I would never lie about being law enforcement."

Ricky said, "Well, I did, and it worked great. Jenn fell for it. I said our DC office had learned she was investigatin' the sleeper agent Ricky Domingo. We didn't want her ruinin' our case."

"Then you appealed to her ego. Told her you needed her evidence and her help."

"Yes, ma'am, I did. Worked like a charm."

I had to keep him talking. I tried to look my most curious and asked, "Why the park so late at night? You could have broken into her house, killed her and taken the papers."

"I thought about it. But I'd have to spend time huntin' down all her evidence. It was easier to let her bring it to me."

"Why not a place farther from town. Maybe a business park?"

"Familiarity. I'd been surveilling her since Andy started visiting. That time of night, the park was nice and empty. I wouldn't have to drive a car that would get picked up on CCTV. Lots of dark spots the gazebo camera didn't reach."

"As one pro to another, kudos. It was a good clandestine meeting spot. It even made Jenn feel safe. Why didn't she shoot you when she saw it was a ruse?"

"I called her and said I was already at the park. I'd insisted she walk so I could follow and check for someone tailin' her. She was standin' there all confused about where I was when I came through the bushes behind her. By the time she saw me, it was too late."

"And then there was the Andrew Cunningham problem."

He nodded. "After Albrecht was gone, I knew I had to kill Andy, too. He knew too much. She got him all whipped up about Iranian spies during that exercise. I knew from my handler that she'd been looking at Iranian Americans in all the nuke plants."

"So how did they get onto you?"

"Cunningham asked me about that issue in my security report when he hired me. When the others washed out, he must have mentioned my case to her. They were meeting all secret like at her house."

"Why didn't you kill him the morning after Jenn? Why wait a day?"

"You know why. My handler said the best way to kill him was poison. I had to check how the police responded to finding her body, so I was late to work and missed our morning meeting where I brought the tea."

"So that next day he knew about you, but went through the motions of having a morning meeting?"

"Yup. He didn't know I'd been surveilling them. Since the guy she thought was FBI killed her, he was trying to figure out who to talk to. He thought he had time. Andy's death was on her. This attack's on her, too."

"I told the Command Center about your attack. They're closing down the reactors."

"What makes you think they believed you?"

"I can be very convincing."

"Yeah, I suppose you can. They think they're closin' 'em down. Their gauges don't report properly."

"Stuxnet code?"

"Of course. America deserves to see it in action. I'm almost done dismantlin' the rest of the fail safes. You plannin' to stop me by yourself?"

"Yes."

He laughed and went back to typing in code. He didn't look up when he added, "The wind's perfect today. Blowin' from the southeast. I'll get D.C."

I channeled all the Jackie Kennedy poise I could muster to keep from reacting. In my quiet, almost Jackie voice I asked. "Ricky, why? I know Qods Force groomed you to do this, but you could have said no. You had a fantastic life here."

His smile was rueful. "Blood's thicker than fake citizenship. I guess I'm one of your weeds. I never belonged here."

We both nodded. I stood, then slowly took a step toward him.

"Stop Minxy. I don't wanna hurt you."

"But you do. Have you already forgotten last night?" I had to stop his typing, even if only for a little while.

"You shot at me. I didn't think you had it in you."

"You don't know me all that well."

"Well, that was then, this is now. I didn't ask you to come."

Ricky outweighed me by eighty pounds. I could try fancy jujitsu moves, but he was probably trained in hand-to-hand combat, too. I only had one effective play. I grabbed his access badge and ran from the room.

Thirty-Five

TUESDAY, JUNE 27, LUSBY, MD

My gambit took Ricky by surprise. I was out the door and running to the other office before he could react. When he launched, he closed in on me fast.

I used his card to badge into the other supervisor's office. The door was pneumatic, and I pushed it to hurry its closing. Before it shut, he grabbed the handle and pushed hard with a shoulder. I threw my weight into it, but it wasn't enough. I jumped out of the way before the door crashed open.

My heart raced as I dove into a connecting room and slammed the wooden door. It wasn't pneumatic so it shut fast. Without an access card Ricky couldn't open it. My interfering with Ricky's goal to gut punch America had him furious. He hit the metal door hard with his fists and screamed in frustration.

As he began kicking the door, I searched the room for options. It was an office. Desk and chair. No window. Only one door. *Trapped.*

I scanned the room for something, anything, to use as a weapon. All the while Ricky was kicking hard, and the door was weakening with each blow. I pulled my walkie-talkie off my belt, "Bryce where's security and the Sheriff?"

He answered immediately, "Security is waiting for the Sheriff, who's through the front gate. He's being directed to you."

"Tell him to hurry."

The banging on the door became fiercer. Ricky was ramming something metal against the lock. *Bam. Bam. Bam.* I saw the door jamb bend, then crack and the door gave way. Ricky fell through it growling.

I threw everything on the desk at him as a distraction to buy time. He batted each item away without notice, continuing to advance. I circled, trying to keep the desk between us. Instead of following me, he lunged across it, grabbing my throat. We tumbled into a heap on the floor. His momentum was enough to make him land hard on me, both his hands around my neck, squeezing.

He scrambled to his feet, picked me up, and held me so my feet barely touched and I was eye to eye with him. "You wanna know how Albrecht died. I'm gonna show you." He shifted my throat to the crook of his arm and pulled me out the door. My feet dragged the floor, but I couldn't get them under me. He pulled me into the workshop.

I was seeing sparks of blue, and my vision was growing dim. I clawed and scratched at him, trying to reach a soft and painful spot, but my efforts proved useless. He was strong and the gleam I'd seen in his eyes told me he was fueled by the most dangerous of intoxicants: a cause.

He walked deliberately, although I couldn't see where we were heading. As he passed machinery, he intentionally banged my body into it as he moved forward. I reached out and felt for anything I could use as a weapon on counters and benches with tools. I found a heavy wrench and tried hitting Ricky's head. In my fog I heard his laughter as he swatted it away.

Finally, he slowed, grabbed me around the waist, and threw

me onto a hydraulic hole punch bench as long as I was tall and almost as wide as a twin bed. Above my head was a massive press with circular cutting tools that punched holes in metal. The sight of those blades set off the turbo setting on my already activated survival mode. I gave it everything I had, pushing and fighting to get away. He released the pressure on my neck and shifted to holding me down with his arm over my midriff as he pressed buttons to start the machine.

I gasped in lungs full of air. He noticed my eyes clearing and smiled. It wasn't kindness. He wanted me fully awake for what was coming next—just like Jenn had been. My chest convulsed as I dragged in air as deeply as possible. He didn't feel the movement of my arm. I searched the bench for anything I could use as a weapon. I felt oily rags. Attached measuring guides. Paper-like patterns. Scraps of metal too small to use. Then my fingers felt the six sides of a pencil. I forced my fingers to grasp it, and slowly they obeyed. I held my fist close to my body so he wouldn't see it and waited for my moment.

The hole punch machine was warming up. He shifted his body and paid more attention to the control panel in an effort to speed the process. The pressure pinning me down diminished.

My eyes sought Ricky's carotid, and my arm followed that path with the pencil. The lead point pierced his skin. I pushed harder to embed it as far as possible.

I didn't wonder for long if I'd hit my mark. Blood geysered from the wound. Ricky pulled away, releasing me.

I didn't hesitate. I rolled off the hole punch table, hitting the floor hard on my hands and knees not far from Ricky. Getting to my feet, I saw Ricky was wide-eyed in disbelief. He started pulling out the pencil, and I felt a rush of sympathy for him. "Don't do it. Keep that in. It's slowing the bleeding."

What was wrong with me. I shook my head to clear it. *Why*

was I caring about the person who almost killed me? Oh Maya, this therapy has gone too far.

Ricky roared in disbelief and frustration. He stepped back from the pneumatic machine, now slamming its razor-sharp blades down against the workbench where I had been moments before. I moved unsteadily backwards, putting space between me, Ricky, and the machine. My eyes met Ricky's.

He said, "What have you done? I was so close."

I leaned on an engine case. I nodded to his throat. "Put pressure on that. We can save you."

He was incredulous. Stumbling toward me, his legs gave out and he crumpled to the floor. He hitched himself upright, leaning against a cabinet door. Blood streamed down his shirt. "Only one mistake..."

I kept backing until I hit a wall. I slid down it eight or so feet from Ricky. "The ring. Without Jenn's research, I would never have put it together. The pictures of the Ayatollah's and Gen. Soleimani's rings convinced me you were Iranian. Here use this." I grabbed a towel and threw it to Ricky, who pressed it to his throat.

With effort, Ricky held his other hand up and examined the ring. "It was my only break in cover. My father had worn it all his life. It was from the Qods Force. A reminder of our purpose. A gem from the same mine as the Ayatollah's."

I nodded, "I understand."

His face was graying.

I said, "Andrew's heart attack was drug induced. From foxglove and oleander... "

"Natalia Rostikova's recipe. Foolproof. Well almost. You and your revenge gardenin'." He started a chuckle, but it brought on rattling coughs.

I pulled the walkie-talkie off my belt. "Bryce are you there?"

"Of course. You okay?"

"Yes, but Ricky needs an ambulance. Tell them to hurry. He's losing a lot of blood."

"No need; the Sheriff brought some. He isn't with you?"

I said, "No. Is he close?"

"Very. Hang in there."

Ricky was staring at me. He smiled and let out the slightest of breaths. Almost an amused chuckle. His eyes fluttered, then closed. I could see the pulse in his throat. It was weak but still beating.

Then security officers in black with huge guns crashed into the room. I heard Jack's voice from behind them, "Minxy, we're coming in. Are you armed?"

"No, I lost it in the fight."

The officers secured Ricky, but Jack headed in my direction, eyeing the pounding hole punch a few yards away. "What the Sam Hill happened here, Minxy?"

"Ricky's an Iranian operative and was trying to blow up the reactors. I stopped him, and he almost killed me on that." I pointed to the hole punch machine. "I was lucky."

Jack looked at Ricky, then took his walkie-talkie off his belt. "Get the EMTs in here stat."

He stepped carefully across the floor, avoiding the blood, then squatted in front of me. "Is that a pencil in his neck?"

My throat was damaged, and it hurt to talk. "All I had. He killed Jenn Albrecht. I've got a tea mug saved for you with traces of poison that caused his boss's heart attack. It'll have Ricky's fingerprints on it. The EA will testify Ricky brought the tea the morning he died. Ricky's also the guy who broke into my house both times. It was his blood on my floor."

He looked baffled. "*Why? Just why?*"

"It's the Iranians, Jack. Ricky was deep cover. You should call the FBI."

Still crouched beside me, he gently touched my neck. "Are

you hurt anyplace besides your throat? You're getting seriously black and blue."

"Dings all over, maybe a cracked rib or two."

The EMTs raced in, and Jack pointed at Ricky. "Him first."

Jack stood, then reached under both of my arms and lifted me to my feet. He watched to see if I was stable, then he put his arm around my shoulders and walked me out of the room. "The man at the door, Carlo, thinks you're FBI. You didn't tell him that, did you?"

I shook my head. "That would be illegal. I think he misread my creds."

"Come on, we'll get you checked out. On our way to the ambulance, could you walk me through what all this means?"

I smiled, "That's easy. It means you owe me a crab dinner. Are you going to cuff me? It was self-defense..."

He chuckled. "Nah, just *try to behave*. Where's that mug?"

"Cunningham's office in the admin building. His wife and the EA are there with it waiting for your people."

"I'll send one of the deputies to get it. I'll let the boys know they can process multiple crime scenes."

Thirty-Six

TUESDAY, JUNE 27, LUSBY, MD

Jack walked me to the back of an ambulance. A female EMT saw us coming and jumped down from the back.

She said, "You look terrible."

I said, "It's been one of those days."

She helped me up the step at the back and onto the stretcher. After checking me head to toe, back to front, she gave me a generally clean bill of health, except for my throat which would need some gargling and rest. She verified that two of my ribs probably were cracked, but said they would heal on their own with time. She had a no nonsense look when she said, "Go see your GP tomorrow. That guy banged you up pretty bad. You have bruises on top of bruises."

"Absolutely. Tomorrow I'll go to my doctor. For now, I need to get home and drink at least two martinis."

The EMT grinned. "Great idea. I think you'll be fine...in a while."

She helped me climb out of the ambulance where Jack was waiting.

"So, are you arresting me?"

"No. Like you said, it was self-defense. I'm sure the prosecutors will have tons of questions for you, but not today."

"Well then, my car's here and I gave Barbara Cunningham a ride from her house. I need to take her home."

He smiled like I'd said the most ridiculous thing he'd ever heard. "Oh no, I'm driving you home. You've been oxygen deprived. One of my deputies will follow us in your little green roadster. Believe me, they are fighting over that duty."

I probably shouldn't be driving. He had me on that one. "But Barbara…"

"I already have a deputy taking her statement and securing the mug. He's driving her home."

"But I need to thank her for her help."

"Call her when you're both home. I need a few minutes to make sure my guys have this, but then I'll be back for you. Stay here. Promise?"

"I promise."

I sat outside the entrance of the administration building on a bright orange metal bench and pulled my cell out of my pocket. I started a video chat with my high-dollar lawyer Michael Grayson in New York. He'd kept Father on the right side of the law for decades. Over the years he had kept me out of significant trouble as well.

I told him about the "incident" at the nuclear plant, and I might have used someone else's badge to access parts of the plant to stop a killer from blowing it up. Some of the people I interacted with had mistaken me for an FBI agent. The killer was now seriously injured by my hand in self-defense.

Sitting behind his ultra-modern desk and in front of some impressive abstract art, he asked, "What was the instrument you used to injure the gentleman this time?"

"A pencil, Michael. Only a pencil."

He didn't flinch. Writing it down, he nodded, and then asked, "Did you bring it with you or did you find it at the scene."

"It was a chance encounter, while stopping him from punching holes in me."

"Excellent. No premeditation. You should be fine. Oh, and flip those Private Investigator credentials a little slower, just as a habit—not that someone else's misunderstanding is your problem. Let me know if they ask leading questions that insinuate your actions weren't self-defense. Otherwise, I think you'll be fine."

"Fantastic."

After the call with Michael, I noticed I'd missed a dozen calls from Celia. I dialed her and said, "Hey girl. I'm okay."

"Everyone we know is in your house watching the fracas on TV. News helicopters show a lot of Sheriff's cars at the plant. We saw you climb into an ambulance. You stopped Ricky?"

"Yeah. The plant's secure. Ricky's hurt but the EMTs are working on him. He's in custody."

"I have a million questions..."

"Save them for happy hour. I see Jack heading this way. He's giving me a ride home."

Celia said, "The Sheriff is giving you a ride? Where's your car?"

"I'll tell you when I get home. Gotta go. Bye."

Jack held my purse under his arm like a quarterback with a football. I fished out my keys for a grinning young deputy who grabbed them and dashed to my car.

Jack walked me to the passenger door of his SUV and deposited me in the passenger seat. We headed out with lights and sirens. The Deputy trailed us out of the plant parking lot.

As we flew up Route 4, Jack said, "So, I always thought you were wasting your life running around West Beach solving gnome thefts."

I didn't look at him but smiled, "I may have heard that from more than one of my friends."

"I'm liking PI Banks way better. You used your giant brain to do a lot of good today."

"Thanks Jack. I'll be honest. It feels great."

I filled him in on the twists and turns of our investigation. He would need the documents from Jenn's office, but not today.

We parked in front of my house, and the lights and sirens brought everyone out to greet us. Celia wasn't kidding. A lot of people had showed up at my house to check on me. Jack refused my invitation to come inside, but insisted on helping me out of the car, his arm under mine for support.

Celia ran down to meet me and went in for a hug.

Jack held out a hand and stopped her. "Watch the ribs."

She patted Jack on the arm. "Oh my." She looked me over appraising my condition. "I'll take her from here, Jack. Thanks for taking care of her." The happy hour party flowed through my front door, filling the porch. They all cheered and waved goodbye to Sheriff Jack and his deputy with the giant grin, who'd parked my undamaged car in the garage. At a respectable speed, they drove off into the evening.

Celia put her arm under mine as Jack had done and walked me to the side gate and the back patio to avoid the stairs.

As I looked around the yard, I realized almost everyone I knew was in my backyard. News coverage of a threatened reactor meltdown got everyone's attention, and gossip had placed me at the scene. The cameo of me climbing into the ambulance had sealed their suspicions. West Beach remains a small town where it's hard to keep secrets, but Ricky had proved you could if you were a professional.

Jerry was talking with Lars. Walt was talking to The Miscreants. Cassie had a martini in her hand and was talking to Eli,

Danny, and his mother. I even had a quick glimpse of Sal, but he didn't hang around long. Sue was petting Mr. Magoo.

Astrid came from behind me with my martini, then sat next to me patting my arm every few minutes.

Emma appeared worried and knelt beside me. "Minxy what happened today? The nuke plant set off the emergency evacuation sirens for real. Not a test. That's never happened since I was born. TV news said it was an attack and they showed a guy on a stretcher being wheeled out."

I put my hand on Emma's and looked up at Tyler who stood behind her. "Hi Miscreants. I'm glad you're here." I raised my glass and while looking at Astrid and Celia, I said, "My voice is gone. You two explain it." I sat quietly and sipped my very fine martini.

Celia said, "Not so fast." She propped the whiteboard on the table in front of me. Astrid handed me the eraser. She said, "We thought you might like to erase this. This case is over."

Even though it hurt to lean forward, I did. I wiped every mark off but asked Celia to hand me a marker. On the blank whiteboard I wrote *Chesapeake Crime Club*. "Now tell them!"

Thirty-Seven

WEDNESDAY, JUNE 28, WEST BEACH, MD

I woke up feeling the physical aches and pains of my attack. I slipped on a silk kimono Theo had given me. He was in the front of my mind. I held the fabric to my nose and could smell his musk. It was comforting.

As I descended the stairs heading for the kitchen, I catalogued the places that were bruised, just so I'd know if I got another ding during the day. Ricky had whacked me around hard while he was dragging me through the workshop. The ribs were particularly sore, but I'd cracked one before. They would heal.

First things first. I filled Magoo's food and water bowl, pushed his pain pill into a cube of cheese, and took it back upstairs to him. Placing both on the floor by his bedroom doggy bed, I gently placed him beside them. He ate a few bites, then rolled to his tummy and drank enthusiastically. He rolled back over thumping his curly tail on the Moroccan rug.

I was ready for coffee. As I walked into my kitchen, I noticed Jenn's copy of *The Old Man and the Sea* sitting on the baker's rack. It wasn't in my office and hadn't been stolen with the rest of the evidence. While the coffee was dripping into my mug, I opened the book to the pictures that I now understood. The ones of Jenn and her former lover, Andrew Cunningham. I flipped to the front of the book. It was inscribed to Jenn with love from Andrew. She'd kept both the pictures and the gift as a secret reminder.

I compared it with the picture of Andrew and Barbara on my phone. It was the same man. Pocketing the device, I looked at Andrew and Jenn at a beach. My best guess was this photo was less old than Cunningham's oldest son. They'd had an affair. Some failed relationships linger like a scar. The wound heals, but the scar never goes away. I bet this was one of those.

The plant exercise must have stirred up old feelings. That was the reason Cunningham and Jenn were eager to meet at her house. If they'd needed privacy to talk about Ricky, they could have done that in Andrew's office.

Combine the reunion with the thrill of flushing out an Iranian spy together, and they must have been emotionally intoxicated. He'd been upstairs in Jenn's office, leaving his gum in her trash cans, including the one in her bedroom. It explained why she'd been so frazzled that she left her windows down and forgot to take her trash cans to the street. It seemed likely to explain Jenn's needing time to accept Walt's proposal.

I ripped the pictures into tiny pieces, walked to the powder room, and flushed them down the toilet. I shelved the book in the living room. Nothing useful would come from Walt or Barbara finding out there had still been a spark between those two.

I took my breakfast and coffee out to the deck. Seated on a lounger, I pulled my phone from the kimono pocket. I was eager to see what the *Washington Post* had figured out about yesterday's incident. The headline story was "DC Narrowly Avoids Radiological Disaster." They had good sources. They got a lot of the story correct. Best of all, they spelled my name right. My inner narcissist loved seeing my name in print.

I took a bite of cheese and bread. If they only knew how close it had come.

"Hey, Minxy."

Looking in the direction of the voice, I saw Walt sitting on Jenn's deck similarly drinking coffee. "Walt. You stayed at the house after the party."

"First time I could bear it. It was hard at first, but then I was surrounded with all the happy memories, and I got through it."

"I understand. You keeping it? The house I mean?"

He shook his head. "I'd never move on if I lived here. It'd be like living in Jenn's tomb. She wouldn't want that."

"No, she wouldn't. She was practical."

Walt said nothing, but he nodded.

The wind was swirling like it did before a storm and I caught a whiff of Jenn's roses. I took it in slowly and with enormous pleasure. The three bushes were covered in pink blossoms. The color I'd once described as 'barf pink,' now seemed vibrant. Then something hit me. "Walt, I said I'd do your case for free, but there is one thing I'd like you to give me."

"Name it." he said.

"One of Jenn's rose bushes. Especially if you're selling the house."

Walt chuckled and cut his eyes up at me, "I think you've finally learned to appreciate Jennifer and her roses."

I harrumphed, but he wasn't fooled. After a moment of reflection, I said so honestly it surprised me, "I respect her. She was brave, relentless, and smart. I didn't realize that soon enough."

"I'll love knowing one of her roses is in your garden. I'll dig up the best one and plant it for you today."

In the mid-afternoon, I had dressed in a sleeveless summer dress that flattered my coloring and was sitting on the front deck outside my bedroom, reading a best seller about time travel. Magoo was acting achy but seemed better. He'd finished his bowl of kibble from this morning, and sat where my hand could rest on his back. Every few minutes, he nudged the hand with his nose, seeking a real petting. I always complied.

I had *that feeling*. The one I'd had so many times before. Maybe it was a hunch from experience. Maybe it was that entanglement. Whatever it was, I felt it strongly. When I heard the throbbing of the muscular Indian motorcycle engine and the throttling down as it neared, I was not surprised. Excited. Thrilled. Perhaps a lot more but not surprised.

The rider pulled the ruby red monster up to the closed garage, turned off the key, and pushed down the kickstand. Then he took off his helmet and looked up at me. I saw the angelically beautiful face of Theo. Carmel brown eyes, wavy dark hair, perfect bone structure. It was a face I couldn't stop looking at.

I said, "Your spider sense is still intact."

He nodded, "I always know when you're in danger. Always." He got off the bike and stood there gazing up at me. "Got room for a field medic who wants to nurse you for a few days?"

The smile crossed my face of its own volition. I put a finger to my cheek. "Let me think. Yes, but I'll have to kick out the Hungarian circus clowns."

"Just as well. You can't trust that lot." He grabbed a distressed leather satchel and climbed the stairs. I met him at the front door.

We searched each other's eyes as a first step to our reconnection. I felt like the world was right again. All the planets were aligned in their orbits and the balance of the universe was restored. I leaned forward and let my lips linger on his for an extended moment, then I kissed him so gently that if his eyes weren't open, he might have mistaken my lips for butterfly wings. He met my kiss with a far more moving one.

Arm in arm we entered the house, an electrical storm of emotion passing between us. I got a strong whiff of Jenn's roses again, just as Theo closed the door.

THE END

www.ingramcontent.com/pod-product-compliance
Lightning Source LLC
Chambersburg PA
CBHW030119010826
48973CB00002B/339